THE
Beach
BAR

THE Beach BAR

KATE McCABE

POOLBEG

This novel is entirely a work of fiction. The names,
characters and incidents portrayed in it are the work of the
author's imagination. Any resemblance to actual persons,
living or dead, events or localities is entirely coincidental.

Published 2007
by Poolbeg Press Ltd.
123 Grange Hill, Baldoyle,
Dublin 13, Ireland
Email: poolbeg@poolbeg.com

© Kate McCabe 2006

The moral right of the author has been asserted.

Copyright for typesetting, layout, design
© Poolbeg Press Ltd.

1 3 5 7 9 10 8 6 4 2

A catalogue record for this book is available from the British Library.

978 1 84223 263 7

Typeset by Patricia Hope in Bembo 11.3/14
Printed by Litografia Rosés, Spain

www.poolbeg.com

About the Author

Kate McCabe lives in Howth, County Dublin where she enjoys walking along the beach. Her hobbies include travel, cooking, reading and dreaming up plots for her stories. This is her second novel.

Also by Kate McCabe

Hotel Las Flores

Acknowledgements

Another year, another novel.

Once again my heartfelt thanks to my family for their continuing support; to all at Poolbeg Press, particularly Paula Campbell, Claire, Emma and Aoife for their professionalism and encouragement; to Gaye Shortland for a superb edit (Gaye, I think the Garda Detective Unit could avail of your services – you have a genuine talent for nosing out inconsistencies!); to Marc Patton, my computer therapist; to Claire and Gaye, my style consultants, to my best friends the booksellers; and finally to all those discerning readers who bought *Hotel Las Flores* in their thousands and propelled it into the Bestsellers list.

I hope you enjoy *The Beach Bar* just as much.

For Maura

1

When she was still at school, Emma Dunne had dreamed of a glamorous career as a model or an actress. With her cloud of blonde curls and angelic face, she pictured herself floating around Dublin surrounded by a posse of admirers. Men would queue up to date her. Club owners would fight over her and doormen would roll out the red carpet. Her photograph would appear in all the glossy magazines. She would be written up in the gossip columns. She would wear the best clothes and eat in the finest restaurants, always with a handsome man on her arm. It seemed the perfect life and she was the perfect girl to fill it.

But as she got older Emma came up against reality. Even though she was very attractive, with soft blue eyes and a slim figure, it soon became obvious that, at five feet five inches, she was too small to be a model. The agencies seemed to want girls six feet tall whose legs went up to their armpits. As for acting, Emma quickly discovered that she would have a quieter time training Bengal tigers than she would competing with the aspiring young things who wanted to get into the movies.

In any case, an accident intervened and she ended up running the family business.

Her father, Joe, had built up the Hi-Speed Printing Company from scratch, starting in 1970 with a small office in the inner city. He ran off handbills and posters and invitation cards on an old press that regularly threatened to break down just at a crucial moment when a large rush order had to be delivered.

He had combed the city for business, a virtual one-man band, knocking on doors, phoning concert promoters, calling at bingo halls – anywhere there was the prospect that someone might want a printing job done. He left for work at seven o'clock each morning and often didn't return till after midnight. Joe Dunne was a determined man but he wasn't proud. He would never turn down an order, no matter how small. It was all money and it paid the bills.

And the business prospered. Joe slowly gained a reputation for fine quality work and reliability. And his prices were always keen. In time, he was able to afford a new state-of-the-art press that could produce glossy colour brochures and catalogues by the thousand at the touch of a button. His orders grew and he hired more staff – master printers whose work was the best in town. The business expanded and he moved from his cramped little premises in Talbot Street to a spanking new facility in an industrial estate in Baldoyle.

Joe drove a BMW, took the family on holidays to Florida for three weeks every June and bought a new detached house with gardens by the sea in Sutton, where they had views of the Dublin mountains. He didn't go around boasting but he liked to think that all the hard work had finally paid off and now he had arrived.

But while those were his glory years and Joe liked to look back on them with a nostalgic smile, Emma and her mother were convinced that was when the damage was done. It was the pressure of those early years – the long working days, the rushed fast-food meals, the threatening deadlines, the near disasters, the nerve-racking crises when the old printing press threatened to collapse – that caused the heart condition that eventually forced Joe to retire from the business at fifty-eight and hand it over to Emma.

She was preparing for her Leaving Cert when the news broke about her father's heart. He had been complaining about breathlessness for some time but he was one of those men who paid little attention to his health. Even though his wife, Nancy, had badgered him for months to go and see Dr Fagan, Joe kept putting it off. He was just a bit overweight, he would say. Why take up the doctor's valuable time when there were more deserving poor devils with real problems to complain about? Besides, Dr Fagan would think he was a hypochondriac if he went running to see him every time he was a little bit out of breath.

Matters came to a head one bright Sunday afternoon on the seventh hole at Deerpark golf course, where Joe liked to play a round of golf with his pals. He had just teed off when he felt a sharp pain shoot along his left arm and into his chest. Next minute he was lying on the ground and someone was beating on his breast while someone else attempted to give him mouth-to-mouth resuscitation. Joe didn't remember any more till he woke up several hours later in the cardiology department of Beaumont hospital.

It turned out that the main artery to his heart was almost blocked with atherosclerotic plaque. He remained in hospital for two weeks while the surgeons performed a triple-bypass operation to allow the passage of blood to his heart. After the operation, a consultant sat down with Joe and had a long talk with him. He told him he was lucky to be alive. He would have to change his busy lifestyle. He would have to slow down and take things easy.

After he was discharged, the family held a council. They sat around the big dining table while they tried to decide what to do. Joe was reluctant to take the doctor's advice. He felt he could still continue to run the company if he just cut back a little and delegated more responsibility. But this time Nancy was determined to put her foot down. Joe had worked hard for long enough. The time had come to retire completely from the business and hand it over to someone else.

While he had been in hospital, the day-to-day running of the company had been taken over by George Casey, who was Joe's deputy. But while George was a competent manager, he didn't have the drive and vision that Joe possessed. It was obvious that he could only be an emergency stopgap. Someone else would have to be found to run the firm in place of Joe. And it would have to be someone from the family.

The oldest boy, Peter, was in his second year as a junior doctor in St Vincent's hospital. He had never shown the slightest interest in the business and was horrified at the suggestion that he might give up medicine to run the family printing firm. His brother Alan was two years younger and was a sports reporter in RTÉ. And while Alan was certainly willing to help out in this sudden emergency that had arisen, it was clear to everyone around the table that he didn't have a clue about business. Nancy could see situations where Alan would be negotiating a printing contract with a client while his mind was on Liverpool's chances of winning their next game against Arsenal in the Premiership. It would never work.

Which left Emma. She knew before anyone said a word

that the job was going to fall to her. She was eighteen and planning to go to college once she had completed her exams. The lingering dreams of a life in modelling or acting had evaporated by now but she still had hopes of an exciting career in publishing or marketing. Now all that would have to be set aside while she mastered the technicalities of offset printing and discounts and margins and VAT and delivery dates. It was hardly the glamorous future she had hoped for.

"You're the obvious person," her brother Peter said, aware of her reluctance and eager to make sure that the responsibility was shifted onto someone else. "Can't you at least give it a shot?"

Emma thought of what would be involved. She would have to learn the business from scratch. She would have to work long hours. She would spend much of her time in an office instead of enjoying the busy social whirl with her friends. She was only eighteen and would be entering a trade that was still dominated by men. Would she be able for it?

Her father smiled softly and gently pressed her hand. "I'll teach you everything I know," he said. "You can do it."

Emma looked at the expectant faces around the big mahogany table where they had all gathered for Sunday dinner since she was a child. The business had provided them with a good life. It would be a tragedy if it had to pass out of their hands. In a strange way, she believed she owed it to the rest of them.

She took a deep breath and bit her lip. "All right," she said. "I'll give it a go."

It was agreed that Emma would take over as managing director and George Casey would continue as her deputy while her father taught her the intricacies of the printing trade. In addition, she decided to enrol in a part-time evening course at the Dublin Institute of Technology so that she could learn the management skills she knew she would need in the years ahead.

Some of her friends felt sorry for her. Instead of enjoying the excitement of college life, she had gone straight from school into the pressurised world of business. While they were out pubbing and clubbing, Emma was dealing with accountants and suppliers and negotiating with clients. In the evening while her friends were heading out on the town, she was trooping off to the lecture hall with her notebooks and folders.

And all the time, hanging over her was the dreadful possibility that she might fail and drive the company into bankruptcy. She knew that some so-called friends would be delighted if this was to happen. But Emma didn't allow herself to brood about this. No matter how hard she had to work, no matter what setbacks she might encounter, she was absolutely determined. Now that she had taken the helm at the Hi-Speed Printing Company, she would work her fingers to the bone to make it a success.

Of course, there were many people who were impressed by her pluck.

One of the first friends she made at evening college was an ambitious young man called Tim Mulhall. Tim had a degree in Computer Studies but he had decided to switch to management. Now he was working by day for an information technology company while he tried to get his qualification by studying at night.

One evening after the lecture had ended, he invited Emma for a drink. Over a couple of beers, he outlined his plans to her.

"The way I see it, everybody wants to get into computers," he said, "but because the industry is so young, there is a shortage of people with management skills. In a few years' time they'll be crying out for managers."

"What are you planning to do?" Emma asked.

"Start my own company. I want to work for myself. How about you?"

"I already do," she said.

Tim was amazed. "You work for yourself?"

"Well, my father started the company. But now I'm running it. Or, to be more precise, I'm learning to run it."

Tim's jaw dropped. "I think that's fantastic. You're so young. I mean . . ." He flushed with embarrassment.

"I know what you mean. I've just turned nineteen and I know I have a lot to learn but I'm very determined."

"And how do the others react to you? Don't they think you're maybe a little wet behind the ears?"

Emma thought for a moment. "Not really. I think they accept me."

He sat back and whistled softly. "That's brilliant. Running your own company at nineteen years of age. I'd give my right arm for an opportunity like that."

Tim's reaction was like sweet music to Emma's ears. Maybe taking on the company wasn't such a burden after all. Maybe it was a glorious opportunity. Maybe she should consider herself fortunate to be the managing director of the Hi-Speed Printing Company, even if she was barely nineteen.

But she hadn't been entirely truthful with Tim. Several of the older workers *did* have problems with someone so young being in charge and some of them adopted a surly resentment towards her. They regarded her as an amateur who didn't know what she was doing. But Emma taught herself to be patient and, above all, to listen to advice. These people knew the printing trade and she had a lot to learn from them. Until such time as she had mastered the complexities of the business, she was determined to take a softly-softly approach and not to antagonise anyone.

It paid off. Her father stayed by her side for about nine months, gradually easing himself out of the company while Emma assumed more and more control. At last he let go completely and gave himself over to a life of golf and healthy eating and frequent holiday breaks. After a career spent slaving to build up Hi-Speed Printing, Joe Dunne seemed content to enjoy himself. Emma took it as a vote of confidence. And she knew if a difficult problem did arise, he would always be there to turn to for guidance.

There were to be many problems in the years that lay ahead. Because she was a young woman, there were plenty of clients who thought she would be a pushover when it came to business. Blonde curls and big blue eyes didn't help and she often cursed the fact she didn't look more severe. They threatened and cajoled and attempted to bully her. They were late with payments. They complained about the standard of the work and demanded discounts and rebates. Emma knew she was on probation. She knew if she showed the least hint of uncertainty, it would be taken as a sign of weakness and the demands would escalate while word went around that Joe Dunne's daughter was a soft touch.

So she held her ground. She dealt with each client personally so that she could get to know them. She listened to their complaints and if there was merit in their arguments she was prepared to negotiate. She knew that rigidity could be seen as just as much a sign of weakness as simply caving in at the first sign of resistance.

Gradually she earned the respect of clients and staff alike. She was particularly pleased when word filtered back to her that one of her most awkward customers had been heard to say in company that Emma Dunne was a chip off the old block – firm but fair, an iron fist in a velvet glove. Emma had smiled with satisfaction when she heard that remark.

But running the Hi-Speed Printing Company took its toll, particularly on her social life. By now, she had moved out of the family home and bought a smart apartment in Howth with a large terrace overlooking the marina. It meant she was close both to her parents and to work and she liked the freedom that Howth gave her: the mountain walks, the sea, the intimate village life, the yacht club and the friendly pubs.

After she graduated from the Dublin Institute of Technology, she continued to see Tim Mulhall, who was still pursuing his dream of starting his own computer business. They would regularly meet for a drink or go for a meal in one of the fish restaurants in Howth. Emma enjoyed the relaxed nature of their relationship and she particularly liked their long walks across Howth Head, during which Tim would outline his plans for future glory when he eventually succeeded in persuading some bank to lend him the cash to start his own business. She tried to give him advice, for she really wanted him to succeed, but it gradually became obvious that unless he came up with a good idea and a clear business plan, no financial institution was likely to risk its capital with him. And while his studies had earned him promotion and a junior management position, as the years passed it became clear that the job he was doing was really a dead-end.

One evening, in frustration, Tim told her he was throwing it all over.

"Have you got something else lined up?" Emma asked anxiously.

"I've got an offer of a job in California," he said proudly.

"Wow!" she said, slightly shocked.

"The Yanks appreciate initiative. They like people with a bit of get-up-and-go. I reckon I'll be running my own company within six months."

"What is this job you've got?"

"It's something similar to what I'm doing now. I'll be responsible for a small team of programmers. It's a great opportunity, Emma."

"But sometimes far-off fields seem green," she said with a note of caution.

"I've got to go," Tim said. "I'm thirty-two. If I don't do it now, I'll wake up some morning to discover that I'm a middle-aged man looking back on broken dreams."

Emma felt a sadness take hold of her. She looked at Tim as he sat beside her, his handsome eyes flashing defiantly. Something told her that nothing was going to change for him. The job he had been offered would turn out to be just another cul-de-sac. But the weather would be better and the experience might stand to him in future years. He was right to pursue his dream, even if nothing ever came of it. At least he would have tried.

She took his face in her hands and stared into his brooding eyes.

"I wish you luck, Tim. You're doing the right thing."

He shrugged and smiled. "I'll miss you," he said.

"And I'll miss you."

"I'll keep in touch. I'll mail you and let you know what's going on."

Emma gently squeezed his hand. "I'd like that." But she doubted he would.

Emma had a succession of men friends but none of the

relationships lasted for very long. Some of the men were clearly fortune hunters, attracted by her position and hoping to get a slice of her money. But they were easy to spot and she quickly gave them short shrift. Occasionally, she met someone who interested her but her hectic working schedule played havoc with her social life. Usually the men she met were older than her, as she typically met them in the course of work – from the start the demands of her job had cancelled out the possibility of clubbing or nights out on the town with the girls.

Often, the men she met were at an age when they were interested in a steady relationship and the idea of marriage was at last making inroads on their consciousness. But cancelled dinner appointments, late arrivals, irritating phone calls at a romantic moment, these would try the patience of the keenest admirer. One by one, the romances petered out. Emma found herself in a cleft stick. She was forced to concede that, while her lifestyle ruled out relationships with free and easy younger men, finding an older man who would put up with playing second fiddle to Hi-Speed Printing was not going to be easy.

She did develop a steady friendship with one man. At forty-two, Conor Delaney was the owner of the Clear Skies Holiday Shop and one of her main clients. Twice a year, in spring and winter, Emma printed his brochures for him. It was a big order: 100,000 glossy magazines packed with enticing photos of beautiful people lounging on sun-kissed beaches or splashing in pools or having a drink at some quaint little bar. Every time the job came around, Emma found those photos tugging at her heartstrings and she would wish she was off with those beautiful people instead of stuck here in noisy, grey, depressing Dublin on yet one more rainy day.

11

The brochures were vitally important to Conor Delaney. They were his shop window and his big hope was that the pictures would have the same effect on thousands of potential holidaymakers as they had on Emma. He took infinite care with them, choosing the photos carefully, spending days writing the text with catchy headlines like *Let Clear Skies Banish All Your Cares* and *Relax in the Magical Surroundings of Sunny Lanzarote.*

When Conor was finally satisfied, he would throw a launch party and bring all the travel writers and representatives of the trade and Emma was always invited. Conor usually had his brochure launch in some nice restaurant and there would be lovely food and gallons of wine and the travel writers would get sloshed and promise to give him a big write-up in their next article.

Emma thought Conor had a wonderful job, much more exciting than her mundane existence at Hi-Speed Printing. He was always flying off to check out some new destination to see if it was suitable to add to his list. From time to time, he would invite Emma to come along too.

"You deserve a break," he'd say. "The company can get along without you for a few days. Why don't you come along and just chill out?"

Although Emma was often tempted, she always said no. She was attracted to Conor. She wasn't in love with him but, then, she was beginning to think that would never happen for her. For one thing, there just wouldn't be time. In that light, Conor wouldn't be such a bad deal – he was tall and handsome and affectionate and wonderful company.

But there were things about Conor that set off alarm bells. For a start, he was reputed to have a wife and three children somewhere in Killiney, from whom he was separated and whom he never mentioned.

And there was a boyish irresponsibility about him that worried her. For all his forty-two years, it was as if he had never grown up. When he was out with the travel writers, he would stay up half the night drinking and the following day his mobile phone would be switched off till after lunch. It really wasn't the best way to run a business.

But while Emma resisted any romantic entanglement, she was still very fond of him. She used him as a sounding board when she had small problems that she didn't want to bring to her father and he was always available to accompany her to a dinner party or a social occasion that required a male escort. If only he was a bit more reliable, she would sigh, if only he would lose his wild streak, he would be an ideal partner. But Emma had learnt enough about life to know that the leopard seldom changed its spots.

By the time her thirtieth birthday passed her by, she had not only mastered the intricate mysteries of the business but had also expanded it. She had installed another new press and, along with the general run of printing work, she had won an important contract to print a string of freesheet newspapers. This contract alone earned the company nearly as much as all its other work put together. Hi-Speed Printing was beginning to excite envy and admiration in equal measure from her competitors so she wasn't surprised when, from time to time, she was approached by intermediaries with offers to invest in the company or buy her out completely.

The most attractive offer was made one day in June 2005, over a delightful lunch at Patrick Guilbaud's restaurant in Merrion Street. The man who made it was called Herr Gunther Braun and he was the representative of a large German printing firm wishing to expand into Ireland.

Herr Braun spoke perfect English and he had perfect manners. He resolutely avoided all talk of business till the meal was finished and they were drinking coffee. Then he laid his cards on the table.

"We are prepared to offer you €3 million for the company and to retain your services as a consultant for five years at a salary of €150,000 per annum," he announced.

Emma almost choked. She had no intention of selling and had agreed to meet Herr Braun largely out of curiosity. But the generosity of his offer took her breath away. She struggled hard to retain her composure and not reveal her surprise.

"Who would run the company if you took it over?" she inquired.

"We would."

"You would put in your own management team?"

"Of course."

"So what would be my role?"

"You would act as an advisor and you would also recruit new business. You know the local scene. People here trust and respect you."

"And when my contract expires in five years' time? What would happen then?"

"We would review the situation. If we still required your services, naturally we would renew the contract for a further period."

Emma nodded gravely. Her head was spinning. She wished she had ordered a brandy instead of coffee.

"I'm very gratified by your interest," she said, "but I need some time to consider your offer."

"Of course. I will be in Dublin for one more week. I'm staying at the Westbury Hotel. Contact me at any time if you wish further clarification."

"Thank you," Emma said.

She rang the office and told her secretary to say that she had an urgent business appointment and to log all phone calls. Then she drove straight home to Howth, ran a hot bath, poured a glass of chilled white wine and luxuriated in the tub while she tried to digest the information that Herr Braun had just given her.

She had no idea that the company was worth so much. And she also knew that it was only the Germans' initial offer. She had no doubt that if she got into serious negotiation, she could persuade them to increase it further. And a salary of €150,000 as a consultant was tempting to say the least! Even if they decided to dispense with her services after five years, she would still have earned a handsome sum.

She was now thirty-one. She had worked for the company for the past thirteen years. It had practically taken over her life. If she accepted Herr Braun's offer she need never work again. Her parents would naturally get a portion of the purchase price and they already had a comfortable personal pension fund.

Her brother Peter was now a senior consultant in the Mater hospital and rarely ever mentioned the company, while Alan was the sports editor on a national newspaper and seemed to be in his element reporting rugby and soccer and horseracing events. They all had lives. They all had happy careers. Why should she be the one to tie herself forever to the Hi-Speed Printing Company, especially now that she had a very profitable way out?

But it was a big move to make. What would the staff think, all those hardworking people, including George Casey, who had given years of loyal service? And what about her father? He had founded the company and spent his entire career building it up. Would he think she was deserting the ship? And would she miss it? Despite her gripes and grievances, the company was the only job she knew. Even though there were times when it wore her out, there were plenty of other occasions when she got a great buzz of satisfaction from winning a contract or seeing a job well done.

Emma lay in the bath till the water began to grow cold. This was not a decision she could take lightly. She needed to think long and hard. She needed to consult. She needed to get advice. And there was one person she could turn to who would give her that advice and also be discreet. Conor Delaney. She would ring him at once and see if he was free.

She stepped out of the bath and was beginning to dry herself when she heard her mobile go off.

"Hello," she said, the bathwater dripping onto the floor.

"It's Conor." He sounded out of breath.

"Hey! That's a coincidence. I was just going to call you," she said.

"I need to talk to you. Urgently. I'm in trouble."

She arranged to meet him in the lounge of a nearby hotel and quickly got dressed. What kind of trouble could he be in? Had he crashed his car? Had he lost his credit cards? Was someone suing him? When she got to the hotel, she found him nursing a large glass of whiskey and by the look of him it wasn't the first. His tie was askew, there was sweat glistening on his forehead and stubble darkened his unshaved chin.

"You look like you've been sleeping under a haystack," she said. "What's the matter with you?"

He took a large gulp of whiskey. "I've got terrible news. My company's going bust."

For a moment, it felt like Emma's heart had skipped a beat. Was he serious? But Conor never joked about things like this and, while he had been drinking, he certainly wasn't drunk. She quickly forgot about her own good news. She sat down beside him and gently stroked his arm.

"Tell me what happened."

"Where do I begin?" he said, spreading his hands wide. "I'm being undercut by these Internet firms and then you've got all these people who own their own apartments and aren't interested in package holidays any more. Plus the competition has become fierce. I've booked a thousand hotel rooms that I can't fill. The bottom line is, I can't pay my way. I'm putting the company into liquidation." He turned his sad eyes to Emma. "I wanted you to be the first to know."

"Is there anything I can do?" she said, trying frantically to think of some way out. She hated the thought of Conor going bust after all the hard work he had put into his business.

He smiled grimly. "No. There's nothing. It's kind of you to offer. But I'm afraid I'm beyond salvation. Tomorrow when the word gets out, the vultures will swoop and pick my carcass clean."

"Oh, Conor," she said, "don't talk like that."

"It's the truth. You know what they're like."

He took another drink of whiskey. "I haven't paid you for the last two sets of brochures. € 40,000, I think it is."

"Forget it," she said. "That's the least of your worries."

"No, I won't forget," he said stubbornly. "You've always been very decent to me, Emma. I can't pay you, of course, but I have another suggestion to make." He reached into his pocket and took out a couple of official-looking documents. "These are the deeds of a beach bar I own on the Costa del Sol. It's a little investment I made when things were going well. It's not worth a lot but it's something. I want you to take them in payment for the brochures."

She quickly pushed the documents away. "For God's sake, Conor! What do you think I am? I couldn't possibly take your bar from you."

"Please, you'll be doing me a favour. You'll allow me to retain some dignity. And if you don't take it, the liquidator certainly will. At least I'll know that you got something out of the wreckage." He lifted the deeds and pressed them into her hands. "Tomorrow morning I'll meet you in my solicitor's office and I'll give him power of attorney to complete the transfer. Now I don't want to hear another word. I'm going to sit here and get gloriously ossified. Will you allow me to buy you a drink?"

"I'll have a glass of white wine," Emma said and felt her heart flood with sadness for him.

The following morning, she woke early. She had been thinking about the developments overnight and now she knew exactly what she was going to do.

As arranged, she met Conor Delaney at his solicitor's office and they both signed the documents that would give her legal possession of the bar.

"Where is it anyway?" she asked.

"Fuengirola. Right now, I have a Spanish lady running it for me. It's ticking over but I've no doubt with a bit of effort it could do much better." He looked sad and hung-over.

"What are you going to do?" she asked.

He shrugged. "Don't worry about me. I'll survive."

She flung her arms around his neck and kissed his cheek. "Good luck," she whispered. "And stay in touch."

Next, she drove out to her parents' house in Sutton. Her father was sitting in the conservatory reading a newspaper while her mother pottered about in the garden.

"I've got something I want to discuss with you," she said to her father.

He pointed to a chair beside him. "Sit down."

Joe Dunne listened carefully while she outlined the offer Herr Braun had made to buy the company. When she had finished, he said: "Do you think we should accept it?"

"What do you think?"

"It's a very good offer. You should consider it seriously."

"How would you feel?"

"My feelings are irrelevant," Joe said. "You stepped in to run the firm when I got ill but I didn't think you'd be doing it forever. The others have satisfying careers. It's time you thought about yourself for a change. You're still a young woman. Maybe you might want to settle down and get married."

Emma smiled at the assumption she would give up work if she married and patted her father's cheek. "You think a good man would straighten me out?"

"He might," Joe said with a twinkle in his eye.

She stood up. "I'm not going to do anything for a while. And before I make my decision, I'll come and talk to you."

She made an appointment to see Herr Braun at midday. They met in the coffee bar of the Westbury Hotel.

"I need more time to consider your offer," she said.

"How much?"

"A month."

Herr Braun looked surprised but his good manners didn't falter. "It's a long time."

"It's a big decision. I have to think deeply. There are people I must consult."

"All right," Herr Braun said at last. "One month. But if you haven't decided by then, we will look elsewhere."

"I will have decided," Emma said.

She took George Casey out for an early lunch and outlined her plans to him. She said nothing about the German offer.

"I'm taking a break and I'd like you to run the place while I'm away. You'll be paid, of course, for the extra responsibility. How do you feel about that?"

"How long will you be gone?"

"A month," Emma said.

George Casey thought for a moment. "I can do it. In fact, I'd be glad to do it."

"You won't be entirely on your own. I'll keep in regular touch with you. You'll be able to reach me if you need to."

"There's no problem," George smiled. "Everything will be fine."

Emma went home to pick up her luggage. She had already booked a flight to Malaga and a hotel in Fuengirola. The flight left at four. She would be in Fuengirola by seven o'clock.

She felt the blood racing along her veins. It was as if she was being released from all her problems and cares, all the pressures of her busy life. It was as if she was starting out on a glorious adventure. A month in Spain would give her ample time to decide where her future lay.

She rang for a cab and finished packing her carry-on holdall. Half an hour later, she was speeding along the motorway towards Dublin airport.

2

Mark Chambers was forty, tall, dark, handsome . . . and heartbroken. But it hadn't always been so. There had been a time when he was the happiest man in Dublin, the envy of his friends and colleagues, because he was married to a wonderful woman who turned men's heads when she came into a room or simply walked along the street. People used to say he had a marriage made in heaven and Mark knew they were right. Yet he had met Margot Hennessy entirely by accident and in the beginning things had not gone smoothly.

He could remember the occasion clearly, as if it were only yesterday. It was November and very cold. The car radio had said there was a threat of snow and he had gone into work that morning wrapped up in his heavy overcoat, hat, scarf and gloves. By the time lunchtime came around, he was looking forward to a steaming bowl of minestrone soup in Bewley's Café in Grafton Street. But when he got there, all the tables were full.

21

Except for one. It was by the window and the solitary occupant was a young woman with her head buried in a book. Mark approached and politely asked if she would mind if he joined her. She glanced up quickly and he found himself looking into the most beautiful brown eyes he had ever seen.

"Pardon me?"

"I asked if I could sit here."

"Of course," she replied and immediately began to remove her handbag to make more room. Once he was seated, she continued reading.

Mark gave his order and while he waited his eye wandered to the book she was reading. It was *The Woodlanders* by Thomas Hardy. This was a coincidence. It was one of his favourite novels. He had read it at school and had enjoyed it so much that he had gone straight to the library and devoured every Hardy novel he could find.

She seemed to sense that he was watching her for she slowly lowered the book and stared across the table and he was able to study her face again. A thin face, a long delicate neck adorned by a simple silver chain, fine skin that gleamed like porcelain, a mass of brown curls and those dark brown eyes that so enraptured him and were sparkling now with mischief.

"Well?" she said cheekily. "Have you seen enough?"

Mark put on his best smile. "I'm sorry. I was just wondering if you were enjoying your book, that's all."

"I'm not sure yet. I'm trying to make up my mind."

"Do you like Hardy's novels?"

"I don't know. This is the first one I've read. I just picked it up by chance."

"How far have you got?"

She held out the page for him to see.

"Keep reading," he said. "It gets better. But be warned. Don't expect a happy ending."

Suddenly her dark eyes blazed with annoyance. "Now you've gone and spoiled it for me!"

"No, I haven't."

"Yes, you have. Who asked for your opinion, anyway?"

Just then, the waitress came with his soup.

"I'm sorry," he said. "I didn't mean to spoil it."

"Well, you have and I hate people who tell you the end of things." She closed her book and buttoned up her fleece-lined jacket as if she were about to leave.

But something in her manner encouraged him.

"Why don't you stay?" he said. "Have a cup of coffee?"

She hesitated for a moment and then stood up. "I can't," she said, pulling on a cream woolly hat that made her look even more adorable. "I'll be late for work."

He watched her stride confidently to the exit, her skirt swaying as she went. When she got there, she turned and smiled at him and lifted her hand in a little wave.

The door closed behind her and she was gone.

"Women," he muttered as he turned to his soup. "I don't think I'll ever understand them."

Mark was twenty-three at the time. He had come up from Athlone a year before to work as a trainee copywriter with an advertising agency and lived alone in a bed-sit off Leeson Street. That night he could hardly sleep for thinking about the girl he had met in Bewley's Cafe.

He thought she was the most wonderful creature he had ever seen. Not only was she beautiful, she had spirit. He thought again of those dark flashing eyes and the finely sculpted structure of her face and the mass of brown curls that crowned her forehead. She had entered his life and just walked out again and he didn't even know her name.

Realistically, what were the chances of meeting her again? For all he knew, she might live down the country somewhere. Maybe she was only visiting. And then he remembered a remark she had made. *I'll be late for work*. His hopes rose.

Over the next few days, Mark thought about her constantly. He replayed their brief conversation in his head. He regretted that he hadn't been bolder, that he hadn't impressed her with some smart remarks. And now she was gone and he didn't know where to find her.

And then he hit on a bright idea. Next day at lunchtime, he went into Easons bookshop in O'Connell Street and bought a copy of the most famous Hardy novel, *Tess of the D'Urbervilles*. He wrote his name just inside the front page and added his office phone number. For weeks, he carried the book around with him in the hope that he might meet her again. He went back every day to Bewley's Cafe. He sat at the same table, desperately hoping that the door would open and he would see that lovely face again. But always he was disappointed.

As the weeks turned into months, his optimism began to fade. Dublin was a big city. Christmas passed and by March the days were lengthening. The daffodils were a brilliant sea of yellow light along Stephen's Green. The trees were bursting into bud. Spring was in the air.

One day in early May, Mark found himself in a music store looking for a present for one of his friends. He had just completed his purchase and was turning away when he saw something that made his heart leap.

He couldn't believe his eyes. The girl, *his* girl, was standing inside the counter dealing with a customer. At once, he began to push his way through the crowded store but as he neared the counter she came outside it and went to place some cassette tapes on a stand. He walked right up behind her. Tentatively, he reached out and touched her arm. She quickly spun around to face him.

"Excuse me," he said.

"Yes?"

"Don't you remember me? I met you in Bewley's Cafe before Christmas. You were reading *The Woodlanders.*"

She studied him for a moment and then a flicker of recognition crossed her face. "Yes, I do remember you."

"Did you finish the book?"

"Oh, yes."

"Did you enjoy it?"

"Maybe *enjoy* is not the right word. I thought it was very sad."

"But that's the whole point about Hardy," Mark said. "His novels are tragedies. I told you not to expect a happy ending."

A playful smile engulfed her lovely face. "That's right. So you did. And your big mouth almost spoiled it for me."

He reached into his pocket. "You know, I just happen to have another Hardy novel on me," he said, bringing out the copy of *Tess* he'd been carrying around for months. "I think you'll like it too." He tried to give it to her but she quickly pushed it away.

"I can't possibly take it. I don't even know you."

"I'm Mark Chambers. What's your name?"

She hesitated for a moment. "Margot Hennessy."

"Take it, Margot. It would please me very much."

Slowly, she reached out till her fingers gripped the book. "I really have to go now," she said. "I have customers to attend to."

"Please read the book," Mark said. "I know you'll like it."

He felt like he was walking on air as he strolled back to

his office. Now he knew her name and where she worked. *And* she had accepted the book from him. This was enormous progress. But he would have to play his cards carefully. He could upset her if he started harassing her by turning up unexpectedly at the store. Besides, he didn't want to scare her away by letting her see just how eager he was. She had the book and it contained his name and phone number. The best thing to do was wait and leave the next move to her.

But it wasn't easy. As the days went by, doubts began to creep in. Maybe she had a regular boyfriend? A good-looking girl like Margot was bound to have lots of men chasing after her. Businessmen with expense accounts who could take her out to fancy restaurants and buy her expensive presents. Why would she be interested in a lowly copywriter like him?

But she had smiled at him, hadn't she? And told him her name. And accepted his book. If she didn't have some feelings for him, why would she do that? His mood would swing from elation to despair, sometimes in the space of a few minutes. He couldn't get her out of his mind. He would be walking along O'Connell Street and he would suddenly see her face in the lunchtime crowds or staring at him from a passing bus. At night, he would dream about her and then wake to the cold reality of his lonely room.

In the end, he couldn't wait any longer. He decided to go back to the music shop the next day and take his courage in his hands. He would ask her to go out with him some evening. What was the worst that could happen? She could say no. And devastating as that might be, at least he would be out of his misery.

That night he tossed and turned, fretting about the outcome and about what best to wear to make the right impression. Should he be smart but casual? Should he get dressed up to the nines – show her how he scrubbed up? Yes, he decided at last, that would be the best idea. The next morning he polished his shoes till they shone. He chose his best suit, which was dark grey, with a brand-new pale-blue shirt. He agonised over a choice of tie, discarding this one and that as too conservative or too loud and so on, eventually playing it safe with a fairly discreet maroon and silver one.

At eleven o'clock, instead of going for coffee, he nipped along the street to the barber's shop and had his hair trimmed, even though it had been cut the week before.

He couldn't wait for the minutes to pass till it was lunchtime and he would see her again.

He kept busy with work. Finally, at twelve thirty, he left his desk and quietly slipped away. He hurried towards the music store where Margot worked. He kept rehearsing in his head the things he would say when he saw her again.

But when he got to the store, she wasn't there.

Frantically, Mark looked around. Maybe it was her day off. God forbid, maybe she was ill. He caught the attention of another sales assistant and asked where Margot was.

"She's gone," the young woman said.

"To lunch?"

"No. For good. She's left."

Mark was stunned. "When?"

"Couple of weeks ago."

"I have to find her," he said urgently. "It's very important. Do you know where she is?"

"Afraid not," the assistant said and turned away to attend to a customer.

Mark was heartbroken. He cursed himself for not being bolder when he had the chance. Why did he wait? Why did he not just ask her out when he met her that day in the store?

Now she was gone, swallowed up in this big city of a million people, and he would never find her again. He was a fool – a stupid, cowardly fool who had let a wonderful girl slip through his hands because he hadn't the courage to ask her out.

He felt utterly dejected and threw himself into his work in an effort to wipe all thoughts of Margot from his mind.

One afternoon, a few weeks later, he was immersed in an advertising campaign that had to be completed in a rush when he saw the office secretary wave to catch his attention.

"What is it?" he asked.

"Phone call."

"Who?"

"Some woman. She didn't give her name."

Mark quickly grabbed the instrument and cupped it to his ear.

"Mark Chambers speaking."

"I loved *Tess*," the voice said. "It was the most beautiful book I've ever read. I cried all night."

Thus began the love affair that was to dominate his life. For their first date, he took her to a fancy restaurant in Dame Street and afterwards to a club off Dawson Street. They had a brilliant time. It was after two in the morning when he finally deposited her outside her parents' house in Raheny.

"That was a great night," she said.

"Why don't we do it again?"

"Okay."

There was an awkward pause and then he took her in his arms. She closed her eyes and leaned her face into his.

Mark pressed his warm lips to hers and felt his body tingle all the way down to his toes.

They began to meet regularly. Margot had a new job in

a fashion shop in George's Street that was close to Mark's office. He would meet her after work and take her for something to eat. At weekends they went into town or drove over to Dalkey and climbed Killiney Hill and gazed out at the sprawling city bustling below them. Soon he was spending all his spare time with her.

But they still hadn't slept together. She hadn't even been in his flat. He wanted it that way. This was too important to rush.

As the August bank holiday approached, he asked her to spend it with him.

"What exactly do you have in mind?"

"I thought maybe we could go off somewhere. Make a long weekend out of it."

"Where?"

"I don't care. Galway? Just so we can be together."

"Let me see if I can get time off."

She rang back a few minutes later to say that everything was arranged. They could go on Thursday evening and come back on Monday night. Mark could barely hide his excitement.

"Your parents won't mind?"

"Why should they? We're adults, for God's sake."

They decided to take the train. A railway journey would be fun and it would avoid the hassle of driving. The carriage was packed and they were lucky to get seats together. Mark held Margot's hand as the train rattled out of the station and gathered speed as it thundered across the plains of Kildare towards the West.

"Are you happy?" he asked her.

She nodded. "And you?"

"Rapturous," Mark replied. "If we were going to hell in a bucket, I'd be happy. Just as long as I was with you."

It was dark by the time they got to Galway and the lights

were twinkling like stars all along the bay. They had no accommodation arranged so they asked at a guesthouse near Eyre Square. The landlady gave them a quick inspection and allocated a double room.

Once inside, Margot threw herself on the bed and doubled up with laughter.

"Do we look that old and established?"

"How do you mean?"

"To be married, I mean! She obviously took us for man and wife."

Mark cupped his hand behind her neck. "Does it bother you?"

"No, of course not. I was hoping it might happen."

He looked into her eyes. It was still there, that mischievous gleam that he had seen the first time they met. He began to undo the buttons on her blouse but she stopped him.

"Tell me what I want to hear."

"That I love you?"

"Yes."

"You know that already, Margot."

"But I want to hear you say it."

"I love you."

"And I love you too."

She threw her arms around him and pulled him down, and he covered her face and neck and breasts in wild, sensuous kisses that set her blood on fire.

They were married the following June. It was a quiet affair with just family and a few close friends because they didn't have much money. But when his boss heard about it, he gave Mark a raise so they rented a flat in Clontarf while they looked around for a house.

Those early months of married life were sheer bliss. Margot seemed to blossom in her role as a wife. Someone had given them a set of cookery books as a wedding present and every Saturday night they would invite friends for dinner and experiment with a new recipe. They would sit around the table in the kitchen and drink bottles of wine and try Margot's Beef Wellington or Chicken Chasseur and talk and sing till the elderly couple in the flat above banged on the ceiling for them to keep quiet.

On Sunday afternoons, they went house hunting. They had both agreed they wanted to live near the sea. Mark said he would like an older house with a bit of character that you could do things with; and besides, they were cheaper. But Margot wanted something new. There were too many problems with older houses, she argued. The plumbing never worked and there were draughts and the insulation was bad and they cost a fortune to heat. So Mark, who really just wanted to keep Margot happy, gave in. After months of searching, they finally settled on a three-bed semi-detached redbrick in Malahide.

That was when Mark got his first shock. The property boom hadn't yet taken off but the house still cost £95,000 and then there was stamp duty and legal fees on top of that. By the time they had negotiated a mortgage, he realised they would be repaying the building society £600 a month. His next shock was the cost of furnishing it. Mark had no idea that furniture cost so much. To save money, he suggested they go to an auction and buy some second-hand stuff but Margot was scandalised at the very idea.

"Are you out of your mind? You would have us sleeping in somebody else's old bed? Maybe the bed they died in. And what will my friends think when they see the place stuffed with the sort of furniture your granny would throw out?"

"Well, maybe we could buy a new *bed* but I'm told some of the furniture at those auctions is almost brand new."

But Margot was determined. "We're getting new furniture for the house or I'm not living in it. And that's my final word on the matter."

Mark had to give in again. He watched with mounting horror as the delivery vans began to arrive with new carpets and drapes and tables and chairs and kitchen appliances. And after the delivery vans, the bills came. In no time at all, their debt burden had risen by a further £15,000. He had to go meekly to the bank and beg them to give him a second mortgage.

But when they had finished, the house looked beautiful. Margot had excellent taste and Mark could see the envy and admiration on the faces of their friends when they came to visit and the evident pleasure it gave his wife. There was a little patch of lawn at the front of the house and a larger garden at the back. They came to an agreement to divide the labour. Margot would look after the house and Mark would take care of the garden.

He went at it with a will. He got some books out of the library and read up on roses and flowering cherry trees and hardy annuals and how to maintain a lawn in good condition. The first fine spring day, they went out to the garden centre and stocked up on plants and shrubs and Mark spent the following five weekends getting his garden in order. By Easter, the lawn was a smooth green carpet and the tulips were in bloom and the buds were opening like tiny starbursts on the cherry trees.

They were deliriously happy. They fell into a simple daily routine. Each morning at seven the alarm-clock in the bedroom would go off. Mark got up first and went down to the kitchen and made tea and toast while Margot used the shower. They had breakfast together and by eight they were driving into Dublin.

On those days when Mark didn't have to see a client to discuss an advert, they would meet for lunch. Most days it was just a sandwich in a coffee shop. But for special occasions, he would take her again to the restaurant where they had their first meal together.

Some nights Margot had to stay late for stocktaking and other nights Mark had to finish work for a client but whichever of them got home first prepared dinner for the other one. They would eat together and later watch television or sometimes they would wander down to the pub and meet a few friends. By midnight, they were safely tucked up in bed.

They looked forward to the weekends. They would get up late and have a big fry-up for breakfast and drive over to Dún Laoghaire and wander round the shops. Or they would stroll in Stephen's Green and feed the ducks in the pond and later take in a movie. Or go wandering through the Liberties and end up eating fish and chips from Burdock's on a bench in the shadow of Christ Church Cathedral.

Mark thought he was the happiest man alive. He had everything he ever wished for. He was absolutely besotted with Margot. When they were apart, he would think about her constantly and couldn't wait till they were together again. During the day, he would ring her at odd moments just for the pleasure of hearing her voice. She was the only person who mattered to him. He knew that he loved her more than anything else in the world.

The only thing that made him uneasy was the level of debt they had taken on. So he started to work harder to earn bonuses. He took on extra projects. He worked late at night to get commissions completed on time. It meant that often he didn't get home till nine or ten o'clock at night, tired and hungry and out of sorts.

Margot would gently scold him. "You're leaving me alone too much. Do you want to drive me into the arms of a secret lover?"

"But I'm doing it for us. What's going to happen when you get pregnant? Then we'll have another mouth to feed and one less pay-packet."

Margot would laugh and throw her arms round his neck. "We'll cross that bridge when we come to it, Mark Chambers. In the meantime, why don't you lighten up? I don't like to see you get so stressed."

Mark's hard work didn't go unrewarded. Two years after they were married, a senior partner in the firm retired and it was decided to reorganise the operation. Mark was promoted to Projects Manager, with responsibility for attracting new business. His salary was increased and he was given an expense account for entertaining clients.

They were delighted. It seemed that Mark's career was on the threshold of big things. They were able to pay off the second mortgage. Now if Margot got pregnant, they would have no financial worries. If she wanted, she could give up her job to care for the baby.

But as time passed, no baby came. Margot started reading articles in health magazines. She studied charts to identify her fertile days. She mentioned it to her doctor, who examined her and told her she was perfectly healthy and there was nothing to worry about. He told her not to think about it so much. She would get pregnant in due course. Worrying about it might even be counter-productive.

Still nothing happened. They decided to see a specialist. She asked them a lot of questions and carried out more examinations. She took blood samples and arranged for

Mark to have a sperm test. Margot couldn't wait for the results to come in. She was sick with apprehension. The day came for their next appointment. Mark took the morning off work and they drove out to the hospital.

It was a dull morning in March. There was a cold wind blowing and the sky was heavy with big, dark rain clouds. Their appointment was for eleven thirty but the specialist was running late and they had to wait till after midday before she was able to see them.

She was a young woman with a confident, professional manner. She tried to put them at ease but the news she had to give them didn't inspire much hope. Mark's sperm count was normal and Margot was perfectly healthy. She could find nothing to indicate why they hadn't succeeded in having a baby.

They went for lunch at a nearby restaurant while they tried to come to terms with the news. Neither of them had much appetite. They had been hoping that the specialist would be able to identify the problem and deal with it.

Mark tried to be upbeat. "She *did* say that diet might help."

"And they're developing new fertility treatments all the time," Margot said, eager to agree.

He smiled and grasped her hand as he looked at the food growing cold on their plates.

"We'll do it," he said. "You'll see."

At the first opportunity, they went away on holiday. They wanted somewhere sunny and warm to escape from the miserable Irish weather, so they chose Lanzarote. They relaxed by the pool every day and went swimming and walking. Each evening, they chose a different restaurant for dinner. In the afternoons, they went to their room and made love.

But gradually the joy began to go out of their sex life. The passion of their early married life seemed to have disappeared. Margot grew tense and moody. Now that it appeared to be out of reach, having a child became the most desirable thing any woman could do.

She found herself looking enviously at young mothers with squawking babies in their arms. Would she ever have a child of her own? Would she be able to watch them grow from baby to toddler? Was she doomed always to be childless? These thoughts made her depressed and she would break out crying at unexpected times and then feel embarrassed that she had lost control of herself.

Mark didn't know what to do. He blamed himself. He buried himself in his work. He told himself it was for Margot and their life together.

One afternoon, he rang her at work. "Got anything planned for this evening?"

"Just the usual. There's a good movie on television. I'll probably watch that."

Mark caught the edge in her voice, the slight hint of resentment that she would have to spend another evening alone at home while he worked late at the office.

"Well, I have something important to tell you."

"Yes?" she asked.

"Not now. This demands an occasion. I'm buying you a fabulous dinner tonight. Where would you like to go?"

She was intrigued. "Wherever you like. You know all the best spots, Mark."

"The Lemon Tree. It's a new place on Baggot Street. I'll pick you up when you finish work."

He was waiting for her with a single red rose. He presented

it with a flourish and bent to kiss her. She felt his lips soft and warm on her own. It was just like old times when they first began to go out together.

"Do you mind telling me what this is all about?" she asked, flattered and pleased.

"I've been neglecting you and I want to apologise. Now I'm about to make it all up to you."

He insisted on a table at the back, where they could be alone. He ordered a bottle of champagne. After the waiter had popped the cork and poured, Mark raised his glass in a toast.

"To the future!"

"What exactly are you up to? You're driving me crazy with suspense."

He filled their glasses again and smiled triumphantly. "I've got an important announcement to make."

"For God's sake, what is it?"

"I'm going out on my own."

"You're what?"

"Starting my own company. I've given it a lot of thought. I've talked to the bank and they're prepared to advance me the capital. And most important, I've persuaded several of our major clients to come with me."

Margot was shocked. She had no idea he was thinking of something like this. "Is this a good idea, Mark?"

"Of course it is."

"But you'll be giving up a safe job. They think so well of you. Sooner or later, they're going to put you on the board."

"Why should I wait? Nobody ever got rich working for someone else."

"Won't they think you're being treacherous? Taking their clients away?"

"But they're not their clients. They're *my* clients. I was the one who recruited them in the first place. I'm the one they want to work on their advertising campaigns." He put down his glass and took her hand. "You don't sound very enthusiastic, Margot."

"Oh, Mark! You know I'll support you in anything you do. I'm just worried about the risk involved. And I don't want to see you work any harder. You're working too hard as it is."

"But don't you see? This is my chance to make some serious money. And if I have to work hard to begin with, I'll be able to relax later when I've recruited good people to manage the business. You've got to trust me, Margot. I know what I'm doing."

She snuggled closer and laid her head on his shoulder. "You know I would trust you with my life."

When she looked up, the waiter was hovering over them, pen and notebook to hand, ready to take their order.

Mark *did* make serious money. In his first year, Chambers Creative Artists had a turnover of £350,000. By the end of the second year, this had grown to £900,000. Mark's photograph, in dress suit, glass in hand and Margot on his arm, began to appear regularly in the trade press. He designed a successful advertising campaign for Tyrone Malt Whiskey that won a prestigious award that brought him more attention. He got invited to press functions and product launches.

Before long, the business was expanding. Mark's name was on everyone's lips. He began to hire new staff: bright young design artists and clever copywriters who came up with snappy slogans and brilliant concepts. The company won more awards. They attracted new clients. It seemed that Mark's success knew no boundaries.

They moved house. They sold their semi and bought a large detached house with two acres of grounds overlooking the sea at Howth summit. Mark had to hire a couple of gardeners to tend the lawns.

He bought a little red sports car for Margot and a new Mercedes for himself. She gave up her job and took up with a group of ladies who met regularly for lunch and gave sparkling dinner parties. They went on holidays three times a year: to the Canaries in the winter, Paris in the spring and the Côte D'Azur in August.

It seemed to the casual observer that they were the perfect couple: always turning up to first nights at theatre events, dining at the best restaurants, sharing a joke with politicians and television stars in the owners' enclosure at the races. But behind the brittle exterior, there was unhappiness. Beneath the smiles on the covers of magazines, there was a melancholy of the heart. Mark and Margot desperately craved a child.

No one in their hectic social set commented on the fact that they hadn't yet started a family. Many professional women were postponing pregnancy as long as possible to concentrate on their careers. It was not uncommon to see women in their late thirties and early forties announce blithely that they were pregnant. And Margot was still only thirty-five.

They discussed adoption. But it was harder than ever now to adopt children. There were so many hoops to jump through, so much red tape to unravel. And to seek to adopt a child was an open admission that they couldn't have children of their own. Neither of them was prepared to face that possibility as they clung desperately to the belief that one day, perhaps, a miracle would occur and Margot would conceive.

It was a difficult time for them. But there was no recrimination and no blame. They supported each other with the same love that had sustained them from the day they were married.

Mark continued to seek out vitamin supplements and wonder drugs. Margot went on strange diets. They tried different positions when they made love. They approached each cycle as if engaged on a military campaign, concentrating on those days when the calendar and the thermometer said that conception was most likely to occur. But still nothing happened.

And then one evening Mark came home from work to find Margot in a state of high excitement.

"I was watching a television programme," she said breathlessly, "and there's this clinic in London —"

"Yes?" he said, catching the excitement himself.

"It's a fertility clinic. They treat childless couples. They have a very high success rate. Something like eighty per cent, the man said."

Mark put down his briefcase on the dining-room table. "Did they give an address or a phone number?"

"Yes," Margot said, "I wrote them down."

Mark took the piece of paper. He read it and then looked at the face of his wife, as she struggled to contain the hope that was surging in her breast.

"Maybe this is it," he said. "Maybe these are the people who can help us."

They made contact with the clinic, which pointed out that due to the publicity generated by the television programme they were overwhelmed with inquiries.

But a few weeks after, they got a phone call inviting

them to come to London for a preliminary discussion. They were given an appointment and Margot immediately set about organising plane tickets and accommodation.

The clinic was in a restored Regency building in Knightsbridge. They were interviewed by an elderly man with glasses and thinning hair who introduced himself as Dr Grant. He listened sympathetically to their medical history and took notes.

At the end of the interview, Dr Grant arranged for a series of tests to be carried out. He asked how long they intended to stay in London.

"Three or four days," Mark said. "We thought we'd take a break. Do some shopping, catch some West End shows."

"Good. I'll be able to discuss this matter with you further when I've seen the results of the tests. Can you come again on Thursday afternoon at two thirty?"

"Do you think you'll be able to help us?" Margot asked anxiously.

Dr Grant smiled. "I can't say that for certain till I've had a chance to study the results. But rest assured, Mrs Chambers, if it's possible to assist you, that is exactly what we shall do."

Margot was ecstatic. When they got outside, she gripped Mark's arm. "I've got a feeling about this. I just know it's going to work. Oh, Mark! Isn't it wonderful?"

"You're going too fast," he said, laughing. "Let's wait till we hear what he's got to say."

"But weren't you impressed? He certainly seems to know what he's doing. And they have a very high success rate. The television programme said that."

"Let's wait," Mark said.

They spent the next few days sightseeing, going to the theatre, visiting museums and art galleries.

On Thursday afternoon, at two thirty precisely, they

presented themselves once more at the clinic. Dr Grant was waiting for them.

He discussed the results of the tests. They showed there were no major physical problems and then he outlined the possible causes of their difficulties.

"Mrs Chambers, I'm going to put you on a course of a new drug called Clomiphene. It's had very good results in clinical trials in the United States. It should enhance your fertility. I want you to pay strict attention to the prescribed dosage and contact me at once if you suffer any side-effects."

"Is that all?" Margot asked, surprised.

"For the time being."

"And will I get pregnant?"

Dr Grant laughed. "That's entirely up to you young people. I want you to continue with your sexual life as normal. And don't be discouraged if it doesn't work immediately – it may take a while to have an effect. Come and see me again in three months' time."

Margot was in great humour as they flew back to Dublin that evening. The visit to the clinic seemed to have restored her old spirits.

"He called us 'young people'. Did you hear him?"

"What's wrong with you?" Mark chided jokingly. "Can't you take a compliment?"

"But 'young people' means kids in their twenties."

"No, it doesn't. It's one of these elastic terms. You can be young in your fifties. Youth is just a state of mind. Besides, he's older than us so we're young to him."

He went back to work and Margot resumed her social activities. Everybody commented on how giddy she had become.

Dr Grant had given her a three-month supply of the drug, which she took religiously according to the directions. They resumed their lovemaking but this time a new confidence seemed to have entered. However, at the end of the first month, Margot's period arrived as usual, right on schedule. She couldn't hide her disappointment.

"You have to give it time," Mark urged. "Dr Grant said it may take a while. Just relax, Margot. Everything is going to be all right."

Meanwhile, he was busier than ever. Each week brought new commissions so they could scarcely keep up with the demand. It seemed that everybody wanted Chambers Creative Artists to work on their advertising campaigns. He decided to reorganise the company with a small group of senior designers concentrating on the major accounts.

The increased workload meant he was away from home longer. He had meetings to attend, interviews to conduct, clients to entertain. The promise he made to Margot to withdraw from the business once it was successful seemed to have been forgotten.

But she never complained. It made Mark feel guilty. He compensated by buying her presents and taking her out to dinner in expensive restaurants. And he told himself that in a year, two at the most, he would honour his promise and begin to wind down.

One evening as he was working late, she rang him at work.

"Any idea when you might be home?"

He looked at his watch and swore. "I'm sorry, Margot, I didn't realise it was so late."

"Can you come home now? It's just that . . ." She seemed to hesitate. "It's just that I've got something to tell you."

"Shoot."

"I was going to wait till you got home . . ."

"Don't keep me in suspense! What is it?"

"My period's overdue."

"*What?*"

"I didn't want to say anything immediately in case it was a false alarm. But it's now four days, Mark. And it's *never* been this late before."

"Halleluja!" Mark shouted and jumped up from his desk. "I'm on my way. I'll get champagne. That's the best news I've heard in years."

He put down the phone and grabbed his jacket.

A young designer called Larry Dolan looked up from his work. "Somebody win the lottery or something?"

Mark's face burst into a wide grin. "No," he said. "It's far better than that."

Margot got a home pregnancy-test kit and the result was positive. They could barely contain their excitement. But she was the one who urged caution. She was well aware that many pregnancies ended in miscarriage in the early stages. They decided to wait for one more month before getting a medical opinion.

For the rest of the month, she got kid-glove treatment. Mark took time off to look after her. He fussed. He made sure she was eating a good, healthy diet. He insisted that she got plenty of rest.

"For God's sake," Margot protested, "I'm not an invalid, you know."

"We're not taking any chances."

Her period didn't come the next month either and they breathed a sigh of relief.

They decided that Margot should see her own GP immediately rather than wait the two weeks for their appointment with Dr Grant in London.

Mark took the day off work and they went together. He sat in the waiting room while Margot went in alone for her consultation. She was gone a long time. He watched the big clock on the wall above the door as the hands seemed to crawl along. After what felt like an eternity, the door opened again and Margot reappeared. He studied her face for a sign that everything was okay.

Their eyes locked and she smiled. She slowly raised her fist and gave a thumbs-up sign.

Mark felt his heart explode with joy.

"When are we going to tell people?" Mark wanted to know, when they got home and the initial flush of excitement had subsided.

"Not just yet," Margot insisted. "Let's just keep it our secret a little while longer."

"I'm sure they're all wondering. I'm sure the tongues have been wagging."

"Who cares? That just means they're going to get an even bigger surprise when we finally tell them the news."

But Margot couldn't even keep her own counsel. Within a fortnight, she was sending off for catalogues of baby clothes and taking surreptitious trips into town to look at baby buggies. She began to discuss names with Mark. He wanted something traditional but she was determined to have a modern name.

"Some of the traditional names are enjoying quite a vogue," Mark said. "Adam, for instance, was a very popular boy's name last year according to *The Irish Times*."

After weeks of discussion, they drew up a compromise list of six boys' names and six girls' names.

"But this might alter," Margot warned. "These are only preliminary. I retain the right to change my mind."

She bought books on child-rearing and got hours of pleasure reading about the various theories of parenting. She decided she would like to develop a relationship with her child that would be based more on friendship than a strict adult-child arrangement.

"We'll grow up together. I'll rediscover my own childhood," she told a baffled Mark one evening at dinner.

"I'm looking forward to seeing it," he said.

She had monthly appointments with her gynaecologist, who monitored her diet and blood pressure and reassured her with the comforting news that everything was fine and right on schedule for a healthy delivery.

She began to put on weight. Soon it would be impossible to keep her condition a secret. They decided to hold a drinks party to announce the news to their friends. But first, they would have to tell their parents. Margot said it was only diplomatic that they should know before anyone else. Imagine the indignity if you were to discover you were about to become a grandmother from someone you met in the supermarket.

So the parents were told and the following Sunday they held the party. It was a warm July day but there was a cool breeze blowing up from the sea. Mark decided to light the barbecue on the lawn. People came and drank wine and beer and ate hamburgers and said what a perfectly original idea to hold a party to announce your pregnancy. But that was Mark and Margot. They were always coming up with bright schemes.

Some of Margot's girlfriends cornered her and said she

just had to come out to lunch with them next week. She had been hiding herself away recently. She protested that she wanted to take it easy now that she was five months pregnant but they insisted. It would be an opportunity to swap gossip and pass on some useful baby advice. Reluctantly, she agreed.

The lunch was arranged for Wednesday; a new bistro in Malahide that was getting rave reviews. She explained to Mark that she had been ambushed but he surprised her by saying he agreed with her friends.

"You *have* been cooped up too much. It'll do you good to get out of the house. Ring me later and let me know how it goes." He set off for work as usual at eight. Since his return from London, he had thrown himself back into the business with a vengeance. He planned to put a new management team in place and then gradually withdraw from running the company once the baby was born. But first, he had to secure the position of Chambers Creative Artists as Ireland's leading advertising agency.

He worked on projects all morning and then had lunch with a rising young copy-editor he was hoping to recruit. By the time he got back to the office there was more business to attend to, so it was almost four o'clock before he realised that Margot hadn't called.

Must be a cracking lunch, he thought. I know what it's like when that lot get together. No doubt, a lot of ears will be burning. Rather than call Margot on her mobile, he decided to wait till she got home.

He never got the chance. At ten past five, his secretary came to him with an ashen face.

"The Malahide police are on the line for you," she said.

Mark took the call. He knew before they said anything that it was bad news.

"Mr Chambers, there's been an accident."

He felt a bolt of white-hot fear go shooting through him.

"Where is she?" he said, his voice rising.

"Beaumont hospital."

"I'm on my way."

He would remember the next words for the rest of his life.

"Mr Chambers, you should prepare yourself for the worst."

He learned later what had happened. The lunch had been a big success and Margot had stayed later than she planned. But at three thirty she decided it was time to go home. She got into her red sports car and drove along the coast road. She was stone cold sober. She had been drinking mineral water all through the lunch.

On the narrow Baldoyle Road, she came across a parked delivery van. She slowed down, indicated and pulled out. But as she did so, a heavy truck bore down on her in the oncoming lane. The truck driver saw her and stomped on the brakes. But it was too late. His truck slammed into Margot's red sports car and smashed it to a pulp.

There was a massive turnout for the funeral. The newspapers and television covered it with pictures and reports. Mark and Margot were well known and the tragic death of the mother-to-be was a good human-interest story.

Mark was distraught. He thought his own life had come to an end. All he could feel was an aching emptiness; all he could see was a long, lonely void where his life had once been.

After the funeral, he returned to work. But he couldn't concentrate. He lost weight. He couldn't sleep. He had no interest.

Everything in the house remained exactly as Margot had left it. Her clothes still hung in the closet; her perfumes and toiletries remained on the bathroom shelf. Even the book she had been reading about parenting still sat on the bedside table. Every week, Mark visited her grave and brought fresh flowers.

For months afterwards, he was stricken by grief. The weeks moved slowly into spring, then summer.

One day in June, a friend told him about this priest he knew who was based at the Mount Argus monastery in Dublin. The friend suggested that Mark should go and talk to him. He had a wonderful reputation as a counsellor and he might be able to help Mark deal with his grief. The priest was called Father Michael.

Mark went to see him. He was an elderly man with bright eyes and a kind, sympathetic face. They talked for a long time about Margot and what had happened. The priest said he couldn't explain why God had allowed her to die so tragically.

"What do you think she would want you to do now?" the priest asked at last.

"I don't know."

"She would want you to be happy. She loved you. Surely you can believe that?"

"Yes."

"So you must stop grieving. You must pick up your life again. That's what she would want you to do. You must let go of the past and look to the future."

"I can't, Father. I have no interest in my life or my work any more, and everything reminds me of her."

"Then let it all go for a while. Go somewhere new – somewhere different. Where you can rest, relax, allow yourself time to heal." The old man smiled. "Preferably in the sun."

The idea struck Mark as a good one. He would get away somewhere; at the very least a change of scenery would distract him.

He rang his local tourist agent and asked what was available.

"The Costa del Sol is very good this time of year. Plenty of sunshine, nice restaurants, golf if you're interested."

"Where do you recommend?" he asked.

"There's a little place called Carvajal. It's on the sea, close to Fuengirola. Malaga is the nearest airport."

"All right," Mark said. "Would you book something for me?"

3

Claire Greene stared at the advert that had just jumped off the page of the *Irish Independent* to grab her attention. She had been sitting in the little kitchen at the back of the office enjoying a welcome cup of tea when she spotted it.

Give Yourself a Break! Enjoy a Carefree Holiday in Sunny Fuengirola!

Immediately, she stopped reading. Her mind flooded with glorious images: the unbroken expanse of clear blue sky, the shimmering sea, the burning sand, the nightlife, the music, the fun, the excitement. It would be magic. No more rain, no more cloud. No more dull boring days. Claire had golden memories of the last time she was on the Costa del Sol, four short years ago, just after she had graduated from Trinity College with her degree in Legal Studies. It had been the happiest time of her life. She had been young, free, unattached and her future had stretched before her like a bright shining path.

And then another thought came rushing into her head

to shatter her reverie. She put the paper down. There had been a darker side too. Something had happened back there that still cast a long shadow on her life. She closed her eyes and let her thoughts drift back.

It was the autumn of 2001. Claire was twenty-two. The dowdy tomboy in jeans and denim jacket had blossomed into a tall, attractive young woman with long black hair and dark, intelligent eyes. At five feet nine inches, Claire had outgrown all her friends and, by dint of some seriously hard work in the last six months of her final year in college, had managed to secure a pretty good degree: a 2.1 Honours. There had only been five of them awarded that year and one First, which went to Patricia Smyth who everyone agreed had spent every waking minute of every day with her head stuck in a book and consequently had no life whatsoever.

"Poor Patricia!" they sighed over their strawberry daiquiris in Banana Joe's bar, where they had all gathered to celebrate their exam results. Was it worth it? To sacrifice four years of your life for a First? Never to have been to a dance or a Rag Day or the Trinity Ball? Never to have been kissed by a man? Or a woman, Philip O'Neill of the rugby club put in to hoots of laughter from the men.

It *wasn't* worth it, they all agreed. University was about more than just studying. It was about growing up. It was about savouring new experiences. It was about self-discovery. And how were you going to do that if all your time was spent swotting? Mind you, they were forced to concede that Patricia would walk straight into a good job in a top law firm. In no time at all, she would be earning buckets of money. There *was* that to be said in favour of a

First Class Honours degree in Legal Studies from Trinity College.

The question of what to do with her own degree was to consume a lot of Claire's thoughts in the coming weeks. More precisely, it was to consume a lot of her mother's thoughts. Mrs Greene was one of those fussy, overpowering women who believed that her role in life would never be complete till she had guided, browbeaten or manipulated each of her three children into secure careers and advantageous marriages.

She had succeeded with her first two. Thomas, who was the oldest at thirty-two, was the deputy head of the Life division of a major insurance company and was married to Paula, a distracted, nervous woman whose family were large dairy farmers in Tipperary and had grown fat on the proceeds of the Common Agricultural Policy. Mrs Greene talked proudly to her friends and acquaintances of the couple's beautiful home in Dalkey on a road near the sea where their next-door neighbour was a minor rock star.

Orla was the assistant principal of a national school in west Dublin and had married John, who owned a successful bookshop in Blackrock. They had agreed to postpone having a family till Orla became principal, which was expected any day soon, as the incumbent, Mr Breen, was showing distinct signs of wear and tear. Mrs Greene predicted a glittering future for them too.

Which left Claire, who was the youngest child and by far the most difficult. Claire was a bright girl, Mrs Greene agreed, but she had inherited a streak of independence from somewhere. It certainly hadn't come from Mr Greene, who was a principal officer in the Department of Fisheries and Food and played absolutely no part in the upbringing of his children. He had long ago accepted that his wife could more than adequately fulfil that function for both of them and had retreated to the front parlour where he completed crossword puzzles and listened to Brahms quartets on the stereo and left all the major decisions to his wife.

It was Mrs Greene who had decided that Claire should apply for Legal Studies as she approached her Leaving Certificate exams.

"The law is the place to be," she said bluntly. "It's a licence to print money. Some of those barristers are earning £1000 a day. It's like owning a piece of a goldmine. And you're bound to meet a nice class of man from a good family."

Mrs Greene had also specified Trinity College. She came from that generation that had been prevented from going to Trinity by the Catholic Archbishop of Dublin and as a result she held it in very high regard. Mrs Greene wouldn't admit it publicly but she believed Protestants had more class and better manners and were generally more reliable than Catholics. Not that there were that many Protestants left at Trinity. Recently, the place seemed to have been overrun by Catholics. Still, she was firmly convinced that a degree in Legal Studies from Trinity would be much more valuable than a similar document from any other university.

Claire had gone along with her mother's plans simply because she had no better ideas of her own. But she had proved a disappointment. She had not managed to snag an aspiring young legal eagle as her mother had fervently hoped. Mrs Greene believed that the way to win a man's heart was for a girl to be totally subservient and to make herself pretty and agreeable at all times.

"They're not looking for female Einsteins," she told Claire. "They're looking for someone who will bolster their self-confidence and make them look good in front of their friends. All that other stuff can wait till later, when you've got the ring safely on your finger."

But Claire's independence got in the way. She couldn't see why she should play second-fiddle to some silly idiot just because he happened to be a man. And she couldn't bring herself to simper and smile at the nonsense that some of them talked and the juvenile behaviour they indulged in like the beer-drinking contests during Rag Week when they got maggoty drunk and were sick all over the place.

Claire found the very idea sad and demeaning. And anyway, she was in no rush to get married like her sister and brother. She was confident that she would know when the right man came along. So she drifted through college with only an occasional short-lived flirtation while her mother fretted with frustration and muttered darkly about Claire missing the boat completely if she wasn't careful.

But any regret that Mrs Greene felt about Claire's failure to find a suitable partner was as nothing compared to the panic that set in once she had got her degree. She was privately disappointed that Claire hadn't managed a First but she reluctantly accepted that a 2.1 was a pretty good second-best. Particularly since it was from Trinity. Now she had to put it to good effect and get a job. But as the weeks ticked away without any prospect of even an interview, Mrs Greene started to get worried.

"What are you waiting for?" she demanded to know. "You can't just sit around in the hope that someone will come knocking on the door. You've got to get out there and sell yourself."

"I need time to think," Claire said wearily.

"What is there to think about? Are you going for the Bar or do you want to become a solicitor? It's one or the other."

"I don't know," Claire said irritably. "I don't even know if I want a career in the law at all."

Mrs Greene, who believed there was a limited number of jobs just as there was a limited number of eligible men and was convinced they were all being snapped up while Claire sat at home and twiddled her thumbs, exploded in exasperation.

"You're letting the grass grow under your feet. Do you want to end up packing bags in Tesco?"

Claire wouldn't have minded packing bags in Tesco while she tried to make up her mind but she knew her mother would die of embarrassment at the very thought. Yet she was determined not to be bounced into something she might regret. She had gone along with her mother's wishes so far but now that she was facing a major life choice, she wanted to think it out clearly.

It was at this point that fate intervened. Claire got a phone call one morning from her friend Róisín Murphy to meet her for coffee in town as she had something great to tell her. Claire jumped at the opportunity. The atmosphere at home was growing increasingly fraught, with Mrs Greene now resorting to cutting adverts from *The Irish Times* appointments section and placing them on the kitchen table along with Claire's cornflakes each morning.

Claire met Róisín at a sidewalk café in Grafton Street. She looked excited. Don't tell me she's just landed a big job, Claire thought glumly. Mum will never let me forget it. Róisín waited till Claire had sat down and ordered a café latte before announcing her news.

"I'm going to Spain," she said.

Claire blinked. What was the big deal? People went to Spain all the time these days.

"A holiday?"

"Well, sort of. A kind of extended holiday. I intend to work."

"Aren't you applying for jobs here like the rest of them?" Claire asked.

Róisín, who was one of the staunchest advocates of university as a life-enhancing experience, gave a curious smile. "I've decided to take a year out. Why rush into something that's going to tie me down for the rest of my life? The way I see it, I've got my degree. Now it's time to enjoy myself and see a bit of the world. The jobs will still be waiting when I get back."

Suddenly it all made sense to Claire. Of course, Róisín was perfectly right! It wasn't as if the job market was going to dry up in the next couple of weeks. She had spent four years studying for her degree and before that another fourteen years at school. She had been on the educational treadmill practically since she had learned to walk. Didn't it make sense to take time out to reflect?

"When are you going?"

"Next week."

It took Claire a split second to make up her mind.

"I'll go with you," she said.

The pair spent another couple of hours deciding how they would do it. In the end, it was agreed that they would get the ferry to France and make their way to Paris and then south to Marseilles before crossing the border into Spain. They would travel light and stay at cheap hostels while they made their leisurely way. It was summer; the weather was fine. They might even sleep out under the stars and wake up to eat fresh pears in some rural orchard, Róisín said brightly.

Claire felt the excitement surge through her as they plotted what would be the biggest adventure of their lives.

They had all the time in the world. They could stop off at pretty little towns along the way. It was the holiday season and they spoke English, so they could easily get work in bars and restaurants.

"What will we do about money?" Claire asked. "We're going to need some and I know I'm broke."

"We can take out a student loan. It's no problem. The banks will be delighted to lend us some dosh. Especially now that we've got our degrees."

The plan was finalised. They would go the following week. It would give Claire time to take out a loan and get her passport and ferry ticket organised. Now came the hard bit. She had to tell her mother.

Mrs Greene exploded at the news. She ranted and raved. She said it was the craziest thing she had ever heard – to walk away and leave all those lovely jobs to people with second-class qualifications from inferior colleges. And what about the disgrace? What was she going to say to people when they asked about Claire? How was she supposed to tell her friends that her daughter with her good degree was off picking grapes with Andalusian peasants on some dusty Spanish hillside while *their* children were settling their fat bums into nice cushy positions? She even dragged the long-suffering Mr Greene into the dispute, suggesting that Claire was clearly having a nervous breakdown and needed urgent psychiatric attention.

But Claire stuck to her guns. If anything, her mother's reaction just strengthened her determination to get away from Dublin as fast as possible. In the end her mother had to accept that she wasn't going to change her mind. She went into a sulk and moped around the house, muttering about the ingratitude and the fact that Róisín Murphy was a bad influence and she hadn't liked her from the very first day she set eyes on her.

On the morning of Claire's departure her mother tearfully drew her aside and gave her a little lecture.

"I think you understand that I totally disagree with this but for God's sake take care of yourself. Watch those foreign men, especially the Italians."

"We won't be going anywhere near Italy," Claire pointed out.

"They're all the same," Mrs Greene said. "They're only after the one thing and I needn't tell you what it is. They enjoy nothing better than taking advantage of innocent Irish girls like you."

"I'm twenty-two, Mum, and I'm not as innocent as you think."

"It doesn't matter. They can't control their hormones like Irishmen. And for God's sake don't allow them to buy you drinks under any circumstances. They put drugs in them and the next thing you know you wake up in bed with no clothes on. I read an article about it in a magazine just the other day."

Claire had to smother a laugh. "I'll bear that in mind."

"And don't wear tight trousers. It drives them crazy."

Her father gave her a kiss and a hug and an envelope stuffed with €50 notes.

"Good luck," he said. "Keep in touch. You can always reverse the charges when you're phoning home."

"Thanks, Dad," Claire said as she shouldered the knapsack she had bought and headed down the drive to where the taxi was waiting.

She felt an enormous sense of liberation as the taxi carried her away. She knew her parents loved her. And she knew her mother meant well and had her best interests at heart. But she had to escape. The atmosphere at home had become stifling. It was like living in a hothouse. She had to breathe a little. She had to live. She had to start making decisions for herself. And if she made mistakes, so be it. At least they would be her own mistakes.

But that sunny August morning as she journeyed to the train station where she had arranged to meet Róisín, mistakes were the last thing on Claire Greene's mind.

From the moment she settled into the train that was to take them down to Rosslare, Claire felt like an explorer setting off to discover new worlds. This would be the longest period she had ever spent away from home since the time she went to the Connemara Gaeltacht when she was fourteen. And this would be a whole year! It was a glorious opportunity. She was going to do new things and meet new people. She felt a tingling excitement as she settled back in her seat and watched the countryside go flashing by.

By seven they were in Cherbourg. It was too late to travel any further. Róisín found a cheap hotel near the railway station and they left their luggage with the owner and went out to get something to eat. They were determined to guard their money carefully but, even so, they were able to have a fabulous dinner of mussels and salad and fresh bread and a carafe of red wine for what they would spend in a burger joint back home. After the meal they had glasses of Cointreau with their coffees. Claire felt light-headed. The world they had left less than twelve hours ago already seemed like a million miles away.

She sat back in the little wicker chair and breathed in the sea air.

"Can't you just smell it?" she asked.

"What?"

"The freedom."

Róisín laughed. "I know what you mean. Isn't it marvellous? To think we have no more lectures! No more exams. We can do what we want. Go where we like."

"I don't know why I didn't think of this."

"Because your mind was focused on getting a career. You had been brainwashed into believing that was your natural destination in life."

"You're so right."

"You were getting caught up in the rat race."

"The mouse race, you mean."

They threw back their heads and laughed and the plump proprietor smiled from her seat behind the bar. She had seen it all before. They came to France and immediately their personalities changed with the weather. Still, it was good to see her customers enjoying themselves.

They were up early the following morning. They had already decided to get the train directly to Paris. They would spend a week there before beginning their journey south. They had a breakfast of fresh rolls and hot chocolate, paid their bill and made their way to the station. By midday, the train was pulling into the Gare du Nord.

There were lots of cheap hotels near the station. They found a place that looked clean and reasonably priced and Róisín, who spoke decent French, was able to negotiate a good rate. After Cherbourg, they found Paris crowded and noisy and the heat sticky and oppressive but it didn't matter. This was the first time either of them had been in the city and they were determined to extract the last ounce of enjoyment from the experience.

They spent the next seven days wandering through the streets and along the banks of the Seine, stopping at tiny restaurants when they were hungry, resting in the little parks with their tinkling fountains and grand statues, having a nightcap in one of the many bars that littered the streets near their hotel.

They did the usual tourist things: visited Notre Dame and the Louvre, strolled in the Luxembourg gardens, took the train out to Versailles to see the splendid palace of the Sun King. Before they knew, their wonderful week in Paris had come to an end and it was time to move on.

The morning they left, it was raining. They took the metro to Porte de Vincennes and emerged into the fine drizzle with their knapsacks on their shoulders and stood at the slip-road to the motorway while they waited for some kind driver to give them a lift. Maybe the rain helped. Within twenty minutes, a truck driver had taken pity on the sodden figures and they were ensconced in the warm cab and heading south towards Dijon.

It took them another week to reach Marseilles but they were in no hurry. If they arrived in a town in time, they booked a hotel room; otherwise they bunked down wherever they found themselves. The weather had turned warmer the further south they travelled. It was no problem to unroll their sleeping bags in a barn or in the shade of a bush and go to sleep with the stars twinkling above them. Next morning they would waken to the sound of birdsong and walk to the nearest village to breakfast on fresh-brewed coffee and hot baguettes with ham or great melting slices of Camembert cheese. Claire loved it. It was all part of the adventure. Some days she hoped they would miss a town just for the experience of sleeping rough.

Marseilles was big and crowded and noisy, a smaller version of Paris but with the sea and a distinctive Mediterranean feel. They spent a night there in a rowdy hotel where people kept coming and going all night long and they got little sleep. The following morning they were amused to discover that it doubled as a bordello. They packed their bags quickly and headed along the coast towards Perpignan. Two days later they were in Barcelona.

Claire had read about Barcelona but it still took her breath away. She marvelled at the easy-going nature of the inhabitants, the cosmopolitan atmosphere, the wide-open squares, the pavement cafés, the broad sweep of the Ramblas with its banks of flowers, its covered markets and the bustling port waiting to surprise the visitor at the bottom of the hill.

She could have stayed longer in Barcelona but Róisín was anxious to press on further south to the Costa del Sol. Already, their money was beginning to get low and Róisín believed it would be easier to find work along the Costa with its thousands of tourist visitors. After four days, Claire reluctantly packed her knapsack and they were off again.

They reached Fuengirola in the middle of September. Róisín wanted to go on a little further to Marbella but a quick inquiry about accommodation soon convinced them. Marbella was ritzier and more upmarket but so were the prices. They would do better to stay where they were. The holiday season was coming to an end. Traffic was beginning to trail off. It made sense to spend the winter in Fuengirola and review their options again in the spring.

They left their knapsacks in the left luggage at the bus station and set off to find somewhere to stay. And here again, fate took a turn. After trooping around the dozens of rental agencies along the seafront, they finally arrived at a little office in one of the back streets of the old town.

The man who came to talk to them was in his late twenties perhaps – tall, dark-haired, blue-eyed, tanned and dressed in a smart navy pinstriped business suit, shirt and tie. He spoke with a brisk London accent. He reminded Claire of one of those ideally handsome dummies in fashionable shop windows – but much more animated. In fact, he was a bundle of energy.

Yes, he had accommodation. Yes, it was quiet and well-maintained. How long did they want it for?

"Three –" Róisín began.

But Claire quickly intervened. "Six months."

"Well, that changes things slightly. If you're prepared to stay for six months, I can let you have it at a reduced rate."

"How much?" Claire asked.

"Four hundred euro a month."

"Three hundred."

His face broke into a broad smile. "Don't you want to see it first?"

"Of course. But before we proceed, I want to make sure that we're all singing off the same hymn sheet. There's no point wasting each other's time."

He drove them to the apartment, which was only a few streets away. It was in a modern block, had two bedrooms, a sizeable sitting-room, bathroom, kitchen and a balcony overlooking the street. He explained that it was owned by a French woman whose husband was ill and consequently wasn't able to use it. It was perfect for what they wanted.

"What do we get for the rent?" Claire wanted to know.

The man looked amused. "You get the apartment, of course."

"What about utilities?"

He let out a loud laugh. "My God, you drive a hard bargain!"

"The holiday season is coming to an end," Claire said. "It could be lying empty all winter. At least this way you're getting some return."

It was agreed that the rent would include water, gas and electricity charges and that they would pay him a month's rent in advance.

On the way back to the street, he asked, "What are you young ladies planning to do in Fuengirola?"

"Work," Claire said.

There was a twinkle in his eye. "Do you think you could sell property?"

"What would be involved?" Claire wanted to know.

"Call at my office in the morning. I'll have your lease made out. I'll explain it all to you then." He pushed a card across the table. *Matthew Baker*, it read. *Sales Director, Gateway Properties Ltd*.

That evening they ate paella with salad and warm bread in a lively square near the church.

"That was a smart move to tell him we'd be staying for six months," Róisín said.

"I suspected we'd get a better deal that way. Anyway, who knows? Maybe we will be."

They tapped their glasses together and gazed across the square. The lights were coming on and the strollers were beginning to appear – whole families with the grandmother and children in tow. A crowd was starting to gather round an acrobat in a clown's outfit.

Claire felt a warm glow spread through her. She was going to like it here. She knew it in her bones. Already things were falling into place. They had a nice apartment; and tomorrow a promise of work. She drained her glass and uttered a small sigh of contentment.

The following morning at ten they made their way back to the rental agency. The air was already warm and it promised to be a hot day. A young woman who looked like she had just stepped from the pages of *Vogue* flashed a dazzling white smile and asked them their business. When they told her, she brightened even further and said in a cool, professional voice: "Mr Baker is expecting you."

She led them to the back of the premises and pushed open a door.

Matthew Baker was on the phone. In a silver-grey shirt so crisp it looked like it had just been taken out of its packaging, he looked every bit as debonair as he had the previous day. How on earth do they do it, Claire thought? Do they have some built-in air-conditioning system that keeps them cool? Already she could feel the prickly heat cause beads of sweat to stand on her forehead.

Matthew Baker put down the phone and invited them to be seated. He pushed two leases across the desk and asked them to sign. Then he signed himself and gave one back.

"Aren't the signatures supposed to be witnessed?" Claire asked.

He grinned and waved his hand dismissively. "We're all friends here." He looked at her more closely. "At least I think we are."

His playfulness caused Claire to smile. "You said you might have work for us."

"Yes, I might. You've already shown considerable sales skills in the way you managed to reduce the rent, Ms . . ." He glanced again at the lease.

"Greene," Claire said. "What would we have to do?"

"Like I said, sell property."

"How?"

"By stopping people on the street."

Róisín burst out laughing. "You're joking, of course."

"No, I'm not."

"But that's not how you sell property."

"Why not? It's a cultural thing, that's all. The Spanish have a more aggressive approach to sales. Have you seen how they operate at the local market? Anyway, you won't actually be selling anything. I'll be doing that. Your job will be to persuade the clients to come back here to this office. Then you leave the rest up to me."

Over the next fifteen minutes, he explained how the scheme worked. Róisín and Claire would be armed with brochures showing the attractions of a new apartment development being built on the outskirts of the town. They would engage people on the street and by charm and persuasion get them to come back to the office where Matthew Baker would be waiting.

The women exchanged a glance.

"Is this legal?" Róisín asked. "We don't want to get arrested."

"It's perfectly legal. You don't think the Spanish authorities would allow me to run this office for five minutes unless everything was above board? And there are rules. You must only approach couples. We don't want one partner agreeing to buy and the other one coming back the next day and tearing the whole thing up. And they also get a guaranteed cooling-off period during which they can change their minds."

He got up from the desk and pulled a large easel across the room. On it was a plan of the development, with *Apartamentos Vista del Mar* displayed in bright letters.

"These are the properties. Now let me explain their features so that you know exactly what you're talking about."

When he had finished, Claire asked: "What do you propose to pay us?"

"One hundred euros a week, plus a bonus of another hundred each time you bring a prospective client back. Plus a further bonus if we make a sale."

Claire did a quick calculation. The basic wage was peanuts. They would get more on the dole back in Ireland. But it would pay the rent and there was the prospect of more if they were successful. She looked at Róisín, who nodded reluctantly.

"Okay, we'll give it a try."

Matthew Baker clapped his hands. "Excellent." He opened a drawer and took out a couple of mobile phones. "Ring me the minute you have someone interested. And bring them back in a taxi. It creates a better mood. And don't let them out of your sight or let up on the sales spiel until you've handed them over to me. Now when can you start?"

"This afternoon?" Claire suggested.

"Perfect. I'll meet you here at two." He allowed his eye to travel over the two women from head to toe. "And ladies, no offence, but could you freshen up a little? Wear something a little more striking? First impressions are everything."

Claire didn't know whether to be insulted or amused by Matthew Baker's parting remark but she had already seen how much store Gateway Properties placed on appearance. Matthew and his receptionist could have been James Bond and his latest sexual conquest.

They spent the rest of the morning at a nearby supermarket stocking up on provisions and then had lunch at a little restaurant. God only knew when they would get the chance to eat again.

"What do you make of it all?" Róisín asked over the grilled sardines.

Claire tossed her mane of dark hair. "It sounds like it could be hard work. But at least it's a job. It will give us a chance to find our feet. And if we don't like it, we don't have to stay."

"I've never sold anything in my life," Róisín said glumly.

Claire could see that already she was beginning to have doubts. "Neither have I. But there's a first time for everything."

She thought briefly of her mother back in Dublin. She would have an apoplectic fit if she thought her daughter was standing on a street corner trying to sell apartments to complete strangers. It would convince her that Claire had gone stone barking mad.

The sun had come out and was bathing the street in golden light. She gently patted her friend's arm.

"Cheer up. I checked the weather forecast on the Internet this morning. It's raining in Dublin."

Matthew Baker drove them to a pitch near the seafront, which was conveniently positioned close to a taxi rank. He gave them each an armful of glossy brochures showing the apartments in all their magnificence. His cool demeanour hadn't waned nor had his energy level.

"All right, ladies. You're on your own. Just remember, you've got to make them feel that you're doing them a favour. And the minute you get a bite, pop them in a cab and whisk them round to me. Easy as falling off a log!"

Claire was to remember that phrase in the hours that lay ahead. There was nothing remotely easy about what they had undertaken. In fact, nothing she had ever done in her life had prepared her for what she was about to experience.

Matthew Baker had told them to put on a big cheery smile and open the conversation by asking where the clients were from and how they were enjoying their holiday. But after a while the muscles in Claire's cheeks were aching from the effort and she hadn't succeeded in even getting past the first sentence. People she approached immediately stiffened and waved her away or they brushed past aggressively as if she was a beggar. She began to wilt under the unremitting torrent of rejection. And the sun just seemed to get stronger and brighter as the day progressed, till her legs began to throb with pain and she felt her skin starting to burn. She cursed the fact that, in the rush, she had forgotten to apply her sun-block.

Róisín was faring no better and the fake smile on her face had long faded to a fixed grin. This was like working in hell. No wonder Matthew Baker had been so eager to employ them without experience or references or any of the usual formalities that Claire expected from a job interview. He couldn't get anyone stupid enough to take on the work. That was why.

And then, just as she was about to pack it all in and dump the brochures in the nearest litter-bin, a middle-aged couple stopped.

"Good afternoon," Claire said, frantically trying to remember the sales spiel she had been taught. "Where are you from?"

"Liverpool," the husband said brightly.

"Ah, Liverpool! The unofficial capital of Ireland."

The man laughed. "My mother was Irish. God rest her soul."

"Well, isn't that a coincidence?" Claire babbled on. This was the longest conversation she had managed with anyone in the past three hours. "Are you enjoying your holiday?"

"So far," the man's wife replied. She was a small birdlike woman with bottle-blonde hair.

"Don't tell me you're missing the dreary English weather?" Claire said quickly, wondering if she'd been taken over by spirits. She had never spoken like this in her life before. But they seemed to like it, for they both laughed this time.

Now for the killer punch.

"Are you interested in Spanish property by any chance?"

The couple looked at each other. There was a pause that seemed to last forever.

"We might be," the man replied at last.

His wife was nodding her head. "John's taking early retirement in a few months. We were thinking of looking around for a nice apartment. Not too expensive, mind you."

Claire could scarcely contain herself. "Well, in that case, I might just have the very thing for you," she said sweetly, producing one of her brochures.

Five minutes later, she had herself and the pair safely tucked up in a taxi. She gave directions to the driver and continued the sales patter. She had been warned not to let them out of her sight till they were safely delivered to the office of Gateway Properties, where Matthew was waiting to make the sale.

He succeeded. An hour later, a very satisfied John and Emily Morton emerged from the office having paid a deposit and signed an agreement to buy a two-bed apartment in Vista del Mar. Claire felt delirious. She had helped to make a sale but, equally important, the Mortons were happy. She had been nursing a lingering doubt about pressurising people into buying something they might not want. But this certainly hadn't happened in this case. They seemed genuinely delighted with their purchase.

That evening, after they had been home to shower and change, Matthew took them to celebrate in a lovely little restaurant in the old town.

"It must be your Irish blarney," he said as he filled their glasses with ruby-red Rioja. "That was one of the fastest deals I've ever concluded."

Claire blushed. She was feeling rather proud of herself. "Just put it down to my natural friendliness."

"Well, whatever it is, it worked." He took out a pocket calculator and did a quick tot.

"You've just earned yourself €500 on top of your basic."

Claire was thrilled. She looked across the table to Matthew. He looked very handsome in the evening light, his dark hair and white shirt bringing out the radiance of his tan.

His blue eyes twinkled as he flashed a broad smile. "Think you can do it again tomorrow?"

"I'll certainly try," she said.

She didn't. She stood all day on the hot pavement and failed to interest a single person. She felt her confidence begin to ebb away and the old despondency return. But the following day, she managed to bring two couples back to the office and one of them bought. She ended the week having earned €1300, which was pretty good by anybody's standards. She began to think that maybe, after all, she had a flair for sales.

Róisín, however, had no such luck. The closest she got was one couple who were about to get into the taxi when they suddenly changed their minds. It completely shattered her morale. At the end of the second week, she decided to get out and seek something more amenable, like bar work.

"At least you don't have to stand out on the street and stick pints of beer in people's hands. When they come into the pub, they've already decided they want a drink."

"That's true," Claire admitted.

She tried to comfort her friend. "Look, you shouldn't take it personally. I was just lucky. That's all."

"No," Róisín shook her head, "you have a natural talent for it. People seem to trust you. I could stand out there for a year and nobody would buy an apartment from me."

Matthew didn't seem too disappointed by Róisín's decision. He was clearly only interested in people who could sell and since someone who was unhappy wasn't likely to make a good salesperson there was no point keeping them on the payroll. Besides, he still had Claire and two young Scottish girls who had joined the previous Monday. Before long, Claire was averaging six referrals a week and two sales. It meant she was earning a very decent salary. And since the cost of everything was so much cheaper than back home, for the first time in her life she felt well-off.

But it was hard work. For six days, she stood at her pitch and switched on her bright smile. She had developed a few little sales techniques of her own. She capitalised on the general goodwill that seemed to exist towards the Irish and milked it for all it was worth. But she was always glad when Sunday came round and she could take the day off and just lie on the beach and top up her tan.

Róisín, meanwhile, had found a job in a beach bar called Pedro's. It served food and drinks and Róisín seemed to enjoy meeting the people who drifted in and out of the place. Usually, when she had finished her stint, Claire would stroll along the beach to the bar and have a beer and a sandwich while she caught up on the day's gossip from her friend. She got to know the regulars: Maria, the elderly Spanish lady who ran the bar and always wore black because she was a widow; the Spanish lifeguards; the retired English colonel who liked nothing better than to tell her about his war adventures while he held her hand and gazed into her eyes and his grey moustache bristled with excitement.

It was a happy existence. As the winter approached, the weather got a little colder but it was still much warmer than at home. You could still eat out at a pavement café every evening and bathe in the sea most days. The days continued clear of clouds and filled with sunshine. Claire wrote a long letter to her mother extolling the wonderful life she was enjoying and enclosing a little business card that Matthew had got printed up. In gold letters, it read: *Claire Greene, Property Negotiator.* She knew it wasn't a patch on the Senior Counsel that her mother would have preferred, but at least she could show it to her friends as evidence that her daughter wasn't begging on the streets.

She had begun to see quite a lot of Matthew as the weeks rolled by and learnt all about him. He was from Fulham in west London, was a youthful twenty-nine and had been living up and down the Costa for four years. He had got involved in investment property in the same way she had – making a pitch to people on the street. He had got promoted and ended up managing the firm for the real owner, a man called Sid Robbins who lived in London and only visited Fuengirola twice a year.

As time went by, Matthew came to rely more and more on Claire. First he used her to train the new recruits, the eager young hopefuls who were sent out each day with bundles of brochures and dreams of making their fortunes. Occasionally, when he had to take a day off, he asked her to stand in for him. He shared his problems with her and sought her advice.

Eventually, they became lovers.

It seemed to Claire the most natural thing in the world. It was a starlit night and they were both slightly drunk after a gorgeous meal. But she didn't use these things as an excuse. She had known for some time that it was going to happen. It was just waiting for the right moment. When she woke up the following morning in his bed with the sun streaming in through the big balcony windows, Claire had no regrets. It was like coming home.

He wanted her to move in with him but she refused. She wasn't ready for that kind of commitment and, anyway, she had to think about Róisín. Unlike Claire, she was struggling to survive on the money and the tips she was earning at the bar. If Claire left, she would have to find a replacement, which might not be easy. To walk out on her friend would not be fair.

But she spent most of her free time with Matthew and several nights a week in his bed. It was like having the best of both worlds. She had her independence and her relationship. Several people had warned her about getting too closely involved with her boss but Claire did not regard Matthew as a conventional boss. He had been her friend and now he was her lover.

But she was totally unprepared for the announcement he made one evening just after Easter. The weather was turning warm again and the visitors were starting to appear in serious numbers. It meant increased work for Gateway Properties after the slack winter period.

Claire and Matthew had been to a concert in Marbella and afterwards had dinner in one of the pretty restaurants in Orange Square. She was eating her starter of prawns and avocado when he dropped his bombshell.

"How would you like to come to London with me?"

Claire thought she had misheard him over the chatter from the surrounding tables.

"Are you visiting your family?"

"No doubt I will. But that's not the primary purpose."

She was intrigued. She put down her knife and fork. "For God's sake, Matthew. Don't talk in riddles."

He smiled awkwardly. "I'm moving to London."

Claire's jaw slowly dropped. "You mean permanently?"

"Yes."

She was shocked. She had never stopped to consider that one day her blissful existence in Fuengirola might come to an end. "But why?"

"Because Sid wants me over there. He thinks the Spanish property bubble is about to burst. They're building too many apartments and it's getting more and more difficult to find buyers. He's pulling out."

"I don't understand."

"Sid wants me to run a shop for him in Chelsea. They have a job for you too."

"Doing what?"

"Assistant manager. He'll be paying good money."

"When?"

"Couple of weeks. He's already surrendered the lease of the office."

Claire gasped.

Matthew gently took her hand. "I'd love you to come with me. Selling property is the same the world over. It's just that you have to be a little bit more sophisticated in London. But you'd love it, Claire. And Chelsea is a fabulous spot. Lots of very interesting people."

Claire looked around the little square. People were sitting out under the stars eating at tables. The fuchsia and bougainvillea were in bloom and filled the night air with their heady scent. A couple of itinerant musicians were making their way round the tables, serenading the diners with soulful Spanish love songs. Did she have to leave all this behind? And what about Róisín? What was going to happen to her?

"I need time to think," she said.

She spoke to Róisín, who was equally surprised.

"Do you want to leave?"

"No. I wish this life could go on forever. I love it here."

"But you want to stay with Matthew?"

Claire slowly nodded. "I think I love him, Róisín."

"Then you must follow your heart."

"What will you do?"

"I'll stay till the end of the season. I'll get someone to share with. Don't worry about me."

"Are you sure? I feel like a heel for leaving you like this."

Róisín hugged her friend. "I'll survive. We'll keep in touch. I'll phone and email you with all the news. Maybe you might even get out again for a visit?"

"Of course I will."

Matthew eventually called the staff together and told them they were closing down. He thanked everyone for their loyal service to Gateway Properties. They would be paid a special bonus. Then he took them all for a boozy dinner. But it was a bit of a disaster. One of the Scottish girls drank too much wine and started to cry and everyone felt gloomy and relieved when the dinner was over.

There was some paperwork to be completed, leases and contracts to be handed over to the company solicitor and then they were ready to go. Claire had to purchase a suitcase for all the clothes she had bought since she had come here six months earlier. But at last they were ready to depart. Róisín came with them to the airport and kissed them goodbye and waved as they went through security to the departure lounge. It was a brilliantly sunny morning, the sky like a vast sheet of blue. Claire felt an ache in her heart. She hated to leave. Two hours later, they were touching down at Gatwick airport.

The next few weeks were hectic, as they struggled to find accommodation and then to get the new office up and running. Sid Robbins had already found premises in Vere Street, in the heart of Chelsea, with a big front window, which he said was the most important feature of an estate agent's office. You need to be able to display your wares, he kept saying. That's what brings the punters in. He had turned out to be a plump man with a weakness for flashy ties and thick smelly cigars and immediately put Claire in mind of a fifties Hollywood film producer. He seemed to take a shine to her and said, with more and more women buying property nowadays, a female touch was exactly what they required.

Eventually they were ready. There was a grand opening with champagne and photographs of dignitaries for the local papers. Sid had even managed to rope in a few ageing actors to add a bit of faded glamour and then they were open for business. Meanwhile, Matthew and Claire had found a nice apartment in Battersea, only a short drive away from the office.

Matthew was right. Selling property in London was not the same as selling apartments on the Costa del Sol. There was no question of standing on the street with armfuls of brochures trying to inveigle people to buy. Instead they had to wait for the clients to come to them. And when they did come there were numerous inspection tours and then weeks of haggling over prices before a sale was agreed. But the profits were much greater.

Claire was astounded at the kind of prices being secured for what looked like mediocre properties. One and a half million pounds was not unusual for a two-bed apartment with a twenty-year lease. Even by the standards of the property boom in Dublin, these prices were astronomical. And of course, Gateway always secured their two per cent commission.

She quickly got the hang of it and settled down to life in the big city. She exchanged her T-shirts and shorts for smart business suits and crisp white blouses and with her tall willowy figure and long dark hair, she made a striking presence. She learned how to promote the best features of a property, to stress the gardens and the sunlight and the bright airy kitchen and to gloss over the defects like the cramped garage space or the dry rot that threatened to devour the floorboards.

And people loved her. They said she had such charm and patience and such bright good humour. She didn't mind taking time out of her busy day to spend hours showing a property for the third or fourth time to a client who couldn't make up her mind. They said they never felt pressurised when dealing with Claire, unlike some other agents who just wanted you to sign a contract before you even had time to draw breath. As a result she was successful. She sold properties and earned hefty commissions. It wasn't long before clients were asking specially to deal with the tall, attractive Irish lady because some friend they knew had recommended her.

Her life in London was very different to the life she had lived on the Costa. It was all business. There were lots of dinner parties where she was expected to dress up and swanky drinks parties given by property developers who were anxious to promote some scheme they were engaged in. But there was a lighter side too. There were the concerts and the galleries and interesting restaurants and the little parks where she and Matthew would go walking on a Sunday afternoon after they had seen the most recent movie in some West End cinema.

But she often found herself thinking about Fuengirola, especially as the autumn passed into the grey depths of winter and the weather turned cold and the rain clouds blanketed the sky.

Róisín had finally left her job in the bar and returned to Dublin to settle down to corporate life in a busy public relations agency. Now she talked of targets and deadlines. Claire realised that the rat race had claimed her friend at last.

She grew into a comfortable relationship with Matthew. She knew now that she loved him. But she often asked herself what she would say if he ever asked her to marry him. She was now almost twenty-four. Some of the friends she had met in Trinity were engaged; a few had actually married. One was the mother of twins. But Claire wasn't certain that she wanted to make such a huge commitment. Not just yet. She was perfectly content with the life she had. She could think of marriage a little bit further down the line.

Just before Easter, Sid Robbins sent her to a property conference in Bournemouth. It began on Friday night and continued till Sunday. She planned to keep in touch with Matthew by email and text and call him in the evening when the conference was over, just for a cosy chat. But early on Saturday morning she discovered that she had left some notes behind. She decided to ring and get him to fax them over to her. But when she called the number of their flat, the phone was answered by a young female voice.

Claire was confused. Had she called the wrong number? She checked her mobile and it showed that indeed she had called the correct number.

"Who are you looking for?" the voice asked.

Before she could think straight, she blurted out: "Matthew Baker."

"He's in the shower," the young woman said.

Claire felt a cold shiver run down her spine.

"Would you like to leave a message?" the voice continued, trying to be helpful. "Who shall I say called?"

"No message," Claire said and switched off the phone.

She sat down on the bed. She saw that her hand was shaking. There could be no mistake. Matthew had a strange young woman in the flat. She checked her watch. At eight thirty a.m.!

Immediately her mind flooded with possibilities. Maybe it was innocent. Maybe there was some simple explanation. But no matter how she tried to view it, it looked bad. In fact, it looked terrible. Claire felt an awful feeling of hurt and humiliation build up inside her.

Almost at once the phone rang again. It was Matthew.

"You were looking for me?"

"Who was that?" Claire demanded.

"Who?"

"The woman who answered the phone earlier. Who is she? What's she doing in our flat at half eight in the morning?"

"Calm down," he said. "I can explain."

"It better be good."

"It's only Angie from the office. We were all out at a party last night and, well, she got plastered and rather than trust her with some cab driver, I let her sleep it off on the couch downstairs."

"She sounded very bright and cheerful for someone with a hangover."

He let out a loud sigh. "For God's sake, Claire! Be reasonable. It's totally innocent. I was only being a Good Samaritan."

"Why didn't you let someone else look after her?"

"Because I'm her boss! I felt responsible for her."

It sounded plausible. Claire desperately wanted to believe him.

"Do you want to speak to her?" he asked.

"No, I do *not*."

"Look, I'm sorry if it upset you. Why were you looking for me anyway?"

Claire took a deep breath. "I left some notes behind. They're in a folder in the sitting-room. I wanted you to fax them to me."

"Of course. No problem. How is the conference going?"

He sounded like sweet reason and Claire felt her anger melt away.

"So far, so good. I'll talk to you this evening."

"I'll tell Sid you called."

"Okay."

"And Claire?"

"Yes?"

"You know I love you."

When she returned to London, Matthew was especially pleasant. He went out of his way to be nice to her. She decided to put the incident behind her and resume the relationship as it had been before. But she couldn't forget it. Her confidence had been damaged and some of the magic was gone. Now she was more wary, more distrustful. And as time passed, she began to notice many little inexplicable things about Matthew's behaviour that did nothing to rebuild her confidence. Fearful that she was simply imagining things, she didn't confront him about any of it – instead, on a few occasions, she asked for an explanation and listened to his excuses.

The year moved on, into the summer and autumn.

By now, the agency was well established and business was extremely good. Sid Robbins was talking about opening another one in South Kensington and putting Claire in charge.

It looked as if she was about to take a leap forward in her career. The new job would mean a big rise in her salary and perks like a car and expense account. It would be a major challenge but she was ready for it.

And then came the day when she had to go to the wardrobe in search of a business card that she had been given by a client at dinner a few nights before. She was sure that Matthew had put it into one of his suit-pockets, as he often did. As she fumbled in one of his pockets, her fingers became entangled in something inside. She withdrew the object and was amazed to find she was holding a woman's thong.

She was shocked. She stared at the thong. It was purple with a sequinned design at the crotch. She didn't own any such thing. Who did it belong to then? And why did he have it in his suit-pocket?

Claire felt her heart hammering in her breast. How was he going to explain this away? What excuse would he give her this time? She quickly made up her mind. She didn't have the energy for a confrontation. She didn't want to hear any more lies. She didn't even want to see him.

She got out her suitcases and packed as many of her clothes as she could cram in. She would have to leave many of her possessions behind: books, CDs, shoes. But she had to get out. She just wanted to put as much distance as possible between herself and Matthew Baker. She rang Sid Robbins and told him she had to go back urgently to Dublin. Ninety minutes later, she was at the airport.

Her mother was delighted to see her. Did this mean she had

finally given up all these silly notions and was now going to settle down and get herself a real job? Possibly, Claire said through gritted teeth.

But first she had to field numerous pleading phone calls from Matthew and a visit to Dublin when she reluctantly agreed to meet him in the Westbury Hotel. He begged her to come back. He gave her a cock-and-bull story about the thong – that a mate she had never heard of had put it in his pocket as a joke but that now the mate had gone back to Glasgow and he didn't have his phone number, otherwise he'd ring him up and give him a good telling-off . . . she knew immediately it was a pack of lies. It just confirmed her suspicions and doubts.

To get rid of him, she said she needed time to think. But she knew she was never going to take him back. After a few weeks, she called Sid Robbins and resigned her job. He didn't ask her to reconsider. Sid was a shrewd old fox and undoubtedly suspected what was going on. But he did send her a glowing reference. Now Claire was faced yet again with the challenge of what to do about a career.

She couldn't stay at home. Already her mother was beginning to drive her mad with daily promptings about the opportunities out there in the legal world. Tribunals of Inquiry were now springing up like mushrooms and barristers were making a fortune. It was like a new Klondike. With her good 2.1 degree in Legal Studies from Trinity, she would be mad not to grab a slice of the action while the going was good.

Claire had money saved from her time in London. She paid a deposit on a one-bed apartment in Sandymount and found a position with a small local estate agency. She put Matthew Baker out of her mind and tried to get on with her life. She resumed her friendship with Róisín, who was now an account executive with her public relations agency and came to lunch dressed in expensive business suits. She had a number of short-lived encounters with men.

Time went past and one year slowly merged into the next.

But sometimes Claire asked herself if she was happy. She was now twenty-six. She enjoyed her job and her independence and her cosy existence. She had money and a car and her own apartment. On her visits to see her parents, her mother would frown disapprovingly but Claire knew that her mother would never be satisfied till she became President of the Supreme Court or something equally grand.

Yet there was something missing. Occasionally Claire would find her thoughts drifting back to that wonderful time she had spent in Fuengirola when she had just graduated and the world was fresh and young and everything seemed possible. It would be great if she could recapture some of that excitement; if she could sit again in a little restaurant under the stars and smell the scent of mimosa on the balmy night air.

And then she spotted the advert in the *Irish Independent*. She had holidays due to her and leave that she had accumulated. Altogether she could probably stretch it out to four weeks. She was tired. She had been working too hard. She needed a break.

Dammit, she thought, I'll go. I can afford it. It will be interesting to see the place again. I wonder how much it has changed?

She sat down immediately at her computer and began to check out air fares.

4

Kevin Joyce quickly tossed back the sheets and jumped straight out of bed. The bright sun had wakened him. Now it was streaming into the room and bathing it in a warm yellow light. From the balcony of his apartment, he could see the beach and the tide gently lapping at the edge of the sand. Already the parasols were going up and the deckchairs were being set out. A few energetic souls were splashing about in the waves. Kevin glanced at his watch. It was eight thirty on a fine summer morning. A big wide grin suffused his handsome face.

Dammit, he said to himself. Another hellish day in paradise!

This year, Kevin would turn thirty. His early boyish good looks had matured and now he was a tall, handsome man with a shock of dark curly hair and deep dark eyes that often sparkled with a mischievous grin that women found wildly appealing.

Sometimes he found it hard to believe that the time had flown so quickly. He had been living in Fuengirola for two years now, ever since his father had died suddenly back in Galway and his life had been turned completely upside down. Kevin had never got on very well with his father. It was the major regret of his life. But he had still been devastated to discover that he had been cut entirely out of his will.

It was a long story, the relationship between Kevin and his father, and he wasn't sure exactly when it all started. For generations, the Joyce family had run a small drapery business in a side street off Eyre Square. It catered for men, women and children and, while it wasn't one of the most fashionable shops in the city, it did a regular trade with the more conservative customers from the outlying countryside.

It sold everything from shoes to First Communion dresses. It did a steady line in men's suits – not your trendy lightweight garments that would barely survive a good cleaning but strong, heavy, hardwearing suits that a farmer could be sure to get five or six years use out of and still be able to wear to Mass on a Sunday morning. It sold thick women's coats that would keep you warm on a cold day on a chilly Connemara hillside. It sold sensible underwear and not this flimsy nonsense that some of the department stores were going in for nowadays. It sold thick worsted socks and heavy brogues and warm cotton vests. It sold good, sensible clothes for shrewd, sensible people.

The shop had been started by Kevin's grandfather back in the depression year of 1934 with the proceeds of a small farm he had been left. He had worked hard to build it up and it had been in the family ever since. Kevin's mother ran the Ladies' Department till the children demanded her time and then she had hired a middle-aged lady called Miss Broderick, who presided over the stock of dresses and coats and intimate garments such as corsets and stockings.

But the shop had barely changed over the years. The Joyces knew their market well and made sure to cater to it.

Kevin was the oldest of three children. His brother Cormac was a year younger and then came the baby, his sister Nora, who right this minute was probably coming off night duty at the Mater hospital in Dublin where she worked as a nurse. Almost from the time he was able to walk, Kevin knew he was destined for the shop. It was never spelled out in so many words. It was just taken for granted that, when the time came, his father Seán would retire and hand the business over to him and he would stand behind the counter and smile at the farmers who came in looking for a nice hard-wearing jacket or a pair of sensible trousers.

This was what lay at the heart of the difficulties between them. While many children would have been delighted to learn that they were going to inherit a prosperous business that would provide a good living, Kevin knew it was the last thing in the world that he wanted to do. From the age of ten, when he would be brought into the shop to help with stocktaking or display, Kevin resisted. He showed no interest in the catalogues his father would give him to study or the delicate negotiations with suppliers that he was obliged to endure as part of his apprenticeship. Kevin resented the whole thing. He resented the fact that he was taken for granted and that nobody ever stopped to ask him what *he* wanted to do.

But a big part of the problem was that Kevin didn't actually know what he wanted. At the age of twelve he was despatched to the local Christian Brothers' school to receive his secondary education. The Brothers were tough men but they were excellent teachers. His father, who had also been educated by the Brothers, swore by them. He scoffed at some of the other shopkeepers in the city who sent their sons to fancy boarding schools like Clongowes Wood that were run by the Jesuits or the Cistercians. He considered it a sinful waste of hard-earned money. There was nothing that the Jesuits could teach Kevin that he couldn't learn from the Brothers.

One thing Kevin did learn at the Christian Brothers' school was a love of sport. By now he was shaping up to be a tall, broad-shouldered young man and he was quickly selected to play for the college GAA team. This was something that he really enjoyed. He loved the training sessions, the camaraderie and the banter and the games themselves, when they would fight like tigers against their opponents for the glory of the school. Kevin thrilled to the roars of approval from the spectators and the glorious feeling of achievement whenever he managed to struggle past the opposing team to score a point.

By the time he was sixteen, he was heading for six feet tall. He was a strapping young man with a mass of curly black hair and a good-natured smile that won him approval wherever he went. People were charmed by Kevin. His schoolmates looked up to him. The girls from the nearby convent regularly developed crushes on him and competed with each other to flirt with him while they waited after school for the bus to take them into town.

In fact, Kevin was universally admired except at home, where matters were rapidly going from bad to worse.

At seventeen, after he finished his Leaving Cert. exams, he left school altogether but instead of going into the shop, he joined a rock band. They called themselves Bang and Kevin played an electric guitar he had managed to buy with the pocket money he had saved. Bang played in the pubs around Galway and the outlying towns. Kevin was in his element in front of a noisy audience. He loved the applause and the adulation. It was even better than scoring points on the football field.

But at home his father was growing very angry.

"When are you going to settle down and learn the shop?" he demanded one Sunday afternoon after they had finished lunch.

His mother, who hated family quarrels, stared at Kevin with a pleading look in her eyes. Cormac and Nora lowered their heads and remained silent.

"Eventually," Kevin said, trying to avoid the looming confrontation.

"What does that mean?" his father demanded.

"It means I'm not ready yet. I want to spend more time with the band."

"That's just tomfoolery."

"No, it's not," Kevin protested hotly. He knew his father didn't understand their music but it stung him to hear it described as tomfoolery.

"You're just being selfish. Am I supposed to slave behind that counter till I drop down dead? I'm fifty-five years of age. I can't go on forever."

"Could you not give your father a hand out on Saturdays?" his mother asked, attempting to play the role of mediator.

Kevin turned to look at her. "Saturdays is when we rehearse."

"I've spent good money on your education and you end up like this, acting the jackass in front of a crowd of drunken yahoos."

"You don't know what you're talking about," Kevin said, angrily. "You've never made the effort to go to one of our gigs."

"Gigs? Gigs? What sort of language is that you're talking?

I'm sure the Christian Brothers never taught you to speak like that."

Kevin banged down his knife and fork and stormed out of the room.

His mother went rushing after him and caught him in the hall. "Why don't you make peace with him?" she pleaded. "He's right, you know. He's not a young man any more. It's time you started helping him in the shop."

Kevin, who deep down was beginning to feel guilty, stared at his mother. "I can't do it, Mum. I'd go crazy standing behind that counter all day waiting to sell wellington boots to farmers."

His father stopped speaking to him and they went around the house avoiding each other. Kevin hated it. So did everyone else in the family. He wished his father could see his point of view. The world was a big wide place and there were loads of opportunities. People didn't have to do what they didn't like. They didn't have to spend their lives in a drapery shop if they didn't want to.

But somebody had to do it and, after Kevin's refusal, Cormac was drafted in to take his place. Every Saturday he helped his father. Saturday was the busiest day of the week and while Kevin rehearsed with his band, Cormac was in the shop wrapping purchases for customers or measuring their shoulders for a new suit. A year later, he left school and joined his father full-time in the shop.

Meanwhile, Kevin's band was meeting with some success. They were signed by a record label and brought up to Dublin, where they spent a fortnight in a studio cutting an album. The band members were excited. They all believed this was going to be their big breakthrough. Once the album was in the charts, their name recognition would spread and they would build a bigger fan base. That would lead to better gigs and television appearances. It was the road to stardom.

But because of some marketing wrangle, the album was never released. Kevin felt terribly disappointed but some older musicians told him he shouldn't get upset. The music industry was full of sharks. What had happened to the band was not unusual. Maybe they'd have better luck next time.

All the while, the atmosphere in the house was becoming poisonous. To avoid friction, his father and Kevin ate their meals separately. Everybody walked around as if they were treading on eggshells. His mother, particularly, suffered, torn as she was between her husband and her son. Eventually Kevin decided to move out altogether and into a flat he shared with another band member, Snuffy Walshe. Now he could do as he pleased without the constant criticism he endured at home.

Moving out was a big step. It was like cutting the ties that bound him to his family. It was particularly painful because of the circumstances. But he kept in touch with them. He rang his mother once a week for a chat and to let her know that he was well and eating properly and looking after himself and doing all the things that mothers think it vital to do. He kept in contact with Cormac too and one night was surprised to find him in the audience at a performance in Slattery's pub. They had a drink and a talk afterwards and Cormac told him he was enjoying working in the shop and didn't mind doing it at all.

His sister Nora was growing into a pretty young woman and was proud of her brother, who all her friends said was going to be an enormous rock star one day. She was making very good progress at school and planning to study nursing when she left. She came to visit and told him their mother was heartbroken about the row between him and his father and that she was complaining about stomach pains and was being sent to a hospital in Dublin to have tests carried out.

By now, Kevin had a lot of things on his mind. Snuffy Walshe had a friend in London who had promised to find work for the band over there. He said it was the right thing to do if they wanted to achieve their big breakthrough. Snuffy was keen to go and so was Kevin but the other two members of the band weren't so sure. They had jobs in Galway and were loath to give them up. Eventually they had a meeting about it. Kevin said Galway was too small. They could play there for the rest of their lives and never get recognition. London was far bigger and there were more opportunities. The band decided to give it a try.

None of them had been to London before and the city seemed vast and hugely exciting. Snuffy's friend had arranged a flat for them in Kilburn, where a lot of the older Irish had settled. He had also found work for them performing in some of the local pubs. It all looked very promising.

Kevin took to London like a duck to water. There was so much to do, so many people, so many new experiences. Soon the band was playing five nights a week. They got a manager who arranged venues for them and negotiated fees. He arranged for a photographer to take publicity shots and kept promising that he would clinch a deal with a record company that would set them on the road to fame.

They worked hard but Kevin loved it. During the day they would rehearse new material and at night they would play. Sometimes the gigs didn't end till one and then they would all pile into the van and go off to a party. There were always girls who seemed attracted to musicians like moths to a candle. There was plenty of alcohol. And there were drugs.

Kevin had experienced drugs before. He smoked

cannabis and hadn't always said no to ecstasy. It was all part of the music scene. But the drugs that were available at the parties they attended were in a different league altogether. He saw people snorting cocaine and, on several occasions, in bathrooms and bedrooms, saw them injecting what he assumed was heroin. It was scary. Drugs seemed to be everywhere. Everybody seemed to be using them. You'd start a conversation with someone and you'd know immediately they were on some kind of high. Nobody seemed to think it was unusual.

By now, the band was getting plenty of work and earning good money. They began to appear as support acts at concerts for big-name stars. Everybody was having a ball. But while there were more opportunities in London, the competition was fierce. New bands were appearing all the time. And the music kept changing. No sooner would they have mastered a whole set of material than the mood would shift and something else would become fashionable. It was very difficult to keep up with the trends. And despite his promises, their manager never succeeded in getting them their album contract.

Still, no one complained. It was all going to happen. It was just a matter of time. Meanwhile everyone was enjoying himself. Life in London was so much better than back home in Galway. There was so much excitement, so much buzz. And everything was on a much grander scale. They never had so much money in their lives and they never spent it so fast on new clothes and new cars and anything that took their fancy.

One day, about eighteen months after they had come to London, Kevin got a phone call from Nora during rehearsal with the band. It was bad news. She said that their mother had been diagnosed with stomach cancer and only had a short time to live. Kevin was shattered. He had been enjoying himself so much that he rarely thought about his family back in Galway.

"How long has she got?"

"It's just a matter of weeks."

"Oh God, Nora, I'm devastated."

"We're all heartbroken. Dad is taking it very bad."

"I'd better come home at once," Kevin said.

"Please do, Kevin," said Nora tearfully. "She keeps asking about you."

He told the others immediately he came off the phone. Alarm registered on their faces. It would mean they would have to cancel engagements.

"When are you going?" Snuffy Walshe wanted to know.

"Next weekend."

"But that's our big Wembley gig!" Jimmy O'Driscoll almost shouted. "Jesus, we can't cancel that! There'd be blue murder. They'd never give us another date if we did that."

In his distress he hadn't thought of that. "But what can I do?" he said, his heart sinking further.

"Could you not put it off for a week?" Snuffy Walshe asked.

"My mother is dying," Kevin said.

"I know. But we've got all these gigs lined up. If you could just wait until after the weekend, we'd do Wembley and then maybe get somebody to stand in for you for a while!"

Kevin eventually agreed. He couldn't let his mates down – or himself. They had waited so long for this kind of exposure.

The Wembley concert was a huge success. They played in front of a crowd of 20,000 fans as a support act for an international tour. It was the biggest audience they had ever entertained and their manager was ecstatic. He kept telling them that this could be the breakthrough they'd been waiting for. He had arranged big write-ups for the band in the music press and spots on television shows.

Afterwards, they went to a party. Everybody wanted to take their photograph. They drank champagne and brandy till the wee small hours. When Kevin got back to his flat he was exhausted. He found a message from Nora on his answering machine.

Mum died this evening at ten o'clock, it said.

The funeral was very impressive. The Joyces had a big customer base and were well respected. The priest who conducted the service spoke of Bridget Joyce as a devoted wife and mother who had carried out countless acts of charity privately, out of the public gaze. She had borne her recent illness with true Christian acceptance and would be sadly mourned by her many friends and acquaintances.

Kevin helped to carry his mother from the church to the nearby graveyard. He poured a shovelful of earth on the coffin and listened as it rattled off the lid. Since getting Nora's message, he had been in a state of shock. Now it was giving way to remorse and grief. He had caused his mother so much distress and at the end he couldn't even be with her at her deathbed. She had died without saying goodbye to her eldest son.

After the funeral, there was a reception at the house for family and close friends. His father turned his back on him and refused to speak. Kevin was distraught. He wanted to talk to his father and ask his forgiveness. He wanted to explain what had happened and how he couldn't get home because of the concert. But how could he do that without causing a scene?

He spent the night at Nora's flat.

"Was she in much pain?" he wanted to know.

Nora shook her head. "Not in the last few weeks. They gave her morphine."

"But she must have known she was dying?"

"Oh yes," Nora said. "She knew that for a long time. It's a pity that you couldn't have seen her before she died. She would have liked that."

"I was going to come home when you called me. But we had a big concert date arranged and the others persuaded me to stay."

Kevin's eyes filled with tears.

Nora gently took his hand. "Don't blame yourself," she said.

"But I do. And what about Dad? He still won't speak to me."

"Dad has taken it very badly," Nora said. "I don't think he will ever forgive you."

After a few days, Kevin got fed up hanging around Galway. He got tired of people coming up to him in the street and commiserating about his mother. And he suspected that others were whispering about him, criticising him for not seeing her before she died. He went back to London and took up again with the band. But something had changed. If it hadn't been for the band, he would have been with his mother when she was dying. Now he had to live with the thought that he had put the band before her.

He felt a resentment building up against them and the lifestyle he was leading. It was all so self-absorbed. He began to regard the people he was mixing with as shallow and unreliable. They were forever making extravagant promises and two days later they would be forgotten. He felt now that the album contract would never materialise. And even if it did, what did it matter? It would just mean more of the same. It would be a continuation of the relentless pursuit of money and success. And he was getting worried about the behaviour of some of the band members. Snuffy Walshe was starting to dabble in hard drugs. How long would it be before he was addicted?

Kevin made a decision. It was time to get out.

He told the others a few weeks later when they were all relaxing after a gig. They were shocked.

"Why do you want to do that?" Jimmy O'Driscoll wanted to know. "Sure isn't everything going just fine?"

"And we've been promised the album deal in a couple of months," Snuffy Walshe added. "Then we'll really hit the big time."

"I've had enough," Kevin said. "I've just got tired of it all."

"You're upset about your mother's death," Snuffy Walshe said. "That's understandable. You just need time to get over it."

"It's more than that," Kevin said. "It's the whole thing. It's like chasing moonbeams. Where's it all leading?"

"Beats shovelling cement on a building site in Salthill," Jimmy O'Driscoll said sagely and ordered another drink.

In the end, he agreed to continue with the band for a few months more to give them time to find a replacement. From time to time they tried to coax him to stay. But he was adamant. When he finally left, he had some money saved. He sold his guitar. He was going to have no further need for it.

He took a number of casual jobs just to earn money. He hadn't yet decided what he was going to do. Meanwhile, he tried to make contact with his father. He rang home several times but when his father heard his voice he put down the phone. In the end, Kevin wrote him a long letter apologising for the part he had played in the breakdown of relations between them. He tried to explain what had happened when his mother was dying. The letter was returned to him unopened.

This was a very difficult time. But Kevin never wavered in his belief that he had done the right thing about the shop. If he had followed his father's wishes, it would have been a disaster. He would have been a terrible businessman and working in the shop would have made him desperately unhappy. He just wished he had been more diplomatic with the old man, that he had taken the time to sit down and explain to him. Now it was too late.

In the end, he got a job as a barman in a pub where he used to play with the band. It was tiring work, standing on his feet all day long, but he enjoyed it. He liked meeting people and talking to the regulars who came in. And the job enabled him to keep track of the band. They had found a replacement for him but there was still no sign of the long-awaited album contract.

One afternoon, Snuffy Walshe came in and sat down awkwardly at the counter. Kevin knew immediately that he was stoned out of his mind. He told Kevin he had made a big mistake by leaving them. They were about to make their breakthrough. All their hard work was going to pay off. He talked in rambling, incoherent sentences and then he fell asleep. Kevin ordered a taxi for him and sent him home.

Kevin had a succession of girlfriends. He was a handsome young man and had lost none of his boyhood charm. Women fell for him left, right and centre. But despite a procession of females who trooped through his bedroom door, he never settled down. He never fell in love. He never met a woman he wanted to commit to and make his life's partner.

Then one afternoon he received a phone call from Nora to say that their father was dead. He had succumbed to a massive heart attack after coming home from his morning walk. There had been absolutely no warning that anything was wrong. Kevin packed his bag and prepared to make the journey back to Galway once more.

It was a sad crowd who gathered in the family home for the wake. Cormac was presiding over the funeral arrangements. He seemed to have changed since Kevin had seen him last. He looked more stooped and serious, as if the burden of the business was weighing heavily on his shoulders. And he had married. He introduced Kevin to his wife, a local girl he remembered from his schooldays. Kevin noticed that she was pregnant. And Nora was there too, straight up from Dublin where she was in her final year of nurse's training.

People said the usual things – that their father was a decent, hardworking man who would be remembered for his kindness and generosity. But there was something more to add to the doleful conversation. They commented on the sad fact that Seán Joyce had died so soon after his dear wife. It was an added burden of grief for the family to bear.

One by one, they came to Kevin and shook his hand and said it was a sorrowful occasion but it was good to see him again looking so fresh and healthy. One or two asked about the band and how they were all getting on over in London and when could they expect to see them on television. Kevin gave non-committal answers. He said the band was doing well but the music industry was a tough business and you didn't become a success overnight.

The day after the funeral, he got a phone call from the family solicitor to say he would like to speak to him, privately. The solicitor was an elderly man, probably older than their father, and dressed in a well-tailored suit with a corner of starched white handkerchief peeping from his breast pocket. Kevin was certain he hadn't bought the suit in their shop.

He began by offering his condolences and then he got straight down to business. He explained that the old tradition of reading the will in front of everyone no longer applied. Now it was the solicitor's responsibility to contact the beneficiaries individually. He coughed into his fist to clear his throat.

"In this case, I thought it best to speak to you in confidence," he said, "because I find myself in a rather embarrassing situation."

Kevin was puzzled but he waited for the man to continue.

"You see, your father has left you nothing in his will."

Kevin sat back in surprise. He had expected that the shop and the house would go to Cormac, who had taken over the business. But it was a shock to discover that his father had left him nothing at all.

"Nothing?"

"I'm afraid not," the solicitor said. "He has specifically excluded you."

Kevin felt his face grow red with embarrassment. He felt as if he had been publicly humiliated. He gathered himself together and stood up.

"I'm very grateful for your consideration," he said.

"I'm sorry. But these were your father's wishes. He was quite adamant about it."

"That's all right," Kevin said. "I understand."

He was hurt, not so much that his father had left him no money but that he would make it so clear in his will that he should not benefit. He hadn't fully realised till now the depth of antagonism that his father felt towards him.

The others must have learnt about it from the solicitor. The following day, Nora took him aside and talked to him.

"You can challenge the will, you know," she said.

"What would be the point of that?" Kevin asked. "It was his money. He could do what he liked with it."

"But I think it's natural justice you should get something. Even though you had a row with him, I don't think it's right that he should just cut you out like that."

Kevin tried to be stoical. "But I didn't make any contribution. Cormac worked in the shop. It's only right that he should get what is due to him."

"I didn't work in the shop and I was left money," Nora said fiercely. She seemed to feel the injustice more than Kevin did.

"Look, Nora, I'd prefer to forget about the whole business. It's very embarrassing for us all. I don't want to add to the difficulties by taking it any further."

He went back with her to Dublin and stayed overnight at her flat.

"What are you going to do with yourself now that you've left the band?" she asked.

"I don't know. I've got a job in a bar. It pays the rent."

"Are you going to stay in London?"

"Probably."

"You can always stay with me if you decide to come back to Ireland."

"I'll remember that."

"Do you think the band was a good idea?" she asked.

He thought for a moment before replying. "It probably was at the time. But we all change, Nora. For better or worse."

A few weeks after he returned to London, he got a letter from Cormac. Enclosed with it was a cheque for €50,000.

Cormac said he agreed with Nora that their father's will was unfair. He wanted Kevin to have the money that he believed he was entitled to from the estate. Kevin's first instinct was to return the cheque to his brother. But after a while, he changed his mind and lodged it in his bank account. Maybe Cormac was right. Maybe he was entitled to it. Besides, it might come in handy some day. He wrote his brother a long letter thanking him for his generosity and wishing him and his new family well for the future.

Kevin was now twenty-eight. Both his parents were dead and the family was broken up. Cormac and Nora had chosen careers for themselves and seemed content with the paths they had taken. But what was he going to do? He decided to take a holiday to give himself a chance to think. He realised that in all the years he had been with the band he had never taken a break. The local tour operator suggested the Costa del Sol. Kevin decided to go.

From the moment the plane touched down at Malaga airport, he felt himself relax. The sun was shining and the flowers were in bloom. Above him, the skies seemed to stretch forever with not a hint of cloud. The hotel where he was staying was beside the beach in Fuengirola and every morning before breakfast he went for a swim. His days were spent lying in the sun. In the evening, he visited the bars and restaurants in the old town, eating under the stars while the sound of guitar music filled the balmy night air.

It was so different to the life he had known in London: the hustle and bustle, the noisy streets, the traffic, the constant rattle and hum. Here, life was more leisurely. Time seemed to move more slowly. For the first time in his life, he was at peace with himself.

There was a little bar he would visit during the day. It was called Pedro's and served snacks and drinks to the passing visitors up and down the beach. Kevin liked to perch on a high stool under the shade of the awning and sip cold beer while he engaged in conversation with the staff and the regulars who dropped by for a drink. The bar was run by an elderly Spanish woman called Maria but he quickly discovered that it was actually owned by an Irishman. He lived in Dublin but he was so busy that he only came to visit a couple of times a year.

Kevin grew fond of Pedro's Bar. He would eat his lunch there every day and chat with Maria while she stirred the big pan that cooked the paella or sliced ham for the crusty *bocadillos* that were a favourite with the visitors. That's how he learned that she was looking for a barman.

"You know anyone?" she asked with a twinkle in her eye. "A man who is not afraid of hard work?"

"I might," Kevin said.

"Must speak good English."

"What sort of wages do you pay?"

"Very good wages. Very good tips. And food. No need to spend money on food if you work here."

That evening, while he ate dinner at a little restaurant off the Paseo Maritimo, Kevin turned the conversation over in his head. He could easily do the work. He had the experience and while the wages would be less than he was earning in London, his costs would be less too. Everything was so much cheaper here. The more he thought about it, the more he became convinced. It would be perfect. And every morning he would wake to that glorious sun.

The following day he raised the subject once more with Maria.

"When would you want this barman to start work?"

"As soon as possible," she said. "As you can see, we are very busy."

"Two weeks?"

She made a frowning gesture. "It's a bit long. But for the right man, maybe."

"I could do it," Kevin said.

They discussed the terms. He would work five days and the wages would be about half what he was earning in London. But there were the other benefits that she had mentioned. He could easily make ends meet. And he had the money that Cormac had given him. He could always fall back on that if there was an emergency. He would need to find an apartment and register with the Spanish authorities. And he would have to return to London and tidy up his affairs.

He went back the following weekend. Before he left, he opened a bank account and transferred his funds. He found a small one-bed apartment overlooking the beach about ten minutes from the bar and paid a deposit of two weeks' rent. Kevin felt a surge of excitement that he hadn't experienced for a very long time. He knew with total conviction this was the right thing to do. Two weeks later he stepped off the plane once more at Malaga airport. The following day, he started work at Pedro's Bar,

That had been two years ago and he had never regretted a single moment. He loved the life here. He loved the job and the wonderful people he met. He loved the food and the atmosphere and the glorious weather. Since coming to work at Pedro's Bar, he had found peace and contentment.

Kevin pulled on his swimming shorts and grabbed a towel from the bathroom. He would have a swim in the sea before breakfast and then he had better get ready for work. The new owner was arriving today to inspect the place: a woman called Emma Dunne. He would need to be on time. And he would need to look his best. Kevin wanted to make a good impression.

5

Emma adjusted her sunglasses, pushed back her blonde hair and strode boldly through the airport doors into the blinding sun of a Malaga evening. She had been one of the first people off the plane. Even though she planned to stay here for a month, she was travelling light. She had brought a simple holdall containing everything she would need for the next few days. She would use the holiday to catch up on her shopping. No need to overburden herself when she could buy a whole new wardrobe and cases to put it in with a flash of her credit card.

A line of sleek white taxis was waiting. She marched confidently to the first one and a young man with olive skin and jet-black hair stepped out smartly and held open the back door for her. She slid onto the cool upholstered seat while he settled behind the steering wheel.

"Where are you going, *señorita*?" He flashed her a bright smile.

Emma hadn't been called "Miss" since she was a schoolgirl

but she didn't mind a bit of mild flattery, especially when it came from such a pleasant young man as the one who was now sitting directly in front of her and switching on the air-conditioning before turning to stare dreamily into her eyes.

"Fuengirola. Hotel Alhambra."

At the mention of her prestigious destination, his expression immediately changed to one of deference.

"*Sí, señorita.*" He smiled again to reveal a perfect line of glistening white teeth. "In a jiff, as you say in English."

"Jiffy," Emma corrected him.

He nodded politely and started the engine. "Jiffy. I must remember that."

Emma chuckled quietly to herself. She was only five minutes on Spanish soil and already she was giving English lessons to this charming taxi driver.

"English is a strange language, is it not?" he said.

"Even to some of those who speak it," Emma said wryly.

He laughed and swung the car out of the airport onto a slip road. A few minutes later they were on the motorway and heading south along the coast in the direction of Fuengirola.

Emma felt the car flood with cool air as she caught her first glimpse of the Spanish countryside. From the window she could see the dark brooding hills studded with little whitewashed houses. Ahead, she could see the high-rise hotels of the resorts dotted along the coast while to her left the sun sparkled off the long expanse of sea. She put her head on the upholstered cushion and closed her eyes. Already she felt relaxed. Already she felt the cares of the last few days just melt away. She knew she was going to enjoy this holiday. But she planned to do more than sun herself and go shopping. In the next month, she would make some serious decisions that could alter her life.

The taxi driver was chatting away in his broken English, pointing out items of interest as they sped along. He was being polite but Emma was only half-listening to him. She was thinking of the Hotel Alhambra and what it would be like. The man in the travel agency had said it was one of the top hotels on the Costa. It catered for the very best class clientele and provided every luxury. Emma hoped he was right. She was paying € 1200 a week for the privilege.

When she got there, she planned to have a long soak in a hot tub, dress in something light and cool and go out and see a little bit of the town. Her guidebook had spoken very highly of Fuengirola. It said the town had a lot of history: a Moorish castle, several old churches and markets and miles of long sandy beaches. It also boasted hundreds of restaurants and bars to cater for every taste. She would probably walk around the old town and find some quaint little bodega where she would have a glass of wine and some *tapas*. She would have an early night and then tomorrow she would inspect the bar she had acquired from Conor Delaney. He had already phoned the manager, a lady called Maria, to tell her she was coming.

The bar was something else she had to sort out. She still hadn't decided what she was going to do with it. It had come completely out of the blue and was something of a distraction from the main focus of her concern right now – Herr Braun's offer to buy her business. It was his proposal that was going to consume much of her thoughts in the weeks ahead. She couldn't help thinking how her life had suddenly been shaken up in the last few days. Maybe it was a portent. Maybe it was a sign that she should change direction. Emma found a smile playing round her lips. She was beginning to think like one of those silly people who couldn't decide which shoes to wear in the morning till they had first consulted their horoscope.

The taxi was entering the outskirts of the town. From the window, she could see people sitting outside bars and restaurants, chatting with their friends or simply relaxing in the evening sun.

At last, they swung off the road into the immaculate grounds of the hotel. She could see lawns and palm trees and the sparkling blue water of a swimming pool. The taxi driver came to a halt outside the imposing entrance and pulled open her door before a uniformed commissionaire could reach her. The commissionaire scowled and retreated back to his post.

"How much is the fare?" she asked, stepping out of the cab.

"Eighteen euros."

She found her purse and gave him a €20 note. "Keep the change."

The driver smiled and bowed. *"Muchas gracias, señorita."*

"De nada," Emma said, proud of the fact that she had learnt some Spanish from her phrase book.

The commissionaire stood to attention like a guardsman and doffed his top hat as she went sailing into the hotel.

It was stunning. In the centre of the lobby, a cool fountain was sprinkling water from the mouths of two reclining mermaids. Huge urns trailed plants and flowers. Classical statues gazed down at her from their plinths. Somewhere in the background she could hear a piano tinkling. She stood for a moment like an awestruck tourist taking in the magnificent scene, then walked briskly to the reception desk.

A smiling male receptionist was waiting.

"Emma Dunne. I have a reservation."

"Sí, Señorita Dunne."

The receptionist quickly tapped a few keys on a

110

computer and raised his eyebrows. "*Sí*. Suite 80. A very good suite – with views of the ocean."

I should think so at the price I'm paying, Emma thought to herself.

He gave her a register to sign, asked for her passport and slid a key across the marble desk. "We will hold your passport for one day. It is a requirement of the police. Tomorrow you can have it again."

"*Gracias.*"

A uniformed young man appeared beside her and lifted her bag. The receptionist gave him instructions and he marched off in the direction of the lifts with Emma following in his wake. Two minutes later they were outside her room. He inserted the key, opened the door and deposited her bag on a little stand. Emma gave him some coins. He thanked her profusely and disappeared as quickly as he had come.

She looked around the suite. It was splendid. A comfortable couch faced a huge television set; a table held a large bouquet of flowers and a bowl of fruit; a small writing desk and chair sat beside a wide window from which she could see the blue curve of ocean.

She opened the windows and stepped onto the terrace. The air felt warm and balmy. She could see the huge orange sun hovering over the sea. She breathed deeply and smelt the sweet bouquet of scented flowers come drifting up from the gardens. This is wonderful, she thought. I feel like royalty. She stood a minute longer, then went inside and quickly unpacked her holdall, frowning as she saw how creased some of the clothes were – a session with the iron provided by the hotel might be necessary. She hung what needed to be hung and thrust the rest into drawers. Then she went to the little bar in her bedroom, uncorked a miniature bottle of chilled white wine and ran the bath. Five minutes later, she was luxuriating in the tub.

She lay in the bath sipping her wine and felt all the tension ebb from her body. It had been quite a busy day with a lot of things to do before she even got to the airport. She had seen Conor Delaney, her father, Herr Braun and George Casey all in the space of four hours. Tonight, she would sleep well, but not before she had seen something of Fuengirola. At last, she pulled the plug and let the water drain away. She stepped out of the bath and reached for a towel.

Back in the bedroom, as she dried her hair, she wondered what to wear. There wasn't a lot to choose from. She had brought one dress suitable for formal occasions and a light suit in case she had to complete any business transactions and wanted to impress. The rest of the clothes in the holdall were casual summer wear. Although it was evening, it was still quite warm out there – she wouldn't need a jacket. She chose a chocolate brown A-line skirt and a pale pink sleeveless T-shirt, both somewhat creased from their journey.

She slipped on a pair of sandals and then examined herself in the full-length mirror. Her blonde hair nestled in a mass of curls around her neck and her blue eyes sparkled. She looked casual and relaxed, which was exactly how she felt. And who cared about the creases? She had only herself to please. Who else did she know in Fuengirola, after all? It wasn't as if she was going for dinner in the Four Seasons Hotel in Ballsbridge. She applied a little lipstick and mascara – no need for more than that. Satisfied, she closed the door and walked quickly along the corridor towards the lifts.

Outside, the streets were crowded and the shops were open again following the afternoon siesta. She wandered aimlessly along the seafront, stopping here and there if something caught her attention. She came to a children's play park with a big wheel and flashing lights and hurdy-gurdy music. Further on there was a large open-air fish restaurant with groups of people sitting at long tables chatting and laughing as they ate their meal.

The town vibrated with life and noise but it was different to the clamour she was used to back in Dublin. This was the sound of people who were enjoying themselves, not the frenetic activity of people rushing around to get things done. She had a month to do exactly as pleased. It was a wonderfully liberating feeling. She couldn't remember the last time she had felt so free.

The enticing smells from the restaurants began to stir her appetite and she realised that she hadn't eaten anything since lunchtime. At last she found a little bar that served seafood. A sign above the door announced its name: *The Bodega*. All the outdoor spaces were taken so she went inside. The waiter quickly swooped and led her to a table near the bar. She ordered calamari and a half bottle of white wine. The calamari came perfectly cooked in oil and garlic and served with salad and scalloped potatoes.

As she ate, she gazed around the room. It was small and crowded with people. Some of them were gathered round the bar, drinking at the counter. A voice nearby caused her ears to prick up. It came from one of the people at the bar, a tall young man with dark curly hair. He was chatting animatedly with his friends. Emma tried to place the accent. It was from the west of Ireland somewhere – Galway perhaps?

As she stared, the man suddenly turned towards her and smiled. Emma instinctively found herself smiling back. He was really quite handsome. She felt a little frisson of excitement run along her spine. What if he spoke to her? What would she do? It might be interesting to have a mild flirtation with a good-looking man on her very first night. There was something romantic about it, like an incident you might read about in a novel.

This wine must be going to my head, she thought. I'm a respectable businesswoman, not some giddy teenager looking for a holiday romance. So, instead of encouraging him, she looked away and bent her head once more to her plate. He was only a stranger. Fuengirola was full of people like him. She was here for a month. There was plenty of time for interesting things to happen.

6

Unfortunately, Mark didn't have Emma's happy experience at the airport. While she was travelling light, he had burdened himself with a large suitcase and a set of golf clubs, which meant he had to wait at the luggage carousel after passing through passport control. And as luck would have it, his case was late coming off the plane. As a result he was one of the last passengers to leave the arrivals lounge. And now it looked as if he had missed all the taxis.

He stood in the shade of the main airport building and tried to get his bearings. No doubt if he waited long enough, a cab would come along. There were flights coming into Malaga airport all the time from all over Europe. Or perhaps he could get a bus? But the travel agent had told him the hotel he was booked into was a little bit out of the way so perhaps the bus didn't go there. Mark decided it was better to wait for a taxi after all.

He looked around him. Even though it was almost seven o'clock in the evening, it was still very warm. He saw a large electronic board beside the airport entrance that recorded the date, time and temperature. Twenty-six degrees. When did they get heat like that in Dublin? What would it be like at midday, he wondered, slightly apprehensive. Still, it will make a pleasant change, he thought. And once I get to the sea there's bound to be a breeze.

Up till now, everything had gone very smoothly. There was no delay at Dublin airport and the flight had left on time. The journey itself had been a brief two hours. And he had left his business in good hands. While he was away, Chambers Creative Artists was being looked after by Ted Cunningham, a thrusting thirty-two-year-old manager who had been delighted at the opportunity to take the reins while his boss was away. It would do him no harm, Mark thought. It would give him a chance to prove what he could do. Anyway, the hotel he was going to had broadband and fax facilities, so they could keep in touch. If there was any problem, Ted knew where to find him.

Mark knew this trip was going to be something of a trial. It was the first time he had ever taken a holiday abroad without Margot. But he had made up his mind to enjoy it. There was going to be no more brooding and no more grieving. He recalled the words of Father Michael: "*She would want you to be happy.*"

He planned to spend the next few weeks unwinding. He would get in some golf practice and a maybe a bit of scuba diving – that was something he had got interested in back in his college days and there were good facilities here. And, of course, he would find some nice restaurants. He had spent the entire flight engrossed in the travel guide he had bought at the airport, learning about the culinary delights that awaited him: fine wines, hams, cheeses, pork, fresh vegetables and fruits and excellent seafood. According to the guide, Spanish seafood would require a book on its own. If only Margot were with him . . . what a time they would have!

He shook off that thought as a cab swung into view and pulled up beside him. The driver hopped out, opened the boot and deposited Mark's suitcase and golf clubs inside. He slammed the boot shut and Mark climbed into the back seat.

"Where to, *señor*?"

"Hotel Sevilla. It's at Caravajal."

"*Sí, señor.*"

The driver started the engine and prepared to pull out and leave. But right at that moment, a tall, dark-haired young woman came hurrying from the airport lounge into the blinding sunlight. Like Mark, she was pulling a heavy suitcase. She looked around, distracted, saw the taxi and immediately began to wave her hand.

Mark quickly leaned forward and tapped the driver on the shoulder. "Would you mind waiting for the lady, *señor*?"

The driver looked confused but did as he was asked.

The woman leaned into the cab and saw Mark sitting on the back seat. At once, she began to apologise. "I'm very sorry – I didn't realise the taxi was taken."

He recognised the accent immediately – Dublin. She had dark brown eyes and exquisite features. She was really quite attractive.

"It's all right," he said. "Where are you going?"

"Fuengirola."

"That's in my direction, I think. Would you like to share?"

She hesitated.

"You could be waiting for a while," he prompted.

This helped make up her mind. She pulled open the door and got into the passenger seat, while the driver took her luggage and stowed it with Mark's in the boot.

"This is very kind of you," she said, putting on her seat belt.

"Forget it. I've just been waiting myself. Where are you from?"

"Dublin."

He smiled. "I thought I recognised your accent. You must have been on my flight. We just got in?"

"Yes. But I had to wait for my luggage."

"Me too. I noticed that the clever passengers were just carrying hand luggage. They were able to march past the carousel with their noses stuck in the air while we poor suckers had to wait around. That's what I'll do the next time."

The young woman laughed and Mark stretched out his hand.

"I'm Mark Chambers."

"Claire Greene."

"Are you coming here on holiday, Claire?"

"Yes, I'm taking a break for a few weeks."

"Been here before?"

"I used to live here."

"Really?" Mark said with interest. "That must have been very exciting."

A misty look seemed to come into her eyes. "It was four years ago. I had just graduated from college and I landed up here with my friend. It was a kind of working holiday."

"And how did you survive?"

"We sold property on the street."

Mark looked at her with surprise. "That sounds like hard work. Did you have much success?"

"Quite a bit. But you need a brass neck to stop people you've never seen before and persuade them to buy a Spanish apartment."

"I'd say you do. What do you work at now?"

"I sell property in Dublin," she said with a grin.

"So it was good training?" he said.

They both laughed.

"What do *you* do?" Claire asked.

"I'm in advertising."

"Now *that* must be an exciting job."

"It has its moments. It's not all glamour. There's a lot of stress and pressure and deadlines. But I love it. And I get a tremendous buzz from designing advertising campaigns, particularly when they work."

They continued chatting as the cab sped along the motorway past Torremolinos and Benalmadena.

"You must have many happy memories of this place," Mark said.

She turned to look at him. "Yes, I do. I was younger then. And everything seemed so fresh and new."

"And then you got older."

"That's right."

"And now you want to recapture some of that time?"

"Yes."

"I know exactly how you feel," he said.

The taxi driver was turning off the motorway down to the coast.

"Where are you staying?" she asked.

"Hotel Sevilla."

"It's a nice quiet place. You'll like it. It's best if we go there first."

The cab pulled up outside the hotel and the driver got out to retrieve Mark's luggage.

"Thanks for your company," Mark said to Claire. "I enjoyed talking to you. It shortened the journey."

"Thank *you* for the lift."

Mark paid the driver. And then a sudden thought struck him. He turned again to Claire.

"You know this place. Can you recommend a good fish restaurant?"

"There are so many."

"The best one?"

"Well, Felipe's is very good. It's down at the port."

He paused as a crazy thought popped into his head. Claire might be just the person to mark his card and give him some tips about the resort. After all, she had lived here.

"Would you do me an enormous favour?"

"What?"

"Would you come with me?"

Later, he was amazed at his own audacity. It was a bit much to ask someone you had only met to come to dinner with you. He wouldn't have been surprised if she had told him to take a running jump. But she had accepted and now he felt quite cheerful as he unpacked his bags, had a quick shower and shave and prepared to pick her up. They had agreed nine o'clock.

He didn't know what to expect, how she would dress or how formal the restaurant would be. He should have asked her – as it was, in this new environment, he didn't know whether to wear beach shorts or a suit! He decided chinos with a dark-green shirt were the best bet – smart enough if Claire dressed up, but he could roll up the sleeves and take his tie off if he needed to look casual. He'd take along his navy blazer in case it got chilly later.

This was the trouble with being in a new country, he reflected as he dressed – things one didn't even stop to think about at home required great deliberation. Well, in a week he'd know the ropes.

Of course, he had always had Margot to advise him what

to wear. He pushed that thought away immediately and, grabbing up his keys and wallet, left the apartment.

Claire met him at the entrance to her apartment block, wearing a red low-necked dress in some flimsy material that swirled around her calves and a kind of light black shawl – the kind they called a pashmina. He thought she looked gorgeous and actually rather Spanish with her dark colouring. He was glad he hadn't dressed too casually.

"Is this restaurant very busy? Are you sure we'll get in?" he asked as she settled into the back seat of the cab beside him.

"I know the chef."

"Well, that might help!"

"Let's hope he's working tonight."

It worked like a charm. The chef, who was called Carlos, came out to see her and she was welcomed like a long-lost friend with many kisses and smiles and handshakes. They were escorted to one of the best tables in the room, where they could look out over the ocean and hear the gentle lapping of the tide against the shore.

"I'm very impressed," Mark said, once they were seated. "You got star treatment."

Claire shrugged and tossed her long black hair. "Carlos is an old friend. He's one of the best in the business as you'll see when we eat."

Mark let his eye travel across the restaurant floor. It was rapidly filling up with diners, which was always a good sign. But the design was plain and simple: just a few potted palms and plain wooden tables with crisp white tablecloths. Whatever was drawing the crowds, it certainly wasn't the décor. It had to be the food.

He turned his attention back to Claire. "Tell me what it was like living here."

The misty look he had noticed earlier was back in her eyes. "It was fantastic. Each morning brought a clear blue sky. The days seemed to stretch forever. And the nights . . ." She sighed. "The nights were magic – the stars, the music. I have so many happy memories. Is this your first visit?"

"Yes. It was a sort of last-minute decision."

"You're going to love it. Most people do. Fuengirola is a very lively place. You'd have to be a crank not to like it."

The food came. He had taken her advice and ordered hake. Claire had sole. To wash it down, they had chosen a nicely chilled bottle of white wine.

"Mmmm," Mark said, eating a forkful of fish. "This is delicious. Your friend certainly knows how to cook."

"I'll tell him. He'll love hearing that. Chefs are like actors. They thrive on praise."

"Here's to your holiday!" he said, offering a toast.

"And to yours! How long are you staying?"

"Four weeks. It's all the time I could spare from work – I need a really long break."

"Are you going to hire a car?" she asked.

"Probably."

"You'll need one if you really want to get the best out of your time here. But car hire is cheap here. You should visit Marbella. And Mijas. It's a beautiful little village up in the mountains. And Malaga is well worth a visit. Did you know it's the city where Picasso was born?"

"No," Mark confessed.

"There's so much to see. You can get a coach tour to Seville and Granada. You can visit Cordoba and Ronda."

"I don't know what I would have done if I hadn't met you," Mark said. "I would have been totally lost."

She smiled and her brown eyes twinkled. "No, you

wouldn't," she said playfully. "A good-looking man like you would just have met some other woman."

He didn't respond and she wondered about the shadow that passed across his face.

It was after midnight when he finally got back to his hotel after dropping Claire off at her apartment. He stood on the balcony and stared at the dark ocean, thinking about Margot and wishing she was with him.

But there was no denying his first day in Spain had been a tremendous success. He was glad he had come. He had just had a lovely meal with a beautiful woman. He had enjoyed her company enormously and tomorrow he was meeting her again for a drink. He took out the piece of paper where she had written down the directions. Pedro's Bar. It was on the beach somewhere. He should find it easily.

But now he felt tired. Mark closed the balcony doors and prepared for bed. He would sleep well tonight.

7

Kevin emerged from the sea, picked up his towel where he had left it on the beach and started to dry himself. It was only nine o'clock but already the sun was high in the sky and it was beginning to feel quite warm; by midday it would be over 30 degrees. Kevin loved his morning swim. There was nothing like half an hour splashing about in the ocean to set a man up for the day. He found the salt water invigorating. Now he would get dressed, grab a quick cup of tea and head into work. Most days he walked but this morning he had decided to cycle. It would save him a few minutes and today it was really important to be on time. The new owner was coming and he wanted everything to be prepared.

He wondered what she would be like. All Maria was able to say was that she had received a phone call from Conor Delaney to tell her that the bar had been transferred and the owner would be coming to see it. The great thing about Conor was that he had left them alone. In fact, Kevin had only met him twice and both times they had spent the occasion drinking beer and admiring the young women who were stretched out on the beach in their bikinis. Conor Delaney hadn't been interested in making massive profits. He devoted all his energies to his travel business. As long as the bar managed to tick over, he was content.

Kevin hoped the new owner wasn't going to start turning the place upside down. Pedro's Bar had been in existence for more than twenty years. It had begun life originally as a beach hut selling soft drinks and sandwiches to the tourists. Pedro, the man who had started it, also had the concession for the deck chairs and beach umbrellas. Between the two activities, he had managed to make a good living.

It was his son, Antonio, who had seen the potential and developed the bar. He had been quick to realise that the sunbathers on the beach didn't relish the long trek through the busy traffic on the Paseo Maritimo every time they fancied a beer. So he obtained a drinks licence and expanded the menu to provide hot food as well as rolls and sandwiches.

Now the bar sold beer, wines and spirits and a range of cooked food like paella and steaks as well as hamburgers and chips. Antonio had eventually sold the bar to Conor Delaney and opened a restaurant with the proceeds, making a nice profit on the deal. But the family connection remained. His mother, Maria, still ran the place.

Pedro's was a magnet for the tourists and the sun-worshippers who spent the day on the beach getting bronzed from the sun. They could have their lunch there or just grab a cold beer when they were thirsty. People met for a chat over coffee. The bar did a steady trade, particularly during the summer months. It could do with a lick of paint and some refurbishment but Kevin would hate to see it pulled apart to make way for some fancy burger joint.

As he cycled along the seafront, his mind travelled back to the previous night and the young woman he had seen eating in The Bodega. This was one of his favourite haunts and he often ended up there for a nightcap before going home to bed. There was usually a gang of his friends hanging around the counter, chatting and exchanging banter.

Her pale skin told him at once that she was a tourist. It was amazing how quickly you could spot them. And she was on her own, which was unusual. Normally they hung around in groups or with their husbands or partners and it was rare to see them in a Spanish bar. They seemed to prefer the English pubs that sold good solid British grub like roast beef and steak and kidney pie and roly-poly pudding.

That wasn't the only unusual thing about her. Kevin reckoned she was in her early thirties but she seemed confident and self-assured beyond her years. She wasn't nervous the way so many tourists were, afraid that they would make a mistake and order the wrong thing. And she was very attractive with her mass of blonde curls and her trim figure. With her looks and poise, she could easily have been a successful model. She wasn't tall enough for catwalk stuff but he could just envisage that angelic face on an advert for perfume.

He was sorry now that he hadn't gone over and spoken to her. It would have been interesting to find out what she was doing here in Fuengirola and why she was on her own. He had learned from working at Pedro's Bar that tourists liked being drawn into conversation. It broke the isolation and put them at ease. And of course, he might have been able to help her – give her some tips and advice about what to look out for and what to see.

But he had been too slow and the moment had passed. The woman had finished her meal, paid the bill and disappeared into the night with her head held confidently in the air. From his perch at the bar, he had watched her go and admired the swing of her hips as she sailed through the door and out of his life.

Pedro's Bar was now coming into view. Kevin slowed down and swung off the bicycle as it came to a stop. A plump matronly figure in a black dress was busy chopping vegetables and slicing bread rolls to make the *bocadillos*.

"*Hola, Maria!*" he cried as he parked the bicycle at the back of the bar and chained it to the wall. "How are you this morning?"

"Very busy," she said, continuing to chop furiously. "You too. The new *señora* is coming today."

"I know that. What time are you expecting her?"

"At midday she will come. We must be ready."

"Midday?" Kevin was surprised. "That's going to be right at the lunchtime rush. Who told her to come then?"

Maria shrugged, shoved a broom into his hand and indicated the floor and the surrounding wooden catwalk. Kevin took the broom and began to sweep. When he had finished, he took the tables and chairs from where they had been stacked beside the bar and began to set them up on the sand. Maria gave him a big basin of soapy water and indicated that she wanted the counter and the bar surfaces scrubbed clean. Kevin could see that he was in for a strenuous time and it was still only half past nine.

He worked steadily. When he had finished with the tables, he took each of the spirit bottles down from their rack and polished them till they shone. He did the same thing with the glasses. Meanwhile, the sun was climbing steadily in the sky. The beach was beginning to fill up. Several people came ambling up to the bar for their morning coffee. Maria served them but today she had no time for her usual small talk. She was brisk and businesslike, taking the money and moving on to the next task

Kevin finished his jobs and went behind the bar to help with the food. Each day, they prepared a big pan of paella, which was a particular favourite with the lunchtime crowd. He filled the pan with chopped onions and peppers and garlic. Then he added oil and shredded chicken and the seafood that made it special. He tossed in fistfuls of prawns and mussels and diced fish. When it was all simmering nicely, he added the rice. An enticing aroma rose up from the pan in a cloud of steam. The paella would now cook on a low flame till it was ready to be served.

"Have you any idea what *Señora* Dunne looks like?" Kevin asked Maria, who merely shrugged again in reply. He could see that the impending visit of the new owner had unsettled her. She was a hard worker but she liked routine. Anything that disrupted her schedule tended to make her nervous. Kevin also knew that she needed the money that this job brought in. She was probably worried in case the new owner took a mad notion to fire all the staff and bring in her own people.

He smiled and tickled Maria under her plump chin. "Don't worry, Maria. Emma Dunne will probably turn out to be just like Conor Delaney. She'll have a beer, look around the place and then you won't see her again till next year."

Maria scowled. She was far from convinced. "What if she turns out to be like *Señora* Thatcher, throwing her ways around the place?"

"Her weight, Maria. Throwing her weight around."

"Yes. What if she turns out like that?"

"Relax. She won't be anything like Mrs Thatcher. Anyway, Mrs Thatcher is retired now. She doesn't scare people any more."

"How you know what the new *señora* is like? You've never met her."

"I just know, Maria. You have to trust me. Now just do your work as normal. Everything will be all right."

But Maria's pessimism had now infected him. What if she was right and the new owner turned out to be a tyrant who made their lives hell? The cosy existence he had enjoyed at Pedro's Bar would be no more. He was beginning to form an image of a stern middle-aged lady who would set them impossible demands and poke her nose in like a busybody and generally interfere in everything. Kevin wasn't sure if he could work for someone like that.

By now it was almost twelve o'clock but there was no sign of Emma Dunne. A crowd of teenagers descended like hungry locusts, demanding hamburgers, chips and cokes. Kevin put the buns in the toaster, turned on the chip pan and flipped the burgers on the hot plate to cook. Maria had already prepared a basin of chopped onions and tomatoes. By the time he had finished, four young men with tattoos and beach shorts sat down on the stools and asked for beers.

What was required was some music. Kevin selected a U2 tape and stuck it into the sound system. Soon the music was booming out over the beach and the young men at the bar were tapping their fingers in time. A few minutes later, a group of young women sat down beside them and ordered glasses of wine.

Soon they were all laughing and joking together. Kevin smiled knowingly. He had seen it all before. As well as everything else, Pedro's Bar had become an ad-hoc dating agency. He glanced at his watch. They were getting close to lunch hour when things would really get hectic. He wondered who had suggested midday for Emma Dunne's visit. It was the worst possible time to arrive.

He went in behind the bar and poured himself a beer. Maria was still frantically fussing around the kitchen, repeating jobs that had already been done.

"Why don't you go and sit at one of the tables?" Kevin said. "I'll bring you a coffee. You've been working hard all morning. I'll take over for a while."

Maria looked at him uncertainly but she allowed him to lead her to a chair on the sand. He adjusted the umbrella so that she was sitting in the shade.

"Now, what would you like? A café leche? A *cortado*? Maybe a little shot of brandy?"

Maria waved her hand. "I'll just sit here and rest."

She closed her eyes and stretched her legs. In the sky, the sun had become a giant ball of fire. It was going to be a scorching hot day. When he returned to the bar, Kevin found more people waiting to be served but thankfully it was just beers. He lined up the glasses and flipped on the taps. Then he quickly set down a line of beer mats and a bowl of nuts.

He took the cash, rang it up on the register and gave the change. Out of the corner of his eye, he saw a young woman in dark glasses, wearing a white T-shirt, slide gracefully onto one of the bar stools. He wiped the counter with a damp cloth and looked at her again. She was very attractive. And vaguely familiar.

She removed her glasses and shook out her blonde hair. Immediately he gave a start. He was staring into the face of the woman he had seen last night in The Bodega. "*Buenos días*," Kevin said, flashing his best smile. "What would you like, *señorita*?"

"I'm Emma Dunne," the young woman said. "The new owner. Who are you?"

130

8

It was Conor Delaney who had suggested midday as a good time for Emma to visit Pedro's Bar. Of course, if he had known *anything* about the place, he would never have advised her to arrive in the middle of the lunchtime rush. But Conor, who had only visited the bar about a dozen times in all the years he had owned it, was probably the worst person to give advice. And to make matters worse, Emma was already running behind schedule.

She had slept well. Indeed, the moment she slipped under the cool white sheets the night before she had fallen into a deep slumber and only woke up when the hot sun came streaming in through the bedroom window. She sat up in bed and realised she had forgotten to draw the curtains the previous evening. And she had also forgotten to ask the reception desk to provide her with an alarm call. By now it was half past nine and it was time she was up and doing things.

She lay back on the heaped pillows. She had slept for

nine solid hours, which was something of a record for her. Normally she managed to function quite well on six. As a special treat, she might lie on for seven hours. But nine hours was unheard of. It just showed how tired she must have been. She had certainly been working very hard in recent weeks. Maybe all that stress had been catching up on her without her realising.

She let her eye travel around the room. In the broad light of day, it appeared very chic: pale pastel colours on the walls, a crystal chandelier hanging from the ceiling, china table lamps, tasteful scenes of Spanish rural life in gilt frames, soft carpeted floors. She certainly couldn't complain about the décor and the standards. And the service last night when she arrived had been exceptional, doormen and flunkies tripping over themselves to look after her. All in all, the €1200 a week she was paying looked like a good investment.

She got out of bed, slipped into a fluffy white hotel robe and went out to the terrace. There were two large terracotta pots filled with blood-red geraniums at each end of the tiled floor and a little wrought-iron table and chairs. It would be perfect to sit here in the evening and sip a glass of ice-cold wine. And the view was spectacular. In front of her was the wide expanse of ocean shining blue in the morning sun, the vast canopy of sky devoid of a single cloud and, to her right, a range of mountains, grey and brown in the distance.

Emma breathed deeply and filled her lungs with pure, clean air. This was magnificent. It made every fibre in her body feel alive. She looked out over the vast ocean to the yachts looking like mere children's sailboats in the distance and the sleek liner heading south towards Marbella. That's a place I must visit at the earliest opportunity, she thought as she turned away from the terrace and went back into the bedroom. She had heard there was some good shopping to be done there.

She wondered if she should order breakfast to be sent up or go down to the dining-room. And then another thought struck her. She had two and a half hours before her appointment at Pedro's. She would go and explore the leisure centre. The hotel brochure had boasted of a gymnasium and sauna as well as a swimming pool. A short spell in the sauna would be an excellent way to start the day. She fished a bikini out of a drawer and put it on, then wrapped the robe around her and made for the leisure centre, which was in the basement. She went down in the lift. When she got there, the doors glided open without a sound and she stepped out into a large hall. She could see the gym with its rows of benches and training equipment and a few eager beavers already pumping weights. An attendant in a crisp white jacket smiled as she approached.

"Do you have your room number, madam?"

Emma showed him her key and he wrote down the number in a ledger, then asked her to sign.

"Do you have any valuables you would like to leave in the safe?"

The only really valuable thing Emma had in her possession was her watch, which her parents had bought her as present for her thirtieth birthday. She had already removed it and placed it in the safe in her room along with her credit cards. Her departure had been so abrupt she hadn't even thought of bringing a camera. She shook her head.

"Which way to the sauna?" she inquired.

The man pointed to a door. "Do you know how to use it, madam?"

"Yes."

"Be careful not to put too much water on the coals. It can make too much steam. Then it gets very hot." He smiled politely.

"*Gracias*," Emma said and wondered at the very good English spoken by all the staff she had encountered so far. The hotel obviously made it an employment requirement. I really must learn some more Spanish phrases, she thought, as she proceeded towards the sauna. It's only good manners that I should try to speak some of their language.

There was no one in the sauna so she had it all to herself. She took off her robe and hung it on a peg, then took a ladleful of water from the wooden bucket and tossed it on the hot coals. At once a huge cloud of steam rose up and filled the little room. She sat down on the bench and felt the perspiration break across her forehead. In a short time, the sweat was cascading from every pore.

She leaned back and closed her eyes. It felt so good. She imagined the perspiration cleaning the toxins from her body, removing the impurities, toning her skin. But after ten minutes, she'd had enough. She left the sauna and approached the plunge pool. This was a small, deep pool filled with ice-cold water. Emma gripped the bars of the steel ladder and lowered herself in. Then she let go and sank into the freezing depths.

It was the most incredible feeling. She felt the shock waves from the cold water go shooting through her system. When she surfaced again, her body was tingling all over with the most invigorating sensation. When she had dried herself and put on her robe, she felt wide awake, bursting with energy and ready for anything the day might bring.

It was time for breakfast. Emma decided to eat on her terrace. She rang room service and ordered fruit juice, cereal, some ham, rolls and coffee. A few minutes later, she heard a gentle knock at her bedroom door and a white-gloved waiter arrived bearing a silver tray. She indicated the terrace and the man set the tray on the little table, bowed and left the room. She sat down and let out a loud sigh of satisfaction.

She wondered how she had managed to work for thirteen years without ever taking a decent holiday. The longest she had been away, apart from hurried weekend breaks, was ten days in Tuscany three years ago. She had just been too busy with the demands of Hi-Speed Printing to spare the time. She must have been crazy. She could see now that a good holiday was an investment. It recharged the batteries. It provided an opportunity to relax and think clearly and plan ahead. It increased a person's productivity. Indeed, the more she thought about it, a good holiday should be *compulsory*. She ought to have been treating herself to a holiday like this every year. But now that she had sampled the delights of Hotel Alhambra, Emma knew that she would certainly be back.

Over the coming weeks she would give serious consideration to Herr Braun's offer to buy the company. She would take her time and weigh up all the angles. She knew she had made the right decision by asking him to wait. And the fact that he had agreed so readily indicated just how keen he was. It had taken a long time to build up the Hi-Speed Printing Company. Emma certainly wasn't going to decide its fate overnight.

But first, she had more immediate business. She had to decide what to do about Pedro's Bar. Her instinct was to sell it – find a reliable estate agent and put it on the market. After all, she didn't want the burden of looking after a bar hundreds of miles from home and she knew, if she decided to keep it, Pedro's could easily become a burden that would consume her time and attention. But before she did anything, she had to see it. Conor Delaney had told her that midday would be a good time to call and had also given her directions on how to find it.

She finished breakfast and glanced at her watch. It was now eleven fifteen. It was time she left. The sun was climbing higher in the sky and, despite the breeze coming in from the sea, it was going to be hot. She felt like wearing shorts but thought perhaps she should wear something formal to fit the image of new owner. No, that would be overdoing it – it was a beach bar after all! She compromised with a white fitted T-shirt and a cotton wraparound skirt patterned in shades of blue. Minutes later, she was ready. She locked the door and took the lift down to the lobby, left her key at reception and walked out into the blinding sunlight.

She strolled along the Paseo Maritimo in the direction of the port. She had been told the bar was somewhere near here. She was sure she would find it easily enough. Already the streets were buzzing with activity, the restaurants were getting ready for lunch and the beach was filling up. Out on the ocean, the yachts were bobbing like corks and she could hear the drone of a speedboat towing a water-skier. Further out, a hang-glider was drifting in the clear blue sky.

It was twelve thirty when the bar eventually came into view. She hated being late for appointments but already the holiday mood had gripped her. As she approached, she let her eye travel over Pedro's Bar. At first glance, it wasn't much to look at: a square wooden structure with a canopy and awnings and a counter with high stools. Surrounding the bar on the sand was a number of little chairs and tables with chequered tablecloths held in place by plastic pegs.

She noticed that a crowd of people had already gathered at the counter. So business was brisk. She wondered what the turnover would be.

By now, she was thirsty. She would enjoy a cold beer. She sat down on the first available stool and waited till the barman had finished serving some other customers. Then he turned to her and Emma immediately gave a start. It was the young Irishman she had seen last night in The Bodega. She saw the look of surprise on his face as he recognised her too.

"*Buenos días,*" he said with a big smile. "What would you like, *señorita?*"

"I'm Emma Dunne, the new owner," she said, introducing herself. "Who are you?"

The young man was startled at this but he quickly recovered his composure, welcoming her warmly and making a fuss over her. It turned out that his name was Kevin Joyce and he was from Galway. Now that she had an opportunity study him up close, Emma could see that her first impression had been correct. He was extremely handsome, with clear blue eyes and a mop of unruly black hair. He poured her beer and brought her to the table where Maria was already sitting.

"This is the real boss of Pedro's Bar – *Señora* Maria Rodriguez de Hernandez!" He gave a playful bow and a grin as he introduced them.

Immediately Maria got confused and tried to stand up.

"No, please sit down," Emma said kindly. "There's no need to disturb yourself. I'm only passing by." She glanced at the crowd who were now swarming like bees around the counter. "By the look of things, this was not a very good time to call. You seem to be very busy."

"It's the lunchtime rush," Kevin explained.

"I'm very pleased to meet you, *señorita,*" Maria managed to blurt out as she grasped Emma's hand and shook it vigorously. "We were expecting you to call."

Emma could see that the old lady was nervous. She tried to put her at ease. "I'm very glad to meet you too, Maria."

"Would you like something to eat?" Maria asked, trying her best to please.

"I've just finished breakfast," Emma replied.

Kevin glanced nervously at the people waiting at the bar to be served. "Look, why don't you ladies get to know each other and I'll go back to the bar. You stay here, Maria, and talk to *Señorita* Dunne."

Maria looked panic-stricken as Kevin departed and left her alone

"How long have you been manager of the bar?" Emma asked in a soothing voice.

Maria shrugged. "Thirteen years. A very long time, *señorita*."

Emma gently patted her hand. "Why don't you call me Emma?" she suggested.

"Emma? This is a nice name."

"I'm glad you like it."

For the next hour, the two women talked under the shade of the parasol while Kevin worked like a slave behind the bar, serving snacks and beers to the lunchtime crowds. But he didn't seem to mind. Every so often, he would wave encouragingly as he tossed hamburgers and pulled pints.

Maria told Emma the history of the bar: how her husband Pedro had built it from a beach hut and then died of cancer at the young age of fifty-seven. Her son Antonio had taken it over and developed it and then sold it to Conor Delaney. Now it was Maria's sole means of income.

As she talked, Emma formed the impression that relations weren't all they should be between Maria and her son, who now ran a successful restaurant from the proceeds of the sale. Maria was careful not to say anything that was directly disparaging about Antonio but it was the things she didn't say that gave the clues. There was no warmth and little of the pride that might have been expected from a parent of a successful child.

She looked more closely at Maria. She thought she must

be at least seventy. It was a time when she should be retired and playing with her grandchildren, yet here she was working hard in the hot sun to run the bar. Emma could see that disposing of Pedro's Bar might not be so simple. She could hardly turn Maria out on the street. She began to realise that she had come to Fuengirola to sort out one problem and now she had inherited another.

Maria must have read her mind. She looked at Emma with pleading eyes. "What are you going to do with Pedro's Bar?" she asked.

"Nothing yet," Emma said. "The first thing I would like to do is have a look at the accounts. Could you arrange that for me?"

The nervous look was back in Maria's eyes. "Accounts?"

"Yes, you keep accounts, don't you? Papers to show how much you earn and how much you spend?"

Maria seemed to grow even more nervous. Then she had an inspiration. She pointed a finger at Kevin, who had finally disposed of the crowds and was now wiping the counter. "I will ask him to get them for you."

"Good," Emma said, getting up. "I'll go and arrange it."

She spoke to Kevin, who said he'd be happy to get her whatever information she required.

"Why don't I meet you somewhere quiet where you can study them in peace?" he suggested.

"Okay," Emma said. "Have you anywhere in mind?"

"Maybe you would let me buy you dinner in The Bodega?" he said with a twinkle in his eye.

"I've got a better idea," Emma replied, brushing a lock of blonde hair from her face. "Why don't *I* buy *you* dinner? I'm now your boss, after all."

"Sounds good to me," Kevin said. "How does tomorrow suit?"

"Tomorrow is fine."

They arranged to meet for dinner in The Bodega the following evening.

Just as she was about to leave, Emma noticed that a tall man had just sat down on the stool next to her and ordered a beer. His face looked vaguely familiar but she wasn't sure where she had seen him before. He turned to her and smiled but, before he could speak, he was joined by an attractive young woman with long dark hair who hopped up onto the stool next to him.

"Hi, you're looking fabulous," he said to the new arrival.

"You look good yourself!"

"Must be the weather – what would you like to drink?"

"Can I have a beer, please?"

Both their accents were Irish.

Kevin was already preparing their order.

"From Ireland?" Emma heard him say.

"That's right," the man responded. "How did you know?"

"Well, you sure didn't pick up those accents in Hong Kong," Kevin replied with a grin and they all laughed.

Emma looked at the man again. She had definitely seen his face before.

"I used to live in Fuengirola years ago," the dark-haired young woman said. "In fact, I had a friend who worked here at this bar."

"That's amazing," Kevin replied.

They were settling down for a cosy chat. Emma didn't want to appear to be eavesdropping. Besides, she wanted to explore some more of the town. She turned away and walked quickly up the beach.

9

While Emma was paying €1200 a week for her luxury suite in Hotel Alhambra, Claire had managed to snag a one-bed apartment for the ridiculous sum of €250 for the entire month she planned to stay in Fuengirola. She was feeling quite pleased with herself. The rent was even less than she had paid for accommodation when she first came here with Róisín four years ago. Of course, her networking skills had proved invaluable.

Once she'd made up her mind to come, Claire had immediately got on the phone to Johnny Parkinson, an estate agent friend she had got to know in the days when she was working here.

"Hi, Johnny," she said. "It's Claire Greene. Remember me?"

"Remember you?" Johnny said, sardonically. "How could anyone forget you? I think there's still a police warrant out for your arrest."

"Very funny," Claire said. "How are things in sunny Fuengirola?"

"Still sunny, thank God. What can I do for you?"

"I'm coming for a month and I'm looking for an apartment. I want something cheap."

"You're coming for a month? Do you think they'll let you back in?"

"Ho, ho, bloody ho!" Claire said.

"How much are you prepared to pay?"

"Not so fast, Johnny. You know that's not the way we do business. What have you got to offer?"

She heard him give a loud laugh.

"You haven't changed one bit, have you?" he said.

"I've got older and, hopefully, wiser."

"I can let you have a nice one bed for €400. Quiet apartment. Good neighbours. No rowdy parties."

"Sound like it's off the beaten track. It's not halfway up a mountain, by any chance?"

"It's on the second line. Five minutes from the beach."

"How about two hundred?" Claire said.

"You *haven't* changed. Just because I have a soft spot for you, I'll let you have it for three."

"Two fifty."

"You're breaking my heart," Johnny said.

The apartment was in an eight-story block with no view of anything but the street below. But it suited Claire perfectly. It had a bedroom, bathroom, living-room and kitchen.

Across the hall was a chatty English woman called Maggie, who called in to introduce herself and claim Claire as her friend the morning after she arrived.

Maggie was about thirty with shoulder-length brown hair and bright hazel-coloured eyes.

"Looking for work, are you?" she asked, making herself at home on the living-room sofa.

"No. I'm just here for a break."

"Oohh, that's nice." She quickly looked around the room. "Here on your own, are you?"

"Yes," Claire replied, taking a brush to her long black hair.

"Much better, I always say. You've only got yourself to please. Anyway, if you feel lonely, I'm just across the hall. You can always drop in for a nice cup of tea."

"That's very kind," Claire said politely, wishing Maggie would go and allow her to get on with her unpacking.

Maggie described herself as an entertainer, which was a grand way of saying that she did a Tina Turner impersonation show in various British bars in Fuengirola. Claire found this a little surprising since Maggie was small and squat and didn't remotely resemble Tina Turner. She told Claire she had been living here for the past five years.

"I used to live here too," Claire said. "Four years ago. It's odd that I didn't run into you before."

"No, it's not," Maggie said defensively. "I was probably going through my Dolly Parton phase back then. I've only being doing Tina Turner for the last eighteen months. Would you like me to give you a demonstration? It will only take a few minutes to put on my wig."

"Not just now," Claire said quickly. "I've got to rush off to meet some people."

Maggie looked disappointed. "Maybe tomorrow," she said. "You'll enjoy it. I knock them dead in the Rum Pot Inn every Friday evening."

"That will be something to look forward to," Claire said.

"And if you ever decide you need work, I'm sure I could fix you up. With your tall figure and that beautiful dark hair, you'd easily get a job as a cabaret dancer."

"I'll keep it in mind," Claire said archly.

Cabaret dancer, she thought. Her mother would love that! But she did have people to see. She was going along the coast to La Cala to visit some friends but first she had to call at Pedro's Bar at one thirty to have a beer with Mark. She wondered what it looked like now and if Maria was still in charge.

She thought briefly of Mark. She had really enjoyed his company last night. He was lively and funny and kept up a stream of witty conversation, then occasionally a sombre look would cross his face. There was something about him that intrigued her. She had noticed that he wore a wedding ring, yet he never once referred to his wife. And if he was married, why was he here alone? He hadn't mentioned that at all. Oh well, she thought. That's his business and if he doesn't want to talk about it, well and good.

After finally disposing of Maggie, she had a shower and pulled on an apple-green vest top and a short denim skirt, grinning at the thought that back in Dublin she would be in the office or escorting clients around in a sober business suit. Yes, the old Claire was back!

She applied some lip-gloss and slathered on the sun cream. No point getting burnt on her very first day. Then she tied her hair back into a swinging ponytail, grabbed sunglasses, baseball hat and bag, and left the apartment.

She set off towards the seafront, past the bustling shops and restaurants. As she went, she had this amazing feeling. It was like stepping back in time. Nothing much had changed in the past four years. A few bars had different names and there was a bakery where a small grocery store used to be, but by and large the town was exactly as she remembered it.

Everything was the same, including the cluster of young people near the entrance to the port trying to interest passers-by in time-share apartments. Claire smiled to herself as the memories came flooding back. The work had been hard but it had been a happy time back then, before she fell in love with Matthew Baker and her life had changed.

When she got to the port she turned left along the Paseo Maritimo. This was where Pedro's Bar had stood. She had happy memories of this place too and the lively occasions when she came to visit Róisín after work and they had drunk beers and flirted with the lifeguards and the old colonel held her hand and talked about the war. She wondered if he was still around or if he had died or moved away.

As she approached, she saw that Mark had already arrived and was seated on a stool at the counter. The bar had barely changed at all. It was in need of a repaint but otherwise it was exactly as she remembered it. There was a new barman, a tall, good-looking guy with dark curly hair. He was in conversation with an attractive blonde woman. But Maria was still there in her striped apron, busily washing dishes and glasses in the big sink.

"Hi," Mark said as she joined him. "You're looking fabulous."

"You look good yourself," she replied.

"Must be the weather," he said with a grin. "What would you like to drink?"

"Can I have a beer, please?"

She glanced at the dark-haired barman who smiled back at her.

"From Ireland?" he asked as he began to prepare their order.

"That's right," said Mark. "How did you know?"

"Well, you sure didn't pick up those accents in Hong Kong," the barman replied with a grin in what was clearly an Irish accent and they all laughed.

"I used to live in Fuengirola years ago," said Claire. "In fact, I had a friend who worked here at this bar."

"That's amazing!" said the barman.

Out of the corner of her eye, Claire noticed the blonde woman in the white T-shirt slide off her stool and walk away along the beach.

"*Hola, Maria!*" Claire called.

The old woman stopped her work and, startled, gazed at her.

"Do you remember me? Claire? And Róisín? You remember Róisín?"

A look of recognition slowly crept into Maria's face. She wiped her hands on her apron and came outside the bar to give Claire a big hug. "Of course I remember. How are you?"

"I'm fine."

"And Róisín?"

"She's back in Dublin now. She's working in Public Relations. She sends her best wishes."

"She was smart, that one. I knew she would get a big job some day and earn plenty of money. What do you do?"

"I'm still selling property."

"And did you get married?"

Claire laughed. "Not yet."

"One day you will. A beautiful girl like you doesn't stay single for long."

As they chatted, Claire was able to examine Maria. She seemed old and tired and beneath the gaiety there lurked a hint of sadness.

"How long are you going to be around?" Kevin asked.

"Four weeks. I thought I'd come and see if things had changed."

"And have they?"

"Not much."

Maria went off to clear the tables and Claire used the opportunity to draw Kevin aside and ask him if there was something bothering her.

"She's a little bit apprehensive," he said.

"Oh?"

"We've just got a new owner. She was here when you arrived – the blonde woman. She's from Dublin too."

"Really," Claire replied. "What's her name?"

"Emma Dunne. Maria's afraid in case she wants to turn everything upside down. Or maybe even close us down altogether."

"Surely she wouldn't do that?"

Kevin shrugged. "Who knows? Maria's been here from the beginning. Her husband started this place. Naturally she's worried."

They finished their beers and it was time to leave.

"Don't forget to come back," Kevin said. "We'll be glad to see you."

As they walked back to the Paseo Maritimo, Mark laid a hand on her shoulder: "Did it bring back old memories?"

"Some," Claire admitted. "But that's the trouble with memories. You expect things to be the same but of course they aren't. They change – sometimes slowly and imperceptibly and sometimes quite dramatically. Maria, for instance, is afraid the new owner might close down the bar. That would be a terrible shock for her."

"I'm sure she's wrong," Mark said. "It looks like a lively place. I'm sure it's quite profitable. By the way, thanks again for a great night. It was wonderful to meet someone who has been here before and knows the ropes."

"*De nada*," Claire said, with a wave of her hand.

"What does that mean?"

147

Claire smiled. "It means: 'It's nothing.'"

"Well, it was something to me. And I did appreciate it, especially since I'm here on my own."

For a moment, she thought he was going to elaborate but he didn't.

"It wasn't all one way, you know," she said. "You bought me a lovely meal and I got to see my old friend Carlos again."

"Aren't you going to La Cala this afternoon?" Mark asked.

"That's right."

"Why don't I drop you there? I hired a car this morning."

"But I thought you were planning to play golf?"

"I can do that later."

The car was parked near the port. Claire settled into the passenger seat and soon Mark was cruising along the coast.

"Have you ever driven a left-hand car before?" Claire asked.

"Never."

"But you're so confident."

"You think so?" Mark said. "Tell you the truth, I didn't even think about it."

Ten minutes later, he dropped her at her destination.

"How are you getting back again?"

"I'll get a taxi. I'll probably have dinner with my friends."

"Make sure to enjoy it," Mark said as he drove away.

Claire watched him go. She was no wiser about him. And an instinct told her that, despite his breezy manner, something was bothering him. She put on her dark glasses and looked at the sky. The sun was blazing in the heavens. The air was still except for the lilt of birdsong from the nearby trees. The very sound of it lifted her heart. She thought of poor Maria and her worries about the bar. And Mark too.

Why couldn't everybody feel as happy as I do? she thought, as she began to walk towards the little square where she had arranged to meet her friends.

10

Claire was right about Mark. Something *was* bothering him. The feeling had come over him back at Pedro's Bar. He had thought about Margot and immediately his mood had changed. He needed to get away; to be alone with his thoughts. He needed to talk to her.

It was Father Michael who had suggested that he talk to Margot.

"Just tell her all the little bits of news and gossip," the priest had said. "Tell her your worries and concerns. Margot may be dead but she hasn't ceased to exist. She's alive in your thoughts and memories. Why don't you give it a try?"

So Mark began to talk to his dead wife. He told her what was happening at the office. He confided his problems. It was just like she was still alive. But earlier, when he was chatting with Claire and Kevin at Pedro's Bar, he had suddenly felt guilty that he was having a good time without her. It didn't seem right. It felt almost like an act of betrayal, as if he had deserted her after such a short time.

He tried to shake the thoughts from his head. He knew they were completely irrational. He knew that Margot would have wanted him to relax, make new friends and get on with the remainder of his life. He had been over this ground so many times yet here it was back again. It was just that he longed for her to be here with him to share his pleasure.

Instead of playing golf as he had planned, he decided to go for a walk. He needed somewhere quiet where he could have his little chat with Margot. Once he had talked to her, he knew everything would be all right again. So, after dropping Claire at La Cala, he drove a little bit further along the coast and parked the car at a deserted beach. The sun was past its peak now but it was still hot. Thankfully, there was a cool breeze blowing off the sea, which made it pleasant to walk along the water's edge. He sat down on a rock and took off his shoes and then decided to take off his shirt as well.

"I miss you so much," he said to the empty beach as he started walking towards a distant tower with his shoes tied together and draped around his neck. There was silence, except for the gentle rise and fall of the tide on the shore and the screeching calls of the gulls.

"Last night I had dinner with this woman I met at the airport. Her name is Claire. She's very nice and she was able to give me loads of really helpful information. And I met her again today for a drink at this little bar she knows. It's called Pedro's and it is run by this old lady called Maria. You would have liked it." He continued walking. "And then I started feeling bad because you weren't with me. I couldn't help it. It just came over me. I felt guilty because I was enjoying myself and you weren't there."

As he walked, Mark turned his thoughts over in his mind. If Margot was with him now, this holiday would be perfect. He thought of all the things they would do together. She would love it here with the sun and the sea and the vitality and the life. But it was impossible. He had to move on from where he was and look forward to the future. That's what she would want. Margot had always been kind and generous. She wouldn't want him to mope and feel sorry for himself.

"Am I doing the right thing?" he said. "What do you think?"

For a while, nothing happened. And then, as he gazed out at the wide expanse of ocean stretching as far as the eye could see, he felt a sudden calm come over him. A smile came to his face. He felt the burden lift and a lightness descend on him. He continued walking, a solitary figure on the deserted strand. When he reached the tower, he turned back again to where he had left the car. He was at peace once more, the calm restored to his heart.

He turned his face to the empty sky. The sun burned like a ball of fire.

"Thank you, Margot," he said gently. "You always give me good advice."

Claire's friends were a former bank manager called Pat Ryan and his wife Anne. They were in their early fifties, childless and had been living in La Cala for almost ten years – ever since Pat had been offered an attractive redundancy package and decided to throw up banking and take up painting instead.

They were waiting for her outside a café, a nice bottle of Rioja already opened beside a bowl of olives and a spare glass set aside for Claire.

When they saw her approaching, they both stood up.

Anne wrapped her arms around Claire and hugged her close. "Oh my Heavens! It's so good to see you again after all this time. Let me look at you." She held Claire at arm's length and gazed with affection into her eyes. "You've still got that hint of devilment that made you take off hitch-hiking to Spain when your poor mother wanted you to settle down with a nice comfortable lawyer!"

Everyone laughed uproariously. Claire had often told them the story of how she had first arrived in Fuengirola.

"And now I'm back again," she said.

"Well, I don't think you've changed a bit."

"Yes, she has," Pat chipped in. "She's improved. I think she's looking more attractive than ever."

"I won't disagree with that," Anne said.

Claire smiled as they both kissed her warmly on the cheeks. This was what she liked most about the Ryans. They were always so bright and cheerful. And their good humour rubbed off on everyone around them.

She took a package from her bag. It was a small watercolour painting of the H'penny Bridge in Dublin that she had picked up at an open-air art exhibition. She gave it to Anne. "This is for you. To remind you of what you left behind."

Anne opened it and gave a little gasp. "That's very thoughtful of you, Claire. It's so beautiful. Look at it, Pat!"

She passed the painting to her husband, who took off his sunglasses to examine it more closely. "It's very good indeed. Exactly as I remember the old bridge. Who is this guy?" He tried to make out the signature at the bottom of the picture.

"He's nobody famous, I'm afraid. Just an amateur. But I liked it and I thought you might like it too."

"We struggling artists must stick together," Pat Ryan declared. "I'll put it above my desk in my study. Now why don't you sit down and have a nice glass of wine and tell us all the wonderful things that have happened to you since we saw you last?"

"Yes," Anne said, pouring wine into the empty glass. "How many hearts have you broken since you returned to Dublin?"

"None," Claire said with a grin. "I'm afraid I can't get anybody stupid enough to take me on."

"Nonsense," Pat said, topping up his own glass. "A gorgeous young thing like you? With a figure most women would kill for? And that beautiful mane of jet-black hair? What man in his right senses could possibly resist you?"

Claire blushed modestly but she couldn't help appreciating the lovely compliments. The others laughed again at her embarrassment.

"What about that Matthew fellow who used to follow you around with his mouth hanging open like a demented bloodhound?" Pat continued. "Whatever happened to him?"

For a moment, a dark cloud passed over Claire's face. "That all fizzled out."

Anne noticed the look on Claire's face and gently massaged her shoulder. "We shouldn't be interrogating you like this. Forgive us, Claire."

Claire took a sip of wine. "I don't mind being asked. But I'm sorry to disappoint you. My life has been pretty boring since I went back. I'm still trying to sell property, you know."

"And succeeding admirably, I'm sure," Anne said. "I know you were damned good at it when you were here."

"I hear prices in Dublin have gone haywire," Pat said.

"That much is true. Somebody paid fifty thousand euros recently for a parking space. Did you ever think you'd see the day?"

"Maybe we should have held onto our own place," Pat said to Anne. "Think of the price we'd get for it now."

"Oh, nonsense," his wife replied. "You'd have gone crazy if you had stayed another day in that damned bank."

"How has life been treating you?" Claire asked, taking another sip of wine.

"Pretty boring too, I'm sorry to say. I paint in the morning. Then we have a break for lunch. In the afternoon we go swimming or read a book. In the evenings we play bridge with some ex-pats we've got to know." He was grinning as he spoke. "I don't think you'd be able to stick it, Claire."

"You want to bet?"

"Why *did* you come back?" Anne wanted to know.

Claire paused. "I suppose I wanted to recapture some of that happy time when I first came with Róisín. It was all so wonderful then. I wanted to see if it had lasted."

Pat was nodding knowledgeably.

"And has it?" Anne asked.

"I'm not sure," Claire replied.

For dinner, they took her to a beautiful restaurant perched on a cliff top overlooking the sea. Claire was afraid that she wasn't dressed properly, in her skimpy little vest and denim skirt, but the Ryans soon dismissed her protests.

"You're perfectly dressed," said Anne. "Anyway, nobody cares about that sort of thing around here. Maybe in some of those snobby places in Marbella they might insist on dressing up but here the main point is to enjoy yourself."

"Now what are you going to eat?" Pat asked, putting a menu into her hand.

It was mainly seafood. From the moment she had entered the restaurant she could smell the wonderful aroma of grilling fish. She studied the menu carefully and finally opted for mussels in white wine. Around them on the cliffs the seabirds wheeled and swooped as the golden sun descended into the azure sea.

"This is so beautiful," she said. "How could anyone ever grow tired of watching a sunset like this?"

"You'd certainly have to work at it," Pat replied, pouring glasses of chilled wine.

The waiter took their order and soon their meal arrived. Everyone had ordered fish: grilled calamari for Anne and sea bass for Pat. The dishes were accompanied by salad and potatoes fried in garlic. Claire realised that she was quite hungry. She had eaten nothing since breakfast. She extracted a mussel from its shell and felt it burst with flavour on her tongue.

"Where are you staying?" Anne wanted to know.

"I've managed to get an apartment at a knockdown price. Someone I used to know in the business."

"You could have stayed with us, you know. We have a spare bed."

"That's very kind but it would have been unfair to inflict myself on you for a whole month."

"Nonsense. We're always delighted to see you," Pat said. "And now that you're here we expect to see a lot more of you. I want to show you my work."

"He's getting to be quite successful," Anne said. "He had a big exhibition in Malaga last month."

"She's exaggerating as usual," Pat butted in.

"No, I'm not. You sold €20,000 worth of paintings."

"That was just a fluke."

"Well, if it was a fluke, let's have more of it."

Claire listened as her friends gently argued. The sun had gone down now and the sky was suddenly filled with stars. Around them, the buzz of conversation from the other diners rose to a gentle hum. From the shore below, she could hear the crashing of the sea against the rocks. This is idyllic, she thought. To have a life like theirs must be sheer bliss. She felt a tinge of envy towards her friends who had forsaken the stress and pressure of Dublin to live here and do the things they wanted.

It was almost one o'clock when the taxi finally deposited her back at her apartment. Climbing the stairs she saw the light was still burning in Maggie's room. As she put the key in the lock she heard the door behind her open.

"Oh, you're back then?" Maggie said.

Claire felt her heart sink. She was too tired to engage in a lengthy conversation with her neighbour. She just wanted to get under the sheets and grab some sleep.

"Have a nice day, did you?"

"It was very pleasant, thanks," Claire said. "I was visiting some friends in La Cala."

"Oooh, that was nice!"

"Yes," Claire replied.

"While you were out the landlord called."

Claire stopped. "Johnny Parkinson?"

"Yes. He said to tell you someone was looking for you."

11

"How long have you been living here?" Emma inquired, pushing her blonde curls back from her face.

"Two years," Kevin replied.

"You must like it."

"I love it. I could live here forever."

She took a sip of wine. "Well, it certainly has a magic. But there must be some drawbacks. Something I haven't discovered yet. Nowhere is perfect."

"That depends on what you're looking for. I just wanted somewhere nice and warm to escape to. The pace of life here is slow and the weather is excellent most of the time and it's very cheap to live."

He shrugged and gave her that mischievous smile that Emma was beginning to find most alluring. "So, here I am."

"You do an excellent job of selling the place," she said. "Maybe you should be working for the local tourist board."

"Now there's an idea," Kevin said and they both laughed.

They were sitting at a pavement table outside The

Bodega having just finished dinner. It was eight thirty and the place was half empty. Kevin had explained earlier that the Spanish tended to eat later in the evening, which suited Emma perfectly. She just wanted to throw her eye over the accounts of Pedro's Bar to satisfy herself that everything was in order. There was a fashion show scheduled for ten o'clock at the hotel and she planned to be there. They'd had a very enjoyable meal but now it was time to get down to business.

"How did you come to work in Pedro's anyway?" she inquired.

"I just happened to be available."

"So it's that sort of place?"

"If you mean it's casual and laidback, then yes, I suppose it is," he replied. "But that doesn't mean it isn't businesslike. Behind that easygoing façade, Maria keeps it ticking over like clockwork. I think you'll discover that when you study those."

He made a gesture to the thick bundle of papers bound with ribbon that sat on the table beside her.

When he had given them to her earlier, Emma had been somewhat surprised. She had been expecting proper account books.

"Tell me about Maria."

He topped up their glasses from the wine bottle. "What do you want to know?"

"Well, let's begin with her age. How old is she?"

Kevin gave her a quizzical look. "Do you always begin with the most difficult questions? Maria's age is one of those great mysteries. Like the Third Secret of Fatima. Your guess is as good as mine."

"I'd say she's at least seventy."

"On the other hand, she could be eighty."

"Oh no, I don't think so. I don't think a woman of that age would have Maria's energy."

"Are you kidding?" Kevin responded. "Some of those old Spanish ladies have amazing energy. They're as tough as old boots. Some of them live to be over a hundred."

"She told me her husband, Pedro, died at fifty-seven. And that was around thirteen years ago."

"How do you know she's telling the truth?" Kevin asked. "Don't you know she has a motive for making herself younger than she really is?"

"Oh?"

He frowned. "Of course. She's terrified that you're going to close down the bar."

"And why would that be such a terrible thing?"

"For one thing, she'd be out of a job. So would I. But the difference is, I would easily find another one. Maria wouldn't."

"Whatever her actual age, she *is* an old lady," Emma pointed out. "Don't you think instead of working every day in the hot sun she'd prefer to be at home with her family? I know I would."

Kevin slowly put down his wineglass. "Do you know about her family?"

"Of course not. I know absolutely nothing about her. That's why I'm asking you."

"Well then, I'll tell you. Maria has only two living relatives: her sister Rosario and her son Antonio. Rosario had an accident about ten years ago, shortly after Pedro died, and she is now an invalid. She's confined to a wheelchair. She lives with Maria, who cares for her."

"And Antonio?"

Kevin let out a loud sigh. "I'm afraid Antonio is not what you would call a dutiful son. Before he died, Pedro wanted to leave the beach hut to Maria as some form of security for her old age. But Antonio persuaded him to change his mind. He told his father he had grand plans to develop it into a bar that would provide a good living for them all. He said Pedro need have no worries about Maria because he would look after her. Well, he did develop the hut – largely with Maria's help it must be said. He got a liquor licence and Maria built up the food side of the business and before long it was a thriving concern. But Antonio had other plans that nobody knew about. Once he had established the bar, he sold it to Conor Delaney and Maria was more or less thrown to the wolves. There was a big row about it and things got very bitter. She didn't get a cent from the sale and only for the kindness of Conor she would have been left with no income at all."

"And now Antonio owns a restaurant?"

"Yes, a very prosperous restaurant called *El Molino Blanco* that caters for the top end of the market. He's a very good businessman, I have to say that. The place is a goldmine. But his mother doesn't get a sniff of any of the profits. And worse than that, the thing that really breaks her heart, he has forbidden her to see her grandchildren."

Emma looked shocked. "That's terrible. I had absolutely no idea."

"Well, now you understand why the beach bar is so important to Maria and why she's so nervous about your visit. Her future is in the balance."

Emma lowered her eyes.

"Have you decided what you're going to do?" Kevin continued.

She shook her head. "Before I make any decision, I need to study these." She gestured to the bundle of papers that Kevin had given her earlier. "You know, I was expecting proper account books. It's what every regular business has."

Kevin gave a helpless shrug. "That's all I was given."

"Tell me something else. Do you know if Maria employs an accountant?"

"I don't think so," Kevin said nervously. "I think she left that end of things to Conor Delaney."

"But are all taxes and duties paid up to date? The bar isn't carrying any debts?"

He hesitated. "I'm afraid that's something I can't confirm because I just don't know."

Emma felt a sinking feeling in the pit of her stomach. What exactly had she taken on with Pedro's Bar? She tried to conceal her growing concern. "Well, that's something else I need to find out. Would you tell Maria I'll call to see her again in the morning? Tell her I must know exactly where we stand with regard to tax and insurance and all outstanding debts. I can't make an informed decision about the bar until I have all the information. In the meantime, I'll take these with me and study them."

"Do you mind if ask?" Kevin said, cautiously. "How come you bought a bar without even seeing it?"

"I didn't buy it," Emma said.

He gave her a look of surprise. "But you own it?"

"You might say I acquired it. I know absolutely nothing about the bar trade. My business is printing. I run a company in Dublin."

"You mean you have no experience?"

"None whatsoever. I'm a complete novice."

He looked incredulous.

"It's too complicated to explain," Emma said as she picked up the bundle of documents and called for the bill.

"How are you getting back to your hotel?" Kevin asked.

"I'll take a cab."

They stood awkwardly for a moment and then Emma extended her hand.

"Thanks for taking the time to meet me and fill me in on the background."

"It was a pleasure. And thank you for a lovely dinner."

The captivating smile was back again on his lips. On another occasion, Emma might have been tempted to go with him to some little bar to share a nightcap. But not tonight. Tonight, she had important business matters on her mind.

"Tell Maria I'll call in the morning," she said as she turned on her heel and strode quickly towards a waiting line of taxis.

Back at the hotel, she dismissed her plans to watch the fashion show. She went straight to her room and put through a call to Conor Delaney. She got his message minder. She left a message to ring her urgently, then ordered a pot of coffee from room service and sat down at the little desk and began to trawl through the bundle of accounts.

They only added to her growing sense of alarm. Whatever about the Spanish authorities, she knew for sure that the bundle of paper in front of her would never be accepted by the Revenue Commissioners in Dublin.

But after a while she began to make some headway. Slowly she started to make sense of the receipts and bills and invoices that passed for accounts. To her great relief, it appeared that the bar was trading well and returning healthy profits. But she still needed to know about possible debts and charges. The material she had been given made absolutely no reference to anything like that.

Just then, her phone rang. She quickly picked it up and heard Conor's voice.

"You were looking for me?" he said in a slurred voice that told her immediately he had been drinking.

"Thanks for calling, Conor. How are you?"

"Banjaxed," he replied. "Just like I predicted, the vultures have started to pick my bones. The way things are going, I won't be left with a pot to piss in."

"You mustn't be too downhearted. I'm sure things will work out."

"I wouldn't bet on it. Now what can I do for you?"

"I'm in Fuengirola."

"So you got there all right? I wish I was with you. Say hello to them all for me. They're a good bunch. How's old Maria?"

"She's fine, Conor. That's the reason I rang you. I'm trying to get a handle on the accounts. Can you tell me if there is a professional accountant looking after those affairs?"

His answer caused a chill to run along her spine. "I never bothered with any of that stuff. Left it all to Maria. I used to go over a couple of times a year and pick up a cheque for my share of the profits. As long as she kept the show on the road, I left her alone."

"But I need to know if things are up to date. I don't want to be hit with a massive bill for unpaid taxes."

She heard him give a loud hiccough. "Take my advice and don't worry about that sort of thing. Everything is different in Spain. Why don't you simply adopt my system? Call for your money a couple of times a year and leave everything else to Maria."

She could see there was no point in arguing with him. "Well, thanks for calling, Conor. And good luck!"

"Don't forget to tell them I was asking about them."

"I won't."

She put down the phone. Adopting Conor Delaney's system would be a recipe for disaster. It was exactly what had got him into his present mess and she had no intention of following him. She went into the bedroom and poured a stiff brandy and sat with it on the terrace.

The stars were out but they brought her little joy. Instead, she felt a grey foreboding settle over her. It looked like her worst nightmare was coming true. The little bar on the beach could turn out to be a millstone round her neck.

She needed to talk to Maria urgently – first thing in the morning, as soon as Pedro's Bar opened for business.

12

Claire's initial reaction to Maggie's information was mild surprise.

"Johnny Parkinson said someone was looking for me?"

"That's right."

"Did he say who?"

Maggie shook her head.

"Did he leave a phone number?"

"Afraid not," Maggie said. "He just called and asked if you were in and when I told him no, he said to tell you someone was looking for you."

"I suppose he meant he got a phone call – or did someone actually call into the agency?"

"I don't know, to be honest."

"I hate messages like this," Claire said, shaking her dark hair in irritation.

"Blimey, I'm sorry."

"No, it's not your fault. I just wish people would be more specific."

"It's all very mysterious, isn't it?"

"It's all very annoying," Claire said. She was feeling tired after her trip to La Cala. Now she wanted to get to bed. "Thanks anyway, Maggie. I'll see you in the morning."

She went into her apartment and firmly closed the door. Who could have been looking for her? Must be someone here in Spain who knew her from before, someone who heard she was around again. Her family and close friends in Ireland had her mobile number and, anyway, with the cost of calls to Spain she knew that few people would be ringing just to have a chat. They all had her email address and that was how she planned to keep in contact. She had spotted an Internet café at the bottom of the street and tomorrow she would call in and check her messages.

Which reminded her: she hadn't called her mother since she left Dublin. She had better do that tomorrow as well before her mother got on to Interpol to say she had been kidnapped by aliens.

She got undressed, had a hot shower and slipped into bed. She'd had a long day. It was great to see the Ryans again and to know that they were happy. But now she was dog-tired. She hoped she hadn't been too abrupt with Maggie but she really was not in the mood for a lengthy chat about Tina Turner. Maybe tomorrow.

As she closed her eyes, another thought popped into her head. Why had the person called the landlord? Hardly anyone knew she had managed to get the apartment from her old contact in the estate agency – unless Kevin Joyce had spread the word around? It really was very mysterious, as Maggie had said. Oh, well, she thought as she snuggled down into the cosy bed, if it's really important, they'll make contact again.

She slept till ten. She was wakened by the sound of Maggie banging on the door. When she opened it she found her standing in the hallway with a bread knife in her hand. My God, Claire thought, I must have really offended her last night.

"So you're up then?" Maggie said.

"I am now," Claire said, nervously eying the bread knife.

"I'm making pancakes for breakfast and I thought you might like some."

Claire rubbed the sleep from her eyes. "That's great, Maggie. I'd love pancakes. Just give me a few minutes to get ready and I'll be right over."

She went back into the apartment, had a quick shower and pulled on a top, skirt and sandals. Then she rejoined her neighbour across the hall. The delicious smell of fresh-brewed coffee and cooking pancakes met her at the door.

"This is very kind of you, Maggie."

"Well, I thought you might be sort of lonely seeing as how you've just arrived and everything." She put a big plate of pancakes in front of Claire at the table along with a jar of syrup. "Did you find out who was looking for you?"

"Not yet."

"I was thinking. It could have been this mad axe-murderer who's going round killing people. He murdered two women in Marbella last week."

"I don't think so."

"No?"

"I don't think he'd ring me up to tell me he was coming."

"I never thought of that. But he might have been checking you out. They say he goes in for brunettes like you."

"But how does he know I'm here?"

"He might have been following you. Do you think we should tell the police?"

"Not just yet," Claire said, tucking into the pancakes. "I think I'll call first to the landlord and see if he can tell me who it was."

"That's a good idea. But I don't think you should take any chances. I think you should lock your door at night."

"I do that already," Claire said, pouring a large steaming cup of coffee.

For the next half hour she listened while Maggie debated the merits of switching her cabaret act from Tina Turner to Madonna.

"Madonna's got a broader appeal," she said. "Tina Turner's sort of limited to older people, don't you think?"

"Oh, I don't know about that."

"And I'm not really tall enough. If I was like you now, it would be different. You're nice and tall. I think men prefer tall women."

"I'm not certain about that either," Claire replied, starting into another pancake. "I'm sure you make a perfect Tina Turner. And I know she has lots of fans."

"Really? I could easily make myself up to look like Madonna. Maybe it's time for a change."

"But can you sing like her?" Claire asked.

"What's that got to do with it?"

"Well, you're supposed to be impersonating her."

"But I don't actually sing. I just mime to backing tracks."

"I see," Claire said, suddenly realising she had a lot to learn about the cabaret scene. "Well, in that case. Maybe you should go for it."

Eventually, she made her escape after promising to come over to Maggie's flat some evening to watch her perform as both Madonna and Tina Turner and help her decide which suited her best.

The Internet café was run by a pleasant Egyptian man who

led Claire to a computer at the back of the room and insisted on giving her a cushion to put on the seat.

"You know how to work it?"

"Yes," Claire said.

"Where are you from?"

"Ireland."

"Ah, my favourite country."

"Really?"

"Oh, yes. I love Ireland. I love Bono. Do you have Internet cafes in Ireland?"

"Loads of them," Claire replied.

"Maybe I will come to Ireland and open another one."

"You'd be very welcome."

"Do you think I will meet Bob Geldof?"

"Not really."

The man looked disappointed. "Why not?"

"He lives in London," Claire said, logging on and beginning to check her mail.

There were six messages, all from friends and contacts back in Dublin. It took her twenty minutes to read them and send replies, assuring everyone that she was having a wonderful time and the weather was marvellous and the food was delicious and she was really having a ball. She signed them all: *Message from Sunny Fuengirola* after checking the international weather forecast and confirming that it was dull and overcast in Dublin.

Now it was time to ring her mother. She had left this to the last because she knew it would be the most difficult. There was a row of cubicles along the wall, each one containing a wooden counter, a seat, a meter and a phone. Claire stepped into the nearest one and closed the door. She took the phone from the wall, breathed deeply and rang the number.

She listened as the phone rang in a hallway thousands of miles away across land and sea. After a minute, there was a click and the call was picked up. She heard a polite female voice announce: "Greene residence. Who is calling?"

"It's me, Mum, Claire. I'm just ringing to tell you that I've arrived safely and everything is fine."

"Oh, thank Heavens," her mother burbled. "I was half distracted with worry about you!"

"Well, why didn't you phone my mobile, Mum, if you were that worried?"

"But sure that wouldn't be working in Spain, would it?"

"Of course it is, Mum!"

"Anyway, are you alright? Is it safe where you are? What's the weather like?"

"It's 32 degrees, Mum. It's so hot I have to sleep with the windows open."

"My God! You're trying to frighten me. Shut them at once. What if some crazed sex maniac broke in and attacked you in your own bed?"

"I'm six storeys up. He'd have to be Batman."

"I can't bear to think about it. Why did you have to go back there? And why did you take four weeks? You're just leaving the employment front wide open for the competition. What's going to happen if a big promotion comes up and you're not here to apply? And you with your 2.1 Honours degree in Legal Studies from Trinity College?"

Claire bit her lip.

"Just try to relax, Mum. I'm sure they'd let me know if anything like that was about to happen. I'm perfectly safe and I'm having a really relaxing holiday and there's nothing for you to worry about."

"You're breaking my heart," her mother said. "Why could you not be like your sister Orla with her nice home and her happy marriage? Did I tell you she's going to get the principal's job in her school?"

"No."

"Well, she is."

"What happened to Mr Breen?"

"He finally had a nervous breakdown. He thought he was being pursued by Martians who were after his job."

"Poor man. And it was really only Orla all the time. Give my regards to Dad. I'll ring again next week. Byeee!"

Claire put down the phone and let out a loud sigh of relief. Thank God that was over. There was no doubt. Her mother was getting worse. She would get on really well with Maggie with their shared interest in sex maniacs and crazed axe-murderers. But she was never going to change. She wouldn't be happy till Claire was nicely tucked up in a wig and gown and safely married to some legal eagle; or even some legal robin redbreast. Just as long as he made plenty of money.

She paid the kind Egyptian owner and went outside to the blinding sunshine. She needed a drink. The beach was just a few blocks away. She decided to stroll along to Pedro's and have a beer. Maybe Kevin would be there and she'd be able to catch up on the gossip.

But when she arrived, there was no sign of him. And Maria was still down in the dumps and in little mood for conversation. She wasn't going to get any gossip here. Nevertheless, Claire sat at the counter and ordered a beer. The frantic lunchtime rush had ended but a few bronzed sun-worshippers remained, drinking pints of Dorada and arguing about football.

Claire waited till the old lady had finished her chores before asking: "Where's Kevin today, Maria?"

"He's taking a break. Be back later."

"Did you have a busy day?"

Maria shrugged. "Every day is busy at Pedro's."

"But that's good. It means people like the place. If it wasn't busy *then* you could complain."

The old lady shrugged again but didn't reply.

Claire felt sorry for her. It was no joke working in the hot sun at her age. "Cheer up, Maria!"

Maria gave a loud snort. "You say cheer up. How I can cheer up when the new *señorita* might close down the bar? Then what am I going to do?"

Claire reached out and touched her arm. "Don't think like that. Think of all the good times we used to have. Think of all the laughs."

For a brief moment a flicker of a smile passed over Maria's wrinkled face. "Yes," she said, "you are right. The times we had were good. Maybe they will come again."

It was after four o'clock when Claire finally left Pedro's. She had nothing planned for the evening. She would find a nice place to eat and then go back to the apartment and curl up on the settee with a good book. Maggie wouldn't disturb her; she had told Claire earlier that she had several engagements tonight at pubs around the town.

But first she would call into the estate agency and find out who had been looking for her. The agency had its office down near the port. When she arrived they were preparing to close up for the day.

"Hello," she said breezily to the young assistant. "Is Johnny still around?"

"Who shall I say is asking for him?"

"Claire Greene."

The receptionist left her desk and disappeared into a

smaller office at the back. A moment later she reappeared with Johnny Parkinson, sporting his usual year-round sun tan.

"Ah, Claire! Good to see you. How are you settling into the apartment?"

"Fine, thanks."

"Everything to your satisfaction?"

"I've no complaints."

"I couldn't interest you in a nice villa in Puerto Banus for a mere million euros?"

"Do you never stop working?" Claire asked with a grin.

"You know this business. Yesterday I sold a penthouse to a man I was playing golf with. Clinched the deal at the nineteenth hole. What can I do for you?"

"My neighbour told me you said someone was looking for me."

A thin smile crossed his face. "That's right. An old friend of yours. I was speaking to him on the phone and I happened to mention that you were in Fuengirola. He said to give you his regards and tell you he'll be here himself next week on business and he'll look you up."

"Who is it?" Claire asked, hoping against hope that she wouldn't get the answer she feared.

"Matthew Baker."

13

Mark walked briskly along the seafront towards the port. It was just after nine o'clock and he was feeling better than he had done for months. After his chat with Margot on the beach, he had felt his spirits revive. He felt somehow that she was happy he was getting back his capacity for enjoyment – almost as if she was enjoying this bright, beautiful Mediterranean world through him.

Yesterday he had taken out his golf clubs and played eighteen holes at a magnificent course in the hills above the town and later joined a group of Irish golfers at the bar where they raised a lot of eyebrows with their hearty renditions of "The Fields of Athenry" and "Dicey Reilly". It was after one by the time he managed to climb into bed. But he had slept soundly and now he felt energised.

It was a glorious morning with a big bright sun dominating a cloudless sky. Dressed in shorts, navy T-shirt and running shoes he strode past the little restaurants and cafés with their tables set out and the smell of fresh-brewed coffee wafting onto the street. The town was already bustling. The joggers were out, the sun beds were being spread on the sand and the bathers were splashing about in the waves.

He decided he would drop in to Pedro's Bar, have a morning coffee and then head back to his hotel. Maybe he might even run into Claire again there. He had really enjoyed their dinner together at Felipe's restaurant the other night. Perhaps he might persuade her to join him again?

But when he arrived at Pedro's, he was met with a surprise. The place was locked and shuttered, the tables and chairs stacked neatly at the back wall. There was no sign of life except for a solitary figure standing at the counter waiting for the bar to open. As he drew closer, he recognised the young blonde woman he had seen talking with Kevin the last time he was here.

"Good morning," he said, cheerfully, as he approached. "Bar closed?"

"I'm afraid so," the woman replied.

"What time does it open?"

"I don't know. In fact, I was hoping you might have been able to tell me."

"I haven't got a clue." He checked his watch. "Nine thirty. Time for morning coffee, I would have thought."

"Me too. But so far there's been no sign of life."

"If you're looking for a coffee, there's a place across the street."

He pointed and the woman turned her head to look. A café on the Paseo Maritimo was already open and doing a brisk trade.

"You're right," she said. "The opposition aren't wasting any time."

"No, they're not. Pedro's would need to get the finger out."

She looked amused. "I'm the new owner of Pedro's Bar."

"Oh, no offence!"

"None taken," she smiled. "I've just come to talk to the manager. But I'm afraid I don't even know the opening hours."

"You probably don't remember but I saw you here a couple of days ago. You were sitting at the counter when I arrived. You were talking to the barman."

"I do remember. You were with a tall, dark-haired woman, right?"

"Yes," Mark said.

"Very attractive too, if I might say. Your wife?"

"No." He hesitated, then continued, "Her name is Claire. She used to live here. Her friend worked at the bar. She wanted to say hello to Maria."

He stuck out his hand. "I'm Mark Chambers, by the way."

"Emma Dunne."

"So you're the new owner?"

"That's right," she smiled. "And I can't even get a cup of coffee at my own bar."

"Look," Mark said, "I've just been out for a walk and I was looking forward to a coffee too. Would you care to join me across the road at 'the opposition' as you call it? You can keep an eye on Pedro's from there and when Maria comes along you'll spot her."

"That's a good idea," Emma said. "And I can kill two birds with one stone. I can check out the competition while I'm there."

"Pedro's seems very popular with the beach crowd," Mark said once they had seated themselves at a pavement table and given their order to a brisk young waiter in a white waistcoat. "It was certainly doing a roaring trade when I was there. When did you take it over?"

"Just a couple of days ago. Came straight out here on an inspection tour."

"But you'd seen it before – in the past?"

"No, never been here before."

"Really?" Mark said. He didn't want to appear inquisitive but it struck him as an odd way to do business – buying a place without looking it over first.

"You probably think I'm mad," Emma continued.

"Why would I think that?"

"To begin with, I know nothing about the bar trade. And I know even less about the Spanish bar trade."

"So why did you decide to invest?"

"I didn't, that's the whole point. I sort of acquired it from the previous owner. In payment of a debt. I hadn't even seen it till a couple of days ago."

"Well, if you don't want to run it, why don't you sell it again? I'm sure you would get a good price for it."

Emma let out a loud sigh. "I wish it was that simple. But there are problems."

"What sort of problems?"

She waved her hand. "You don't really want to listen to this stuff. It's boring."

"No," Mark insisted. "I find it interesting."

"Well, first there's the question of what to do about the staff. I can't just throw them out on the street. Particularly Maria. Managing the bar is her sole means of income and she has a sister who's an invalid and depends on her."

"Hmmm," Mark said. "That *is* tricky. But maybe if you sold it, the new owner would want to keep them on."

"That's possible. But it's by no means certain. The new owner might just as easily want to bring in new staff."

At that moment, the waiter appeared with their coffees.

Mark used the opportunity to examine Emma more closely. She was very pretty with a mass of curly blonde hair tumbling to her shoulders, soft blue eyes and a slim figure that he found very appealing. But there was something else he noticed about her. Behind that pretty face there was a quiet confidence, a toughness even. He was certain that Emma Dunne would be quite a determined lady.

She stirred her coffee and took a sip. "Mmmm – this is good. I must check the coffee at Pedro's and compare." Now that she had a receptive audience in Mark, she suddenly was eager to talk. She went on: "The second problem is potentially far more serious."

"Yes?" he prompted.

"I told you I had no experience of the Spanish bar trade but what I have seen so far doesn't inspire me with confidence. Things seem to be run on a very ad-hoc basis. I asked to see the accounts for Pedro's and I was given a bundle of receipts and invoices. It's the sort of thing that would never be accepted back home."

"What exactly do you do back home?" Mark prompted.

"I run a printing business. Hi-Speed Printing. Have you heard of us? "

He shook his head.

"We're a medium-sized company but quite successful. So you see, I'm used to dealing with accountants, keeping proper books and records, paying PRSI, dealing with the Revenue. All that sort of thing. To tell you the truth, I'm worried that Pedro's might not have been paying their taxes and I could be hit for a massive bill."

"Surely Maria will be able to put your mind at ease?"

"Well, I certainly hope so. That's why I decided to get out here early and talk to her. The trouble is, her English isn't great."

"It will all work out for the best," Mark said soothingly. "You're probably worrying over nothing."

"I hope you're right. A problem with Pedro's is the last thing I need just now."

She finished her coffee. So far, Mark hadn't even touched his, he had been so engrossed in their conversation. He lifted his cup and took a sip.

"Would you like another one?" he asked.

"Oh God, no. Too much coffee gives me the jitters."

He saw her examining him.

"You know, I'm sure I've seen you before," she said.

"You met me at the bar the other day."

"No, somewhere else. What do you do for a living?"

"I'm in advertising."

Suddenly, a smile broke across her face. "Of course! Now I recognise you! Chambers Creative Artists, right?"

"That's right," Mark said.

"You must be very busy. Every time I open a newspaper, I seem to see a reference to you. In fact . . ." She quickly put a hand to her mouth. "Oh my God, I'm terribly sorry." She stared at him in horror.

"My wife died recently," he said. "You don't need to feel embarrassed. I'm slowly getting used to it. It's the reason I've come here."

"I'm so sorry. It must have been dreadful for you."

"There's no point pretending," Mark said sadly. "It was devastating. I loved her very much. And it came right out of the blue. She was expecting our first child."

Emma placed a comforting hand on his arm. "I can't imagine the grief you must feel. And here am I, babbling on about my silly little problems while you have this major trauma in your life. Please forgive me."

He rushed to reassure her. "There's nothing to forgive. Really. I've enjoyed talking to you."

He took a pen from his pocket and scribbled on the back of a napkin then gave it to her.

"Look, that's my hotel number. Give me a ring if you think I can be of any help with the bar. Two heads are always better than one and I have some experience of business. In fact, give me a call anyway. I'll buy you a drink and you can tell me how everything worked out."

At that moment, he saw Maria's plump form step out of a cab and begin to make her way along the beach towards the bar.

"There's your pigeon now," he said. "Why don't you grab her before she opens up?"

Emma quickly got to her feet. "Thank you for listening to my moans and for the coffee. I'll be in touch."

She skipped quickly across the road and began shouting and waving to Maria to attract her attention.

Mark stared at his coffee. It had grown cold. He called to the waiter to pay the bill. Maria was going to be tied up with Emma for a while so there was no point hanging around. He decided to head down to the port. He had been thinking of going scuba diving. He'd go and check out the possibilities.

14

Maria stopped and looked around when she heard the voice calling her name. Then a frown came over her face. It was the Irish *señorita*. Kevin had rung to say she was coming and Maria sensed it would mean trouble. She forced herself to smile as Emma caught up with her.

"*Hola*, Maria!" Emma said.

"*Hola*, Emma!"

"How are you this morning?"

"I'm late for work. My sister, Rosario, was sick this morning and I had to take care of her."

"I'm sorry to hear that. Is she all right now?"

Maria shrugged.

"Don't worry about the bar for a moment, Maria. I need to talk to you. Why don't we go over there to that bench and sit down?"

The look of concern returned to the old woman's face but Emma hastened to reassure her. "It's nothing to worry about. I just need to ask you a few questions."

182

Emma led Maria to a bench beside the footpath. It wasn't ideal but at least it would provide them with some privacy while they had their conversation.

When Maria had settled herself, Emma began. "I spoke with Kevin last night and he gave me the accounts. I've had a chance to study them and I was delighted to find that Pedro's Bar is running very well. That's very good, Maria."

A brief smile reappeared on Maria's face.

"We seem to be trading well and making a good profit," Emma continued. "But there are some things I need to know."

"Yes?" the old lady asked.

"Can you tell me if you pay any taxes?"

A look of confusion came over Maria's countenance. "I don't understand."

"Every business must pay taxes. The government always looks for money," Emma explained patiently.

"I don't know about taxes," Maria said. "I just buy the food and pay the bills for the beer and the vino and pay the wages. I asked Kevin to give you all the papers I have."

Emma felt her heart sink. It was looking exactly as she had feared. She tried to keep her face expressionless so as not to alarm Maria. "This is important, Maria. Do you have an accountant?"

Maria looked baffled.

Emma struggled to recall the word she had located in the Spanish dictionary she had borrowed from the hotel receptionist this morning. "*Contable.*"

"*Ah, contable!*"

"That's right, Maria. Do you have a *contable*?"

"*Sí! Señor Martinez Sanchez.*"

The old lady suddenly looked so relieved that for a moment Emma thought she was going to throw her arms around her.

"He is *contable!*" Maria made a scribbling motion with her hand to indicate that she understood what it was that Emma was looking for.

"That's excellent, Maria. That's what I needed to know. Now I have to talk to him. Can you give me his address and telephone number?"

"Of course."

Maria led the way back to the bar. She took a bunch of keys from the pocket of her dress, opened the flap and burrowed inside. There was a rasping noise as the shutters were suddenly lifted up and Maria appeared again on the other side of the counter.

"*Un momento!*" she said as she opened a drawer and withdrew a small red notebook. She flicked the pages till she found what she was looking for, then wrote the information on a piece of paper and gave it to Emma. "*Miguel Martinez Sanchez.*"

Emma studied the paper. It had his address and phone number. She recognised the street. It was beside the old town.

"Thank you, Maria. This is exactly what I want." She put the piece of paper safely inside her purse. "Goodbye now, Maria. See you later."

"*Buenos días, Emma.*"

Emma turned to go, then swung back again. "Maria, I want you to know that you are doing a very good job and I am very pleased with your work."

The old lady's face lit up. "*Gracias, señorita.*"

"*Buenos días, Maria.*"

Emma's first impulse was to go right round to the accountant's office and speak to him now. She could be there in fifteen minutes. But as she walked back along the Paseo Maritimo, she changed her mind. It would be better to begin their relationship on an entirely professional footing. There was too much casualness already. She would ring first and make an appointment. She would do it from her hotel.

She got him at the first attempt. He sounded flustered. But then he seemed to gather himself together. He explained that he had business this morning but would be happy to see her at two. It was now almost eleven o'clock. Emma decided to spend the rest of the morning sunbathing at the swimming pool. She had been here three days and hadn't had an opportunity yet.

The pool was located in the gardens and shielded from the road by a high wall. The sun beds were laid out in neat rows and already a number of people were stretched out tanning themselves. She found a spot near the wall, took off her sarong and applied a liberal covering of the special sun cream she had bought. Being blond and fair-skinned, she was only too aware of the dangers. She recalled a horror story she had once been told about a woman who fell asleep in the bright midday sun and woke up covered in blisters. The poor creature had to spend the remainder of her holiday in the Burns Unit of the local hospital.

Well, that's not going to happen to me if I can help it, she said to herself as she stuffed her hair into a baseball cap, put on her shades and lay down with a contented sigh.

So far, so good. She had established that the bar did indeed employ an accountant. It was a relief to know. She would check with him that everything was in order and encourage him to put the accounting system on a more orderly basis. While invoices and receipts were important backup evidence they were no substitute for proper account books. If Maria couldn't do it, perhaps she could persuade Kevin to take on the task. Once she had got that problem resolved, she would be in a better position to decide what to do with the bar.

The sun was warm on her face. She thought how pleasant it was just to lie out like this for a while. Most of the people stretched around the pool probably had nothing more pressing to think about than what wine to drink with their lunch. Once again, Emma thought of the dramatic way her life had been turned around: first the offer from Herr Braun to buy the company and then gaining ownership of Pedro's. A week ago, she was discussing print orders with her customers and now here she was stretched out in the sun in Fuengirola with two big decisions on her mind.

Between swimming and sunning herself, the morning flew quickly and it was time to leave. She stuffed her towel and toiletries into her bag and went back up to her suite. She had a quick shower, then dressed in the cream linen suit she had brought with her and put on her make-up. Since this would be her first encounter with the accountant, she wanted to create a good impression. Slipping her feet into cream high-heeled sandals, she examined herself in the mirror. She looked cool and sophisticated and her skin already looked tanned against the cream of the suit. She put on her gold stud earrings and a simple gold chain. Then, satisfied, she left and took the lift down to the foyer.

Outside the hotel, a row of taxis was waiting. Emma got into the back seat of the first one and gave her destination.

Ten minutes later she was deposited in a narrow street off the main square. She checked the number again. It was a shabby doorway beside a small grocery store. Emma was surprised. She had been expecting something more grand. She pushed open the door and was confronted by a flight of rickety stairs. A hand-painted sign with an arrow pointing upwards said: *M. Martinez Sanchez.* The sign gave no indication that he was a *contable.*

With growing unease, she proceeded upwards till she came to a glass-panelled door with the name displayed again. She knocked and entered. A middle-aged woman sat at a computer screen. She looked up as Emma entered.

"I'm Emma Dunne. I have an appointment to see *Señor* Martinez Sanchez."

The woman pointed to another door and indicated that Emma should go in.

She entered and immediately felt her spirits sink further. An overweight man in a loud suit was rising from his desk to greet her. He had sleek black hair and thick, heavy cheeks. His hand was outstretched in welcome. He smiled to reveal a mouthful of gold teeth.

"*Señorita* Dunne," he said. "So good to meet you."

Emma took an instant dislike to him.

Mark had gone scuba diving before and it was something he enjoyed. He found a kiosk at the port that advertised trips and provided all the gear and equipment. As luck would have it, there was a boat going out in twenty minutes. He decided not to go back to his hotel after all. But instead, he paid the fee, changed into a wet suit, put his clothes in a locker and took his place with the other divers in the bow of the boat. Half an hour later, they were out on the broad ocean and ready to commence diving.

There were six of them altogether: three Germans, a Dane and a small, tanned Frenchman. The instructor gave them safety directions, urged them to keep together and one by one they put on their goggles and breathing apparatus and tumbled out of the boat and into the water.

It was an amazing experience. The boatman had taken them to a spot where there was an abundance of rock and as Mark swam down into the cold depths of the ocean he was thrilled at what he saw: beautiful underwater plants, shoals of brightly coloured fish, crabs, lobsters, starfish and now and then a giant squid that went sailing past without paying him the slightest notice.

He could have gone on forever exploring the ocean floor but after ninety minutes the boatman gave them the signal that it was time to return to the surface. When he regained the boat, the others were already there but he realised that the Frenchman was missing. A few minutes later, he surfaced a short distance from the boat and swam effortlessly towards them.

Once back at the port, Mark changed out of his wet suit, took a hot shower and got dressed. It was now almost four o'clock and he was feeling peckish. The exercise had given him an appetite. He decided to call once more to Pedro's Bar. If Claire was there he would ask her to join him for dinner. They might even round off the evening at a night club. An evening spent in her stimulating company would be a fitting end to the day.

He left the port and walked along the beach towards the bar. As he approached, he realised he was in luck. Claire was perched on one of the stools at the counter and was chatting animatedly with Kevin.

"Hi, you guys!" Mark cried, plumping himself down beside her at the counter.

She turned towards him. Immediately, he could see there was a downcast look on her face.

"Oh, hello, Mark," she said without much enthusiasm. He sensed there was something bothering her but decided not to pursue it.

Kevin, however, was in exuberant spirits. He immediately put down the glass he was polishing and grinned at Mark. "Beer?"

"Yes," Mark replied.

"Have you been up to anything exciting?"

"Just been scuba diving."

"Fantastic. You know, that's something I've been meaning to do and never got round to."

"There's a guy at the port will take you and he doesn't charge an arm and a leg. He provides all the gear as well."

Kevin put down Mark's beer. "I'll have to check him out."

Mark gave him a €5 note and spoke to Claire. "What about you? Want a refill?"

She slowly shook her head. "I'm okay, thanks."

"You're sure?"

"Yes. I'm not staying long. I was just having a chat with Kevin."

"Where's Maria?" Mark asked.

"She's gone home. Her sister isn't well," Kevin said, giving Mark his change.

"Nothing serious, I hope?" said Mark.

Kevin shrugged. "Who knows? Maria doesn't like to talk about it."

Mark took a long drink from his glass. "Things look quiet," he ventured.

"For the time being," Kevin laughed. "It always slows down at this time in the afternoon. Just as well or we'd all die of exhaustion."

The conversation tailed off. Mark gazed out along the beach. It was still crowded with sun worshippers, children playing on the sand, bathers splashing about in the sea. It occurred to him that he might have interrupted something between Claire and Kevin. The atmosphere had certainly turned cool. He lifted his glass and finished his beer. No point hanging around where he wasn't wanted.

"Better go," he said with a cheery smile. "See you around."

"Talk to you," Kevin said as he picked up the empty glass.

Claire forced a smile. "See you, Mark."

He started back along the Paseo Maritimo. So much for his plan to take Claire out to dinner. She clearly wasn't in the mood and Mark wasn't a man to push at a closed door. But he felt a little bit disappointed as he made his way back to his hotel. He enjoyed her company a lot and hoped she hadn't tired of his. Now it looked like he'd be dining alone tonight.

When he reached the hotel, he presented himself at the reception desk and asked for his key. The smiling receptionist walked to the bank of pigeonholes, took out the key and with it a cream-coloured envelope with the crest of Hotel Alhambra embossed on the back.

Whatever can this be? thought Mark as he tore open the envelope.

It was a scribbled note:"*Please contact me as soon as is convenient. I would appreciate your advice.*" There was a phone number and a simple signature: "*Emma.*"

"When did this arrive?" Mark asked.

"About an hour ago, *señor*. It came by courier."

Sounds like trouble, Mark thought as he stuffed the envelope in his pocket and headed for his room.

15

Claire *was* feeling downcast. The news that Matthew Baker was coming to Fuengirola had filled her with shock and surprise. It was two years since she had spoken to him, even longer since she had seen him. In the meantime, she had put him completely out of her mind; although, of course, she had never forgotten him. He was the only man she had ever loved and he had left a big impression on her. They had had some wonderful times together. But in the end, he had betrayed her. And next week he was coming here and was going to look her up. What should she do?

She wondered if the story Johnny had told her was true. She wondered if it was just a coincidence that Matthew Baker was coming or whether it was because he had learnt that she was here. Was it purely a business trip or was he coming with the specific intention of seeing her? She had made it abundantly clear that she wanted nothing more to do with him. But Matthew was persistent. She knew that he

191

didn't give up easily. It was one of the qualities that had made him such a successful businessman.

Thoughts of Matthew Baker had been on her mind all day. And they were on it now as she walked along the Paseo Maritimo in the bright evening sunshine. She thought again of the happy times she had experienced four years ago in Fuengirola. Was it just her memory playing tricks or were those times really better than what she was experiencing now? She had been younger, of course, and everything was new and exciting. She had just left university and escaped the relentless pressure from her mother to find a job and a husband in quick succession. Life back then had been a great big adventure. But how much of those happy times were due to the presence of Matthew Baker?

Quite a lot, if she was being honest. He had taught her so much. It was from Matthew she had learned the basics of the property business. And later, when she had fallen in love with him and moved into his apartment, her life had been transformed. She recalled the joy of waking in the arms of the man she loved as the sun came streaming through the bedroom windows to herald a bright new day. She recalled the intimate breakfasts on the balcony overlooking the sea, the roses he sent her, the presents, the compliments, the nights spent beneath the stars eating at some little restaurant, the scent of mimosa hanging in the air and a gypsy troubadour serenading them with a Spanish guitar.

Matthew had been charming and witty and generous and gallant. He was stunningly handsome and he was a wonderful lover. No wonder he had swept her off her feet. But he had also betrayed her with another woman and in the very same bed where they made love together. It was Matthew who had destroyed their dream. She must never forget that. It was Matthew who had poisoned the trust that lay between them. Claire had done the only thing that was possible if she was to retain any shred of self-respect. She had left him. And now he was coming to see her again.

She turned right and found herself in the maze of little streets that formed the old town. The bar that Kevin had mentioned was along here somewhere. She was glad she had called at Pedro's this afternoon. Talking to Kevin had helped to lift her spirits; although, of course, she hadn't mentioned the immediate cause of her gloom. She had just told him she was feeling a bit down in the dumps and he had immediately concentrated on cheering her up and getting her to smile. And when it was time to go, he had invited her for a drink at The Bodega at eight o'clock, which was where she was heading now.

She did regret one thing, however. In the middle of her conversation with Kevin, Mark had arrived and she had been rather cool with him. But she just didn't think she could handle him with the mood she was in. He had quickly got the message and left and afterwards Claire had felt guilty. He was such a nice guy. She should have made an effort to be nice to him in return. Instead, she had been downright rude. She made a resolution to make it up to him the next time they met.

After a few minutes, she came upon The Bodega. There were half a dozen tables outside set for dinner but so far no diners. She stepped over the doorway and entered the dim recesses of the bar.

Immediately, she heard a voice call her name. She blinked in the dull light and made out a figure sitting alone at the counter.

Kevin put his arm around her shoulder as she approached and softly kissed her cheek in welcome. *"Buenas noches, señorita."*

193

"*Buenas noches, señor,*" Claire replied.

"What would you like to drink?"

She ordered a glass of wine.

"This is a quaint little place," she said, looking around at the old kettles and cooking pots that hung from the whitewashed walls.

"It's my secret hideaway," Kevin confessed. "I come here quite a lot after Pedro's is closed for the day."

"It's a wonder I never found it before. I thought I knew all the secret hideaways in Fuengirola."

Kevin flashed her the mischievous smile that was one of his endearing features. "You could spend a lifetime and never find them all."

"You never told me why you came to Fuengirola in the first place?" Claire asked, taking a sip of the wine that the barman placed before her.

"To escape from home. To start a new life."

"Oh?"

"Isn't that the reason why most people come?"

"I thought they came because they fell in love with the place."

"There's that too. I know that I certainly fell in love with it. But I needed a spur to get me to move."

He told her about falling out with his father and his time with the rock band.

"Playing with a band must have been very exciting," said Claire.

"Oh, it was for a while. But eventually I got sick of it. It became like a treadmill, constantly pursuing the big breakthrough that would bring us success. In the end, I was forced to ask myself what it was all about it."

"And what was it about?"

"Chasing moonbeams. I realised it was never going to

make me happy. In the end, I just got fed up and decided to get out."

"And this row with your father?"

Kevin sighed. "We owned a drapery shop in Galway. He wanted me to follow him into the business and I refused. I didn't want somebody else deciding my life for me, even if it was my father."

"I know exactly how you felt," Claire said.

He turned his gaze on her. "Do you?"

"Yes. My mother has been trying to organise my life ever since I was a schoolgirl. I know she means well but I have to make my own decisions. Even if I make mistakes."

"And have you? Made any mistakes, I mean?"

She tossed her dark hair and a misty look came into her brown eyes. "One in particular. Although I'm not entirely sure if it was a mistake. I fell in love with a man and he let me down."

"That's sad," Kevin said.

Claire shrugged. "These things happen."

They fell silent, each reflecting on the past.

"I don't regret not going into the shop," Kevin said after a while. "Although I could have handled the situation better. I was very arrogant and I hurt the old man. But I do have one big regret in my life. I wasn't at my mother's deathbed because of the band. My father never forgave me for that. In fact, I never forgave myself."

She reached out and gently took his hand. "You have to forgive yourself. I'm sure you didn't do it deliberately."

"But I did it, nevertheless. And now I have to live with the consequences."

It was after nine o'clock when they finished their drinks and the bar was beginning to fill up with diners.

"What are you doing now?" Kevin asked.

"I was thinking of calling in on my neighbour. She's an entertainer and she's performing tonight in the King's Arms pub."

"I know it," Kevin said. "It's quite close."

"I promised to give her a critical opinion."

"Why don't we both go?" he suggested, brightening up. "We'll give her two critical opinions."

"That sounds like a good idea."

Outside, the night was warm and the streets were buzzing with life. The pub was ten minutes away. It was an old-fashioned English bar selling solid British food and British beer and was a big draw with the tourists. When they arrived Maggie's act was just about to begin.

There were about fifty people crammed into the pub, sitting at tables around a little elevated stage. Kevin got two beers and was just sitting down when the master of ceremonies stepped onto the stage.

"Ladies and gentlemen, the event you have all been waiting for, the major attraction of the evening! At great expense, all the way from the Sands Hotel in Las Vegas, I give you Ms Tina Turner!"

Immediately, there was a drum roll from two large speakers at each side of the stage. A little curtain parted and Maggie suddenly appeared on the stage with a microphone in her hand and began to strut around with quite a bit of leg showing, twirling the microphone and singing "Simply the Best".

Only she wasn't singing. Claire knew she was miming to the backing track. But she did it so well that an innocent onlooker would believe that the words were actually coming out of her mouth.

Claire was very impressed by the performance. Even though Maggie was shorter and plumper than the real Tina

Turner, she had all the singer's stage actions off to perfection so that she gave a very convincing show. When she finally left the stage after half an hour, it was to a deafening round of applause.

Ten minutes later, she came to join them wearing her street clothes. She had a tall, thin, shaven-headed man in tow. He wore a black T-shirt with a vampire logo and had a tattoo of a dragon on his right arm. Maggie introduced him as Ricky Blaine.

"He's my fella," she said. "He's a musician. Plays the guitar in a band called the Black Pimpernels."

Ricky shrugged and they all shook hands.

Kevin was about to say that he used to play in a band too but, before the conversation could develop, Maggie interrupted.

"What did you think of my show?"

"You were absolutely brilliant," Claire said. "You were very professional. You heard the reception you got at the end."

"Yes," Kevin agreed. "If Claire hadn't told me, I would have thought I was watching Tina Turner in the flesh."

Maggie giggled with delight. "My show at the Rum Pot is even better. Of course, they've got a bigger stage so I can move around a lot more. Do more of the actions."

"You were marvellous," Claire reassured her. "You brought the house down."

"You know, maybe I'll just stick with Tina Turner and forget about Madonna," Maggie said.

"You also do Madonna?" Kevin asked with astonishment.

"Not yet," Maggie said, "But I have a routine worked out. I used to do Dolly Parton and that was a big hit. Especially with the boys." She winked at Kevin.

"I'm very impressed," he said. "And you're living in the

same building as Claire? You'll have to come and visit us at Pedro's – I'll let you have a drink on the house!"

"Oooh, I'd love to come!" She glanced quickly at her watch. "Ten thirty. I'd best be going. I'm due on stage at the Mucky Duck in half an hour and they're a very restless audience. See you later."

She grabbed Ricky by the hand and sailed out of the pub, toting her costume bag over her shoulder.

"She's a bit of a character," Kevin said when she was gone.

"Yes," Claire said. "She's a very kind-hearted soul; although there are times when she would wear you out."

"Count yourself lucky. You could have worse neighbours. You could have people who sit up all night playing heavy metal music."

They parted outside the pub and prepared to go their separate ways.

"Drop by tomorrow," Kevin said as he was leaving. "You cheer me up."

"I think it's the other way round," Claire said, "but it's a nice thing to say."

He leaned forward and kissed her. "Goodnight, Claire."

She got home shortly after eleven o'clock. She had a shower, put on her dressing-gown and sat on the terrace with a book. It was a beautiful night. The air was cool and the sky was filled with stars. Tomorrow was going to be another lovely day.

I'm so glad I came back here, Claire thought. It was the right thing to do.

By midnight, she was beginning to feel drowsy. It was time for bed. As she snuggled under the soft sheets an observation suddenly occurred to her.

She hadn't thought about Matthew Baker all evening.

16

As soon as Mark got to his room after collecting Emma's letter, he sat down on the bed and rang the number that was written on the note. Immediately, he heard the sound of the phone being picked up at the other end.

"Emma. It's me, Mark. I got your message. You asked me to call."

"Were you off somewhere?"

"I went scuba diving. I just got back."

"That sounds adventurous. No sharks around, I hope?"

Mark smiled to himself. "The only sharks I know are on dry land."

He heard her laughing on the other end. "Scuba diving is perfectly safe," he said. "And great fun. You should try it sometime."

"Maybe I'll take you up on that."

"I thought you might be in some kind of trouble."

"Well, not trouble exactly." Emma's voice was now quite serious. "But I would appreciate your advice."

"Is it urgent?"

"Let's put it this way — the sooner I talk to you, the better."

"That sounds urgent," Mark said. "I tell you what. I was thinking of going out for something to eat. Would you care to join me?"

"I'd love to, if it's not inconvenient."

"No, not in the least. But first I have to make a reservation. Let me ring you back."

Since his previous experience at Felipe's, Mark had been planning to go back. He rang the restaurant and managed to get hold of Carlos, the chef. Was there any possibility of reserving a table for two at such short notice?

"What time, *señor*?"

Mark checked his watch. "Eight thirty?"

"Excellent. We look forward to seeing you again, *Señor* Chambers."

Mark put down the phone and rang Emma. "I've booked a table for half eight at Felipe's restaurant. It's down at the port. I can pick you up if you like."

"It might be simpler if I take a cab. There's always a string of them outside the hotel."

"Okay," Mark said. "I'll see you there."

It was now ten past seven. Time to start getting ready. He went into the bathroom and ran the shower and ten minutes later he was peering into a clouded mirror as he began to shave. It had been a very interesting day and it wasn't over yet. He wondered what she wanted to talk to him about. No doubt it was something to do with Pedro's Bar. She must have run into some problem with Maria and the accounts. Well, he wasn't an expert on Spanish property law but he would certainly give her the benefit of his knowledge. In his experience there was always a solution to every problem if you knew where to look for it.

He finished shaving, rinsed his face with hot water and went back into the bedroom to dress. This time he didn't have to deliberate. He chose navy chinos and a black shirt open at the neck and again took along his blazer for later. Glancing in the mirror, he thought he looked good.

At eight o'clock, he emerged from the hotel. The temperature had dropped and the evening air felt cool. The Audi he had hired was sitting in the car park. Mark settled comfortably into the driving seat and heard the engine purr into life. Fifteen minutes later, he was pulling up outside Felipe's.

The restaurant was already filling up and people were drinking and chatting at the bar. He was immediately shown to a table in a raised alcove above the main dining area where they could look out over the harbour. And it had the additional bonus of being discreet. They could talk here without fear of being overheard. Mark ordered a gin and tonic and settled down to study the menu.

At eight thirty, he saw her trim blonde figure enter the restaurant. He watched her spot him and approach, smiling. She was wearing a light summer dress with patterns in dark-honey and gold against a pale yellow background, and a little gold cardigan in the bolero-type style he noticed a lot of younger women wearing these days. With her newly acquired light tan, her whole figure seemed to glow.

"How about something to drink?" he asked, rising to greet her.

"I'll have a gin and tonic with you – no, I'm in Spain after all: I'll have one of those pale dry sherries."

He gave the drinks order while she flicked open the menu.

"You look wonderful," he said.

"Thank you," she replied with a small smile. "You look

201

good yourself." She let her eye roam around the restaurant. "This is very nice."

"It's the best in town for fish. I was here a few nights ago and had a brilliant meal."

"How did you discover it?"

"Someone brought me here," Mark replied with an enigmatic grin.

She gave him a quizzical look.

"Remember Claire? She was with me at Pedro's Bar?"

"Of course. The gorgeous dark-haired girl."

"That's her. I only met her at the airport. We shared a taxi. I asked her to dinner so I could pick her brains. She used to live here."

Emma opened her eyes wide in mock amazement. "Do you make a habit of having dinner with every woman you meet? And picking their brains?"

"Only the good-looking ones."

She laughed and turned her attention once more to the menu. "What do you recommend?"

"I'm going to try the sole."

"Okay, that's what I'll have too."

When the waiter returned with Emma's drink, Mark gave their order.

"Did you have a busy day?" he asked.

"You could say that. I came to Fuengirola to relax but since I arrived I've done nothing but chase my tail and as a result I feel extremely frustrated."

"Oh? Do I take it that your little talk with Maria didn't go too smoothly?"

"It went smoothly enough. The problem came later." She stopped and fixed her gaze on Mark. "Are you really sure you want to listen to this stuff? You're supposed to be on holiday."

"Fire away. I don't mind."

"Well, I spoke to Maria and she gave me the name of the accountant – a man called Miguel Martinez Sanchez – so I made an appointment to meet him. He was not like any accountant I have ever seen before. In fact, he looked like he'd walked straight out of a *Godfather* movie. Flash suit, slick hair and gold teeth."

"My God."

"I asked to see the accounts of the bar and he told me they weren't ready yet. When I insisted, he tried to bamboozle me and when that didn't work, he just continued to smile and nod like one of those wind-up puppets. He told me everything was in order and I didn't have to worry my pretty head. I felt like strangling him. Can you imagine? I own the bloody place and I'm being patronised by this fat slob. And I'm probably paying him a fee to do it."

"Go on," Mark prompted.

"I told him I wanted evidence that all taxes were paid up to date and there were no debts on the bar. He just kept smiling and telling me the Inspector of Taxes was his very good friend and everything would be all right. I should go back to Ireland and not worry about it. It was a complete waste of time. In the end, I just got up and left."

She looked straight at Mark. "I could murder Conor Delaney. This is all his fault for not taking a closer interest in the place."

"Did you find out how long that man has been acting as accountant?"

"Yes. He's been doing it since the time when Maria's son, Antonio Hernandez Rodriguez, owned the bar. He just continued when Conor Delaney took it over. I'm convinced he's a crook."

"Don't go so fast," Mark said. "You need to think this

through calmly. You're saying Conor Delaney bought the bar from Maria's son?"

"That's right. But he took no interest in it. His main concern was his travel company. He just came out here a couple of times a year to collect his profits. He left the running of the bar to Maria. And she left the paperwork to the accountant."

"Conor Delaney transferred it to you in payment of a debt?"

"Yes and all these problems along with it." She let out a long sigh. "Sorry – I suppose I shouldn't be looking a gift horse in the mouth but I stand to lose money rather than gain any on this venture."

"I have to say it all sounds very odd," Mark concluded. "Not the way you would expect to run a business."

"But what am I going to do? I've never had to face a situation like this before. I don't know where to turn. I'm being sent round in circles and now I'm beginning to wish I'd never heard of Pedro's Bar."

At that moment, their food arrived and with it the bottle of wine that Mark had ordered.

"All right," he said, when the waiter had departed. "The first thing you're going to do is enjoy your meal. There's a way out of this and we'll find it. In the meantime, put it all out of your mind and start to eat. Agreed?" He leaned forward and smiled into Emma's eyes till she too was forced to smile.

"Agreed," she said.

For the rest of the meal they engaged in gossip about people they knew back in Dublin. Mark had a wealth of funny stories and spicy tidbits. Emma was amazed at the amount of information he possessed behind that innocent-looking exterior.

"Where did you learn all this stuff?" she asked after he had recounted one particular scandalous item.

"I hear things. I'm a very good listener."

"You're telling me this guy was cheating on his wife with *three* different women at the same time?"

"And a young male interior designer his wife had hired to give the house a makeover."

She raised her eyes in disbelief. "You're making this up."

"No, I'm not. I have a keen memory."

"Well, I'm glad you told me. I'll be careful what I say to you."

"*You* don't have to worry," he said with a grin. "Your secrets are safe with me."

She gave him a look. "Remind me not to tell you any."

By the time the meal ended and they were ordering liqueurs, Emma was in good humour. Mark's steady stream of jokes and funny stories had brightened her spirits. They sipped their brandies and gazed out across the harbour at the stars reflecting off the water.

"It's so peaceful here," she said. "Could you ever imagine spending the rest of your life in a place like this?"

"Wouldn't you get bored?" he asked.

"I don't know. I'm sure I could find plenty of things to do."

"I've worked hard all my life," Mark said. "I'd like to slow down but I'd need something to keep me occupied."

"You play golf, don't you?"

"Not every day. It would become a chore."

"And you go scuba diving?"

"You sound like you're trying to sell me something."

Emma patted his hand. "You're quite hard to please, Mark."

A flicker of a smile played around his lips. "Not really. I

think I know what I want. It's finding it that's the problem."

As he was paying the bill, Carlos came out from the kitchen to inquire if they had enjoyed their meal.

"It was perfect," Mark announced and introduced Emma.

Carlos very gallantly kissed her fingers and, with much handshaking and compliments, they finally left the restaurant.

"So you know the chef as well?" she said as they walked to Mark's car. "I'm very impressed."

"I only met him once before," Mark confessed. "The last time I was here with Claire. But he is supposed to be one of the top chefs in town."

Above them, the sky was a bright canopy of stars. The air was cool. From nearby, they could hear the soft lapping of the waves against the harbour wall.

"Thanks for a lovely evening," Emma said. "And for lifting me out of myself. I needed a sympathetic ear to pour out my troubles."

Mark glanced at his watch. It was still only eleven o'clock.

"I've got a suggestion," he said. "Something I've been meaning to do."

"What is it?"

"Would you come with me to a club? I feel like letting my hair down."

She didn't even hesitate. "What a brilliant idea – I'd love to!"

17

It was a hectic morning at Pedro's Bar. At half eight, Kevin had received an urgent phone call from Maria to say that her sister Rosario was having another turn and she wasn't able to get in to open up the bar. Would it be possible for Kevin to go in at once and take over? Maria would join him as soon as her sister was feeling better.

Of course, Kevin agreed. He jumped on his bike and cycled in along the seafront. He was beginning to get worried about Rosario. This was the second day she had been sick recently. And he felt sorry for Maria. She had too much to do, looking after her sister and trying to manage the bar at the same time. Emma had been right about this. Maria should be at home, enjoying what was left of her life. If only she got some assistance from her no-good son, Antonio. But that seemed like pie in the sky.

He arrived at the bar shortly after nine o'clock and hastily opened up, gave the place a quick clean and set out the tables and chairs. He had barely finished when Pablo, the baker, arrived with his daily delivery of bread.

"*Hola*, Kevin," he said. "All alone this morning?"

"Yes," Kevin replied. "Maria's sister is not well."

The baker sadly shook his head. "She should be in the hospital, poor woman."

He left the bag of fresh-baked rolls that would be used to make the *bocadillos* and hurried off to his next customer.

Kevin opened the big fridge where the provisions were kept, got out the vegetables and began chopping furiously. He decided to dispense with the pan of paella this morning. It would take too much time to prepare and was more work than one person could manage. The paella was a favourite with the customers and he would be sorry to disappoint them but it was better to concentrate on running the core business of the bar.

He glanced along the beach. A few people were spreading out their straw mats in readiness for a day's sunbathing. Soon they would begin to appear at Pedro's looking for beer and coffee and something to eat. He had better use the present lull to get things prepared.

He filled the sink with glasses and washed them all furiously, then dried them with a cloth. Thankfully there weren't too many. The bulk of the glasses and cutlery had been washed the previous night before they locked up. He sliced the bread rolls so that the fillings could be easily inserted when the customers wanted something to eat. He chopped a big bowl of onions and tomatoes for the hamburgers that were always in demand and checked that he had enough frozen chips. Then he turned on the deep-fry pan so that the cooking oil would be hot when it came time to use it.

He glanced at his watch. It was a quarter past ten and

already the sun was strong in the clear blue sky. Any moment now, the first customers would start to arrive. He just hoped that Maria would be able to get here soon. He didn't relish the idea of managing the bar on his own through what promised to be another busy lunchtime.

Just then, his eye was drawn to a forlorn figure slowly making his way along the beach in the direction of the bar. He was wearing an old pair of faded jeans and a check shirt and carried a camper's rucksack on his back. As the figure drew closer, Kevin felt himself stiffen in anticipation. This man looked like someone he knew.

The figure came up to the counter, slid his rucksack onto the ground and sat down on a stool.

"Could I have a coffee, please?"

Kevin turned to the coffee machine and began to prepare the drink.

"What are you doing here?" he asked.

"Are you surprised to see me?"

"Of course I am. You look like a ghost."

The man ran his fingers along his unshaven chin.

"I've just got out of rehab," he said.

"How did you find me?"

"Your sister, Nora, gave me the address."

Kevin put the coffee down on the counter and the man pulled a €5 note from his jeans pocket.

"It's on the house," Kevin said. "Have you eaten?"

Snuffy Walshe slowly shook his head. "Not yet."

Kevin took a big bread roll that he had sliced earlier and filled it with ham, cheese and tomatoes and put it on a plate. "Here – get that into you."

Immediately, Snuffy Walshe began to devour the roll.

"What happened to the band?" Kevin asked.

"Broke up. The rest of the boys have gone back to

Galway. Jimmy O'Driscoll is working on a building site in Athenry."

"And you?"

Snuffy Walshe swallowed hard and tore another bite off the roll. "The gear got me in the end. It was inevitable. I finished up so bad I couldn't get out of bed in the morning without a fix."

Kevin nodded grimly. "I could see it coming."

"Then I met a drugs counsellor who said she could get me into a rehab centre if I really wanted to stop. By this stage, I was desperate. I couldn't function without smack. It was the only thing I could think of. So, I agreed to do the programme. I got out ten days ago and decided to start a new life. I knew if I stayed in London, I'd have no chance. Then I thought of you."

"Have you any money?"

"A bit. But I need to find a job. I thought you might be able to help me get back on my feet."

Kevin thought for a moment. Snuffy Walshe was the last person he had expected to see in Fuengirola. But he was in trouble and he couldn't let him down.

"Do you think you could pull pints?"

"Sure. I'm willing to do anything."

Kevin took a key ring from his pocket. "You look a sight. Those are the keys of my apartment. It's about half a mile away." He scribbled directions on a piece of paper.

"Go there and get cleaned up. You can borrow some of my clothes if they fit you. Then get back here as fast as you can. I have work for you. We can talk about the details later."

Snuffy Walshe grabbed the keys and slung his rucksack onto his back. "I'm really grateful," he said. "I won't let you down."

"Let me down and you're out. Get back here pronto — this place is going to be hopping in an hour's time."

He watched Snuffy hurry back along the beach. I wonder if I'm doing the right thing, he thought. But his reverie was disrupted by Manuel, the newspaper seller, demanding his morning *cortado*.

Claire had woken at a quarter to eight. She could hear the birds chirping on the roof of the apartment block next door. She decided to nip down to the bakery at the corner of the street and get some hot rolls and croissants for breakfast. When she returned, she found a note pinned to her door. It was from Maggie. *Let's go to the beach today*, it read.

She knocked on her neighbour's door and a few seconds later Maggie's face peeped out.

"You're up early," Claire said.

"I'm always up at this time."

"Even when you're working? What time did you finish last night?"

"Midnight. I was in bed by a quarter to one. Did you get my note?"

"Yes."

"What do you think?"

"I think it's a great idea. I've just got some rolls. Why don't you come across and have breakfast when you're ready?"

Claire opened her apartment door and marched straight into the kitchen. She set up the coffee percolator, got out a saucepan and broke in three eggs. She added salt, pepper, a knob of butter and some mixed herbs. Within minutes, the kitchen was filled with the aroma of fresh brewed coffee and scrambled eggs.

"My, that smells good," Maggie said coming through the door.

"Sit down and help yourself," Claire commanded. "I think I've set out everything you need. If there's anything missing, just ask."

Maggie poured a cup of coffee and buttered a roll just as Claire set a plate of scrambled eggs before her.

"How did your show go down in the Mucky Duck?" Claire asked.

"Brilliant. The Duck is always good. They get a younger crowd, you see. That's why I was thinking of switching to Madonna."

"But now you've changed your mind."

"For the time being. But I'd still like you to see my impersonation. Audience feedback is critical."

"What does Ricky think?"

Maggie shrugged. "Ricky doesn't really care. He's a cultural snob. He looks down his nose at my stuff. He's more into playing music."

"How long have you known him?"

"Couple of years."

"And is it a steady relationship?"

Maggie smiled. "Who knows? He's handy to have around. But never mind Ricky. That Kevin is a nice bloke, isn't he?"

"Uh huh," Claire said, taking a bite from a roll.

"Is he your chap, then?"

Claire almost spat out the bread. "Whatever gave you that idea?"

"Just a thought. I wouldn't kick him out of bed, that's for sure. And I should know. I've been round the block a few times."

"I only met him a couple of days ago. He's the barman at Pedro's."

"I think he's dishy. Those dark eyes. Deep wells of passion, smouldering deacons of desire."

"Beacons," Claire corrected her.

"Whatever. He's a lovely bloke. And drop-dead gorgeous, if you ask me."

Claire unexpectedly found herself blushing. "What time do you want to go the beach?" she asked, changing the subject.

"Whenever you're ready."

"Let's say eleven o'clock? I want to pick up a few groceries and I've got a bit of laundry to do. Besides, the sun will be nice and hot by then."

"Okay," Maggie said, finishing her coffee. "I'll be ready."

When she was gone, Claire quickly washed the dishes and left them to dry on the draining board. Then she set off for the supermarket. It was only a couple of streets away. She didn't really need very much: just some bottled water, fresh fruit, a tin of tuna and some peppers. But she hated leaving everything to the last minute. Besides, if she let the grocery list build up, she would just have more to carry in the end.

When she returned, she put the laundry into the washing machine while she went into the bathroom to have a shower. She thought of what Maggie had said about Kevin and her being an item. Whatever had put that notion in her head? Did they give off an aura or something? It was probably just because they were both Irish. Still, Maggie was right about one thing. He was very good-looking with his dark curly hair and his mischievous smile. She had noticed that the first time she saw him. But an item? Claire smiled to herself and shook her head. She didn't think so.

She turned on the radio and listened to some music as she got dressed, putting her bikini on beneath shorts and vest. It would make getting undressed on the crowded beach easy. She was going to enjoy working on her tan and it would also be an opportunity to get a swim. When she had finished, she got out a bag and packed the things she was going to need: towel, sarong, underwear, Walkman, a few CDs, a book, hairbrush, make-up, sun-cream . . . she stopped and considered, then added a bottle of water and her wallet containing some cash. Never go anywhere without money unless you happen to be the queen – it was one of the first things she had learned when she came to Spain.

She emptied the washing machine and was hanging the laundry to dry on the balcony when she heard a loud knock on the door. She opened it and gasped at the sight that greeted her. Maggie was standing on the doorstep wearing baggy jeans, a huge yellow T-shirt, big dark glasses and a giant straw sombrero.

"What do you think?" she demanded.

"You look very . . . dramatic!" Claire said.

"The sombrero is to protect my face," Maggie explained. "It burns easily."

"If you're worried about getting sunburnt, why did you suggest the beach?"

"It's only my face. I have to protect my face. It's my livelihood."

"Well, you're certainly doing that," Claire said, slinging her bag over her shoulder and picking up her sunglasses and hat. "Now, are you ready?"

"Yes."

"Right. Let's go."

They set off. The town was wide awake and bustling with activity. The shops were open and people were lounging at the pavement cafés enjoying a late breakfast or a coffee in the morning sun. At the corner of the Paseo Maritimo, they came upon a group of young holidaymakers eagerly consulting a big tourist map they had spread out on a bench.

Claire stopped to give them directions. Ten minutes later they were at the beach. It was beginning to fill up as the sun got stronger. By now, she was feeling thirsty. She promised herself a cold beer as soon as she got to Pedro's. But when the bar came into view, she could see there was already a crowd around it. Kevin was rushing about like a demented greyhound but there was no sign of Maria. Her place seemed to have been taken by a thin guy with blond hair whose pale complexion immediately told Claire he had only recently arrived.

"Who's the blond geezer?" Maggie asked.

"Don't know," Claire replied. "Never saw him before."

"Looks kind of cute, don't you think?"

Claire looked more closely. Maggie was proving to have a strange taste in men. "Do you think so?"

"Yes, I do," Maggie replied. "And I should know –"

"Don't tell me," Claire said, taking her friend's arm and dragging her along the beach. "You've been round the block a few times. Now let's get two pints of cold lager before I expire from thirst."

18

Snuffy Walshe had returned to Pedro's Bar within an hour looking like a different man. He had shaved and washed his hair and had taken up Kevin's invitation to borrow some of his clothes. He had found a palm-tree patterned beach shirt in the wardrobe that fitted him and a pair of jeans and even a pair of runners. Now he looked like a semi-respectable young holidaymaker and not the scarecrow that had first confronted Kevin.

By the time he got back to the bar, the first of the lunchtime crowd was beginning to arrive. Kevin gave him a critical look-over and nodded his head in approval.

"You'll do. Now, put on an apron and I'll show you the drill. The beer is fairly straightforward. It practically pours itself. You just turn on this tap. A pint is €1.50."

"Is that all?" Snuffy Walshe asked in amazement.

"This is Spain, Snuffy. You're not paying London prices any more."

"What about coffee?"

"That's € 1. I'd better show you how the coffee machine works while I'm at it."

Snuffy watched as Kevin demonstrated how to make a cup of coffee and operate the till.

"Spirit drinks are two euros. Anyone asks for a *bocadillo*, they're looking for a filled bread roll. They have already been sliced and are in that big plastic bin. The fillings are in the fridge. They cost € 1.50. And we don't spread butter on them. Nobody expects it so don't go searching for it."

"Right," Snuffy said, beginning to look confused.

"Reckon you'd be able to make the hamburgers?"

"Eh, I've never made them like that," he said, pointing to the grill.

"When someone asks for one, watch how I do it. There's a price list on the door of the fridge. Anything you're unsure about, just ask me. Okay?"

"Okay."

"Any minute now, the customers are going to descend on us like hungry vultures. Just keep working till they stop coming. And one other thing, you're not playing bass guitar in Slattery's pub any more. Don't look so grim. Try to pretend you're enjoying yourself."

Snuffy flashed a smile.

"That's better," Kevin said and stuck a pint glass in his hand. "Your first customers have just arrived."

Four young men in shorts and T-shirts had just sat down at the counter and were demanding beer.

Lunchtime was brisk, with waves of hungry customers looking for food and drink. Kevin worked frantically trying to cope with the demand. But once he got the hang of things, Snuffy mucked in to give him valuable assistance. In fact, he seemed to enjoy the challenge. In the middle of the mayhem, Maria rang to say that her sister was no better. As a result, she would not be able to come in to work today after all.

"How about tomorrow?" Kevin asked. "Do you want me to open the bar again in the morning?"

"Yes, please. Tomorrow I will see. You are a good boy, Kevin."

He told her about his new assistant.

"You are lucky he comes."

Out of the corner of his eye, Kevin watched Snuffy pour five pints in quick succession and toss a steak on the grill.

"I think you might be right," he said. "Don't worry, Maria. I can manage here. I hope Rosario gets well. Give her my regards."

He put down the phone. Poor Maria. She had a lot to worry about. Maybe a couple of days off work might do her some good. But right now he didn't have time to think any more about her. Another posse of sun-worshippers had just arrived demanding hamburgers, chips and beers.

He had no sooner served them than he saw Claire coming along the beach with Maggie, who was practically dwarfed by a giant sombrero.

They squeezed up to the counter and Claire ordered two beers.

"Is Maria still off work?" she asked.

"Afraid so. Her sister's not well."

"Poor woman," Claire said, pushing a stray lock of dark hair from her eyes.

While they were talking, Maggie had fallen silent and was staring intently at Snuffy, who was attempting to get the cork out of a bottle of wine.

"So you've noticed my new assistant?" Kevin said, setting down the beers and taking the money.

"I think I've seen him some place before."

"Not in Fuengirola you haven't. He's just arrived. He's a friend of mine from Galway. Used to play bass guitar in our band."

"Oooh!" she said. "I didn't know you played in a band."

"You didn't give me a chance to tell you." He smiled his cheeky smile.

"What was your band called?" Maggie asked, removing her sombrero and allowing her hair to fall around her shoulders.

"Bang."

"I saw you," she said, excitedly. "You used to play in the Irish Rose pub in Kilburn."

"That's right, we did."

Maggie was now gazing at Snuffy with renewed interest. "Isn't it amazing?" she said. "To think we would meet up again like this."

The two women finished their beers and moved off along the beach to find somewhere to sunbathe.

"Isn't that a coincidence?" Maggie said when they were out of earshot. "I particularly remember Snuffy because he used to sing with the band and I sort of fancied him. Mind you I was only a starry-eyed youngster back then."

"And now you're a starry-eyed adult," Claire said.

The beach was packed with glistening bodies stretched out on towels and sun-beds but they managed to find a space down near the water's edge. They laid out their straw mats and got undressed.

"Are you working tonight?" Claire asked.

"No. I've got the next couple of nights off."

"Do you enjoy your job?" Claire continued, stretching herself in the sun.

"It's a living, I suppose. I know I'm never going to make it to the London Palladium but I get a buzz when I give a good show and people enjoy it. And of course, it pays the rent."

"And you like living here?"

"It beats Clapham Common on a rainy Saturday afternoon. You should know that. You lived here too."

"So I did," Claire said wistfully.

Maggie folded her towel into a pillow, tilted the sombrero over her face and lay down on the mat.

"Did you ever find out who was looking for you?" she asked.

"Yes," Claire said. "An old boyfriend."

"So it wasn't the Marbella axe-murderer, after all?" She sounded disappointed.

"Afraid not. Just a respectable estate agent."

"What did he want?"

"He's coming to see me."

"Really? That's nice. Where does he live?"

"London."

"Aaaaah, I think that's very romantic. He's coming all this way to see you! He must be very keen."

Claire was uneasy with the turn the conversation was taking. Matthew Baker had rarely been out of her mind since she heard the news. And she still hadn't decided how she was going to handle the situation when he got here.

"Well, he's not coming just to see me. He's coming anyway on business and he's going to look me up."

"Still, he must have a soft spot for you. He doesn't have to look you up, now does he? He could just ignore you if he wanted to."

Claire wished that Maggie would talk about something else but she didn't want to be rude. "That's true," she conceded.

"You don't sound too cheerful. Don't you want to see him, then?"

"I haven't made up my mind."

"Did you have a big break-up?"

Maggie had raised herself on one elbow and was gazing down at Claire as she lay stretched out on the sand. It made Claire feel like a patient lying on a psychiatrist's couch.

"It's a long story," she said and closed her eyes to let Maggie know that the conversation was over.

"Sounds to me like he might still be interested," Maggie said and sank back onto her mat.

That was precisely what Claire was worried about: that Matthew Baker hadn't given up despite everything she had said and done to let him know their relationship was over. She dreaded the thought of another confrontation and all the energy it would consume. Why couldn't he just accept that she didn't love him any more and everything had moved on?

But had it? Was that why she was so worried? Did she not trust herself with the charming Matthew when he turned up on her doorstep next week? Was she afraid that she might give in and relent? Oh, no, surely not? Surely she couldn't have any lingering grain of affection for him after what he did? She turned over and buried her face in the towel. Why was he coming back now when everything was going so well? Why was he intent on spoiling her holiday?

She tried to forget him but suddenly he was back, dominating her thoughts once more. Despite her best efforts, she found her mind wandering back to the happy times when they lived together here in Fuengirola. It seemed that, no matter what she did, she couldn't escape the spectre of Matthew Baker. It was making her depressed. She couldn't take it any more. Suddenly, she stood up.

"I'm going for a swim," she announced abruptly.

Before Maggie could reply, Claire was running down the

beach and diving headlong into the surging tide. She swam blindly, as if trying to escape, till eventually she felt her arms grow tired. She stopped and glanced back towards the shore. It seemed so distant, the vast expanse of ocean around her so silent and lonely. Maybe here she could get some peace from Matthew Baker.

She floated for a few minutes on her back and then decided to return. The swim had done her good. Already she was feeling better. At least she had got Matthew Baker off her mind. She buried her face in the waves and struck back for land. But when she looked up again, she was shocked to find the beach was further away than ever. With a feeling of terror, Claire realised that she was drifting further out to sea.

She renewed her efforts but the strength in her arms was failing. Instead of gaining ground, the sea was pulling her further out. Suddenly, she began to panic. She struck out wildly and began shouting for help.

But there was no one to hear. All around the sea seemed to stretch forever. Above her the sky was like a vast blue canopy. The people on the beach were so far away that they looked like tiny dolls. She felt her heart beat faster as a terrible thought came crashing into her head: *I'm going to drown.*

Her arms began to grow cold and stiff; the strength began to seep from her body. Her head went under the water and all she could see was inky blackness. She was never going to make the shore. So this is what it's like, she thought. This is how it feels to drown. She surfaced again and the sky seemed to come down to swallow her up.

Suddenly, she was conscious of a voice nearby. She felt someone grab hold of her and shout out: "*Hold onto me and don't struggle!*" She went limp and allowed herself to be pulled along by the superior strength.

It seemed like forever before she began to hear new voices – concerned, excited voices. Now hands were taking her and pulling her up onto the beach. Someone had brought a blanket and was wrapping her in it. She felt cold and tired as if she just wanted to sleep forever.

She saw a face bend over her and heard a voice say: "You're safe now. You're going to be all right."

She closed her eyes and everything went dark.

19

Mark had woken that morning with the sound of a pneumatic drill going off in his head. My God, he thought, it must have been rough last night. I don't remember anything this bad since my student days. What the hell was I drinking to get in a state like this?

He turned over and buried his face in the pillows but still the loud drilling sound persisted. What was the best thing to do? Order some strong black coffee? Swallow some aspirins? Take a cold shower? He burrowed deeper into the sheets as he tried desperately to remember what exactly he had to drink at the Voodoo Club, where he had ended up with Emma. Whatever it was, it must have been deadly.

As he slowly came awake, the noise grew louder. Now it seemed there were several drills going off at the same time. This is terrible, he thought. This is the worst I've ever been. Maybe I should give up the booze altogether and become teetotal.

He flung himself out of bed and clasped his hands to his

ears in an effort to block out the terrible sound. In desperation, he pulled back the curtains. And then he blinked at the sight that met his eyes. A gang of workmen in blue overalls and hard hats were digging up the roadway in front of the hotel.

Mark fell back on the bed and doubled up with laughter till the tears ran down his cheeks. He didn't have a hangover after all. He was only slightly the worse for wear. It was just the damned roadworks that were causing all the noise. But one thing was certainly true: he did have a good time last night. Now that he was fully awake, he had a vivid memory of the dancing, the music, the lights, the laughter.

"Margot," he said aloud, "I hope you approve of all of this?"

But he had the feeling she did.

Now, he had something to do.

He glanced at his watch. It was half nine. They were an hour ahead here in Spain, which meant it was half eight back in Dublin. He had time for a quick breakfast before he started working the phone. He rang room service and ordered orange juice, coffee and croissants. Then he went into the bathroom and stood under a piercing hot shower. He was just getting dried when a sharp knock on the bedroom door announced the arrival of his breakfast.

He tipped the waiter and took the tray out onto the terrace. The sun was blazing in the heavens. As he ate, Mark gazed out at the clear blue expanse of ocean, practically on his doorstep. He remembered Emma's conversation in Felipe's restaurant. Wouldn't it be nice to wake up every morning to this beautiful sight? Wouldn't it be nice to spend each day relaxing and taking life easy? For years, he had promised Margot to slow down till in the end it was too late. Maybe now, the time was approaching.

He would have to give it more consideration. But right now, he had urgent business to attend to. He finished eating and put the tray aside. Then he went back into the bedroom and rang Dublin.

He got his manager, Ted Cunningham, at the second ring.

"Just checking up on you," he said when he heard Ted's surprised voice.

"What is this? Why aren't you out on the golf course?"

"Because I'm trying to help a damsel in distress."

"*What?*"

"It's a long story that I haven't got time to explain. I need you to give me Terry Kavanagh's number. Can you dig it out for me? It should be somewhere on my desk."

"Have you got a legal problem?"

"I sincerely hope not," Mark said.

A minute later, Cunningham was back with the number of the firm's legal advisors. Mark had a pen and paper handy and quickly wrote it down.

"How are things back there?" he asked. "Managing all right without me?"

"Sure. Everything is ticking along quite smoothly. And you?"

"I'm having a ball," Mark said. "I've just had a delicious breakfast on my terrace and later I'm planning to meet a gorgeous young woman."

"Oh!" Ted said, somewhat taken aback.

"And by the way, the temperature is already 25 degrees in the shade."

He laughed as he hung up. He enjoyed teasing his colleagues and keeping them in suspense. Now they would be scratching their heads trying to figure out what the hell he was up to.

Next he rang Terry Kavanagh.

"Hi," the lawyer said. "How's the holiday going?"

"Brilliantly. The sun is shining and I have nothing to do but relax and enjoy myself."

"You're making me jealous. I hope you're not in trouble?"

"No. Just in need of some advice."

He took a couple of minutes to explain the nature of Emma's problem.

"Sounds nasty," Terry Kavanagh said.

"What I was hoping was that you could give me the name of a lawyer down here who could direct us. Neither of us has a damned clue about Spanish law. We need someone who knows the system and can advise us what to do."

"Luis Garcia Santiago," Terry said immediately. "He's excellent. We use him all the time when clients are thinking of investing in Spanish property. He's the man you need."

"Where is he based?" Mark asked.

"Malaga. Hold on and I'll get you his number."

A few minutes later, Mark put down the phone. Now he had the name and address of a top-class lawyer who could advise them and it was still only half ten. He had time to take Ted Cunningham's advice and play a round of golf before calling on Emma. It couldn't have worked out better. Mark calculated he could get in nine holes before the sun got too strong.

Meanwhile, Emma had been putting in some phone calls of her own. After breakfast, she called George Casey at the office just to inquire how things were coming along.

"Everything's tip-top," Casey replied. "Don't be worrying yourself. Just relax and enjoy your holiday. You worked long enough for it, God knows."

"Okay, George. You know where I am if you need me."

"You'll be the first one I call."

They chatted for a few minutes more and Emma knew from his confident manner that he was clearly on top of things. She came away with a warm feeling of satisfaction. The fortunes of Hi-Speed Printing were in good hands while she was away.

Next she rang home. Her father answered the phone.

"So you arrived safely?" he said. "How are you getting on?"

She decided there was no point worrying him about her difficulties with Pedro's Bar.

"Like a house on fire," Emma replied. "I'm having a wonderful time. I haven't seen a single grey cloud since I got here."

"Met any nice men?"

"Dad!" she protested. "You're so old-fashioned. You seem to believe that my life won't be complete till I find myself some male attachment."

"Well, I know *my* life wasn't complete till I met your mother. Some things don't change, Emma, no matter what you think."

"Where is she anyway? Put her on."

"You've just missed her. She's taken the car down to the supermarket."

"Tell her I called. Give her my regards."

"I will, of course. Have you had an opportunity to consider that offer from Mr Braun?"

"Not yet," Emma said. "I've been too busy." That much was true.

"Take your time. Don't rush into anything. And remember I'm always here if you need any advice."

"I love you, Dad," she whispered as she put down the phone.

She was blessed with her parents. Her mother and father

had always been loving and supportive. They made no demands on her and never interfered in her life. She made a mental note to get them some nice presents while she was here.

It was now eleven o'clock. Mark had promised to call her at lunchtime. It meant she had some free time to work on her tan. She collected the things she would need and put them into a straw shopping bag, then slipped on her bikini and sarong and set off for the pool. Today she would stay in the sun a little bit longer. The trick was to take it nice and easy.

The young clerk at the reception desk smiled politely as she went sailing past, while another young bell-boy rushed to hold open the door as she walked out into the garden. Some determined sun-worshippers had got to the pool before her but there was plenty of room left. She decided to position herself where she had been the previous day. She spread her towel, applied sun cream and adjusted her glasses, then stretched out in the warm morning sun.

It was bliss. The sun was so pleasant that she felt like drifting off to sleep again. Instead, she tried to concentrate on the things she had to do. She had promised herself a shopping trip into Marbella but so far she hadn't been able to manage it because of the hassle with the damned bar. There were times when she felt like giving it up. Yet some fighting instinct made her determined not to be cheated or outwitted. The attitude of the accountant had really got her back up. She would not be treated as some little numbskull just because she happened to be a woman. She was the legal owner of Pedro's Bar and was entitled to know everything about it. And by God, she *would* know.

Gradually, she began to feel better and her thoughts instinctively turned to Mark. She was lucky he had turned up to help her. He had been a godsend. He had been through the mill with his wife yet he had never once complained. She wondered if he would ever remarry. At forty, he was still a young man and quite handsome. Lots of women would find him extremely attractive. And unlike some handsome men she had known, Mark wasn't arrogant or spoiled or selfish.

Last night at the Voodoo Club she had seen another side to him: a playful fun-loving side. He had stayed on the dance floor almost the entire night and insisted that she stay with him, till in the end she was almost dropping off her feet with exhaustion. It had been a wild night and they had thoroughly enjoyed themselves. Yes, she thought as she turned over to get some sun on her back, Mark Chambers is what I would call a really *interesting* man.

By half past twelve, she decided she'd had enough sunbathing for one day. She had a quick shower and got into the swimming pool. Twenty minutes later she had completed thirty lengths. She felt invigorated. She dried herself and repacked her bag and went back to her suite. She had barely got inside the door when the phone rang. It was Mark.

"Having a good day?"

"So far. I've just been lying in the sun for a bit. How about you?"

"Let's just say I've had a very productive morning. Have you anything planned for this afternoon?"

"No," Emma confessed.

"Well, this is your chance to visit Malaga. I'll call for you in half an hour. Does that suit?"

"Yes. Great!"

"Excellent! I have something very special planned."

"What?" she asked, intrigued.

"I'll explain when I see you."

Mark was outside Hotel Alhambra at half one to find Emma

waiting as arranged, looking smart and cool as ever in the blue and white patterned skirt he had seen before and a blue top that brought out the colour of her eyes. She was wearing mules with wedge heels and had a large basket-weave bag slung over her shoulder. Her blonde hair was a riot of curls. He thought she looked stunning.

He could tell at once that she was glad to see him.

"Sleep well?" he asked, pushing open the passenger door.

"Like a baby. And you?"

"Likewise. Till a gang of workmen with pneumatic drills started digging up the road outside my window."

"You can't have everything," she said with a grin. "Now what's the special thing you have planned?"

"We're going to see a man who might be able to help you. I've been thinking about what you told me last night and it struck me that you need some expert advice."

"You can say that again."

"Since neither of us knows the least thing about Spanish law or taxation matters, I decided to find someone who does. His name is Luis Garcia Santiago. He's a young lawyer and he comes highly recommended. He has agreed to see us at three o'clock in his office."

Emma kissed his cheek in excitement. "Oh, Mark, that's fantastic! How did you find him?"

He smiled modestly. "It wasn't difficult. I made a few phone calls to some people I know. Now, I suggest you explain your problem to Luis. Tell him about your meeting with the so-called accountant and your difficulty in getting hold of the accounts. He should be able to advise you exactly where you stand and what action you can take."

"Why are you going to all this trouble for me?" she asked.

"It wasn't a lot of trouble."

"You haven't answered."

He shrugged. "Maybe I have a Robin Hood streak. Maybe I just like to help people in trouble. Especially beautiful women like you."

Emma laughed. "You flatterer! But I'm extremely grateful."

"Say no more."

He leaned forward and fired the engine, then switched on the air conditioning. Ten minutes later they were on the motorway.

The journey to Malaga took about thirty minutes. Emma stared from the window at the coastline far below, the sea like shining silver foil in the bright afternoon sun. In the distance, she could see the dark brooding peaks of the Sierra Nevada stretching eastwards towards Granada. These were places she planned to visit once she had finished with the messy business of Pedro's Bar. Shortly before two o'clock, the spires and domes of Malaga came into view. Ten minutes later, Mark was parking the car in an underground garage close to the cathedral.

"This is a beautiful city," Emma said once they were out on the street. She gazed in admiration at the maze of little alleys and the narrow cobbled squares.

"We could take a short tour if you like once you've finished your business with the lawyer. It should be cooler then."

"Why don't we do that?"

He checked his watch. "And we have just enough time for a coffee while you gather your thoughts."

"Okay."

There was an open-air café nearby, beside a statue of some long-dead Spanish conquistador. They sat down and Mark gave the order for two café leches to the young waiter who quickly arrived to serve them.

"I have to do some shopping soon," Emma said. "I'm running out of clothes. I only brought enough for a few days."

"We can do that too, if you like."

"Oh, no," she protested. "You've done enough already. I couldn't inflict that on you as well. I know how much men hate shopping."

"Well, I could do a bit of sightseeing and meet you afterwards."

"Are you absolutely sure?"

"I'm certain. In fact, why don't we make a day of it? We could find a nice little restaurant somewhere and have dinner."

"Oh, Mark, that would be perfect!"

He smiled and gently stroked her hand. "Nothing would give me more pleasure than to spend the rest of the day with you."

She looked at him and felt her heart stir. She could think of nothing better than to spend the afternoon with him. "All right, then. That's decided. I kill two birds with one stone. I see the lawyer and I go shopping."

"Three birds," Mark corrected her. "You also have dinner with me."

Luis Garcia Santiago was waiting for them in his cool wood-panelled office on the Calle Andalucia. He was a thin, handsome man with jet-black hair and was dressed in a well-cut lightweight suit. Emma calculated that he couldn't be much older than thirty, yet he looked so poised and confident. She couldn't help contrasting this scene with the one she had witnessed yesterday in the dingy office of Miguel Martinez Sanchez.

"Would you like coffee?" he asked once they had introduced themselves and shook hands.

"No, thank you," Emma replied. "We've just had some."

"Sparkling water, perhaps?"

"That would be nice."

Luis lifted a phone on his desk and spoke softly. A few seconds later, the door opened and a young woman appeared with a tray containing three bottles of water and three glasses.

"Now," Luis said when everyone was settled. "Would you like to explain your problem?"

For the next few minutes, Emma outlined the history of Pedro's Bar while Luis sat quietly and took notes.

"So, you are the legal owner of the property?"

"Yes."

"Do you appreciate in Spanish law you are also responsible for any debts it may carry?"

"That's exactly what I'm concerned about," Emma explained. "I have been trying to find out whether all the taxes have been paid but the accountant – Miguel Martinez Sanchez – won't give me a straight answer."

Luis frowned. "He is obliged to give you this information."

"But he won't do it."

"Has he refused?"

"Not point blank. He just told me not to worry about it, that he is friendly with the Inspector of Taxes. You see, in Ireland, I am used to having all my business affairs in order and I find this casual attitude very unnerving."

"I can assure you in Spain we also prefer to have our business affairs in order." Luis gave her a small smile before assuming a brisk, businesslike tone. "There are several things we can do. I can contact the accountant on your behalf and demand the information. Or I can go directly to the tax authorities and ask them for a statement of the taxes for Pedro's Bar. The second option is the best. But I have to warn you. It may take time. How long do you intend to stay here?"

"A month."

"I will start on it right away. In the meantime, I suggest that you enjoy the remainder of your vacation. As soon as I have information, I will let you know."

He was now on his feet and was politely shaking hands with them.

"*Buenas tardes*," he said softly as he showed them to the door.

"How do you feel now?" Mark asked when they were once more out in the bright afternoon sun.

"Extremely relieved. At last I believe I'm dealing with a professional. I feel confident that Luis will get to the bottom of this."

"I hope you heed his advice to relax and enjoy the holiday."

Emma smiled. "Of course I will. What's the point of paying for advice and then ignoring it?"

They parted company at the top of the street with an agreement to meet again at the cathedral at seven o'clock for dinner. Emma skipped off lightly in the direction of the big department stores to do some shopping while Mark wandered off to engage in some sightseeing, tourist guide to the city in hand.

The day had turned cooler and it was quite pleasant to walk. As he strolled through the narrow streets and alleys, he felt a mood of quiet satisfaction settle over him. He was enjoying Emma's company enormously and also the effort involved in helping her solve her problems. He shared her confidence in Luis. He had struck Mark as an efficient young lawyer who would quickly cut through the nonsense and get to the heart of the business. If anyone could sort out Pedro's Bar it would be Luis Garcia Santiago.

As he walked, Mark stopped occasionally to peer into shop windows or to wander into quiet little churches to admire the architecture. At last he emerged from the shade of a narrow cobbled street and found himself in a bright square with a fountain playing in the centre. Gathered around the fringes of the square were a number of young artists displaying their work.

He stopped to admire a series of drawings when a young woman wandered over and engaged him in conversation. She was dressed in a shirt and jeans and had a mop of black curling hair and dark flashing eyes.

"Are you English?" she inquired.

"No," Mark replied. "Irish."

"*Ah, Irlanda!* That is a different country altogether."

"You're dead right, it is."

"Do you like these drawings?" the young woman asked.

"Very much. I think they are quite good."

She beamed. "They are all for sale. Would you like to buy one? Which one would you like?"

"What are the prices?" Mark asked.

"They are not expensive."

"What about this one?" he said, pointing to a miniature of the cathedral. He was thinking that it would make a perfect present for Emma. It would remind her of her visit to Malaga.

The young woman tilted her head. "Twenty-five euros?"

She spoke tentatively as if she was unsure how much to ask for her drawing. He had no doubt if he haggled with her he could get it for less. But he was in a happy mood. He liked the picture and it was a fair price. Besides, the young artist had to make a living.

"Okay, I'll take it."

She lifted the drawing and quickly wrapped it in tissue paper.

Mark took the money from his wallet and paid her.

"What is your name?" he asked.

"Dolores Lopez Castillo."

"That is your signature in the corner?"

"Of course. I always sign my work. Why do you ask?"

"Perhaps some day your signature will be as valuable as that of Pablo Picasso."

The young woman's face lit up with pleasure and amusement. "Who knows? If it is, you will have made a good bargain today."

When he got back to the cathedral shortly before seven, he found Emma already waiting and loaded down with bags and parcels.

"My God," he said. "It looks like you bought everything in the store."

"Not quite. But I did get some lovely things. The quality is superb and they were so cheap I kept thinking the shops were making a mistake."

"Let me think. I've heard this argument before. You're going to tell me that you actually saved money in the long run?"

Emma's face broke into a wide grin "I should have warned you that I have a passion for shopping."

"Passion? This looks like clinical obsession."

He helped her carry the bags back to the car where they stowed them in the boot before locking it.

"Are you hungry?" he asked.

"Ravenous."

"So am I. Let's find somewhere nice to eat before I bite the leg off some innocent passer-by."

There was a restaurant nearby that specialised in Andalusian cuisine. They perused the menu on the blackboard before going inside. Mark ordered pork and Emma opted for roast chicken. To accompany their meal, they settled for a bottle of Rioja.

When the wine was poured, Mark raised his glass and tapped it gently against Emma's. "To a successful day!"

"Yes," she said. "It was very successful. I think it's the best day I've had since I arrived. At last, I think we might be getting somewhere."

Mark presented her with the drawing he had bought at the square. "I bought you something to remember Malaga by."

Emma quickly removed the wrapping paper and uttered a squeal of delight. "It's lovely. Oh, Mark, you shouldn't have spent your money on me."

"Listen to who's talking! You probably maxed out all your credit cards in those stores."

"Seriously, you're so thoughtful! And it's such a beautiful drawing! I'll get it framed as soon as I get home. I know the very place for it too. Right in the hall of my apartment where everyone can admire it."

Their food arrived accompanied by dishes of fried peppers, chopped potatoes and onions and a bowl of salad.

They smiled at each other across the table and Emma suddenly reached out and took his hand.

"You've been so kind to me and yet we've barely met."

"You've been kind to me too."

"In what ways?"

"In ways you might not even realise. Just being in your company makes me feel alive. You're so vibrant and full of joy."

Emma lowered her eyes. "Do you miss your wife?"

"Of course I do. Her death was such a shock I wished my own life had come to an end." He paused. "You might think this strange but I talk to her every day."

She squeezed his hand. "No, I don't think it strange at all. I think it's beautiful."

"I tell her all my news. She knows about you."

Emma looked up again and gazed into his face.

"And does she approve of me?"

"Oh, yes," Mark said. "Very much."

20

Claire woke from a hazy sleep to find herself propped up in bed, her mane of jet-black hair spread on the pillows and her body wrapped in a heavy duvet. At first, she didn't recognise her surroundings. But gradually, as she gained consciousness, she realised she was back in her own bed in her apartment. And sitting across the room, she could make out the plump little figure of Maggie, quietly reading a paperback. Claire was just able to make out the title: *Golden Legends of the Stage*.

As she came awake, Maggie lowered the book and gave her a big warm smile.

"So you're back in the land of the living. How do you feel?"

"A bit groggy."

"Well, thank God that's all."

"I hardly remember what happened. I went for a swim and got into difficulties and after that it's all a blank."

"Difficulties is putting it mildly. We almost lost you. Only for Kevin you'd have been a goner."

"Kevin?"

"That's right. He's the one went in and pulled you out."

"Oh my God!"

Claire sank back on the pillows and closed her eyes. It was coming back to her now. The dreadful nightmare of her last moments of consciousness, the dark swirling waters of the sea and her body going limp and slowly surrendering to the cold expanse of ocean. And then someone had taken hold of her and begun to pull her ashore. So it had been Kevin who saved her.

Maggie was talking again, rapidly recounting what had happened. "We were lying on the sand, relaxing in the nice warm sun and all of a sudden you jumped up and said: 'I'm going for a swim.' Then you ran down the beach and into the sea. Do you remember that?"

"Yes."

"Well, I thought it was odd so I followed you but when I got there, you were already swimming like a mad woman away from the shore. You kept going for ages, getting further and further out. Then you stopped and looked around. I waved but you didn't see me. I saw you float for a while and then you started swimming back again towards the beach.

"That's when things started to go wrong. You didn't seem to be making any progress. You began to flail around as if you were panicking. I ran back up the beach looking for the lifeguards but I couldn't find them. So I made straight for Pedro's Bar yelling for Kevin and Snuffy." Maggie sounded as if she was enjoying retelling this story.

"Kevin ran down the beach with me and saw that you were in serious trouble. He immediately dived straight into the sea. He got hold of you and somehow pulled you back to shore. If it hadn't been for him, God knows where you would be. Probably North Africa by now."

"And is he all right?"

"He was fine. He just got dried and stayed with you till the ambulance arrived."

"Oh yes . . ." Details were beginning to come back to her. Strange Spanish faces leaning over her . . . being lifted . . . the ambulance . . . Maggie holding her hand.

"You were unconscious when you came out of the sea," Maggie went on. "One of the lifeguards turned up – about time for him – and resuscitated you. Then the ambulance arrived and the paramedics wrapped you in blankets and brought you back here. You've been out for the count ever since."

Claire was now feeling totally embarrassed at all the fuss she had caused by her stupid actions. If her mother ever got to hear about this, she'd never let her forget it.

"How long did I sleep?"

Maggie looked at her watch. It was ten past nine. "Six hours."

"And you've been sitting in that chair all this time?"

Maggie shrugged. "It's no big deal. I was reading my book. Anyway, I had my orders – the paramedics told me to watch you."

At once, Claire felt an enormous wave of gratitude engulf her. Good, kind, gentle Maggie had given up her entire afternoon and evening to take care of her. And Kevin. He had saved her life. If it hadn't been for him, she would have drowned.

"How can I ever thank you, Maggie?"

Maggie was blushing now. "You don't have to thank me. It was nothing. Honest."

"Where's Kevin?"

"Don't worry about him. His only concern was that you were okay. He rang a couple of hours ago to ask about you."

Claire started to get out of bed. "I must find him and

thank him. I know where he'll be. The Bodega. That's where he always goes after work."

But Maggie was already shoving her back into bed. "You're not to move. Doctor's orders. You have to stay in that bed till the morning."

Claire sank back helplessly under the duvet.

"You're probably suffering from shock," Maggie went on. "Now you have to take something to eat. I've got a pot of vegetable soup simmering. It's very nourishing. I'm going to stand over you till you've eaten every drop."

Claire weakly nodded her head.

"And afterwards I'll make you a nice mushroom omelette. It will do you good. We can go back to Pedro's Bar in the morning and thank Kevin then. Besides, it will give me an opportunity to have a chat with that Snuffy geezer about the old days in London."

Claire felt weary. She was too tired to argue. "All right," she said.

Maggie fed her the soup and omelette and afterwards sat beside her and read extracts from her book. It was filled with spicy anecdotes about the lives of the great stage entertainers. As Maggie read, Claire felt her eyes grow heavy. Half an hour later, she was fast asleep again.

She was wakened at half eight in the morning by a loud banging on her apartment door. She looked around. Maggie was gone.

The banging was growing more insistent. She got out of bed, threw on her dressing-gown and opened the door. She blinked in surprise at the sight that greeted her.

Kevin Joyce was standing in the hallway with a huge bouquet of flowers.

"How is the patient this morning?" he asked with his trademark smile all over his face.

Claire gasped. He was the last person she was expecting to see and she was acutely aware that she had just got out of bed and must look like a wreck. "I'm fine, thanks. What are you doing with that bouquet?"

"About to give it to you."

"*Me?*"

"Who else? Do you have a flatmate I could give them to?"

Claire felt her face redden with embarrassment. "Come in," she said holding the door wide. "Pardon the mess. I've just gotten up."

He came inside. "I'm not staying. I'm on my way in to open up the bar. Maria's sister is still sick."

"Oh, dear," Claire said. "Poor Maria must be having a terrible time."

"I just dropped by to see how you were doing and to give you these." He thrust the truly enormous bouquet of flowers into her arms.

"How can I ever thank you for saving me yesterday?" Claire asked as she laid the bouquet carefully on the table. "I would have drowned only for you."

Kevin grinned. "Oh, I don't know about that."

"*I* know. I was going under. I had no strength left."

"Why don't you put it behind you?" he said. "You're alive and well and looking like a million bucks. That's all that matters."

Claire lowered her eyes. She couldn't fail to pick up the compliment he had just paid her. "I feel such a terrible fool putting everybody to such trouble. I don't know how I'll ever show my face on that beach again."

"Nonsense. It was an accident. Unfortunately, it happens

all the time. The lifeguards are pulling people out practically every day."

"But I was so stupid. I did the very thing I shouldn't have done. I swam away from the shore."

"Don't beat yourself up about it. It happened and now it's over and you're well again."

"Thanks to you and Maggie and that lifeguard – does anybody know his name?"

"I don't. Maybe Maggie might have picked it up. I know his face though – he's often on duty."

"I must thank him – buy him a gift or something."

"Good idea."

"Are you sure you won't have some coffee?"

"No, thanks. I'd better be going. I have another busy day ahead of me."

"How is Snuffy working out?" Claire asked.

"Brilliantly. In fact, I don't know how I would have managed without him for the past few days."

"Thank him for me. And tell him I was asking for him. And Maggie too. Tell him Maggie sends her regards."

Kevin gave her a knowing smile. "Maggie and Snuffy?"

Claire found herself smiling. "That's right."

"Well, I'll be damned. Okay, I'll do that." He turned to go and then he stopped.

"Come to think of it, there is something you could do for me."

"Yes?" Claire asked.

"There's an open-air rock concert in Mijas tonight. Do you think you'd be well enough to come with me?"

Claire didn't hesitate. "I'd love to," she said.

After he had left, Claire leaned against the door of the apartment and felt her heart hammering in her breast. What a nice, kind, generous guy Kevin was proving to be. He had just saved her from drowning and refused to accept any credit when many men would be expecting a medal.

She took the flowers into the kitchen and placed them in the sink. Then she got out some bacon and eggs and put on the coffee percolator. There was no sound from across the hall. Maggie must be still asleep. She was probably exhausted after all the excitement of yesterday.

A thought struck her. She would surprise Maggie. It would go a small way to repay her for her kindness. She undid the wrapping around the flowers and divided the bouquet in two. Gathering up the larger bunch – it still made a generous bouquet – she went and listened at Maggie's door. Yes, there were faint sounds from inside – Maggie was up.

She knocked. A minute later the door opened and a bleary-eyed figure peeped out.

"These are for you," Claire said thrusting the flowers into Maggie's arms.

"What's all this in aid of?"

"It's in aid of a dear neighbour who showed me the value of true friendship. Just a small way of thanking you."

Maggie looked bashful. "I hope you didn't spend a whole lot of money on them."

Claire grinned. "I didn't buy them. Kevin Joyce dropped by this morning and gave a huge bunch to me so I want to share them with you."

"Oh, I can't take them! Kevin would be offended."

"No, he wouldn't! Besides, I've kept half!"

"OK – they're beautiful," Maggie said. "Let me put them in a vase."

"Go ahead and then come over to my place and have breakfast."

She went back to her apartment and put the bacon on to

cook. Then she set the table on the terrace. It was another glorious day. The sun was high in the sky and was already bathing the street with golden light. I feel so lucky to be alive, Claire thought as she laid out the knives and forks. And to think that only for Kevin my body might be lying in the public mortuary right now. She shuddered at the thought as she returned to the kitchen and began to cook breakfast.

A few minutes later, Maggie joined her. Claire shifted the food onto plates and they carried them out onto the terrace.

"This is nice," Maggie said, pouring herself a cup of coffee. "And you look so much better this morning. That sleep must have done you a world of good."

"Not to mention your wonderful vegetable soup," Claire said, tucking into the bacon and eggs. "I have so much energy that I think I'll spend the morning cleaning up the apartment."

"There's something I've been meaning to ask you," Maggie said. "Why did you do that yesterday? Why did you go swimming off like a lunatic? It looked like you were trying to escape from something."

Claire felt her face redden as she lowered her eyes. "It was just a mood that came over me."

"Well, don't do anything crazy like that again. Kevin might not be around to rescue you the next time. How was he this morning?"

"He was in a rush to get into work. Maria's sister is still sick so he'll be running the bar with only Snuffy to help him."

"I suppose that means Snuffy will be too busy to have a chat? And I was so much looking forward to that."

"Has Snuffy changed much since the time you knew him?"

"He looks different. He seems to be calmer. When he was with the band, he used to be jumping about all over the stage like a lunatic. Now he seems more relaxed."

"He's older," Claire said. "I asked Kevin to tell Snuffy that you sent your regards. I hope you don't mind?"

"Oh, no," Maggie said, brightening up. "I'm glad you did that."

"You're interested in him?"

"Yes, I was before and I suppose I still am. It was eight years ago — I was only twenty-two. When you're that age you think anybody in a band is a sort of god."

"But what about Ricky? You can't just dump the poor guy."

Maggie looked perplexed. "I'll have to think about that."

An idea suddenly occurred to Claire. "Kevin has invited me to go with him to an open-air rock concert in Mijas tonight. Why don't I ask him to bring Snuffy along and we'll make it a foursome?"

Maggie's eyes lit up. "That would be brilliant."

"You're not working?"

"No. I'm off till tomorrow night. I wonder if I should wear my tartan punk outfit and my spiky dog-collar?"

"We'll talk about that later," Claire said. "In the meantime, I'm going to start on the apartment right now while I'm in the proper frame of mind."

"I'll help you," Maggie said, finishing her breakfast. She grabbed the dirty dishes from the table and carried them off.

Next minute, Claire heard a loud female voice emerging from the kitchen.

"Did you ever hear me impersonating Mick Jagger?" Maggie asked. "*I can't get noooooooo — satisfaction!*"

21

Miguel Martinez Sanchez sat in his dingy office and stared down at the busy street below. He was feeling nervous. The feeling had been growing in recent days, ever since that Irishwoman, *Señorita* Dunne, had called on him demanding to see the accounts of Pedro's Bar. Now, he was finding it difficult to sleep at night because of the worry. He jumped each time the phone rang. He scrutinised his mail before he opened it up. He glanced nervously behind him when he walked in the street. The burden was becoming intolerable.

At last he stood up from his desk and put on his suit jacket. He spoke briefly to his secretary to tell her he'd be gone for some time and to log any phone calls, then made his way out of the office and down the rickety stairs. Before stepping out, he looked carefully up and down the street. Deciding that the coast was clear, he proceeded as fast as his fat legs could carry him to a shabby bar that stood at the corner of the adjoining street.

Once inside, he ordered a large brandy and quickly

knocked it back standing at the bar. Feeling the alcohol begin to relax him, he presented his glass to the barman once more for a refill. Then he hunted in his pocket for the stub of a cigar he had squirreled away and lit it in a voluminous cloud of smoke. He surveyed the bar for signs of strangers and, satisfied that there were none, he finally sat down and let out a loud sigh.

He had good reason to feel nervous. The visit of the Irish *señorita* had startled him. When he got the phone call to say she was coming to examine the accounts, he had almost swallowed the pen he was chewing. It was the very last thing he was expecting. It presented him with a terrible dilemma. For the sad truth was, there were no accounts. There had been no accounts since the time Conor Delaney had taken possession of the bar.

He blamed his dilemma on two people – Antonio Hernandez Rodriguez and Conor Delaney. He had never seen a man who was less interested in his business. In all the time he had been the owner of Pedro's Bar, *Señor* Delaney had never once asked to see accounts or anything else for that matter. He was a most trusting gentleman. He came out to Fuengirola two or three times a year and always rang in advance so that Miguel had plenty of warning. Unlike this new *señorita*, who was already behaving like a thief in the night, sneaking up on people and almost giving them heart attacks!

When he knew he was coming, Miguel would arrange for a nice cheque to be ready for *Señor* Delaney, which he would graciously accept and fold into his wallet. Then he would buy everyone a round of drinks. Sometimes he would buy several rounds. Indeed, there were some people who whispered that *Señor* Delaney was too fond of buying rounds. But it was nice to see a gentleman relaxing. He would go off to Marbella to meet his friends for dinner and sometimes he would go to the racetrack at the Hippodroma. And then he would disappear back to Dublin and they wouldn't hear of him again for another four months.

So with an owner like that, what was the point of Miguel breaking his back preparing accounts? The business was ticking over and it was making good profits under Maria's careful stewardship. She was a most diligent manager. Indeed, he couldn't understand why his friend Antonio didn't treat his mother better. He could have used her in his restaurant. But there was bad blood between them over the sale of the bar. Antonio had been greedy and had given his mother nothing and only for *Señor* Delaney she would have been out on the street. Miguel didn't agree with it but he had very good reasons for shutting his mouth and keeping his opinions to himself.

The system had worked well. The staff were happy and *Señor* Delaney was happy and Miguel Martinez Sanchez was extremely happy. As financial overseer, he had fallen into the habit of diverting a little slice of the profits for his own use; although, of course, he was careful not to get too greedy, unlike Antonio. And this was another very good reason not to produce accounts. Miguel had come to believe that the situation would continue forever until he got that shocking phone call from the Irish *señorita* to say she was the new owner and was coming to see him.

He had to put her off, so he told her he was busy and couldn't see her till the afternoon. He had spent the intervening time frantically trying to locate Conor Delaney in Dublin to find out if this nightmare was real. When he finally managed to find him, Conor Delaney sounded as if he had been out again buying more rounds of drinks. But he was able to confirm that Emma Dunne was indeed the new owner and that she was presently in Fuengirola to look over the property. He had the good manners to apologise for not alerting Miguel sooner but said he had been very busy with a temporary cash-flow situation that had taken up all his time. He ended the conversation by thanking Miguel profusely for his sterling service over the years and promised to buy him a drink the next time they met.

Which did absolutely nothing for Miguel's peace of mind. What was he going to do? He couldn't be expected to cobble together accounts at the drop of a hat. And what if she demanded to see the financial records going right back to the time when *Señor* Delaney took over the bar? It was an impossibility! Miguel had a flair for what is known as creative accounting. But he wasn't a magician. He couldn't create accounts out of nothing. And that's all there was in the way of records for Pedro's Bar.

He did the best he could. He bluffed her, told her not to worry, assured her that everything was under control. Don't concern yourself about it, he said. That's what you're employing me for. I'm the guy who has to shoulder this responsibility. Why don't you adopt the practice of *Señor* Delaney and just leave it all in my capable hands? Before you return to Dublin, I will have a nice fat cheque ready for you.

But she wouldn't be put off. She kept insisting that she had to see the non-existent accounts. And he knew he was dealing with someone who was determined and had made up her mind and wouldn't be brushed aside with flimsy excuses. But what really caused the shivers to run down his spine was her inquiry about the tax affairs.

She was demanding to see written confirmation from the Tax Office that everything was up to date and there were no outstanding debts. It was all that he could do not to break down and weep. She had left his office with a face like thunder and as soon as the door was closed, he knew he was in trouble. That's when he rang his friend Antonio and that's who he was expecting any moment now.

He finished his second brandy and glanced out of the door to the street. There was no sign of Antonio. Miguel felt the sweat gather inside the collar of his shirt. He felt like having another brandy but decided against it. He needed a clear head if he was going to think his way out of this problem. So instead he caught the barman's attention and ordered a café leche.

He had known Antonio for a very long time. Their acquaintance went back to the time when Miguel was a young student at accountancy college and Antonio was working for his father running Pedro's Bar. He would always remember the night when Antonio had come to him to ask if he could draw up a set of ghost accounts: something that would look good but wouldn't tell the whole story. Something that would hide the true profits of the bar from the prying eyes of old Pedro and the Tax Office.

Miguel had been reluctant. He hadn't qualified yet. If something like this ever came out, it could mean the end of his career. He would be expelled from college and face prosecution. But Antonio assured him that no one would ever know. It was only a once-off favour. Once it was done, he would never bother him again. In the end, the sight of the large bundle of pesetas in Antonio's hand had persuaded him and he agreed to do what he was asked. And of course no one ever did find out, although Antonio did not keep his word.

That decision had proved to be a turning point in Miguel's life. Within twelve months, Antonio was back again with the same demand and this time there was the subtle hint of blackmail if Miguel didn't comply. And along with the blackmail there was another inducement. Antonio offered him a job: a good well-paid position on the payroll of Pedro's Bar. The salary was more than Miguel could ever hope to earn as a young accountant. It didn't take him long to make up his mind. He gave up his studies and went to work full-time for Antonio.

He faked the tax accounts for Antonio's restaurant; he faked the VAT returns and the income tax returns. When Conor Delaney eventually bought Pedro's Bar, Miguel was kept on and continued to look after the financial affairs of the bar, which basically involved lodging the takings in the bank and making sure there was a healthy cheque awaiting *Señor* Delaney on those rare occasions when he called. Over the years, Miguel had gradually become more and more enmeshed in Antonio's web, owing everything to him and living in total fear of him. And the charade had worked. Up till now. Up till *Señorita* Dunne came calling.

He looked at his hand. It was shaking. He had lain awake all night worrying about how he was going to deal with this bombshell that had landed in his lap. Right this minute, *Señorita* Dunne could be talking to the tax authorities; or worse the police. They could come calling at any time. What would happen to him then? How would he explain his way out of this problem?

At that moment, he saw a shadow fall across the doorway. He turned quickly to see a thin, cadaverous figure dressed in a dark business suit slip into the bar. With a wave of relief, Miguel got quickly out of his seat and went forward to greet him.

"Antonio! How good to see you! How good of you to come!" He took hold of his benefactor's hand and warmly shook it.

Antonio looked at him as if he was an insect who had

just crawled out from under a stone. "What is this all about, Miguel? Why do you disturb me from my busy schedule?"

"Please, Antonio. Keep your voice low. People will hear you." He glanced nervously towards the barman, who was eying them with interest. "Let me get you a drink."

He called to the barman. "*Dos coñacs, por favor.*"

He paid for the drinks and brought them back to the table, where Antonio had now seated himself.

"What is wrong with you, Miguel? You look like you have seen a ghost."

"I have seen a ghost only she is not dead. She is very much alive."

"What are you talking about?"

"I have bad news, Antonio."

"What is it? Spit it out."

"I got a phone call the other day from an Irish lady called Emma Dunne."

"Yes?"

"She is the new owner of Pedro's Bar."

At this information, Antonio's interest suddenly picked up. "And what about Conor Delaney? What happened to him?"

"Conor Delaney has transferred the ownership to Emma Dunne. I think there was some business arrangement involved."

"Hmm," Antonio said and stroked his chin.

"*Señorita* Dunne called to see me. She is a very tough lady. She demanded to see the accounts. She wanted to know if the tax affairs were up to date."

"So why are you worried?"

"You know very well, Antonio. There are no accounts."

Antonio smiled. "So what did tell her?"

"I told her not to worry. I told her everything was under

control. But I don't think she believed me. She was very unhappy. I think she will be back again. What am I going to do?"

"Where is this Emma Dunne staying?"

"Hotel Alhambra."

"A good address. She has taste, this young lady." A strange light had come into Antonio's eyes. Suddenly, he clapped Miguel jovially on the shoulder. "I will give you the same advice that you gave her. Don't worry about it, Miguel."

"But Antonio, if she goes to the tax authorities, I will be in serious trouble. I could end up in jail."

"She won't go there. Why don't you listen to me? Don't worry."

"What will I do?"

"You will do nothing. If she comes back again, tell her the same story."

Antonio suddenly looked at his watch and stood up. He had given Miguel enough of his valuable time. "I must go, Miguel. I have an appointment. I will be in touch with you."

He turned quickly on his heel and was gone.

Miguel stared after him in amazement. Don't worry. What sort of advice was that? How could he not worry when he was staring disaster in the face?

22

The following morning, Mark was up early and decided to go for a brisk walk before breakfast. This time, he made up his mind to take a different direction – to head along the coast towards Benalmadena. It was quieter at this stretch of beach, with fewer restaurants and bars and consequently less activity apart from the squawking of the gulls. The sun was casting spangles of light on the glittering sea. As he walked, he let his thoughts roam over the events of the last few days.

It was interesting the way things had turned out. He had run into Emma completely by accident but in the short time he had known her his affection had grown by leaps and bounds. At first, he had felt sorry for the dilemma she found herself in and wanted to help. Now that initial interest was developing into something much stronger. But it was a pleasant feeling and Mark didn't resist.

She reminded him a little of Margot. She was strong and determined and he admired those qualities in a woman. But she was also essentially feminine; she wasn't afraid to talk about how she felt, unlike his male friends who kept their emotions safely bottled up so that you never knew what they were thinking. Emma was open and honest and Mark found that refreshing. She could also be tender and affectionate. He was beginning to look forward to her company and eagerly wanted more.

It was half nine by the time he returned to his hotel. This morning, he decided to eat in the dining-room. He showed his key to the steward and made his way to the buffet. The brisk walk had sharpened his appetite so he loaded his tray with orange juice, muesli, a couple of slices of bacon, an egg, two pieces of toast and a pot of tea. He carried the whole lot back to a table by the window and sat down. Today he was going to take his time over breakfast and enjoy it

At the adjoining table, a middle-aged couple were talking animatedly in loud voices so that Mark couldn't help overhearing their conversation. It was all about an incident on the beach the previous afternoon when a young woman had almost drowned.

"Swam out too far," the man was saying. "Of course, that's the one thing you mustn't do. Safety First is very clear about this. You must always swim *along* the shore. Then she couldn't get back in again. If it hadn't been for that young man from the beach bar she'd have been a goner."

"Which one is that, dear?"

"Pedro's, I think it's called."

"The one that sells the paella?"

"That's right. Young Irish guy. Regular hero, he was."

At once, Mark's interest picked up.

"Ran straight into the sea and pulled her out. She's a lucky woman that he was around. Otherwise the crabs would have got her."

They continued talking about the incident till Mark had finished his breakfast. There was little doubt about it. From the details he had managed to overhear, they must have been talking about Kevin. He wondered who the young woman was.

Emma was sitting on a bench outside the Alhambra hotel when Mark pulled up in the hired Audi at midday. Today they were going down the coast to Marbella. Emma had decided she wanted to do some more shopping and it would give them an opportunity to see the town.

For the trip, she had chosen to wear baggy white trousers, a white V-necked top and a long white cotton jacket. Mark had a suspicion they were part of the wardrobe she had purchased the day before in Malaga. She wore an amber stone set in silver on a thong around her neck, amber earrings and dark glasses. With her cloud of blonde hair and golden tan, the overall effect was stunning.

"You look fantastic," he said as she slid into the passenger seat. "For a moment, I mistook you for Michelle Pfeiffer."

"You silver-tongued flatterer! I look nothing like Michelle Pfeiffer! Besides, she's older than me."

"How was I to know that?" Mark chuckled. "The point is, you look magnificent."

"Thank you."

"And did you have a good morning?"

"I had an excellent morning. I've done absolutely nothing except chill out at the pool. Thanks to Luis Garcia Santiago, this is the first day I haven't had to think about that damned bar."

"That reminds me," Mark said, as he swung the car into the traffic. "There was some sort of incident on the beach yesterday. I overheard some people talking about it at breakfast. It seems that Kevin Joyce rescued a young woman from drowning."

"Really?" Emma said. "Maybe we should drop by and see how he is. The bar is on our route, isn't it?"

"Okay," Mark said. "Why don't we do that? Wonder who the woman was?"

Kevin was busy pulling pints and a strange young man was cooking hamburgers when they arrived. There was no sign of Maria. Already the lunchtime crowd was beginning to gather. Kevin raised his hand in greeting when he saw them.

"How's tricks?"

"We're only passing by," Mark explained. "We don't want to hold you up. Where's Maria?"

Kevin shot Emma a cautious glance. "Her sister isn't well. She's taken the day off. But I have a replacement." He called Snuffy and introduced him. "He's a friend from home. We used to play in a band together."

Snuffy grinned as he shook hands.

"Getting the hang of it yet?" Emma asked.

"Just about," Snuffy said, glancing appreciatively at Kevin. "I've learned the difference between a *bocadillo* and a *cortado*. One you eat and the other you drink."

They laughed.

"Of course," said Snuffy, "I've also got a very good teacher."

Kevin hit him a playful dig in the ribs. "He's just sucking up to me because I'm his boss."

"I heard you had a spot of drama yesterday," Mark put in.

"Yeah, we sure did."

"And you were quite the hero."

Kevin lowered his eyes and looked embarrassed. "It was nothing, really."

"Are you sure? The way I heard it a young woman would have drowned but for you."

"Who was it?" Emma put in. "Was it a foreigner?"

Kevin shuffled uneasily. "It was Claire."

There was a stunned silence as they gazed at one another.

"Claire Greene?"

"Yes."

"My God," Emma said. "How is she?"

"She's at home in her apartment. I saw her this morning and she's absolutely fine. There's nothing to get concerned about. In fact we're going to a concert up in Mijas tonight."

"What happened?" Mark said.

"She swam out too far and couldn't get back in. It happens all the time on this beach."

"Did she see a doctor?"

"Yes. She's okay. Really."

"Well, thank God for that. Make sure to tell her we were asking after her."

"Will do," Kevin said.

"How are you managing without Maria?" Emma inquired.

"It's a bit of a struggle but we're surviving. Snuffy has been a godsend."

He smiled at his friend.

"Tell Maria I'll call in to see her in a few days' time," said Emma. "Tell her I hope her sister gets better."

"Sure," Kevin said.

A group had arrived demanding beers. It was time to move on. Mark and Emma said goodbye and set off back to the car. Half an hour later they were at Puerto Banus.

The resort was one of the ritziest on the entire Costa and

today it was sparkling in the bright afternoon sun. Along the marina, the yachts dazzled and shone. Crowds of sightseers packed the restaurants and bars and jostled for space in the upmarket souvenir shops. Mark and Emma strolled along by the harbour till they came to a little bar.

"Are you hungry?" he asked.

"Not particularly. But I could use a coffee."

They sat at a pavement table and watched the crowds stroll by. Emma's earlier good humour seemed to have evaporated after their visit to Pedro's. Now a gloomy look had entered her eyes.

"What's the matter?" Mark prompted.

"I'm thinking about Maria. With her sister ill, she won't be able to work and that will be an added strain for her. She's already upset because of my visit – terrified that I might close down the bar. As for Antonio, I can't believe he has treated her so badly. Forbidden her to see her grandchildren and cut her right out of her share from the sale of the bar."

"What a total bastard!" Mark agreed.

"So, you see, I have a responsibility. Not just for the bar but for the people who work there. They're depending on me."

"Look," Mark said, taking her hand, "there's nothing you can do till you hear back from Luis. It's out of your hands now. And remember what he told you. You should relax and enjoy your holiday."

"You're right," Emma said. "But somehow I can't escape from Pedro's. It seems to follow me everywhere I go."

"Put it right out of your head," Mark said, firmly. "Now why don't we drive up to Marbella and you can go shopping while I take a look around?"

She forced herself to smile. "Okay. Let's do that."

"And try not to buy everything you see. Leave something for the other shoppers."

Marbella was quiet when they arrived. Mark found a place to park near the seafront and locked the car. He produced a couple of maps of the town that he had picked up earlier at the hotel and gave one to Emma.

"This map shows all the big department stores, although I've no doubt you would sniff them out anyway. You seem to have a built-in detector system that starts flashing every time you approach a shop."

Emma found herself laughing. "I'm not that bad surely?"

"Want to bet?" He checked his watch. "Why don't I see you back here at five o'clock? That should give you oodles of time."

Emma had already brightened at the prospect of some more serious shopping.

"What are you going to do?"

"I'm going to explore. One thing I most certainly am *not* going to do is venture within half a mile of a store."

Mark set off along the Avenida Ramon y Cajal till he came to a beautiful little park with a magnificent fountain dedicated to the Virgen del Rocio. All around the base of the fountain was a series of little painted representations of other Madonnas from various towns and villages. He sat on a bench in the shade of a palm tree and closed his eyes while he absorbed the tranquillity of the place. It was so peaceful and quiet that he could have stayed there all afternoon but eventually he dragged himself away and walked down the Avenida del Mar to the seafront. At the Club Maritimo, he stood for a while watching the sailing enthusiasts potter about on their boats.

At last he came to a little bar with a terrace overlooking the beach. He ordered a beer while he sat in the sun and watched the waves gently crashing on the sand. Emma was right. There was no escaping Pedro's Bar. It seemed to keep turning up like a bad penny. And it wasn't just the business side of things and whether it was making any money. There was a human dimension that he had barely considered at all. He could understand why Conor Delaney had hardly bothered with the place except to turn up every now and then to pick up his cash.

The easiest solution would be to sell it. But Mark knew that the easiest way wasn't always the right way. He had noticed from their very first meeting that Emma had a social conscience. She cared about people and it was one of the things he admired about her. Whatever she decided to do, she would want to make sure that Maria and Kevin were properly looked after.

Well, one thing was for certain. Until the lawyer came back with more information, there was nothing to be done. He would go back now and meet her and then they would find a nice restaurant and have a lovely dinner.

At ten to five, he saw Emma come striding into the car park carrying several large shopping bags. As she drew closer, he noticed there was a grim set to her jaw and her features were etched with frustration. He got out of the car and hurried to meet her.

"What's happened to you? You look like you're ready to kill someone."

"Look at that," she said, handing him her mobile phone. A text message was emblazoned on the screen.

"*Have just heard you are in town. Would like to meet you urgently to discuss a matter of mutual interest. Antonio Hernandez Rodriguez.*"

"When did this arrive?" Mark asked with surprise.

"Half an hour ago. What should I do?"

It only took Mark a moment to decide.

"Ignore it," he said, switching off the phone. "You're not letting Pedro's Bar interfere any more with your holiday."

23

Emma wasn't alone in her concerns about Pedro's Bar. Kevin was also getting worried, although he kept his thoughts largely to himself. From the phone conversations with Maria he was beginning to suspect that Rosario was sicker than the old woman was saying. Unless she managed to get someone to look after her, Maria could be away from work for a long time.

How would Emma react to that? Already, Kevin could see that she was a sharp businesswoman who was going to leave nothing to chance. She had even paid a visit to that chancer who was supposed to be the accountant, although that was a joke. He wouldn't know an accountancy report if it jumped up and bit him on the leg. He was a sidekick of Antonio's and as far as Kevin could see he was in Antonio's pocket. He would be very surprised if he had ever paid a cent of tax for Pedro's Bar.

All this warned him that Emma would do what he feared most – she would sell the bar. Once she learned the full extent of the problems she had inherited, she would want to rid herself of the whole business. And who could blame her? She knew nothing about running a bar. She had her hands full with her own printing company back in Dublin. Why would she want to keep Pedro's Bar when all it was doing was giving her one headache after another?

He had better get used to the idea. In a few weeks' time, he could be out of a job. And Snuffy too. He watched his friend as he busied himself scrubbing all the surfaces and the utensils in preparation for locking up for the night. He had turned out to be a conscientious worker. He had quickly picked up the routine. He worked hard and showed every sign that he was determined to put his past behind him and forge a new life.

It had been a bit of a gamble taking him on board and bringing him home to live with him. Kevin had enough experience of addicts from his time in London to know they were notoriously unreliable. They meant to do well but often the craving for the drug proved too much for them and they relapsed. And there were plenty of drugs available right here on the Costa if Snuffy ever felt seriously tempted.

But so far he had shown no sign of going back to his old ways. He seemed to welcome the work for the distraction and the therapy it brought. And he had located a Twelve Step group here in Fuengirola that held meetings several times a week. He had been to one last night and had come back to the apartment looking peaceful and contented.

If Emma did sell the bar, Kevin would make sure that Snuffy got a glowing reference. He now had some experience. There were hundreds of bars in the resort and he would easily find another job. As for himself, well, time would tell. He would cross that bridge when he came to it.

He finished counting the day's takings and put them in a

leather bag along with the lodgement slip. He would drop it into the bank on his way home. Snuffy was now folding away the chairs and tables and chaining them to the back wall.

"How's it going?" Kevin called out to his friend.

"Nearly finished."

Kevin looked down along the beach. There was still a good crowd of sun-worshippers but if they got thirsty they would have to go somewhere else. Pedro's Bar was closing. It had been another frantic day and they were picking up the girls at eight o'clock to go to the concert in Mijas. It was being given by a local rock band called Los Desperados. Kevin had heard them play before and they were very good. It promised to be a great evening. Just after lunchtime, Claire had contacted him to see if Snuffy would come along with Maggie and make it a foursome. He had agreed at once. Indeed, he felt sorry that he hadn't thought of the idea himself.

Snuffy finished stacking away the chairs and tables. No point sweeping the wooden walkways till the morning. Kevin checked one last time to make sure that everything was in order, then pulled down the shutters with a bang. He secured the locks and put the keys in his pocket. The two men began walking up the beach to the Paseo Maritimo with pleasant thoughts of the evening that lay ahead.

Around the same time, Claire was emerging from the shower and vigorously towelling her long black hair while she decided what to wear. She had spent the morning cleaning the apartment with Maggie's assistance. Not that it particularly needed cleaning but Claire had woken up with such energy that she had to spend it on something. So the two women had washed and scrubbed and polished till every surface shone like a bright new penny.

Claire was still afraid to go back to the beach till all the fuss had died down so she had taken a bottle of wine from the fridge and they spent the afternoon on the balcony chatting in the bright sun.

"Do you ever think of the future?" she asked Maggie.

"Why would I do that?"

"It can be fun to think where you might be, what you might be doing, who you might be with."

"Not really. I tend to live my life a day at a time. If I think as far as the weekend, I'm doing well."

"I sometimes think of the future," Claire said. "And wonder what my life will be like. Do you believe in the stars?"

"Rock stars or film stars?"

"Horoscopes!" Claire said with a laugh. "Do you believe everything is preordained? Already planned?"

"Oh, I don't know about that," Maggie said quickly. "I think we're responsible for a lot of the things that happen to us through the actions we take. For instance, if it hadn't been for the karaoke competition I wouldn't have become an entertainer."

"What karaoke competition?"

"The competition I won. Didn't I tell you?"

"I don't think so."

"Well, it was like this," Maggie said, taking a sip of her wine. "Five years ago, I came here on holiday. I was only intending to stay a week. Then one night, I entered a karaoke competition in the Bloated Toad pub down in Fish Alley. I ran away with it and the manager was so impressed that he asked if I'd like to do a turn for a couple of nights because the regular girl was away. So I agreed. And I enjoyed it so much that I stayed. I just threw in my job in Clapham and never went back. And that's how I got started in the entertainment business."

"But maybe you were meant to win that competition," Claire said. "It doesn't disprove the theory of the stars."

"Maybe you were meant to get into trouble on that beach yesterday so that Kevin could rescue you and then invite you out tonight."

Claire stroked her chin. "I hadn't thought of that."

"And maybe I was supposed to look after you so you would ask Kevin to invite Snuffy along."

Claire was smiling now. "Hey! I think you're actually proving my theory of the stars!"

"But you like him, don't you?"

"Who?" Claire said, blushing slightly.

"Kevin, of course."

Claire pursed her lips. "I suppose so."

"Well, if you want my opinion, he's a very good-looking bloke. I told you that already. And what's more, I think he likes you."

"Really?"

"Oh c'mon! Don't pretend you haven't noticed. He buys you flowers. He invites you out. Why do you think he'd be doing that if he didn't like you?"

"Because he's such a nice guy."

"He's a nice guy who likes you. And if you've got any sense, you'll like him right back."

"He hasn't said anything."

"Give him time," Maggie said. "He will."

Claire thought about the conversation after Maggie left. She knew the way some girls could make a play for a man but she hadn't done that with Kevin. Things had just sort of happened of their own free will, without any effort on her part. They had just drifted together and here was Maggie already writing them down as an item. But it was a nice idea and privately it made Claire feel very pleased. Maybe their relationship really was written in the stars like she had said.

She pondered these thoughts as she tried to make up her mind what to wear. This was a rock concert. It demanded a certain dress code. She wished she had packed her little black leather jacket but she hadn't thought she would need it and, besides, she didn't have room in her bag.

In the end, she chose her short denim skirt, a dark green vest top and black boots. She pondered whether to wear her dark hair loose around her shoulders. In the end, she pulled it up into a ponytail, leaving some tendrils hanging around her face. She would do. She might not look like a wild-child rock chick but at the same time no one would think she was going for a night at the opera. She just had time to put on a smear of bright red lipstick and a spray of perfume when she heard a car horn sound from the street below. She went to the window and saw Kevin and Snuffy waving to her from a taxi.

Maggie must have heard the horn too, for she emerged from her apartment at the same time as Claire wearing an identical skirt and vest (in purple) but with the addition of a pair of chic dark shades. Damn, Claire thought, I knew there was something else. She was about to return for her sunglasses when she changed her mind. They would be so alike that they would look like the Bobbsey Twins. She grabbed Maggie's arm and hurried down the stairs to the waiting cab.

"You both look really cool," Kevin said as they settled into the back seat of the cab. "You'll be turning heads."

"Yes," Snuffy agreed and Claire saw Maggie snuggle closer to him.

"Feeling better?" Kevin continued.

"One hundred per cent," Claire replied. "No. Make that one hundred and ten per cent. And it's all down to you. I shudder to think what would have happened if you hadn't come along. Tonight I would have been sleeping with the fishes."

"Lucky fishes," he said and gave her arm a gentle squeeze. "Incidentally, Mark and Emma called at the bar today. They wanted me to say they wished you well."

"My God. How did they find out?"

"Search me. They picked up the information somewhere."

"Don't tell me it's all over the resort," Claire said with a stricken look. "I'll definitely never be able to show my face again."

"Relax," Kevin said reassuringly. "It will all be forgotten in a day or two. Just concentrate on enjoying yourself. We're going to have a brilliant night. And afterwards, we'll have a few scoops to celebrate your miraculous recovery."

"I'll vote for that," Maggie said from the depths of Snuffy's embrace.

Mijas was a picturesque village in the mountains and it took them twenty minutes to get there. When they arrived they found the town packed with people and the square jammed with cars noisily honking their horns in celebration.

The concert was being held in the bullring. As they approached, the noise from the sound system became deafening. Claire felt the excitement rise. Kevin took her hand and squeezed it tight. She glanced towards Maggie and saw that Snuffy had his arm around her shoulders. She was clinging to him like a limpet to a rock. Maggie caught Claire's eye and winked happily.

The concert was a wild event. Several thousand people had packed the wooden benches of the bullring and were determined to enjoy themselves. They sang and waved and stamped their feet and Claire found herself joining in. But she noticed the way Kevin and Snuffy paid serious attention to the band, obviously taking a professional interest.

She felt Kevin's arm encircle her and draw her close till she nestled her head on his chest. The music seemed to fill the night air with its frenetic sound. Above her, the sky was a mass of blue and pink as the sun began to go down.

"Thanks for coming," Kevin said. "I've been looking forward to this all day."

"Me too."

"Just being with you makes me feel so happy. I could be on a desert island and I'd feel the same as long as you were there."

Claire could hear her heart fluttering in her breast as he drew her closer and his warm lips descended onto hers. She closed her eyes and felt a warm glow of happiness envelop her.

24

Several days passed and Maria still hadn't returned to work. Kevin was beginning to get seriously concerned. It was almost a week now since she had first rung to say that her sister was ill. The strain was beginning to tell on him. He wondered if he should inform Emma.

He hadn't seen her for days. Not since the morning after Claire's accident when she had called to the bar with Mark. She was obviously still trying to figure out what to do. But the silence was ominous. Perhaps if he told her about Maria it might just tip her into selling the bar. But if he didn't tell her she might think he was withholding information. She was the owner and had a right to know. Kevin ran his fingers through his mass of curly hair. How had he found himself in this situation? Whichever way he turned he was sure to be wrong.

He glanced at Snuffy, who was busily washing dishes and glasses in the big sink. Neither of them had taken a break since Maria's sister got sick. Snuffy had never complained.

He spent his days working at Pedro's and his evenings at Maggie's apartment listening to tapes of Tina Turner and Madonna and helping her to polish up her act. But how long could either of them keep going without getting a day off?

It was now afternoon. The beach was still crowded but the worst of the rush was over. Kevin finished wiping down the bar counter and spoke to Snuffy.

"I've got to ask a favour."

"Go ahead," Snuffy said.

"Do you think you could hold the fort for an hour or so?"

"Sure," Snuffy said. "*No problemo.*"

"I have to go and see old Maria. I shouldn't be long."

"Take as long as you like."

"No, I can't leave you on your own. I'll come right back."

"That's all right," Snuffy said and continued with his task.

Kevin put on his jacket and made his way along the beach to the taxi rank. He had been to Maria's place before. She lived in an apartment block on the edge of town. It would take him about ten minutes to get there. He settled into the first taxi and gave the address.

He wondered if Maria would be upset at him calling on her unexpectedly. But this was an emergency. He had to find out what was going on and how long she was likely to be away from work.

The cab set off through the winding streets till eventually it deposited him outside a decrepit building in a narrow lane close to the motorway. Kevin paid the driver and looked up at the apartment block. The paint was peeling from the walls and lines of washing flapped in the breeze from the balconies. A couple of young boys kicked a ball around the yard. Kevin went to the main entrance and studied the list of the residents till he came to Maria's name. He pressed the buzzer and waited.

It took Maria several minutes to answer. "*Hola?*"

"It's me. Kevin."

She sounded surprised. "*Buenos días*, Kevin. What you want?"

"I thought I'd call and see how Rosario is."

There was a pause.

"Rosario is very sick."

"Can I come up?"

"What for?" she asked cautiously.

"I want to see you."

"This is not a good time."

"I need to talk to you, Maria."

There was another pause before she said: "All right. Wait."

He heard a click and the door opened. He entered a shabby hall. In front of him was a rickety lift. One look told him he might be safer taking the stairs. Maria's apartment was on the fourth floor. He saw her head looking down at him over the bannisters as he approached.

"*Hola*, Maria," he said cheerfully as he approached and stuck out his hand.

He thought she looked tired and worn. She grasped his hand as he kissed her gently on her old wrinkled cheek.

"Come," she said and pushed open the door of her apartment. It was a small flat. To the left was a tiny kitchen, then a bathroom. One door remained firmly closed and Kevin remembered this was the bedroom. Presumably that was where the sick Rosario was.

Maria ushered him into the sitting-room. It was sparsely furnished with a couple of chairs and a settee. A dining table sat in the corner with a vase of artificial flowers in the centre. A few cheap pictures hung on the walls. On the mantelpiece was a big photograph of some smiling kids: Maria's grand-children, whom she was forbidden to see.

"Sit," she commanded and Kevin lowered himself into the settee.

Maria sat on a chair opposite. "Tell me the truth. Did *Señorita* Dunne send you?"

"No," Kevin rushed to reassure her. "I came myself. *Señorita* Dunne doesn't even know I'm here."

"What do you want?"

"I was worried about you, Maria. We haven't seen you. And Rosario. Is she not getting better?"

Big tears began to swell in the old woman's eyes. She took a handkerchief from her sleeve and wiped her face. "Rosario is very sick."

"Did you get the doctor?"

She slowly shook her head. "The doctor will only send her to the hospital."

"Maybe that's where she should be."

"Oh, no!" Maria cried. "She should be here with me. I am her sister."

"But she needs medical care. She'll get better in the hospital. They'll be able to help her there."

"I can help her. In a few days she will be better. Then I come back to Pedro's."

"Can I see her?" Kevin asked.

Maria looked uncertain. She got up slowly from her chair and went out of the room. Kevin heard the bedroom door open. A minute later, she was back. She indicated that he should follow her.

"She is sleeping. You must be quiet."

Kevin followed Maria. The curtains were drawn and the bedroom was dark. There were two beds in the room. In one of them, Rosario lay curled up, her white hair spread out on the pillow. Kevin winced as he bent over her to look. Her face was thin and emaciated, the skin sallow and brittle, the veins in her forehead clearly visible. On her hands, he saw several ugly sores. Her breathing was faint and laboured. As they watched, she twitched in her sleep and coughed up mucus. Maria took a handkerchief and wiped it away.

Kevin was shocked by what he saw. He took in the remainder of the room. A chair had clothes hanging from it. Several bottles of patent medicines sat on top of a chest of drawers. They were the sort of medicines that could be purchased at any pharmacy.

Neither of them spoke. Maria turned slowly and left the room. Kevin followed.

"Have you spoken to anyone about Rosario?" he asked when they had returned to the sitting-room.

Maria shook her head. He wondered if he should mention her son, Antonio. Surely someone should be helping the two old women.

She was staring at him now. He could see the fear and distrust in her eyes. He sat beside her and took her hand.

"I think you should call the doctor, Maria."

Immediately, she began to get agitated. "No. No doctor."

"But she needs attention."

"She is getting better. In a few days, you will see."

"She is very ill. The doctor will be able to help her."

"If he sends her to the hospital, what will I do? Then the *señorita* will be angry. She will sell Pedro's."

"No," Kevin said. "Why would she do that? She will be angry if you don't call the doctor."

Maria was weeping again. He wondered what he should do. Should he call the doctor himself?

"Please, Maria. Let me call the doctor for you. He will be able to help Rosario and then you can come back to work. Rosario will get better and everyone will be happy. That is the best thing. Believe me."

Maria seemed to hesitate.

"She's very sick, Maria. Without help, she might die."

At this, the old woman burst into a flood of tears. She grabbed Kevin's arm and held it tight. "I don't know what to do. I'm afraid."

"I'm your friend, Maria. Do you trust me?"

She nodded her head.

"You know I would never give you bad advice. Now please do as I say. Ring the doctor and ask him to come." He took out his mobile phone. "What is his number?"

Maria told him.

Kevin keyed in the number and waited till he heard someone answer. Then he handed the phone to Maria.

He got up and walked to the window. Outside, the afternoon sun beat down mercilessly and cast long shadows across the street. In the background he could hear the conversation in Spanish between Maria and the doctor. After several minutes she handed the phone back to him. He switched it off.

"He come in half an hour."

The time seemed to drag by.

"Would you like something to drink?" Kevin asked. "Can I make you some coffee?"

Maria shook her head. She sat in the chair as if in shock, the handkerchief clutched tightly in her hand. At last, they heard the buzzer sound to announce the doctor's arrival.

Maria looked up sharply. She rose from the chair and spoke into the intercom. Kevin watched her press the button to admit the doctor to the building. A few moments later, there was a sharp knock on the apartment door. Maria quickly opened it and the doctor walked in.

He was a young man in shirtsleeves and carried an old-fashioned leather medical bag. He glanced quickly at Kevin and nodded politely. Kevin nodded back. Then the doctor turned to Maria and began a conversation in rapid Spanish. There was much gesticulation and Kevin got the impression that he was scolding her for not contacting him sooner. Eventually, she pointed to the bedroom and the doctor turned to go in. Maria followed.

From the sitting-room, Kevin could hear the doctor wakening the sleeping Rosario. Then his voice dropped to a gentle coaxing tone. Occasionally, Maria's voice broke in. A long time seemed to pass before they emerged and when they did, Maria was weeping once more.

The doctor folded away the stethoscope that still hung from his neck. He took out a mobile phone and pressed in a number. Now he was giving instructions in a voice of authority. Maria sat down. Her face looked ashen.

"What's happening?" Kevin asked.

"She's going to the hospital. He's calling the ambulance to come." She gave him an accusing look as if what was happening was his fault.

"Did he say what it is?"

"*Sí. Pulmonía.*"

"*Pulmonía?*" Kevin had never heard the word before. "What is that?"

The doctor snapped shut the mobile phone. He turned to address Kevin.

"In English, I think you call it pneumonia. Unfortunately, the patient is very ill. I am having her transferred at once to intensive care. I understand you persuaded Maria to contact me. You did well, *señor*. You might have saved this lady's life."

Kevin stayed till the ambulance arrived and Rosario was

taken away. Maria wanted to go with her but the doctor refused. He was quite firm with her. He insisted there was nothing to be gained. Maria would only get in everyone's way.

"If you call the hospital in the morning, they will give you information on her condition. When she is well, you can come and visit."

He gave Maria a pat on the back, snapped shut his medical bag and gave Kevin a final nod of farewell. They heard his footsteps echoing down the stairs and then his car revving up outside. Maria now sat with a weary, subdued look on her face as if events had finally overwhelmed her.

Kevin checked his watch. He had been here for nearly two hours. God knows how Snuffy was faring back at the bar. "You did the right thing, Maria. Now Rosario will get the medical treatment she needs. You heard what the doctor said. She is very ill."

She turned her sad eyes to him. "You are going to tell *Señorita* Dunne?"

He hesitated for a moment and then shook his head. "No, Maria. I won't tell her."

25

Maggie's romance with Snuffy was progressing like a runaway train but in the last few days a dark cloud had appeared on the horizon in the shape of Ricky Blaine, her former boyfriend. He turned up at the apartment one morning demanding to know why she was avoiding him. Claire, who happened to be visiting her neighbour at the time, couldn't escape the ensuing argument.

"Who said I'm avoiding you?" Maggie demanded to know, deciding that attack was the best form of defence.

"Well, I haven't seen you for over a week and every time I ring, you have the message-minder on and you never return my calls. I've sent you loads of texts and you never reply. What's going on, Maggie? Are you seeing some other geezer?"

Maggie pretended to be shocked. "Whatever put that idea into your head?"

"I'm not stupid," Ricky replied. "I can see the way they ogle you down at the Mucky Duck when you're doing your

Tina Turner act. I know what's going through their dirty little minds."

Maggie gave a loud snort of contempt. "You know I never get involved with my audience. It's a point of professional principle."

"That doesn't mean *they* don't want to get involved with *you*."

"I've been busy, that's all. Claire and me have been rehearsing my Madonna routine. Isn't that right, Claire?"

Claire gulped. She had no desire to get dragged into this lover's tiff. But she had to support her friend. "Er, yes," she said. "Sort of."

"Well, I heard you were seen with some bloke at the Desperados gig up in Mijas."

"Who said that?"

"A little bird."

"A bleedin' vulture, that's who," Maggie said angrily. "Have you been spying on me?"

"No, of course not," Ricky said defensively.

"That's what it sounds like. You know, Ricky, I can't stand jealous men. And you're behaving like a small boy who's had his Smarties taken away."

She continued to harangue poor Ricky till he began to wilt under the onslaught.

"So, when am I going to see you?" he asked finally.

"Whenever I'm ready. Right now my career is at a crossbar."

"Crossroads," Claire said softly.

"That's right. I'm trying to decide whether I should do Kylie Minogue. So I need time to concentrate. This is a definite moment for me."

"Defining moment," Claire corrected.

Ricky seemed to be mollified. At last he slunk off, his tall, gaunt frame making him resemble an extra out of a horror movie.

"Men!" Maggie spat in disgust, when he was gone. "Don't they make you sick? Always whingeing about something."

"Well, he does have a point," Claire said gently. "If you've taken a shine to Snuffy, you should let Ricky know. It's not fair to keep him hanging around like a mongrel on a leash."

"You think so?"

"Certainly. Try to think how you would feel."

"You're right," Maggie said. "The problem is I like them both. I can't make up my mind."

"Well, you better do it soon. Otherwise, you run the risk of losing them both."

Maggie flung her arms round Claire and hugged her close.

"You always talk common sense," she said. "You're so sound!"

Claire smiled. "That's what friends are for, Maggie. To support each other. And you were a great support to me when I had my accident on the beach."

"Oh, get away with you," Maggie said, blushing. "All I did was make you some veggie soup."

Claire returned to her own apartment but as she opened the hall door, she heard the sound of her mobile phone ringing. It was in her bag where she had left it on the kitchen table. She wondered who it could be as she closed the door and hurried inside. The sound of the phone grew more insistent as she approached the kitchen. At last she managed to dig it out of the bag and pressed it to her ear.

"Hello?"

"Thank God you're all right," her mother's voice proclaimed breathlessly.

For an awful moment, Claire wondered if her mother had heard about her incident on the beach. Sometimes she believed she had psychic powers. But it was something else entirely.

"Of course I'm all right. Why wouldn't I be?"

"Because there's a madman on the loose down there."

"*What?*"

"An axe-murderer. He's going around killing people."

Claire scrambled her brains to think how her mother had got hold of this information. Had she been in secret communication with Maggie? Surely not.

"I read about it in the paper this morning. It says the police have launched a manhunt."

"That's old news. And it's miles away. In a different resort. Where I am is perfectly safe."

"What if he comes down to your place?"

"Relax, Mum!"

"How can I relax when my only unmarried daughter is in danger? And you with your good degree in Legal Studies from Trinity College!"

"I'm not in danger. I'm perfectly safe."

"Don't argue. I saw a programme on television about these people. They're always on the lookout for fresh victims. Tender young female flesh, the reporter said. I immediately thought of you."

"That was nice."

"Well, you're the sort they go for. I think you should stay indoors till he's caught."

"I could do that in Dublin. Why do you think I came the whole way to Fuengirola?"

"You tell me. I don't know where you get these crazy

notions. Why you couldn't have gone to the West of Ireland for your holidays, I'll never know."

"Would you like to start with the weather?"

"Now don't you get smart with me. Bray was good enough for your father and me."

"I wanted a change of scenery. I thought I had explained all this."

"I'll never forgive myself if anything happens to you."

"Mother!" Claire heard her voice rising. "Look, I appreciate your concern for me. But I'm perfectly safe. I'm six storeys up in an apartment block. I've got locks on all my doors. I only go out with friends."

"*Friends?*" Her mother sounded as if she was having hysterics. "Who are these people? Where do they come from? What are their backgrounds?"

"I don't go around asking people for their CVs before I speak to them," Claire shouted down the phone. "They're just people I've met. They are all perfectly respectable. As far as I know, none of them has any convictions for axe-murder. Now why don't you stop worrying? If I run into any psychopaths, you're the first person I'll call."

She finally calmed her mother down and got her off the line. She felt like she'd just been wrestling with an octopus. She was twenty-six years old and still her mother was treating her as if she was a schoolchild on her first bus trip.

Outside, it was another bright day. And it was also Tuesday, which was market day and Claire had been promising herself a visit. She needed to pick up a few items and it would be a good excuse to get out of the apartment and get some exercise. She locked up and set off towards the train station. The market was held at the feria grounds in Los Boliches, which was only one stop away.

Half an hour later she was walking through the crowded stalls, listening to the hubbub all around her.

The market sold everything from fresh peppers to second-hand clothes. She stopped at a vegetable stall to pick up some tomatoes and peaches. At another stall, she browsed among the herbal medicines that promised to treat every ailment from high blood pressure to arthritis. At a third stall she bought some CDs. When she had finished her shopping she decided to relax over a coffee and cake at a nearby café.

As she sat in the sun, her thoughts automatically turned to Kevin. Tonight he was taking her to a club in Marbella. She was really looking forward to seeing him again. In fact, she thought about him all the time and the more they were apart, the more she missed him. What was happening to their relationship? Where was it going?

It was a big question and Claire wasn't sure about the answer. All she knew was that she had grown very fond of him in the short time they had known each other. And he was fond of her. But would it lead to anything or was it just a fleeting holiday romance? In a few weeks she would be returning to Dublin. What would happen then? Would they just kiss and say goodbye? Would he take up with the next young woman who turned up some afternoon at Pedro's Bar looking for a beer?

She thought again of his dark curling hair and his mischievous smile. It was curious that Maggie should have spotted from the beginning that there was some spark between them. But was it wise to pursue it? Kevin's life was here and hers was back in Dublin. She suddenly found herself laughing at the thought of her mother's reaction should she ever bring Kevin home to meet her.

"And what do you do for a living, Mr Joyce?"

"*I serve hamburgers at a beach bar in Fuengirola.*"

Her mother would have a heart attack and would probably never recover from the shame.

Claire finished her coffee, paid the bill and started back towards town. She would do nothing and let fate take its course. If her relationship with Kevin was destined to develop into something more, then so be it. If not, at least she would have happy memories of a beautiful friendship.

She was beginning to feel tired as she neared the apartment. She would have a nice cold shower to cool down and then a glass of chilled wine to help her unwind before she started to prepare for her outing with Kevin. But as she emerged from the lift, she heard Maggie's voice from the open door of her apartment.

"Come in, come in," she said as she ushered Claire into the living-room and insisted she sit down on the sofa. Claire prepared herself for the long-threatened Madonna impersonation. But instead, she got something else.

"When you left this morning, I had a brainwave."

"About what?" Claire asked, bewildered.

"About Ricky and Snuffy. Remember I said I couldn't make up my mind which of them I liked the best?"

"Er, yes."

"Well, I've decided what to do. They're both musicians, right?"

"Right."

"They both play bass guitar?"

"Yes."

"I'm going to hold a guitar competition. Whichever of them wins is the one I'll stay with."

Claire clapped her hands and hugged her friend. "You mean the winner will get your hand?"

"Exactly. What do you think?"

"I think it's brilliant."

"So do I," Maggie said, getting excited. "I think it's very romantic. That's the trouble with blokes today. No romance. Incidentally, Johnny the landlord called when you were out. You seem to keep missing him. He said to make sure to give you this. He said it arrived this afternoon." She handed her an envelope.

Claire tore it open.

It was a fax message from an address in London.

Dear Claire, Arriving Fuengirola this evening. Would like to meet you 10 a.m. tomorrow. Hotel Victoria. Best regards, Matthew.

Immediately she felt a gloom descend on her shoulders like a shroud.

26

Now that the problem of Pedro's Bar had been delivered into the hands of Luis Garcia Santiago, Emma was free to do some serious sunbathing. She had purchased a couple of high-quality tanning creams with sun-blocking agents and a tube of after-sun lotion. As a result, her tan had improved dramatically in the last few days and she was beginning to look healthily bronzed. Unless they were colour-blind, no-one back home in Dublin would be unaware that she had been on holiday.

She was stretched out on her sun bed beside the hotel swimming pool, listening to the radio, when the long-awaited call from the lawyer finally came through.

"*Señorita* Dunne?"

"Yes."

"It is Luis here. I have some information to report about the matter of Pedro's Bar."

Emma sat up straight. This was the first contact with Luis since she had visited him in his office in Malaga.

"It is quite important. Would it be possible to come and see me?"

"Of course. When would you like me to call?"

"As soon as possible."

She checked her watch. It was now half twelve. "I could come right away, if you like."

"That would be excellent. Shall we say two o'clock?"

"Fine. I'll be there."

She hesitated and her curiosity got the better of her. "Can you tell me if the news is good or bad?"

"It's complicated. I would prefer to talk to you face to face."

"All right," she said, reluctantly. "I'll be at your office for two."

She heard him switch off his phone. Immediately, she rang Mark. He had told her he planned to spend the afternoon scuba diving off the port. With a bit of luck she might get him before he set out. On the third ring, he answered his phone.

"Where are you?" she asked. "There's a lot of background noise."

"I'm in traffic. I'm approaching the port."

"I just got a call from Luis. He wants to see me in his office at two."

"That was fast. Did he say if he had found anything?"

"No, he wasn't giving anything away. But he did say it was important."

"That's the way of lawyers," Mark said. "I'll come and pick you up."

"Are you sure? I thought you were going scuba diving."

"That can wait. I'll be with you in half an hour. Why don't you start getting ready?"

"Will do," Emma said

"*Adiós*," Mark said.

He was outside the Hotel Alhambra half an hour later, having stopped briefly at his own hotel for a quick shower and change of clothes. Now instead of shorts and T-shirt, he wore his navy chinos, black shirt and navy blazer. In Mark's experience, a visit to a lawyer's office was always an occasion for dressing soberly.

He gave her a quick peck on the cheek as she settled beside him in the passenger seat.

"How did your morning go?"

"Lazily. I spent it by the pool working on my tan."

"And succeeding by the look of you. You're getting quite dark now," he said with an approving glance. "With your blonde hair and brown tan, you're beginning to look like one of those Nordic sun goddesses – well, a pint-sized one!"

"I take it they were all good-looking women?"

"Absolutely stunning and powerful as well. Those ladies took no nonsense from anyone." He smiled and gave her hand a little squeeze. "How do you feel? Apprehensive?"

"A little," she confessed. "I've managed to put the business of Pedro's Bar out of my mind but it's like a stone in my shoe. It's always irritating me. I just wish the whole damned thing was done and dusted."

"Cheer up," Mark said in a reassuring voice. "Maybe Luis is about to tell you that he has solved your problems."

"That would be wonderful. But somehow I don't think life is that simple."

Half an hour later, the rooftops of Malaga came into view, shining like copper in the bright afternoon sun. They found a space in the underground car park they had used the last time. Mark locked the car and they emerged into the busy life of the city. At five to two they were at Luis's office.

After a short delay, they were ushered in to see him. He sat behind his desk, immaculately dressed and looking cool and relaxed. With perfect manners, he rose to shake heir hands then invited them to take a seat. They declined his offer of something to drink.

The lawyer's face betrayed no emotion as he opened a file on his desk. "Since we last spoke, I have been able to make some progress with your case."

"Yes?" Emma said eagerly.

"I have spoken to the taxation authorities regarding Pedro's Bar." He raised his head and his eyes bored directly into Emma's. "I am afraid the news is not good."

Immediately, she felt a sick feeling in the pit of her stomach.

"They have no record of any taxes of any kind having been paid in relation to the bar."

There was a silence in the room as the three people stared at each other.

"Do they have any indication of how much money is owed?" Emma managed to ask, trying to conceal the tremor in her voice.

"Not an accurate figure. They are still working that out."

"Were they able to give you an estimate?"

"Yes. But this is not exact. With interest and penalties, the tax bill could be as high as € 60,000."

She let out a little gasp and Mark reached out to hold her hand.

"And I am liable for that?"

"Yes. As I explained to you, under Spanish law, you are responsible for the debts due on the property. You assumed these debts when you took ownership."

Mark was clearing his throat. "What is the position of the accountant in this matter?"

The lawyer spread his hands and sighed.

"He was responsible for assessing the tax and keeping the

records up to date. In this regard, he was certainly remiss. You could sue him. But I do not recommend it."

"Why not?" Emma asked.

"Because it will be a long, slow process. It will cost money. You may not win. And even if you do win, you may not get any redress. I have made some inquiries regarding *Señor* Martinez Sanchez. I have to tell you he is not a man of substance. He has no money."

Emma and Mark exchanged a glance.

"We have a saying in Spanish," Luis continued. "You cannot get blood from a stone."

"We have the same saying in English," Mark replied.

The lawyer shrugged. "Then you can see the situation. It is hopeless. I regret to be the bearer of bad news, *Señorita* Dunne."

"So I owe the tax authorities €60,000?"

"Yes. That is the bottom line."

"And there is nothing I can do?"

Luis spread his hands. "Unfortunately, no."

Mark took Emma by the arm as they left the lawyer's office and walked out into the blinding sunlight.

"I think after that little conversation you need a stiff drink," he said.

There was a small bar nearby. They sat down and he ordered two brandies. By now, Emma's eyes were blazing with fury.

"Damn that fool Miguel! I knew the moment I set eyes on him he was a crook. And damn Conor Delaney too! He gives me a bar and it turns out to be a booby trap that blows up in my face. I should have simply written off his debt and been done with it."

She took a gulp of her brandy.

"Look, I know this is a nasty shock for you," Mark said. "But you must try to think rationally."

"It's not such a shock. I've had a bad feeling all along that something like this was going to happen. The thing that really hurts is that I've been taken for a fool."

"You've got to put your feelings aside," Mark said. "The question is: what are you going to do?"

"What can I do? I'll have to pay the €60,000. You heard what Luis said."

"And then what?"

Emma shrugged. "Sell the bar, I suppose. I never wanted it in the first place. I want it even less now."

"Aren't you forgetting something?" Mark said gently. "If you sell the bar it will mean putting the staff out on the street. Whatever about Kevin, we both know that Maria will never work again."

Emma turned her face to him. "Oh, Mark, you know that's the very last thing I want. But do I have any choice? Pedro's Bar is a distraction to me. I have bigger, far more pressing issues to deal with."

He gave her a quizzical look. "What are you talking about?"

She lifted her glass and drained it. "I never told you the real reason I'm here. You never asked because you're just so damned polite. But now I'll tell you."

At the very moment when Emma and Mark were discussing their visit to Luis, Miguel Martinez Sanchez was pacing the floor of his shabby office in Fuengirola like a caged panther. In the last few days, his nervousness had turned into obsession. He couldn't sleep; he couldn't concentrate. He could think of nothing but the terrible threat that was hanging over his head. Just yesterday, he had received the phone call he had been dreading. An official in the Tax Office had phoned to know why no accounts had been submitted for Pedro's Bar.

Miguel had tried to be polite. He had explained that he had a very heavy workload and unfortunately the affairs of the bar had been overlooked as a result. He would attend to them right away. But the official had been insistent. He had proceeded to ask awkward questions, probing this detail and that, till Miguel's head began to spin.

It was with enormous difficulty that he had finally managed to get the man off the line. But the phone call told him one thing. The Tax Office had finally woken up to the situation at Pedro's Bar. And he knew the tax authorities well. Once they got their teeth into you, they never let go. It would only be a matter of time before they were back again. And on the next occasion, they would not be put off so easily.

That steely-eyed Irishwoman, *Señorita* Dunne, was behind it. He had no doubt. She was the person who had alerted the tax authorities. It was what he had feared. There had been no contact with her since she called at his office but she had obviously been busy elsewhere. He had known when she left that his troubles were only beginning. And he had been right. Now an avalanche was about to descend on him and he would be swept away.

Antonio had told him to do nothing. Not that there was very much he could do. But he had found the waiting almost unbearable. Antonio had also promised to keep in touch with him and so far he had heard nothing. Worse than that, Antonio was now refusing to return his phone calls. Since his conversation with the tax official, he had rung his friend at least a dozen times to get his advice. He had pleaded with Antonio's secretary. He had stressed the urgency of his business. He had begged her to let him speak with Antonio or at the very least to get him to call back. And so far, nothing had happened.

Miguel was at his wit's end. He felt like a rat caught in a trap. In his imagination, he saw himself being bundled off by the police to stand in front of a magistrate and be sentenced to a lengthy spell in prison. His career would be destroyed; the little reputation he had left would be in shreds. He would never last in prison. To be locked up with those criminals and thieves and murderers – he would never be able to do it. He would sooner kill himself than go to jail.

The thought caused a shiver of terror to run down his spine. Miguel could stand it no longer. He stopped pacing the floor and opened a drawer in his desk. From it, he extracted a large bottle of brandy and a glass. He filled the glass and drank it down, then quickly wiped his lips and poured another.

The brandy helped him to feel better. At least it kept his wild imagination under control. He frantically tried to assess his options. He could try to fake the accounts for Pedro's Bar as he had faked the accounts for Antonio's restaurant for so long. But the problem was: he had absolutely nothing to go on. He knew that old Maria kept receipts and invoices for expenditure at the bar but they probably didn't go back for more than a year. She certainly wouldn't have any paperwork that was older than twelve months. And it wouldn't be enough to keep the tax authorities satisfied. They would want to see properly audited accounts and no such accounts existed. No, he decided, trying to fake accounts would never work.

He got up and paced the floor again and the more he thought about his difficulties, the more desperate he became.

He poured another brandy and gulped it down. It was useless. There was no escape. He had no choice but to make a clean breast to the authorities and throw himself on their mercy. If he did that, if he co-operated with them, they might show him some leniency. Maybe the magistrate might even reduce his prison sentence. But to make a clean breast would mean telling them the whole story. It would mean implicating others. Could he bring himself to do that?

He thought bitterly of his so-called friend, Antonio, who was refusing to take his phone calls. This was the man who was prepared to stand by and see him sink beneath the waves without raising a finger to help him. Did he owe such a man any loyalty? Should he meekly allow himself to be sacrificed while Antonio got away free?

He poured another brandy. At last, he was beginning to think straight. Now he could see clearly what he had to do. A plan began to form in his fevered brain. He could see a way forward that might salvage something from the wreckage that loomed before him. But it was a plan that Antonio would not like. So be it. These were tough times.

He lifted the glass and polished off the brandy.

27

Claire stared in horror at the fax message she had just been given by Maggie as if it had jumped out of the envelope and taken a bite out of her. In the last few days, Matthew Baker had never been far from her mind. Now, he was suddenly centre stage.

"It's not bad news, is it?" Maggie asked, noticing her stunned reaction.

Claire pulled herself together and tried to smile. "Oh no. Nothing like that."

"That's good," Maggie went on. "I thought by the look on your face that maybe somebody had died."

"Good Lord, no."

"So you like my idea for the guitar competition?"

"Oh, yes. I think it's a great idea."

"Maybe you could be the adjudicator?"

Claire felt an urgent need to get out of Maggie's living-room as quickly as possible and back across the landing to the sanctuary of her own apartment.

"Sure, why not?"

"I'll arrange it for tomorrow night. I'll invite Kevin as well. I'll cook chilli con carne and we'll have a sort of dinner party. What do you think?"

"That sounds marvellous." She grabbed her bags and stood up. "Look, Maggie, you've got to excuse me. I'm meeting Kevin and I've got to get ready."

"Where are you going?"

"He's taking me to some club in Marbella."

"Oooh, that's nice. Give him my regards."

"Of course I will. Byeee!"

Claire hurried into her apartment and closed the door. She sat down on the bed and took out the message and read it over once more. Hotel Victoria. She knew where it was. It was one of the best hotels in the resort, probably costing a packet. But then Matthew always liked style. There had been a time when her heart would have skipped a beat at such a message, when she would have thrilled with anticipation at the thought of meeting her lover. But now she felt only a leaden sense of apprehension. Till now, her stay in Fuengirola had been a relaxing holiday from the humdrum cares of her life. Why did Matthew Baker have to come along and spoil it?

Of course, she didn't have to go. She could tear up the message and ignore it. But would it do any good? If she refused to meet him, Johnny Parkinson would probably give him her address and he would simply turn up on her doorstep. Maybe even cause a scene. She knew Matthew only too well. He wasn't the type to give up easily.

She silently cursed Matthew Baker as she went into the bathroom and began to get undressed. She stepped into the shower and felt the hot water cascade along her body. There was something soothing about a shower; it helped her gather her thoughts. What did Matthew Baker want? If he was still hoping to lure her back, he was wasting his time. If anything, her determination had been strengthened since she had met Kevin. The relationship with Matthew Baker was well and truly over. There could be no going back.

But how could she avoid him? He would simply pursue her till she agreed to see him again. It seemed she had little option but to go along to the Hotel Victoria tomorrow morning and find out what he wanted. But it would be a purely formal occasion: two old acquaintances meeting after a long separation. If he attempted to expand the meeting into anything more, she would be firm. Matthew Baker was the past. Her life had moved on.

She stepped out of the shower and dried herself, then went into the bedroom and began to get ready for the evening. She felt like dressing up for the occasion. She hunted through the clothes she had brought and decided on her most "formal" outfit – the same red scoop-necked dress and black pashmina she had worn that first night for dinner with Mark. Kevin hadn't seen the outfit yet and she remembered Mark's admiring look when he caught sight of her that night. She set about the serious business of getting dressed.

Half an hour later, she emerged from the apartment into the balmy night air. She had arranged with Kevin to meet at The Bodega. She made her way through the little narrow streets till at last she saw the familiar blackboard announcing the dinner specials. She stepped into the gloomy interior and saw him waiting at the bar. He was wearing black jeans with an olive-coloured shirt in a soft, heavy cotton material. He looked so handsome as he leaned against the counter with a glass of beer in his hand and the mass of dark curling hair cascading round his face.

Immediately, she felt her spirits revive.

"*Buenas noches, señorita*," he said playfully as he pulled her close and planted a warm kiss on her lips. "You look amazing tonight."

"I was about to say the same thing about you," she replied.

Kevin laughed. "What is this, a mutual admiration society?"

"Just a woman who appreciates a good-looking man when she sees one."

"You'll turn my head. Now enough of this self-congratulation. What are you going to drink?"

"I'll have a glass of red wine, please."

She glanced around the little restaurant. It was beginning to fill up with diners. José, who acted as chef *and* waiter, was taking an order from a couple at a corner table.

"Has Maria returned to work yet?" Claire asked.

Kevin shook his head. "Her sister is quite ill. I went out to see her. She was in a very bad state. Maria was trying to treat her with stuff she had bought from the pharmacy. I had to persuade her to call the doctor. When he came, he immediately ordered an ambulance and took her off to hospital."

"My God! What is it?"

"Pneumonia. The doctor told me I might have saved her life."

Instinctively, Claire put a hand to her mouth. "I never realised it was anything so serious."

"Neither did I. And I don't think Maria did either. But she was so worried about Emma finding out that she was trying to keep it all hidden. She made me promise not to tell her."

"Should you do that?" Claire asked. "Hasn't she got a right to know?"

Kevin let out a long sigh. "Of course she has. But I've been put in an impossible situation."

"Well, Maria's supposed to be the manager. It shouldn't really be your job to decide these things."

"I know. But unfortunately there's no one else to do it. So I've got stuck with it."

"If Emma knew the truth, I'm sure she'd take a sympathetic view."

"So am I. But I've given my word. The positive thing is that Rosario is now in hospital, where she'll get expert medical attention."

Claire sipped her wine. "So what happens now?"

"God knows. The bar has always been run on a very casual basis. Right now, Emma is trying to sort out the accounts."

"And when she has done that?"

Kevin shrugged. "She'll decide whether to keep it or sell it."

"Which will it be?"

He thought for a moment before replying. "You want my honest opinion?"

"Of course."

"I think she'll sell."

The club Kevin had chosen was called Mischief. From the outside, it looked like a swish, upmarket place, with potted palms and a fake marble façade. They joined the queue at the entrance and slowly made their way past the burly security guards till at last they entered a vast cavern filled with mirrors and flashing lights and a wall of noise. Claire glanced around. The club seemed to be populated by wafer-thin women and strutting peacock men, many of whom appeared to be out of their heads on alcohol or drugs.

"Let's grab a couple of beers," Kevin said, heading towards the bar.

They found a table in an alcove where they could watch the heaving mass of bodies on the floor.

"Been here before?" Claire asked.

"Just once. This is supposed to be the top club on the coast."

"They all seem the same to me," Claire confessed. "Noise and sweating bodies and people stoned out of their trees."

"Me too. Feel like dancing?"

At first Claire was reluctant but the insistent beat coming from the sound system soon persuaded her to venture onto the floor and join the hordes of ecstatic dancers. Before she knew it, she had surrendered to the excitement of the night.

She was enjoying herself so much that the time seemed to fly. One minute she was on the dance floor wildly gyrating beside Kevin and the next he was examining his watch and announcing that it was two o'clock.

"Time to go," he said. "I've got to be at Pedro's in the morning looking bright-eyed and bushy-tailed."

Claire thought briefly of the message she had received earlier. She too had an important appointment in the morning.

"Okay. Let's cut."

They fought their way through the crowds till they the reached the exit doors and the cool night air. A line of taxis was waiting on the road outside. Half an hour later, Kevin was depositing her back outside her apartment building in Fuengirola.

He took her hand and gazed dreamily into her eyes.

Next moment, she was in his arms and his warm lips were enveloping hers.

"There's something I've been meaning to tell you," he whispered.

"Yes?"

"You're the most beautiful creature I've ever met."

28

Mark listened carefully while Emma outlined the terms of the offer she had been made by Herr Braun to buy the Hi-Speed Printing Company. When she had finished, he spread his hands wide and gave a low whistle of amazement.

"What can I say? It's a brilliant offer."

"You think so?"

"Of course. You get €3 million for the company, plus you are kept on as a consultant for a further five years at a salary of €150,000 a year. It's a no-brainer. Have you asked your accountant to run his slide rule over it?"

"He doesn't know about it. In fact, no one knows about it except my father. And I'm trusting you to keep it strictly confidential."

"What does your father think?"

"He agrees with you."

"So? Are you going to accept it?"

"I don't know. I came here so that I would have peace to

think about it. But so far, I haven't had a chance. Most of my time has been taken up with Pedro's Bar."

"Yes," Mark said, toying with his brandy glass. "I can see that the bar has become a major distraction for you."

"It's more than a distraction. It's a bloody pain in the butt. I don't want Pedro's Bar. I never wanted it. And after that session with Luis, I feel like giving it away to the first person who will take it off my hands."

"There's the small matter of the €60,000 tax bill."

"Yes," Emma sighed. "I suppose I have no option but to pay that."

"Unless you want to sue the accountant?"

She shook her head. "You heard what Luis said. It would be a complete waste of time. But the first thing I'm going to do is fire him."

Mark put a comforting arm around her shoulder. "Would you like another brandy?"

"No," Emma replied. "I think I'd better get back to the hotel."

The session with the lawyer had left her feeling defeated and depressed. Right now, she wanted to be alone. She left Mark outside the hotel, with a promise to meet him later in the bar for a drink, then went up to her suite and soaked in the bathtub while she let the tension slowly ebb away.

It had been a bruising day. What upset her most was the knowledge that she had been outwitted and cheated. She had sensed from the beginning that there was something wrong and now she felt a burning sense of injustice at the memory of how Miguel Martinez Sanchez had tried to dismiss her justifiable inquiries by patronising her. Well, she would get some satisfaction tomorrow morning when she rang to tell him he was fired.

Tomorrow was going to be a very busy day. She

considered the various tasks she had to do. First, she would ask Luis to open a Spanish bank account for her and then she would arrange for the funds to be transferred from Dublin. She would also ask Luis to nominate a proper accountant who would deal with the tax authorities on her behalf. Once she had got a final figure from them she would pay it. Then she could set about putting Pedro's Bar up for sale.

It was the cleanest way of dealing with the problem. As long as she kept the bar, she would be plagued with worries and concerns. It had become a ball and chain around her ankles. She wanted to be free from the hassle of staffing problems and all the attendant difficulties with insurance and taxes. She had absolutely no idea what the bar was worth but she would get a property consultant to advise her. With a bit of luck she might even cut her losses and break even.

But she was still left with the immediate problem of the existing staff. Kevin and Snuffy would quickly find new jobs. But what was she going to do about Maria? Who was going to hire an old woman of her age with an invalid sister who depended on her? No, whatever happened, Emma would not have that on her conscience. She could never live with herself if she left the old lady and her sister to the mercy of the fates.

Maybe she could insert a clause in the sales contract insisting that the existing staff be kept on. But would it work? And was it legal? And would anybody want to buy the bar with a condition like that attached? She would ask Luis. He was the man to advise her.

Eventually, she emerged from the bath and dried herself. She put on some comfortable clothes, rang room service and ordered tea and sandwiches to be sent up to her room.

When the food arrived, she took it out to the terrace and ate it at the little table while she watched the evening shadows lengthen and the golden sun hover above the azure sea.

It was so peaceful here, away from the hurly-burly of her hectic business life. She thought of the long hours she had put into Hi-Speed Printing. Most of the time she had enjoyed it. But hadn't she worked hard enough? Wasn't it time to relax and spend more time on herself? She was now thirty-one and she had never had a decent holiday until now. Did she want to wake up some morning to discover that she was an old lady and her life had passed her by?

The offer from Herr Braun was very attractive. Both Mark and her father had said so. After taxes and a settlement to her parents, she might have €2 million left. It was more than enough to live comfortably. If she invested it wisely, she would have a steady stream of income for the rest of her life. And for the next five years, she would have a consultant's salary of €150,000 for doing more or less what she was doing now.

She would be free. She would have reclaimed her life. She would be able to do exactly as she pleased. Maybe she would buy a property here, somewhere she could escape to when the mood took her. For a moment, she let her thoughts dwell on the idea. How wonderful to wake on a dreary winter morning in Dublin and decide to fly off to the sun. She could leave Dublin at 10 a.m. and be here by midday. And if she had her own place, she could stock the wardrobes with clothes. She wouldn't even need to pack a suitcase.

These pleasant thoughts were disturbed by the loud ringing of the phone. Who can this be, she wondered as she got up from her seat and went back into the room. It was her mother calling from Dublin.

"Oh, Emma, how good to hear your voice! I was just talking about you this morning to Ellie Moore. I was telling her you've gone to Spain for a month. She was very envious."

Ellie Moore was one of her mother's cronies. They got a great deal of enjoyment from teasing each other.

"How is everybody back home?" Emma asked.

"They're all well. Alan is going off to Australia next week. I think it's some rugby tournament or something. Your father knows more about it. It's a very long journey by plane. I don't think it would suit me at all."

"What about Peter?"

"You'll never guess what's happened. He's got a girlfriend. A very attractive young woman she is too. Another doctor, if you don't mind. She came to tea last Sunday. That was just to show her off. So I suppose it must be serious."

About time too, Emma thought. Her brother Peter was now thirty-seven and had never shown the slightest inclination to get a steady girlfriend and settle down. And they probably thought the same thing about her.

"What is the weather like over there?"

"It's quite good, thank God. Nice and sunny. We just had dinner on the back patio. Of course, it's nothing like the weather you're getting down in Spain. I hope it's not too hot for you. You know, with your fair skin, you have to be careful."

"Don't worry, Mum. I always make sure to use my sun cream."

"Well, I'm delighted that you're enjoying yourself. You deserve a break. You've been working too hard if you ask me."

"Is Dad there? I'd better say hello."

There was a bit of crackle on the line as the phone

changed hands and next moment she was speaking to her father.

"How are you, love?"

"I'm fine. I'm glad to hear you're getting some decent weather at last."

"Yes. It changed yesterday. Before that we had rain. You know what it's like."

"Good golfing weather."

"Now you've got it."

She paused. "I've been thinking about that offer for the company, Dad."

"Yes?"

"I haven't decided yet but I think I might take it."

"Well, that's entirely up to you. But go into it carefully before you make your mind up. Once you agree, there's no going back."

"Honestly – how would you feel if I sold?"

"I told you – my feelings don't matter. You own the company now. You put in all the work."

"You'd have no regrets?"

"Not so long as you are happy."

"If I did sell, there'd be something for you and Mum."

"Get away with you! Don't be worrying about us. We're well looked after."

"I'll do nothing without talking to you."

"That's all right, love. You know where to find us."

She finished the conversation and put down the phone. She always felt good after talking to her parents. She checked her watch. It was time to get ready to meet Mark for that drink in the bar. Thankfully, she was now in a more cheerful mood. She would enjoy a couple of drinks in the cosy surroundings of the cocktail lounge.

She rifled through the rack of clothes she had purchased

on one of her shopping expeditions. She would have to buy some new suitcases for the return journey to pack it all in. After some consideration, she chose a little knee-length taupe dress – it would look good with the dark-green kitten-heeled shoes she had bought in a sale in Marbella.

She was just putting the finishing touches to her lipstick when the phone rang again. This time it was the reception desk.

"Hello?"

"*Señorita* Dunne?"

"Yes."

"There is a gentleman to see you."

Mark is earlier than I expected, she thought.

"Tell him I'll be down right away."

"*Sí, señorita.*"

She took her bag and her new rose-coloured wrap, checked that the terrace door was locked and let herself out. She rode the lift down to the foyer. As she approached the reception desk, she noticed a thin man in a flashy suit waiting near the desk. But there was no sign of Mark.

As she drew nearer, the man stepped forward to greet her.

"*Señorita* Dunne?"

"Yes," Emma said, slightly taken aback.

"My name is Antonio Hernandez Rodriguez."

"Who?"

"Maria Rodriguez de Hernandez is my mother."

"Oh, yes," Emma said.

"If you could spare me a few moments, I have something important to tell you about Pedro's Bar."

29

Claire woke with the memory of Kevin's kiss still lingering on her lips and his words echoing in her ear. It was ten past nine and already the bright morning sun was flooding the bedroom with light. She lay for a moment, luxuriating in the warm cocoon of the sheets and then suddenly sat up with a start. She was supposed to be meeting Matthew Baker in less than an hour!

She jumped out of bed and ran into the bathroom. As she stood beneath the cascading shower, she asked herself once more if there was any way she could possibly get out of this meeting. Matthew Baker was the very last person in Spain she wanted to see right now. But even as the thought entered her head, she knew it was futile. She had been over this ground several times already. She had no option but to go and get the damned thing over with.

Whatever should she wear? The Hotel Victoria was very fancy and she wanted to look her best to meet Matthew – but not so well that it looked as if she were dressing up for him. It was difficult and she didn't have a lot to choose from. She spotted a dress she hadn't worn yet, a simple lilac button-up with a V-neck. That would have to do.

As she brushed her mane of dark hair, she rehearsed in her mind how she would handle this encounter. She would be cool, of course. But she would have to be polite. There was nothing to be gained by having a blazing row in the grand surroundings of Hotel Victoria, even if she might get some pleasure from his embarrassment. But she would be firm. She would let him know that their relationship was over and that she resented the fact that he had pursued her to Spain. She would leave him in no doubt that there would be no going back.

Twenty minutes later, buoyed up by this resolve, she closed the door of the apartment and made her way down in the lift. The hotel was about twenty minutes away on foot. She would make it just in time. As she hurried through the little cobbled streets, she pondered how much he might have changed since the last time they met. It was over two years. What would he look like now? Matthew had always taken care of himself, with regular visits to the gym and weekend jogging sessions. Even in the hectic atmosphere of London, he had maintained his fitness regime. No doubt he would be the same debonair figure she remembered from all those years ago.

The majestic exterior of Hotel Victoria glittered in the bright morning sun. A uniformed commissionaire politely held the door as she entered the opulent foyer at precisely five minutes to ten. Claire paused to take stock. A tiled marble floor stretched all the way to the ornate reception desk. Glittering chandeliers blazed with light. A fountain played silently in the centre of the vast room.

As she stood and stared, she heard a voice call her name.

She turned at once and felt her heart skip a beat. He was sitting on a sofa beside the wall. He was wearing an obviously expensive dark-grey suit and a crisp white shirt with a copper-and-grey tie. His dark hair was beautifully cut, with a stray lock falling over his forehead. He rose to greet her. He looked exactly as she remembered him – the same tall, lithe man who had once captured her heart. He looked so poised and confident that she felt the breath leave her body.

He caught her hand and kissed her on the cheek. "Claire, it's great to see you again! You look absolutely wonderful."

She stared at him. She felt like a rabbit caught in the headlights of a car.

"Thank you," she said.

She sat beside him on the sofa.

"You're probably wondering why I asked you here?" he said.

"Well, yes, I am."

"I want to offer you a job."

Claire gasped. "A job?"

"Yes, a job." He was smiling now. "Why do you look so shocked?"

"I . . . I wasn't expecting this."

"Before I explain, would you like some coffee?"

"Yes, please," she managed to reply as she struggled to overcome her shock.

He snapped his fingers and a uniformed waiter appeared at his side to take his order. The waiter was back a few minutes later with a silver tray bearing a steaming coffee pot, cups, saucers and a little dish of biscuits.

"How have you been getting on?" Matthew asked as he poured the coffee. "I understand you're still in property?"

"Yes. I'm working for a firm in Dublin."

"You were always very good," he said in his silky voice. "You have the gift. People trust you and that's essential in this business." He smiled again. "I taught you myself. And I could see from the beginning that you had natural talent."

Suddenly, Claire felt totally confused. She had come here expecting Matthew Baker to try to bully her to return to him and instead he was being absolutely charming.

"Thank you," she said. "What are *you* doing now?"

"I'm about to start my own property company."

"You mean you've left Sid Robbins?"

"Yes. But it's all very amicable. I decided the time had come to strike out on my own."

"In London?"

He shook his head as he confidently stirred his coffee. "Here."

Claire could barely conceal her surprise. She felt as if she was being pummelled by one shock after another. "In Fuengirola?"

"Yes. Didn't Johnny tell you?"

"No. He simply said that you were coming on a business trip and wanted to see me. He didn't say what it was about."

"Well, let me tell you. I've recently secured a very lucrative contract with a Spanish developer. I'll be the sole selling agent. We're talking top-of-the-range luxury villas right along the Costa and we're aiming at high net-worth individuals. The days of standing on the street corner with armfuls of brochures are long gone, Claire. This will be West End property methods transferred to Fuengirola. I happened to be talking to Johnny Parkinson last week and he told me you were renting an apartment from him. So immediately I thought of you."

Claire sat dumbfounded. He seemed so different, so much more relaxed than the Matthew she had known. The high-level energy had been replaced by a more controlled intensity.

"You'd be perfect. We always worked well together. And I would make you a very good offer – excellent salary, company car, expenses, sales commission. If things go to plan we could look at making you a partner down the line. And you'd be working and living on the Costa. You always liked it here. Remember how reluctant you were to leave?"

It was all true. She had loved living here. It was the reason she had returned; hoping to recapture some of that old magic. And now Matthew Baker was offering it all back again.

"You're making me a formal offer of a job?"

"Yes. If you agree, we can discuss terms right now. I'll put it in writing for you if you like." He leaned closer and his blue eyes bored into hers. "Tell me you'll say yes."

Claire felt her determination begin to crack. "I c-can't."

"Why not?"

"Because I've moved on from those days. I've built a new life in Dublin. I've bought my own apartment."

But he deftly brushed her objections aside. "Keep the apartment. You can use it for trips home. I expect you'll still spend a lot of time in Dublin. Many of the people we hope to interest in our properties will be Irish."

She looked at him. He was debonair as always with his well-tailored suit, crisp shirt and smooth, finely chiselled features. He looked so suave and self-assured. And he was offering her the job of a lifetime. But was there a catch somewhere? Something that she couldn't see?

"This has come as a big surprise," she managed to say. "I can't give you an answer right now. I need more time to think about it."

"That's perfectly all right," Matthew Baker said. "I'll be

here till the end of the week. If you need any clarification, just give me a call."

He took out his wallet and produced an impressive business card, then wrote his room number and phone extension on it. "That's my card. Contact me at any time."

They stood up and shook hands.

Once again, those intense blue eyes were boring into hers.

"It's been good seeing you again, Claire. I hope you'll say yes. With you on board, I know we're bound to succeed."

Claire left the hotel in a trance. She couldn't believe what had just happened. Matthew Baker hadn't attempted to flirt with her, much less browbeat her into going back to him. He hadn't even referred to their previous relationship. The meeting had been entirely formal and businesslike. And he had been the epitome of charm. That was one thing that certainly hadn't changed.

She thought how well he looked. He was still the same handsome man she had once known: self-assured and confident but more relaxed and mature than before. No wonder she had fallen head-over-heels in love with him. Any girl would have found herself in a spin over Matthew Baker.

Another thought came tumbling into her head. Perhaps she had misjudged him? Perhaps Matthew had moved on too? For all she knew, he could have formed a new relationship, maybe even got married, although she had noticed that he wore no wedding ring. Had she been too arrogant in her assumption that he still wanted her back? What if she had been entirely wrong and Matthew had forgotten all about her till Johnny Parkinson had casually mentioned her name again?

This realisation came as a shock. She had been so wrapped up in her own hurt and grievance that she had failed to consider the wider picture. What if she had been entirely wrong and Matthew had been innocent all along? What if there had been no betrayal? She thought back to the incident that had precipitated their final break-up. She had given him no opportunity to explain himself. She had just packed her bags and left. Had she been too rash? What if her break-up with Matthew had all been a ghastly mistake?

In the end, she didn't know what to think. He had just made her an offer that could change her life. It would be an exciting job and was just the kind of challenge she needed at this point in her career. She knew she could do it. She'd be based here in Fuengirola but with frequent opportunities to return to Dublin. And whatever their personal circumstances, she had always worked well with Matthew Baker. He was right about that. Should she accept his offer?

But her reverie was interrupted the moment she reached her apartment. Maggie was waiting for her at the door of her apartment.

"I've been waiting to tell you. Oooh, I'm so excited!"

"Tell me what?" Claire asked.

"It's all arranged," Maggie announced triumphantly.

"What's arranged?"

"The guitar competition to win my hand."

Claire had been so engrossed in her own situation that she had completely forgotten about Maggie's hare-brained proposal. "The guitar competition?"

"Yes. I rang Snuffy and Ricky last night and I told them I couldn't make up my mind between them and you had suggested they should compete for my affections."

Claire's mouth dropped open. "I didn't suggest it, Maggie. You did."

"Did I? I couldn't remember. Anyway, they've both agreed. They'll be here tonight at eight o'clock."

"They've agreed?"

"Of course they agreed. And I told them that you were going to be the adjudicator and your word would be final."

Claire took a deep breath. What had she got herself into? Whichever of the two men lost would be her mortal enemy for life.

"You know, Maggie, I'm beginning to wonder if this is such a good idea after all."

But Maggie wasn't about to be deflected.

"Of course it's a good idea. In fact, it's a brilliant idea. You said so yourself."

30

Mark was dining alone. It was the first night in almost two weeks that he hadn't been with Emma and he missed her terribly. It was amazing how close they had become in such a short space of time. When he had arrived here a few short weeks ago, he was still in mourning for Margot. He wouldn't have thought himself capable of forming a close relationship with another woman. But it had happened.

Mark knew this wasn't just a case of feeling lonely and wanting some female companionship. It was much more than that. Emma was a special woman, an extraordinary woman whom he had stumbled across quite accidentally. Much the same way as he had met Margot in Bewley's Café all those years ago, he thought to himself. And soon the holiday would be over. He would have to do something. And he would have to do it fast.

He was eating in a little fish restaurant he had discovered near the railway station and the meal had been excellent. But now he wanted to pay his bill and get back to the Hotel

Alhambra, where he was supposed to be meeting Emma for a drink. This afternoon he had come to a decision. After much soul-searching, he had finally accepted what had been staring him in the face for several days. He had fallen in love with her.

He could see now how the feeling had sneaked up on him. At first, it was simply that he enjoyed her company. She was nine years younger but that hadn't seemed to matter. Emma was so full of energy and fun; she was so vibrant. And yet she could also be serious and sensible. And quite tough when the occasion demanded. It was a curious combination and it fascinated him so much that he just loved being with her.

But recently his feelings had changed dramatically. Now his mind was dominated by thoughts of her. He found himself thinking about her all the time – first thing in the morning and last thing at night. When they were apart, he was unhappy till they were together again. When they were together, he felt an excitement set fire to his blood. He wanted to prolong the experience and never allow it to end. Mark wasn't a young adolescent in the first throes of infatuation. He was a mature adult. He had been here before. He knew what he was experiencing. If this wasn't love, he didn't know what it was.

He caught the waiter's eye and called for the bill. The man nodded politely and hurried off in the general direction of the kitchen. Please God he won't leave me hanging around all evening, Mark thought. One thing he had discovered about Spanish restaurants: paying the bill was often the hardest part of the experience. It was as if all their energy went into cooking and serving the meal and paying for it was only a mere afterthought. Perhaps they had their priorities right. But tonight, Mark was in a hurry.

While he waited, he poured out the last of the wine he had ordered with his meal. His thoughts returned to Emma. Of course no one could replace Margot, nothing could ever change that. But he had found he could love someone else while still loving his lost wife. He had told Margot the way his feelings towards Emma were changing. And Margot had approved. He knew because he felt no guilt. He didn't feel he was betraying his wife.

He checked his watch. It was almost nine o'clock. If he didn't get to the hotel soon, Emma would wonder what had happened to him. He looked around for the waiter but now he seemed to have disappeared completely. Mark swirled the remains of the wine in his glass and drank it off. He should have ordered a brandy when he finished his meal. It would have given him something to do while he waited for the damned bill to arrive. He took a deep breath and willed himself to be calm.

He had to declare his feelings to her. If he left it till they were back in Dublin, the opportunity might slip by. Now was the time to do it. He had no doubt how she would react. Unless she had been putting on an Oscar-winning performance for the past few weeks, he was certain she would be pleased. There was something of the romantic in Mark and he wished he could do this thing properly: present her with flowers and pop a bottle of champagne. But the occasion wasn't right. And besides, she had an awful lot of other things on her mind right now. It wasn't exactly the best time. But it was the *only* time. And now that he had made up his mind, he was determined to go ahead and do it.

The waiter had reappeared. Mark caught his eye and ordered a brandy and once again asked for the bill. The man returned a few minutes later with both. With a sigh of relief,

Mark knocked back the glass and felt a warm feeling spread up from his stomach. He took some notes from his pocket and left them on the plate, making sure to leave a decent tip. He left the restaurant and strode out into the balmy night air.

Immediately, he felt better. A confidence entered his step as he walked quickly through the maze of little streets towards the hotel. In a few minutes' time, his life could be changed completely. In his mind, he planned how he would do it. He would choose a quiet corner of the bar, a place where the lights were low. Hopefully the pianist would be playing something soft and romantic. He would wait till Emma was relaxed. And then he would tell her. Timing was crucial as it was in all things.

Ten minutes later, Hotel Alhambra came into view. There was a jaunty swing in Mark's step as he marched up to the door and sailed past the commissionaire into the magnificent interior. He hurried across the busy foyer till he came to the bar. And there, he saw something that made him stop dead in his tracks.

Emma was already seated at a table. But she wasn't alone. She was with a thin-faced man and their heads were locked together in intense conversation. Mark felt his confidence drain away. Who was this man? Why was she listening to him with such rapt attention?

Then another terrible thought came hurtling into his brain. Could it possibly be that he had a rival? Someone she hadn't told him about? He felt a sinking feeling in the pit of his stomach.

He turned on his heel and walked quickly away.

At ten minutes to eight, Claire was disturbed by a loud

banging on her apartment door. She opened it to find Maggie standing in the hallway. She was wearing a long-sleeved dress that covered her entire body from neck to ankles. In addition, she had put on a pair of fake diamond pendant earrings and a string of imitation pearls. Her face was ludicrously made up with mascara and eyeliner, her mouth a crimson bow of bright red lipstick. She looked like an outrageous pantomime dame.

"They're waiting," she said calmly.

Claire blinked. She hadn't really believed that Maggie would go through with her ridiculous plan to have Snuffy and Ricky compete for her hand. But obviously she had underestimated her neighbour's determination.

"Er, right," Claire managed to stammer. "You still want me to adjudicate?"

"Of course. You're the most important person. Apart from me, of course." She gave a modest smile and a little twirl so that her dress billowed out like a parachute. "What do you think of my outfit?"

"It's em . . . very original."

"I thought I should dress up for the occasion. It's not every day you have two fellas fighting over you. Now are you ready?"

"I think so."

"Then come on. They're all set up. And remember, you have to be fair. You can't be taking sides. This has to be totally in parcels."

"Impartial," Claire corrected her.

"Exactly. Everyone is equal."

Claire let out a loud sigh and locked her apartment door. Taking part in this madcap scheme was the very last thing she wanted to be doing right now. But she had promised Maggie and she couldn't let her down. She crossed the hallway and entered her neighbour's apartment. Immediately she was assailed by the smell of cooking food and the loud twanging of guitars. She had forgotten that Maggie had also suggested turning this daft event into a dinner party.

The living-room had been transformed into something resembling a recording studio. Amplifiers and loudspeakers were stacked against the walls, while electric cables ran the length of the room. Ricky, dressed in black shirt, black leather jacket and tight black jeans, sat brooding on a stool in one corner with a Gibson Thunderbird guitar in his lap. In the other corner, Snuffy and Kevin sat like a boxer and his trainer preparing for a bout. Kevin smiled and waved when he saw her, while Snuffy gave a shy grin.

In the centre of the floor, midway between the two contestants, another stool had been placed and at the top of the room a large armchair rested. Maggie pointed to the stool, indicating that this was where Claire should sit, while she plonked herself in the armchair with regal splendour and surveyed the proceedings like a queen reviewing her subjects.

"Now," she said. "We haven't got all night and the chilli con carne is nearly ready, so why don't we start?"

"Who'll go first?" Snuffy asked.

"You can," Maggie said.

"Okay," Snuffy said.

He lifted his Fender Jazz guitar, made sure that it was properly plugged in, struck a few chords and then launched into a blazing version of "Ain't Misbehavin'" that soon had the observers clapping along. When he had finished, he wiped the sweat from his face with the back of his hand. Everyone clapped, while Snuffy nodded across the room to Ricky.

He lifted his guitar and began playing "Blueberry Hill".

All the heads now turned in his direction and Claire felt like an umpire at a tennis match. When he had finished there was another round of applause and Snuffy launched into "Mustang Sally".

Claire was pleasantly surprised at the quality of the musicianship. She could see that she was going to find it extremely difficult to decide between them. Meanwhile, Ricky had started playing "Basin Street Blues", while she noticed that Snuffy was tapping his toes in rhythm and his fingers were twitching round his guitar.

And then the inevitable happened. Ricky finished playing and Snuffy began a spirited version of "I Hear You Knocking". Next minute, Ricky had joined in and the two guitarists were playing in unison.

The room erupted. When they had finished, Ricky immediately launched into "Honky Tonk Blues" and Snuffy joined him. Half an hour later they put down their guitars, exhausted by their efforts, and threw their arms round each other's shoulders.

"That was a hoot, man," Ricky said.

"Cool," Snuffy agreed.

Maggie sat in her armchair, shaking her head in disbelief.

"Bloody musicians," she said. "I should have known they'd end up jamming together."

After that, all idea of a competition was abandoned, which suited Claire perfectly because she would have found it impossible to decide between the pair of them. Instead, Maggie announced that the food was ready. Everyone trooped into the kitchen, where a big pot of chilli sat beside an equally large pot of rice. A bowl of salad, several baguettes and various bottles of wine and beer rested on the kitchen table.

"Why don't you fill up your plates and we'll eat on the balcony?" Maggie suggested. Soon they were all seated round a big table on the terrace, eating and drinking and listening to the sounds of nightlife from the street below. Ricky and Snuffy, who had started out as rivals, were now huddled together like bosom buddies at one end of the table. Kevin squeezed in beside Claire and Maggie.

"This chilli is delicious," he said. "Can you give me your recipe?"

"Sure," Maggie replied proudly.

"I might put it on the menu at Pedro's."

"Hey, that's a great idea. And wait till you taste my dessert. Gooseberry crumble. It's made from a recipe that's been in my family for generations. Did I ever tell you they were old farming folk from Kent?"

"I don't think so," Kevin said.

"Well, they were. Very close to the soil. That's where I get my down-to-earth personality from."

"Right," Kevin said, glancing in amusement towards Claire. "It all adds up."

Claire smiled at him. "How is Maria? Still off work?"

"No. Guess what? She came back today."

"I'll bet you were one glad guy to see her?"

Kevin grinned. "I think you can take that for granted."

Eventually they drifted back inside and there was some more jamming from the two musicians. The evening ended with Maggie doing impersonations of Kylie Minogue and Madonna, while Snuffy and Ricky accompanied her on guitar. It was almost two o'clock when Claire finally made her way back across the landing to her own apartment. Kevin came with her. At the door, he took her in his arms.

"Did you enjoy yourself tonight?"

"Enormously."

"So did I. But poor Maggie still hasn't decided between Ricky and Snuffy."

"Maybe they'll just have to share her," Claire said with a grin.

As she got undressed and prepared for bed, a thought came into her head. It had been a brilliant night. And if she took up Matthew Baker's offer of a job, there would be many more. Nights like this would stretch for ever.

31

"You want to talk about Pedro's Bar?" Emma asked of the man who stood before her flashing an ingratiating smile. She quickly took in the thin, cadaverous cheeks, the loud suit, the gold Rolex watch. He reminded her of a Mafia money launderer.

"That's right," Antonio replied. "I apologise most profusely for not making a formal appointment. I sent you a text message a few days ago. Perhaps you didn't receive it?"

"I did receive it," Emma said sharply. "And I decided to ignore it. How did you get my number?"

"From Miguel Martinez Sanchez. You gave it to him yourself. I am sorry if I have upset you. But the matter of Pedro's Bar is very urgent. I would be most grateful if you could spare me a few minutes of your very valuable time."

Emma hesitated. He had caught her completely unawares. She had been expecting Mark.

He sensed her uncertainty and wasted no time in pressing home his case. "What I have to say may be to your advantage."

Emma began to relent. Maybe it would be in her interest to talk to him after all.

"All right," she said. "I'm expecting someone to join me but we could talk while I wait."

"That will be entirely adequate, *Señorita* Dunne. We can talk here?" He indicated a quiet table in a corner of the bar.

Emma nodded her agreement and he politely ushered her before him and pulled out a chair for her to sit down. Immediately a waiter was at their side.

"May I offer you a drink?"

"I'll have a glass of dry sherry."

"That will be two glasses," Antonio said to the waiter, who bowed and hurried away again.

"This is a very fine hotel," Antonio said, stretching his legs and looking round the room. "One of the best in Fuengirola. I trust you are comfortable here?"

"Very," Emma said tersely.

"And you are enjoying your holiday?"

"Yes, indeed."

"That is good. We always like our visitors to have a good time. They act as ambassadors whenever they return to their own countries. Is that not so?"

She wished he would cut out the formalities and get down to business. But just then, the waiter returned with their drinks. Antonio left a €20 note on the tray and waved the man away.

He raised his glass in a toast. "Your good health!"

"And yours," Emma said. She took a sip of sherry and put down the glass. "Now what is it you wanted to discuss with me, *Señor* Hernandez?"

"I have to tell you that I am concerned with the affairs of Pedro's Bar. As you may know, I was once the proprietor.

It was I who developed it. When my father owned it, it was just a hut, a shack that sold sandwiches and water. I developed it into a thriving business."

"Yes," Emma replied. "I did know that."

"Unfortunately it has been allowed to run down. It makes me sad to see the way it has deteriorated. Are you aware that my mother, who is supposed to be the manager, has not been at work for almost a week?"

"I understood that your aunt was ill."

"Indeed, she is very ill. She has been taken to hospital. The bar is being run by the young Irishman, *Señor* Joyce. He does his best, of course, but it is all very unsatisfactory."

"I know that things are not as they should be," Emma countered, "but you must appreciate that I have just taken over the ownership. And I am aware that the previous proprietor, Conor Delaney, took no interest in the bar."

Antonio looked sad. "That, alas, is true. He only came here to collect his profits. It is not the proper way to conduct business, *señorita*." He looked at her slyly. "One cannot run a busy bar from a long distance. It is a recipe for disaster. To run a bar successfully, one must be always on the spot. That is my opinion. And I am now the proprietor of a very successful restaurant, so I know what I am talking about."

Emma studied him carefully. He was after something but what was it exactly?

"I hear you have been to talk to Miguel about the taxes," he said softly.

"Your information is correct," Emma said. Antonio was turning out to be remarkably well informed.

He lowered his voice. "I will speak to you in confidence. Miguel is not a very reliable individual."

"But he was your accountant," Emma pointed out.

331

"Didn't you appoint him when you owned the bar? I understood that he simply continued when Conor Delaney took over?"

Antonio didn't bat an eyelid. "That is true. But then I was only starting off in business. I was inexperienced and he was recommended to me by a friend." He took another sip of sherry. "Did you find the information you were seeking?"

"No," Emma said.

"I am not surprised."

"But I succeeded elsewhere."

"Yes?"

She wondered how much she should tell him. He appeared to know most of it already.

"I can tell you there are considerable debts on the bar. It appears that no taxes have been paid for many years. As you might expect, I am not very pleased."

"*Madre de Dios!*" Antonio said with vehemence. "This is outrageous! This proves what I have been saying to you. Conor Delaney takes no interest in the bar and this is what happens. What are you going to do about it?"

"I haven't decided."

He took a deep breath. "I feel ashamed. This is not the way a respectable person like you should be treated. And I also feel sad that Pedro's Bar has come to this situation. When I sold the bar to *Señor* Delaney it was a thriving business and now . . ." He made a dismissive gesture. "Now it is a poor shadow of itself. It is becoming a dump. Soon someone will open another beach bar and steal away the remaining business. It is a pity to see that little place come to such a low state. It once had such great potential." He looked directly at Emma. "Now you can see the truth of what I said. To run a business successfully, you must always be there. It cannot be done any other way." He paused.

"Forgive me for being so inquisitive, *señorita*, but may I ask if you intend to come here to Fuengirola to live permanently?"

"No," she said. "That is not my intention."

"Then how do you propose to run the bar?"

In a matter of minutes, Antonio had succeeded in getting right to the heart of the matter.

"That has yet to be decided."

There was silence. Antonio fiddled with his sherry glass.

"If I may be permitted to make a suggestion, *Señorita* Dunne?"

"Yes?" Emma said.

"Again, this is strictly in confidence. If you were to consider selling Pedro's Bar, I might be interested in buying it."

Emma sat bolt upright. "Even though there are debts?"

Antonio waved his hands. "It is rarely in business that everything is completely straightforward. Always there are problems. I am sure we could come to some arrangement. If you agree to sell, you will not find me unreasonable."

This was amazing. He was offering the solution to her problem. If he bought the bar, she would be free to concentrate on the really important business of Herr Braun's offer.

"But why would you want to buy it?"

Antonio smiled. "Because I have a nostalgia for the old place. Maybe I am foolish but it was my first venture in business and I would be sorry to see it fail. Also, I am here all the time. I can keep an eye on it. I can make sure that it runs properly."

Emma quickly tried to think. His offer had taken her completely by surprise. Was it a serious approach or was Antonio playing some deeper game?

"What would you consider a fair offer?" she asked.

"Fifty thousand euro?"

She did a quick calculation. Fifty thousand euro would just about clear her initial debt from Conor Delaney and the legal costs she would incur. The slate would be wiped clean.

"I have to tell you that the unpaid taxes could be as high as € 60,000. You would also assume responsibility for those."

Antonio showed no reaction. "I have already taken that into consideration. I said I would not be unreasonable. Do you find my offer acceptable?"

"I have to say it is a fair offer. But there is one more thing."

"Yes? You may speak freely."

"I would require guarantees about the existing staff."

Immediately, his face clouded over. "How do you mean?"

"Pedro's Bar provides your mother's sole means of income. And she has responsibility for your sick aunt."

"You do not need to worry about her," Antonio said dismissively. "I will look after her."

"But I *do* worry about her. If I agree to sell, I want her job to be guaranteed. And those of the other staff."

For a moment, Antonio looked uncomfortable but the smile quickly returned to his face. "All right. If that is what you want, it can be arranged."

Emma felt a wave of relief pass over her. She had managed to solve the problem of Pedro's Bar and on her own terms. She felt as if an enormous weight had suddenly been lifted from her shoulders. But she kept her feelings to herself.

"In that case, I think we can proceed. I will instruct my solicitor to prepare the necessary papers."

Antonio was beaming. He opened his wallet and took out a business card.

"That is my address. Your solicitor can contact me there."

Emma took the card and, as she turned to place it in her bag, she saw Mark entering the bar. She quickly stood up. "I must leave you now. There is someone I have to see."

Mark had now turned away and was walking out of the bar.

She hurried after him, calling out his name.

"Mark!" she cried. "Wait for me!"

32

At the sound of Emma's voice, Mark immediately stopped. She caught up with him at the top of the steps leading into the gardens.

"Where are you going?" she asked, out of breath.

"I was just about to take a stroll. I saw you were engaged and, rather than interrupt you, I decided to leave you to get on with your little chat."

"Do you know who that man was?" she asked.

"I've no idea," Mark said coolly.

"Antonio, Maria's son."

At the sound of the name, Mark wrinkled his nose in disgust. But Emma could barely restrain herself. "And, Mark, you'll never believe what's happened. He has just offered to buy Pedro's Bar from me."

His eyes opened wide. "*What?*"

"He wants to buy Pedro's."

"Does he know about the debts?"

"Yes. I told him. I think he knew already."

She threw her arms around him and hugged him tight. "Isn't that fantastic news? It means I don't have to worry about it any more. Now I can concentrate on the offer for Hi-Speed Printing."

"But what about the staff? What's going to happen to them?"

"He has agreed to keep them on."

"My God, Emma, that *is* fantastic news! It sounds like you've got everything you wanted."

"Including the price. He has offered €50,000, which will cover my initial debt from Conor Delaney."

"Oh, Emma, I'm really delighted for you," Mark said. "You've been worried about Pedro's Bar from the first day I met you."

"And now I've found a solution."

They strolled out into the gardens. A strong scent of flowers filled the night air. There was a bench nearby. Mark took her hand.

"Let's sit down. There's something I want to say to you."

"Oh? Something pleasant?" she asked as they sat.

"That remains to be seen." He cleared his throat and then began. "We've been seeing an awful lot of each other in the last few weeks."

"Yes, we have."

"And I've enjoyed every moment of it. You're a wonderful companion. You're so lively and full of fun. You're so beautiful. You're so intelligent. You're —"

"Stop," she said and held up her hand.

Mark's face immediately fell, as if he had just been slapped.

"Before you go any further," said Emma, "there's something I want to say to *you*."

"Yes?" he asked apprehensively.

"I've been considering this for some time."

"What?"

"And I've been meaning to tell you."

"For God's sake, what is it?"

"I think I've fallen in love with you."

For a moment, Mark found himself lost for words. Then he flung his arms around her and held her tight.

"You've fallen in love with me?"

"Yes."

"But that's what I was going to say to you."

Emma tossed back her blonde hair and laughed. "But I got in first."

"So you did, you minx!"

He held her close and his lips encircled hers. Next moment, they were locked in a passionate embrace while overhead a myriad stars twinkled in the bright heavens.

Claire stood at the window of her apartment, a mug of coffee in her hand, and gazed down at the street below. Her mind was in turmoil. Matthew Baker was back and his arrival had disrupted the smooth tempo of her life. Despite all her reservations, she was sorely tempted to accept his job offer.

He was offering her a position here on the Costa doing something she enjoyed, along with a good salary, expenses, commission, a company car and the prospect of a directorship. Even her mother would be impressed. If Claire had sat down and written a description of her dream job, she could hardly have come up with anything better.

Yet she still had serious doubts. She was not convinced that everything was as it seemed. Part of her suspected that the job might simply be a ploy to lure her back again. She wasn't sure if she could trust him. And what was much worse, she wasn't sure if she could trust herself.

This was what worried her the most. She had been completely taken aback by her own reaction to the meeting yesterday in Hotel Victoria. She had gone along expecting to meet the liar and deceiver who had destroyed their relationship and betrayed her with another woman. But when she saw him sitting there in the lobby, she had immediately been transported back to the old days. She had seen the Matthew she had fallen in love with, the dashing figure who had stolen her heart. He looked so smart and handsome that he had taken her breath away. Claire was forced to admit that, deep down, part of her had never stopped loving him.

If she went to work with him, she could find herself under pressure every single day. And she knew how persuasive he could be when he wanted. She knew the way he could turn on the charm: the invitations to lunch and dinner, the flowers, the compliments, the little presents. She would have to be constantly on her guard lest she gave in. Because, even if he was no longer in love with her, she could easily fall in love with him all over again.

And where would all this leave her relationship with Kevin? It would be impossible.

What she needed was advice, a trusting friend she could confide in. And fortunately there was someone on hand. She finished her coffee, turned away from the window and walked into the kitchen. Her mobile phone was lying where she had left it on the table. She took it up and rang Anne Ryan.

"Hi," she said when Anne came on the line. "It's me. I hope I didn't waken you up?"

"Are you joking? It's nine o'clock. What do you take us

for? A bunch of ravers who party all night and sleep all day?"

Claire found herself smiling. "It's just that I never know what time to ring people. Some of my friends don't get out of bed till noon."

"Not us, dear. Those days are long gone. Pat has been up since seven o'clock. He's working on a painting about the sunrise. Nature coming alive and all that stuff. We both love the early morning. It's the best part of the day, if you ask me."

"Are you going to be at home for the rest of the morning?"

"Of course. Where else would I be?"

"I was thinking of paying you a visit."

"Well, that would be lovely. And you can stay for lunch."

"I'd like that. I want to ask your advice about something."

"What is it? You've got my curiosity aroused."

"I'll tell you all about it when I arrive. You can expect me around ten o'clock."

"Can't you even give me a clue?" Anne pleaded.

"Afraid not. You'll just have to wait. Byeee!"

Claire switched off her phone. She was lucky to have friends like the Ryans. At least she knew that whatever Anne was going to tell her would be good advice born of long experience and shrewd observation.

She locked the apartment door and started down the stairs. As she passed Maggie's apartment, she could hear the gentle sound of snoring. She was still sleeping soundly after last night's revelry. It took Claire fifteen minutes to reach the station, where she discovered that the bus for Marbella was leaving shortly. Twenty minutes later, she was getting off at La Cala.

The Ryans lived in a bungalow near the beach. When

Claire arrived just after ten o'clock, she found Anne pruning roses in the garden. She left down the secateurs and wrapped Claire in her arms.

"It's so good to see you again. I was just doing a little bit of gardening before it gets too hot. Come in and have something to drink."

She led Claire into the cool interior of the house.

"Pat still painting on the beach?"

"Yes. He should be back shortly. In the meantime, you and I can have a quiet chinwag. Now what would you like? Tea? Coffee? Maybe a cold drink?"

"A cold drink would be nice."

"I've got orange juice."

"Perfect."

Anne poured two glasses and led Claire to the patio at the back of the house, where they had views over the ocean.

"Now," she said when they were both settled. "I haven't been able to relax since I got your call. When people come to me for advice, it usually means one thing: an affair of the heart."

Claire smiled. "You're a clairvoyant as well as everything else. But that's only part of it."

"Spill the beans," Anne said. "I'm all ears."

For the next twenty minutes, Claire outlined her dilemma: how she would love to take the job that Matthew Baker had offered but was concerned about the consequences. When she had finished, Anne pursed her lips and slowly drew her hand across her chin.

"It's a tricky one."

"The job would be perfect. I know I could do it blindfolded. And it would mean I could stay on in Fuengirola to be with Kevin."

"So you're serious about Kevin?"

Claire nodded her head. "We've been seeing a lot of each other in the last couple of weeks."

"Does he feel the same way?"

"I think so."

"And if you turn down the job? What would you do then?"

"I hadn't thought that far ahead. I suppose I would have to return to Dublin."

"And Kevin? What would he do? Would he go with you?"

"We haven't discussed it. I only got the job offer yesterday. Kevin doesn't even know about it."

"Do you think it's something you could discuss with him?"

"Perhaps."

"Well, it seems to me that's one thing you should do. There is another possibility."

"Yes?"

"You could have a frank discussion with Matthew Baker and tell him that you will take the job but only on the strict understanding that it is a purely business arrangement. You could mention your relationship with Kevin if you like, to let him know you're serious."

"You don't know this guy. That wouldn't stop him if he's still interested. He might even see it as a challenge." Claire lowered her eyes. "If you want to know the truth . . . I'm not sure how long I could resist him. I'm terrified that I might even be the one coming on to him. I think part of me is still in love with him."

Anne threw her arms around Claire. "Oh, you poor dear! Listen, Claire. You have clearly been hurt by this man. And you obviously don't trust him. But if you ever go back to him, he'll do it again. Men like Matthew Baker don't change."

"I know that," Claire agreed. "I know I mustn't. But the job – the opportunity to stay here. What should I do?"

"Well, I know what I would do. But I can't live your life for you. It seems plain to me that you have to decide which of these two men you really want, find out if he feels the same – and then rule the other out of your life. If you want Kevin, that means you can't take the job, whatever the advantages."

For the next twenty minutes, Claire helped Anne to prepare lunch, chopping vegetables, making salad, slicing bread, laying the table on the patio, where they planned to eat. At midday, they heard the sound of Pat's footsteps in the hall. He came through the house and out to where the women were sitting.

"Claire! How good to see you. To what do we owe this unexpected pleasure?"

He put down his painting equipment and embraced her warmly.

"She was looking for some advice about a job she's been offered," Anne said, glancing quickly at Claire.

"What? Here?"

"Yes," Claire said. "Guess what? I'd be selling property."

"Well, why not? That's your forte." He moved a chair into the shade and sat down.

"You could do worse than come back here to live. If nothing else, we would see you a lot more often." He took off his straw hat and fanned his face. "That beach was pretty hot this morning. If it hadn't been for the breeze, I would never have stuck it. So, are you going to take this job or not?"

"I'm not sure."

"Pay and conditions okay?"

"Oh, yes."

"So what's the problem? You always liked the Costa."

Before Claire could reply, Anne intervened. "Who would like a drink before lunch?"

"Gin and tonic for me," Pat said.

"Claire?"

"Could I have a glass of wine, please?"

Anne went to get the drinks.

"There are lots of attractions here," Pat said. "Listen to that sound."

Claire looked confused. "What sound?"

A big grin spread over his deeply tanned face. "That's the point. There *is* no sound. Complete silence. It's so peaceful here. And the sun shines all day long. But you know all this, Claire. You've been here before. You know how pleasant life can be on the Costa."

They sat around the table under the shade of a giant umbrella and ate a delicious lunch of lamb casserole and salad washed down by a local rosé wine. Pat talked about his paintings. After the success of the Malaga exhibition, he had been invited to take part in another one in Marbella in a month's time.

"He's beginning to get recognised," Anne said, "but he just won't promote himself."

"You're missing the point," he retorted playfully. "It's not about recognition. Or money. It's about relaxation and creative satisfaction. I don't paint for exhibitions. I do it for myself."

They chatted till the sun grew so strong that even the shade of the umbrella wasn't enough to protect them. Reluctantly, they were forced to abandon the patio and move indoors.

"I'd better be going back," Claire said at last. "My friends will be wondering what has happened to me.

344

Pat kissed her goodbye. "Be sure to let us know what you decide."

Anne saw her to the door. "Would you like me to drive you to the bus stop?"

"It's all right. I don't mind walking. Anyway, you've done enough already. Thank you for a lovely lunch. And for the good advice."

"Remember what I told you," Anne said as she hugged her close.

Claire got a seat at the back of the bus and watched as the coast went flashing by on the road to Fuengirola. Anne was right, as usual. She had to decide between solid, reliable Kevin and the dashing Matthew. And she knew whichever one she chose would decide the future course of her life.

33

Now that Maria was back at work, Kevin had resumed his morning swim. He realised how much he had missed it in the recent stress-filled days. It was the only exercise he got, unless you included pulling pints at Pedro's Bar and washing dishes after the hungry hordes had departed. But now things were beginning to settle down again. Maria had taken up her management duties once more and had even begun to smile and Rosario appeared to be making good progress in hospital. It was a stroke of luck that he had decided to call at her apartment that day – otherwise, who knows what might have happened.

But there was still one dark cloud hanging over them. They didn't know what Emma planned to do about the bar. In fact, none of them had seen her for almost a week. Kevin assumed she was still struggling with the accounts and that crook of an accountant. He wished her well. Dealing with him would be like wrestling with a crocodile.

But the bar was ticking over and Maria's return had

relieved some of the pressure on Snuffy and himself. They had even managed to get some time off. Kevin had used the opportunity to tidy up the apartment and get some laundry done. Snuffy had struck up a friendship with Ricky Blaine and there was even talk of him joining his band, the Black Pimpernels. This evening, they were planning to take Maggie on a trip to Puerto Banus to check out entertainment possibilities in the bars down there.

He smiled to himself. Maggie now had two admirers. But instead of fighting over her, they were all getting on like Mormons. Which brought him neatly to his own situation, he thought as he swam towards the rocks at the edge of the beach where he had left his towel. Recently, his relationship with Claire had moved up a notch. Now he was seeing her every day. They were becoming inseparable. And this was a strange experience for someone who had never been so close to a woman in his entire life.

Sure, he'd had plenty of girlfriends. When he was playing with the band, he had got used to girls throwing themselves at him. He could have had a different woman every night if he'd felt like it. But this feeling for Claire was entirely different. He found it difficult to understand. All he knew was that she seemed to have invaded his consciousness to the point where he could think of nothing else. He was becoming besotted with her.

But there was a problem. What was going to happen when Claire's vacation was over and she had to go home? Would he follow her back to Dublin? Would she want him to? If she did, it would be a big step. It would mean giving up the cosy life he had built up here. But if that was what it took to hold onto her, Kevin was prepared to do it. He had thought it over and made up his mind. Claire was special. He wasn't going to let her go.

He lifted the towel and vigorously rubbed himself down. Then he pulled on his tracksuit bottoms and vest and made his way up the beach to his apartment. He always felt good after a brisk swim. It was the perfect way to start the day. Five minutes later, he was opening the door of his apartment and letting himself in.

Snuffy had already left for work so the place was empty. Kevin had a hot shower and got dressed, then went into the kitchen and put on the kettle to make tea. This was another of his daily routines. While he had no problem drinking coffee during the day, he had to begin his mornings with a nice cup of tea. He had even managed to locate a little shop in Los Boliches where he could buy packets of Barry's Gold Label. He smiled while he poured the hot water onto the teabag and waited for it to draw. Some old habits died hard.

While he drank his tea, his thoughts once more returned to Claire. He wondered if he should ring her but decided not to. She would probably call at the bar later in the day. Instead, he sent her a simple text message which read: *Thinking about you*. Then he finished his breakfast, locked up the apartment and let himself out. Twenty minutes later, he was approaching the bar.

As he drew closer, he sensed something unusual. Snuffy was serving some customers. But he didn't have his usual chirpy grin. Instead, there was a dull frown on his face. And there was no sign of Maria.

"What's going on?" Kevin asked anxiously, as he drew Snuffy aside.

Snuffy shrugged.

"Where's Maria?"

"Out the back."

"Has something happened?"

Snuffy pulled a face. "You'd better ask her yourself."

Kevin walked quickly round to the back of the bar. Maria was sitting in a chair on the sand. She had a handkerchief in her hand and was quietly weeping.

He squatted down beside her and took her hand. "What's the matter, Maria? Why are you crying?"

She turned her red eyes to him. "Antonio rang me this morning."

"Yes?"

"It is very bad news."

"What is Maria? What did he say?"

The old lady burst out sobbing. "He says he is buying Pedro's Bar from *Señorita* Dunne!"

Emma came awake slowly to find the room flooded with sunlight and Mark sleeping peacefully in the bed beside her. She sat up and gazed at him. She ran a hand lightly over his naked back. The muscles were taut as coiled springs, his biceps bulged and his shoulders were powerful. Before last night, she hadn't realised just how fit he was.

That wasn't the only pleasant surprise that had awaited her when they finally fell into bed together. Mark had turned out to be a skilled and patient lover. He had slowly undressed her, all the while covering her body with kisses, which increased in intensity till she was crazed with passion. By the time it was over and they both lay exhausted in the twisted sheets, Emma had experienced a pleasure she had never known before.

She thought of those moments now as she watched him sleep. He appeared so peaceful, his breathing soft and measured. She looked at his face, tanned and handsome, the jaw set firm, the little line of stubble that cast a dark shadow on his cheeks. Emma instinctively knew that she had found the man who would be her companion for the rest of her life.

As she watched him, Mark stirred. He raised a fist and rubbed his eyes.

"Good morning," he said, blinking in the sunlight. "What time is it?"

"Almost ten o'clock."

"Why were you watching me?"

"I was admiring you. I was wondering how you keep so fit."

Mark smiled. "Exercise," he said.

"I was also thinking how fortunate I am to have found you."

"The feeling is mutual."

"We are a lucky couple, aren't we?" She ran a finger playfully through the hairs on his chest. "And to think, if I hadn't met you that morning at Pedro's Bar, we wouldn't be here together now. Did you sleep well?"

"Perfectly."

"So you're well rested?"

"Yes."

"And your stamina has returned?"

"I hope so," Mark said.

"Do you know what's on my mind?"

"Let me guess," he said, pulling her down beside him. "Would it have anything to do with a three letter word beginning with S and ending with X?"

Afterwards, she rang room service for breakfast.

"What do you want to order?" she asked as she held the phone in her hand.

"Just coffee and hot rolls."

"We'll make that two."

While she waited for breakfast, she went into the bathroom

and ran the shower. Apart from her joy at being with Mark, she would have been feeling good this morning. At last she appeared to have solved the problem of Pedro's Bar. And she was coming round to the view that she would accept the offer for Hi-Speed Printing. But not until she had talked again with her father and wrung some more concessions from Herr Braun.

It was Mark who had helped her to make up her mind.

"What have you got to lose?" he argued. "It's a fantastic offer. You'll have more than enough to live on for the rest of your life. And if you ever feel the urge to go back into business, you will have adequate start-up capital."

"What are you going to do?" she asked.

"I might follow your example and sell Chambers Creative Artists. When Margot was alive, I kept promising myself that I would slow down. But I never did. It's one of the big regrets of my life. And now that I've found you, I don't intend to make the same mistake twice."

As she stood under the shower, Emma thought of all the benefits the sale would bring. She would be released from the stress of running the company. She would have financial security. She would have time and money to do the things she wanted. For the first time in her life, she would be entirely free.

There would be many more days like this one, relaxing and enjoying life with Mark at her side. Perhaps she might even buy a house out here, where they could come whenever the cold, dreary Irish winters got too much to bear. It would be idyllic.

But her thoughts were disturbed by the loud ringing of the phone. She heard Mark lift the receiver and answer it. A moment later, he was knocking on the bathroom door.

"It's for you," he announced.

She turned off the shower and wrapped a towel around her.

"Who is it?" she whispered as she emerged from the bathroom.

"Kevin," he whispered back.

Emma took the phone, looking slightly confused.

"Hi," she said.

"Forgive me for calling you like this," Kevin said.

"What is it?"

"I've got a bit of a crisis on my hands and I don't know what to do."

"What sort of crisis?"

"I've just arrived at Pedro's. Maria is very upset. She's just been told that Antonio is buying the bar."

352

34

Claire still had not made up her mind. All night, she had lain in bed, tossing and turning, trying to decide whether to accept Matthew Baker's offer. She had analysed the situation from every possible angle and still she couldn't reach a decision. Now she had run out of time. Matthew Baker would be returning to London later today. Either she told him now or he would make other arrangements.

She sat at the kitchen table and clenched her fists in frustration. Why did life have to be so complicated? She had come here for a simple holiday and instead she had been plunged into a terrible dilemma – accept the job offer with all the attendant risks or go back to Dublin in a few weeks' time without Kevin.

If she took the job she could be putting herself under tremendous pressure. If Matthew was still interested in her, she feared that sooner or later he was bound to wear her down. Particularly because she was still attracted to him.

So did this mean she didn't love Kevin?

"Damn Matthew Baker!" she cried to the four walls of the little kitchen. If only he wasn't involved, it would all be so simple. The job sounded brilliant. She would be doing something she enjoyed and getting well paid for it. She would be able to remain here on the Costa. In time, if they were still together, she and Kevin could get an apartment together. She would be able to make a new life for herself. Everything would be wonderful.

She thought of Anne's advice. The problem was, she didn't really have time to find out how she felt or what either Matthew's or Kevin's feelings and intentions were. Too many unanswered questions to make such a momentous decision.

What was she going to do? Her mobile phone lay on the table beside her. She opened her purse and took out the business card that Matthew Baker had given her. Slowly her fingers reached for the phone and she dialled the number. After a few moments, she heard his suave tones come on the line.

"It's me, Claire."

Immediately, she caught the note of satisfaction in his voice. "Claire! I was wondering when you were going to call."

"I've been thinking about your job offer," she said, a lump rising in her throat.

"Yes?"

"I'd like to take it."

A few minutes later she switched off the phone and felt her heart hammering in her breast. She had done it! She had made her decision! She noticed that her hand was trembling. Matthew had been delighted. He had suggested that they meet for lunch in Felipe's at half twelve to discuss the details. She glanced at her watch. It was now almost eleven o'clock. She had better think about getting ready. Oh, please, God, let me have made the right choice, she prayed as she rose from the kitchen table.

Just then, she heard a loud hammering on the apartment door. She opened it to find Maggie standing in the hallway in her dressing-gown.

"I've just made some French toast," she said excitedly. "I want you to come over and try it."

Claire was about to refuse when something made her change her mind. Maggie had probably gone to a lot of trouble to make the toast and right now Claire needed nothing more than some friendly female conversation.

"I'd be delighted," she said, grabbing the apartment keys and locking the door.

In Maggie's kitchen, she was presented with a mountain of toast. She took a piece and nibbled at it. It was very good but if she was going to do justice to her lunch in Felipe's, she needed to go easy.

"Don't tell me this is another of your family's secret recipes?" she said.

"More or less. With a few little additions of my own. Do you like it?"

"It's delicious," Claire replied, licking her fingers and rolling her eyes.

"Try it with honey," Maggie said, pushing a jar across the table.

"I've already had breakfast!" Claire protested.

"A little bit of French toast won't do you any harm. Go on!" She pushed the honey closer.

"And I've got to meet someone for lunch."

"You can skip dessert. Here, would you like me to spread it for you?"

Claire realised she was trapped. There was no way she could escape from Maggie's apartment without surrendering to her neighbour's demands. She took another piece of toast and smeared it with honey. It tasted heavenly.

"My God, Maggie! This is truly spectacular."

Maggie smiled triumphantly. "You can have as much as you like. I made loads."

"No. This is enough. Honest."

Claire tried to make the toast last while they chatted about Maggie's visit this evening to Puerto Banus. Ricky had phoned earlier to say he had secured an audition for her at the Pig and Whistle pub.

"I'm a little nervous," she confessed. "The clientele down there are a bit on the snooty side."

"But you've got absolutely nothing to be nervous about. You'll slay them."

"You think so?"

"I'd bet on it." Claire glanced nervously at the clock on the wall. "I've really got to go now or I'm going to be late."

"Can't you stay a little bit longer? I love talking to you. You're always so sensible."

"I love talking to you too. But if I don't go now, I'm going to be late for my appointment." She stood up. "Thank you for the toast, Maggie. You must make it again some time."

"I'll make it tomorrow if you like. And we can continue our conversation. Maybe you can help me decide what I'm going to do about these two fellas in my life."

"Tomorrow would be too soon. Your toast is the sort of thing you treat yourself to very rarely. You know, like champagne or caviar."

She edged gingerly towards the door.

"Wait!" Maggie commanded.

Claire stopped dead.

Maggie tore a strip of cling film, wrapped it round the remaining toast and thrust it into Claire's hands.

"Take it with you. You can eat it as a snack later."

Back in her own apartment, Claire frantically set about getting ready for the lunch. First she had to have a shower. She wondered if she should wash her hair. Did she have time?

Ten minutes later, when she emerged dripping from the bathroom, it was half past eleven. What was she going to wear? She hadn't come prepared for something like this. After another search through her limited wardrobe, she decided that this time she should wear something that would look distinctly businesslike, that couldn't be possibly construed as flirtation. But the clothes she had with her weren't those kind of clothes. Eventually she made do with a pair of black palazzo trousers with a white long-sleeved shirt. She tied her hair back. A gold chain, discreet gold earrings. That would have to do as her "business" outfit.

By twelve o'clock, she was ready. She gave herself a final look-over in the bathroom mirror. She would pass. She locked the apartment, hurried down the stairs and caught a cab at the end of the street. Twenty minutes later, she was being greeted by the cheerful head waiter at Felipe's.

The restaurant was beginning to fill up but Matthew hadn't arrived. She was shown to a table near the window, presented with a menu and asked if she would like something to drink.

"I'll have tonic water and ice, please."

She opened the menu. She realised she was feeling quite nervous. To cheer herself up, she thought of the last occasion she was here. It was with Mark Chambers on the very first evening she arrived. That had been a happy, carefree night. She'd worn her swirly red dress and her pashmina. She remembered that she still owed Mark an apology for her brusque manner the last time they met at Pedro's Bar. But she hadn't seen him since. She wondered what had happened to him and how he was enjoying his holiday.

She opened the menu and stared at the printed page. She had no appetite. It wasn't just the French toast she had been forced to eat at Maggie's. It was the thought of meeting Matthew Baker. There were butterflies in her stomach.

Just then, the waiter arrived with her drink and, immediately after, Matthew came striding in. He looked superb in a cream blazer, dark-brown trousers with a knife-edge crease, a coffee-coloured shirt and chocolate tie – all of which screamed designer label. An image of Kevin in his shorts and vest flashed into her mind.

Matthew slung his jacket over the back of the chair opposite her, then bent to kiss her gently on the cheek before sitting down.

"Sorry for being late," he apologised. "I've just spent the morning in negotiations for a new office suite. I'm looking at a place on the seafront near the port."

"Sounds like an ideal location," Claire heard herself say.

"It is. But I'm trying to get them to reduce the rent." He smiled across the table. "You look terrific, Claire. But then you always did."

She found herself blushing. "Thank you."

"I can't tell you how pleased I am that you're coming on board."

"I'm excited too. I hope we can work well together.

"Of course we can. But before we get down to details, why don't we order something to eat? What would you like?"

"I'll just have the prawn salad."

"Oh, you can do better than that! We're in the best fish restaurant in Fuengirola and all you want is a prawn salad?"

"I'm not particularly hungry," Claire explained.

"That's a shame. Something to drink?"

"I'll have some white wine."

He reached across and playfully tickled her chin. The action immediately made Claire recoil.

"That's my girl. Once we get settled in, we'll have lots of these lunches together. You've no idea how much I'm looking forward to working with you again, Claire."

The waiter took their order and returned with the wine. Matthew poured two glasses and raised his in a toast.

"To a fruitful working partnership!" He clinked his glass against hers and raised it to his lips. "We're going to be fantastic together, Claire. Just like the old days."

"Can we talk about the terms?" she asked.

"Sure," he said. "What do you want to know?"

"Let's start with salary."

He suddenly became serious. He fidgeted with his cuffs. "I was thinking of €20,000 to begin."

Claire thought her ears had deceived her. She was earning almost three times that amount in Dublin. "*Twenty thousand?*"

"It's only a starting salary," he said quickly. "Just till we get up and running."

"But I'm earning far more back home."

"This is Fuengirola, Claire. Everything is cheaper here." He then rushed to reassure her. "You'll earn more in time. But I have to keep costs down at the beginning." He smiled. "I might be able to squeeze €25,000. And don't forget you'll also be earning commission."

"But that's not guaranteed."

He suddenly reached across and took her hand. His blue eyes gazed deeply into hers.

"Let's not fall out. I see this as much more than a job. I see it as the beginning of a partnership. It really excites me.

Once I get established, I'll be able to pay you much more. We'll have a wonderful time together."

Just then, he was interrupted by the ringing of his phone. He let go of her hand and pressed the phone to his ear.

"Why, hello," he said, sitting back in his chair and grinning widely.

Claire watched him with growing unease. This lunch was beginning to confirm her worst fears. She listened as he chatted away on the phone.

"Weather is beautiful as always. No, I'm not working too hard. I'm just about to have lunch, in fact." He looked across the table at Claire and winked. "Who with? Just somebody who's interested in a job."

At last, he finished the conversation and switched off the phone.

"Who was that?" Claire asked.

"My secretary in London. Just keeping me up to date on developments."

Claire felt her stomach churn.

Matthew reached across and stroked her arm. "Incidentally, I was wondering. I have to stay on for a few more days. You don't have a spare bed at your place, do you? It would only be for a couple of nights?"

Suddenly, Claire was overwhelmed with loathing. She had made a ghastly mistake. Matthew Baker was still a lying philanderer, probably stringing along some poor woman back in London while he attempted to persuade Claire to work with him for peanuts. And now he was trying to inveigle himself back into her bed within ten minutes of meeting her.

She smacked his hand away. "You haven't changed one bit, have you?"

Immediately, the colour drained from his face. "What do you mean?"

"You're still the same lying bastard I used to know."

He tried to smile. "I don't know what you're talking about."

"Yes, you do. You're a disgusting reptile puffed up with your own self-importance. You think you can come here and buy me a glass of wine and get me to work for nothing while you try to seduce me as a bonus. You've learned nothing, have you?"

Matthew Baker's mouth fell open in shock.

She stood up and tossed her napkin on the table. "You can stick your job. I'm afraid you've picked the wrong woman."

She turned on her heel and strode out of the restaurant, her heels clacking loudly on the floor.

Heads turned to stare.

At his table, Matthew Baker's face was burning scarlet.

35

Once Emma and Mark were dressed, they set off at once for Pedro's Bar. When they arrived, it was almost midday and a crowd of thirsty customers was milling around the counter while Snuffy struggled valiantly to serve them. Mark caught his attention and asked him where they could find Kevin and Maria.

"They're round the back," Snuffy said, indicating with his thumb.

They followed his directions and came across a distraught Maria, sitting in a chair while Kevin held her hand and tried to comfort her. Mark took one look at the scene. "Let's all go across the road and have a coffee while we try to sort this out," he said.

It was the same café where he had first taken Emma. They sat at a pavement table and a brisk waiter quickly appeared to take their order.

"Now," Emma said in a soothing voice to Maria, "tell me exactly what happened."

The old lady looked at her and wiped her eyes with a large handkerchief.

"This morning, I get a phone call from my son, Antonio. He say he has news for me that I won't like. When I ask him, he tell me you are selling him Pedro's Bar." She stopped and looked at Emma.

"Go on," Emma said.

"Antonio say that things are going to change. He say the bar is not being run properly and nobody is in charge. I tell him I am in charge. He laughs and say I am an old woman and should be at home looking after Rosario." She began weeping again.

"What else did he say, Maria?"

"Nothing else. But I know when he buys the bar, he will get rid of me. He will hire new manager. There will be no more job for me." She turned her pleading eyes towards Emma. "What am I going to do, Emma? Why does he behave like this to me? He is my only son. Always I have been good to him."

Emma bit her lip. She glanced at Mark for support. "I don't know why he behaves like this, Maria. But nothing has been decided yet. I am still the owner of Pedro's Bar."

"But is it true what he say? Is it true you are selling to him?"

Emma took a deep breath. "It is true that I have reached an agreement with him about a price and about certain conditions. One of them is that the existing staff will be kept on. That includes you, Maria. But I have to stress that no contract has been signed."

"What does that mean?"

"It means that I'm still the owner. I'm the person who makes the decisions."

"And what about Antonio?"

"He has no say in the matter at this point."

Emma's words seemed to have the effect of pacifying Maria. She sniffed and blew her nose. They finished their coffees and Mark summoned the waiter to pay the bill. Emma turned her attention to Kevin. "I want you both to go back to work now and continue as normal. As soon as I have something to report, I will talk to you again. I promise I will do my best for both of you."

Maria seized her hand and fought back the tears. "Thank you, *señorita*. You are so very kind."

They went back to work. For the next few hours, the pace was unrelenting. About two o'clock, it began to slacken off and Kevin told Snuffy he could have the rest of the evening off to prepare for the trip to Puerto Banus with Maggie. He was washing some glasses when he looked up to see a familiar figure approach along the beach. He stopped as Claire drew up to the counter and plumped down on a stool. She sank her head into her hands.

"What's the matter?" he asked anxiously. "You look sick."

She shook her head. "I feel sick. I feel like a fool."

He came out from behind the bar and put his arms around her to comfort her. "What's bothering you?"

She looked at him. There were tears in her eyes. "Oh Kevin, I almost made the biggest mistake of my life."

He signalled to Maria that he was taking a break.

"Let's go for a walk," he said.

When they were a safe distance from the bar, he took out a paper handkerchief and gave it to her: "Dry your eyes and tell me what has upset you like this."

Claire did as he instructed. "I was offered a job," she sniffed. "I thought it was going to be the job of a lifetime and it would mean that I could stay here in Fuengirola."

"So why didn't you take it?"

"Because it would have been a disaster. The man I would have been working for is an absolute bastard. He's an old boyfriend and a total womaniser. I met him years ago when I lived here. I thought he had changed but he hasn't. If I had taken that job . . ."

She clung to him and began to weep again.

"There, there," he said.

She held him tight.

"But, Claire . . . are you still in love with him? Is that the problem?"

She looked up into his eyes. "Kevin, the strange thing is, the whole nasty experience has just proved something that has been staring me in the face."

"What?"

"*You're* the one I love."

He stopped and looked deeply into her face. "Do you mean that, Claire?"

"Yes, I mean it. With all my heart. You're the one I love."

"Because I love you too."

Claire tried to smile through her tears. "Honestly?"

"Yes. I was trying to figure out a way of telling you."

"Oh, Kevin! How could I have been so stupid?"

She clung to him and their lips met in a long, lingering kiss.

At last they separated.

"Now that you've turned down the job, you'll be going home?" he said.

"I suppose so. What about you? Will you come with me?"

For a moment, he didn't reply. He appeared to be wrapped in thought.

Finally he said: "Do you have any savings, Claire?"

"A little. About €20,000. It's in my account in Dublin. Why do you ask?"

"Just an idea that has occurred to me."

Emma and Mark spent the remainder of the afternoon visiting the pretty village of Nerja to the east of Malaga. It was a trip they had been planning for some time and with the end of Mark's holiday approaching, they had decided to do it now. But it was a gloomy affair. The enthusiasm that Emma had felt when she woke this morning had now evaporated after her talk with Maria.

It was early evening when Mark swung his rented Audi into the car park of Hotel Alhambra. As they came through the doors into the opulent foyer they were met by a familiar voice. They turned to see Kevin and Claire get up from a sofa and come hurrying across the floor to meet them.

"This is a surprise," Emma said. "What are you pair doing here?"

"We've been waiting for you," Kevin said excitedly. "Could we have a word with you?"

"It will only take a moment," added Claire.

"Okay," said Emma.

Emma led the way across the foyer to a quiet alcove where they all sat down.

"Now," she said. "What is this all about?"

Kevin cleared his throat. "I've been thinking about the conversation we had earlier today."

"Yes?"

"Pedro's Bar means a lot to us who work there. We enjoy the job. We like meeting the different customers who turn up. But especially it means a lot to Maria. It's her only source of income. I've spoken to Snuffy and . . . well . . ." He looked up. "If Antonio buys the bar, we couldn't continue to work there."

There was silence for a moment.

"What would you do?" Emma asked.

"Get jobs elsewhere."

"And Maria?"

Kevin shrugged. "God knows what would happen to her. Maria believes if Antonio takes over, her days at Pedro's are numbered. No matter what guarantees he might give, once he has bought the bar, Maria is convinced he will get rid of her."

Emma let out a loud sigh. "Let me be straight with you. I don't like Antonio any more than you do. But he is absolutely right about one thing. The bar cannot be run from long distance. It needs someone who is on the spot and can keep an eye on it. You saw what happened with Conor Delaney."

"Can't you run it?"

"No," Emma said. "I don't have the time or the knowledge. I've made up my mind to dispose of it."

Kevin's face looked grim. "There is an alternative."

"What alternative?"

He threw Claire a nervous glance. "You could sell it to us."

36

Emma stared at Kevin.

"Sell Pedro's Bar to you? Do you know what it would cost?"

"Not exactly. But between us we could raise about €80,000. Everyone is prepared to contribute something."

"Even Maria?"

Kevin lowered his eyes. "Even Maria. She hasn't got much. But she's prepared to put it up to save the bar."

Emma felt confused. "This is all a big surprise," she said at last.

"We'll be here permanently to make sure it is run properly," Kevin went on. "And we have ideas to expand the business and make it more profitable. It's in a perfect location. Why do you think Antonio is so keen to purchase it? Because he can see the untapped potential, that's why."

"But €80,000 would barely cover the debts. They amount to at least €60,000. Then you would have legal costs on top of that."

Kevin's face clouded over. "Maybe we could borrow the rest of the money. But, anyway, whatever you do, *please* don't sell it to Antonio!"

Claire interrupted. "I have an apartment back in Dublin that I could sell."

"And where would you live?"

She turned to Kevin and took his hand. "I'm going to stay here with Kevin. Please. If you just give us a little time, I'm sure we could come up with the cash."

Emma looked from one to the other.

"Don't dismiss our offer out of hand," Kevin pleaded. "At least consider it. I'm convinced it could work."

Emma glanced at Mark, who nodded gravely.

"All right," she said at last. "I'll consider it. Can you be back here tomorrow at midday?"

"Sure," Kevin said, his face brightening up.

"I'll give you my decision then."

Antonio Hernandez Rodriguez gazed out from the little room that he used as his office and let his eye travel over the restaurant floor. All the tables were set with starched white tablecloths; later, as they approached opening time, the waiters would put a spray of fresh flowers on each one. The floors were swept, the mirrors polished and the red carpet that ran from the door to the cash desk had been vacuumed twice. The place looked pristine.

Antonio insisted that these jobs be completed each evening before the staff finished work. He still remembered the occasion when he got an urgent phone call at eleven to say that forty top tourism executives would be arriving for lunch at half twelve. What a mad scramble that had been! But it had taught Antonio a valuable lesson. Now he left nothing to chance.

El Molino Blanco had seating for one hundred and twenty diners and most nights it was full. His restaurant was one of the most successful on the Costa del Sol and was mentioned in all the best guidebooks and restaurant reviews. He counted all the top earners and big spenders among his clients. His investment account was in a healthy balance and his bank manager was happy. And he had built it all from nothing but hard work and good business sense. And he hadn't finished yet. Antonio had grand expansion plans as soon as he got his hands on Pedro's Bar.

He had always regretted selling the bar to Conor Delaney. But at the time, he had no option. He needed the money to open his restaurant. His mother, of course, had created a fuss, demanding that he give her a share of the proceeds. For what? Antonio still felt bitter about the affair. He owned the bar. His father had willed it to him. He was the one who had developed it. If he had given her what she wanted, he would have had nothing left to open the restaurant. And what would she have done with the money anyway? Probably spent it on silly trifles for that sick sister of hers. That's where she should be: at home looking after her.

But things were going to change when he regained possession of Pedro's. Antonio had plans to redesign it as a cocktail bar that would cater for the trendy young tourists who flocked to the Costa. No more cooking paella. No more greasy hamburgers. Instead, they would serve designer drinks at €5 a shot. And the first thing he would do would be to get rid of his mother. She was so old-fashioned that she would be a liability. Despite his promise to the Irishwoman, there would be no job for Maria. Or for any of the rest of the scruffy staff, who looked more like a bunch of beach bums than the kind of smart young cocktail assistants that he had in mind.

But first he had to buy Pedro's and, so far, things were looking good. He had relied heavily on his gut instinct that the Irishwoman would not want to keep it, particularly since she knew nothing about running a bar. He had also stressed the obvious fact that, to manage it properly, the owner needed to be on site. But what had really tipped the scales in his favour was the fact that the bar was so heavily indebted.

That was why he had told Miguel to do nothing about the unpaid taxes. Not that there was anything he could do. Miguel had produced no accounts for Pedro's Bar for years. And Antonio also knew that he had been quietly milking the bar, siphoning off funds for his own use. There was no possibility that he could produce accounts out of thin air. Antonio had guessed that this combination of factors would prompt *Señorita* Dunne to get rid of the bar at the first opportunity. And he was right.

When he made his bid and offered to take on the debts, he had seen her eyes light up like a child in a toyshop. He had given her a way out: a chance to get her money back and be free of Pedro's. Of course, she was going to take it. They had agreed terms and, any day now, he was expecting the contract of sale to arrive from her lawyers. Which reminded him: he would ring Luis Garcia Santiago this afternoon and see what was holding things up. Yes, Antonio was happy with the way things had panned out. He couldn't wait to get started on the redevelopment of Pedro's Bar.

He got up from his desk and walked out into the restaurant. From the kitchen, he could hear the sound of chopping and the aroma of cooking food as the chefs began preparing for lunch. In the meantime, he would just step across the road to the corner bar and have a *cortado* while he had a quick glance at the papers. But when he reached the door, he found his way out to the street was blocked by two tall men in dark suits.

"*Señor* Antonio Hernandez Rodriguez?" the first man asked. He had produced a badge of some sort and was flashing it in Antonio's face.

"Yes?" Antonio said, smiling benignly.

"I am from the Tax Office."

The smile immediately disappeared from Antonio's face.

"My colleague is from the police. We have a warrant to search these premises."

Antonio felt a tremor of fear run along his spine. "A warrant?"

"Yes."

The second man had produced a document and was showing it to him.

Antonio tried to remain calm. There was no point getting angry with these people. It would do no good.

"We also have a warrant for your arrest."

Antonio gulped. "Arrest? I do not understand. What for?"

"Falsifying tax returns. Evading taxes."

Despite himself, Antonio began to protest. "This is outrageous. I am an honest businessman. You can't do this to me."

"We have the warrants, *Señor* Hernandez. We can do it."

"But I have done nothing wrong. I have always paid my taxes."

"That will be for the authorities to decide. But I should tell you that we already have a signed confession from one of your associates."

Antonio felt his heart go cold. "Who is the scoundrel who makes these false allegations?"

"*Señor* Miguel Martinez Sanchez. He has made a full report to us."

Antonio couldn't believe his ears. "Miguel?"

"That is correct. He has told us everything. Now I suggest it is best for you not to resist."

He had produced a pair of handcuffs.

Meekly, Antonio held out his wrists.

Kevin had been up since seven o'clock. He hadn't slept very well, worrying about Emma's reaction to their bid to buy the bar. He just hoped she would show them a little bit of compassion, that was all. But he had his fears. She was a businesswoman after all and, in Kevin's experience, business-people had little time for sentiment.

Now he sat at the kitchen table and drank strong black tea while Snuffy pottered about with the electric toaster.

"How did Maggie's audition go last night?" Kevin asked, trying not to think of the big decision that lay ahead.

"Like a bomb. She brought the house down."

"Did they offer her a gig?"

"Not just one. She's got a regular three-night slot starting next week. At twice her usual fee."

"Well, that's good news," Kevin said.

"And tomorrow night, I begin rehearsals with the Black Pimpernels."

"Are you going to join them?"

"Looks like it. Ricky is very keen. Says another guitar would give the band an edge."

"You're going to be busy. Do you think you can manage all this and still work in the bar?"

Snuffy smeared marmalade on his toast. "Isn't that the point of this meeting with Emma? Are you sure there's still going to be a bar for us to work at?"

Kevin lowered his eyes. "No," he said. "I'm not. But we've got to hope for the best."

At a quarter to twelve, they all gathered outside Hotel Alhambra. Maggie had come along to lend support. On their way, Kevin had made a detour to Pedro's Bar where he stuck up a sign that read: *CLOSED TILL 3 P.M. FOR STOCKTAKING.* Because of the importance of the occasion and the venue, they had dressed in their best clothes – even Snuffy looked quite smart in new jeans and a short-sleeved blue shirt he had borrowed from Kevin. They stood nervously waiting till at last Maria was seen making her way along the footpath in their direction.

She too had dressed in her Sunday best and wore a white blouse and flowing dark skirt. She had put a plain silver chain and pendant around her neck and pinned a large brooch to her breast. But there was no disguising the look of concern that lined her face. Maria was well aware that this meeting was going to decide her fate. In an hour's time, she would know whether she was ever going to work again.

"*Buenos días,*" she said gravely to each of them in turn.

Kevin took her hand and kissed her cheek. "You look splendid, Maria. Maybe you will meet a wealthy businessman who will marry you."

The old lady smiled. "Not any more. Not unless he is also blind."

Her joke seemed to ease the tension and everyone laughed.

Kevin checked his watch. It was now five to twelve. It was time to go in.

"All right," he said. "Everybody ready?"

They nodded their agreement.

374

"Let's go."

He walked past the elegant commissionaire and the others followed. Looks of awe and amazement broke on the faces of Maria and Maggie when they saw the opulence of the vast foyer: the glittering chandeliers, the tinkling fountain, the wealth and elegance of the world they had entered.

Mark was already waiting for them at the reception desk. He came forward and warmly shook their hands.

"Good to see you all. Why don't you follow me?"

He led them along a corridor till they came to a small conference room. He opened the door and stood aside to let them enter. Inside, a number of chairs had been set out facing a small platform. In a corner of the room, a pot of coffee sat on a table beside cups and saucers.

"Help yourselves," Mark said, pointing to the coffee. "Emma will be along shortly. She rang a few minutes ago to say she was on her way."

They looked at each other but nobody moved towards the coffee pot. Everyone seemed to be on edge. Slowly, they pulled out the chairs and sat down. Mark tried to make small talk but it gradually died away. A deathly hush settled over the room as they waited to learn what lay in store.

Emma was running late. Like Kevin, she had also been up early. She'd eaten a light breakfast of croissants and coffee and at nine o'clock rang Luis at his home. She had spent most of the morning in intensive phone conversation with the lawyer while they discussed the finer details of her decision. Now she had to go downstairs and break the news to Kevin and the others.

They were sitting anxiously when she entered the room, like people waiting for a judge to announce his verdict.

Emma walked briskly to the top of the room and opened her briefcase with a loud snap.

"Good morning," she said tersely. "I'm sorry to have kept you waiting."

Their faces watched her closely for some indication of her decision. She reached into her briefcase and took out a bunch of documents.

"Before we begin, I want to explain how I came into possession of Pedro's Bar."

There was a creaking sound as someone shifted in their chair.

"My main business is printing and in the course of my work I came into contact with Conor Delaney, who some of you know was the previous owner of the bar. I won't go into details but Conor Delaney owed me some money for work I had done. He couldn't repay it and he proposed that I take the bar instead. I knew nothing about running a bar. And what is more, I had no interest in it. In addition, I soon learnt that there are considerable debts that the bar has incurred. It was for these reasons that I decided to dispose of it."

She paused and glanced at Maria.

"Recently, I was approached by Antonio, Maria's son, who made a very generous offer to purchase the bar. Antonio was also prepared to assume the debts. I reached agreement with him subject to an undertaking that the jobs of the existing staff would be guaranteed.

"Then, last night, I was approached by Kevin with a counter offer on behalf of you people. I promised to consider it and to give you my response today."

There was complete silence as every eye focused on Emma.

"I have now had time to do that." She paused. "I have to tell you that I have decided not to accept your offer."

There were gasps and groans from her audience.

Kevin rose to speak but Emma waved him down again.

"Allow me to explain," she went on, with a slight smile on her lips. "I know how much you all love Pedro's Bar. And I appreciate the fears you have about your jobs and particularly Maria's job. But if I accept your offer, you will have no money left. You will have no capital to expand the business as Kevin has suggested. You would be burdened by debt and I don't think that would be a good way to start your career in business."

Mark had now moved to stand beside her.

"Instead, I have decided on a different course of action," Emma continued.

The room had fallen silent again.

"I have decided to incorporate Pedro's Bar as a limited company. I will maintain the main holding and will pay off the debts but each of you will become shareholders. The money that you proposed to put up for the purchase will now be invested in the renovation and improvement of the premises. I will take no part in the running or management of the business, which will be the responsibility of Kevin and Maria.

"I have spoken to my lawyer this morning and he is in the process of drawing up the necessary papers. If you are happy to accept this arrangement, we can have the legal documents signed this evening."

Snuffy had risen to his feet. "What exactly does this mean?"

"It means we will own the bar between us. Everyone's job is secure."

Their astonishment gave way to shouts of joy. As the import of Emma's words began to sink in, they jumped up and grabbed each other. Kevin kissed Claire. Snuffy smothered

Maggie in a bear hug. They crowded round a beaming Emma and Mark and warmly shook their hands.

Alone in her chair, Maria sat in a trance, the big tears of gratitude rolling silently down her face.

37

"Fasten your seat-belts. Landing shortly."

The captain's instructions disrupted Emma's enjoyment of the tape she had been listening to on her headphones. She opened her eyes and the sea suddenly came into view like a great pane of blue glass. Then the plane dipped and the brown mountains became visible beneath the cloud. The journey was almost over. In a few minutes, they would be landing in Malaga.

Beside her, she felt Mark's hand reach out to twine her fingers.

"Feeling okay?" he mouthed.

She removed her headphones to hear him.

"Were you sleeping?" he asked.

She shook her head. "Just relaxing to the music."

"Seat-belt fastened?"

She pointed to her lap. "Yes."

"Excited?"

Emma smiled and laid her head on his shoulder. "What

a silly question, Mark. Of course, I am. Since meeting you I've never stopped."

It was true. There were moments when Emma thought she had been hit by a cyclone. In the nine months since she had first set eyes on Mark Chambers, her life had been turned completely upside down. She had finally sold the Hi-Speed Printing Company to Herr Braun, after weeks of intensive negotiations. With Mark's advice and her father's guidance, she had managed to push the sale price well past the initial €3 million offer. The deal had been sealed over several bottles of champagne in the Four Seasons hotel in Ballsbridge and now the Germans were installed in the company's headquarters in Baldoyle.

Despite some trepidation, the transfer had gone extremely smoothly. As part of the negotiations, Emma had insisted that each member of staff be given a goodwill bonus and this had greatly facilitated the changeover. And she was still in position as consultant, although a new management team was being moved into place. Everybody seemed satisfied with the outcome.

It had been a more difficult task to convince her parents to accept the cheque for €1 million that she had set aside as their part of the payout. Her father had argued that they were comfortably off and didn't need the money but Emma had been adamant.

"You started the company, Dad, and you deserve a reward."

"But you built it up."

"On your foundations. If you don't take the money, I'm calling the whole thing off."

Her father sighed. "You always had a stubborn streak, Emma. Now you're trying to blackmail me!"

Reluctantly, he agreed to accept the cash.

Meanwhile, Mark had been making changes too.

On his return from Spain, he had set about reorganising Chambers Creative Artists. He remained as Managing Director but Ted Cunningham had been promoted to Chief Executive, with responsibility for the day-to-day running of the firm. The move allowed Mark to take a back seat and devote more of his time to Emma. Now they spent all their spare time together. She had moved some of her clothes into his house in Howth and spent her weekends there.

Even Conor Delaney had managed to survive. They had run into him one evening in a restaurant in town. He was looking fit and had lost weight and Emma was surprised to see that he was drinking mineral water. He explained that after his company had gone bust he had managed to secure a position as Sales Director with an on-line travel firm and was slowly rebuilding his life. He had also given up the booze.

"What did you do with Pedro's Bar?" he asked.

"I turned it into a limited company."

"You did what?"

Emma was tempted to tell him the whole story but decided not to.

"I brought in some new investors who live in Fuengirola. They'll be able to give it their full-time attention."

It was true. The regular reports she received from Kevin and Claire spoke in glowing terms about the progress the bar was making. They had used their capital to rebuild and expand it and had added a restaurant with seating for eighty people. They had even managed to recruit Carlos, the chef from Felipe's. Now the restaurant was receiving rave reviews and was a runaway success.

It was one of the reasons Emma and Mark were making

this return trip. The other one was to see the new house that Claire had found for them on the outskirts of Mijas. They planned to use it for regular breaks and as a retreat from Dublin. Claire had spent months searching for somewhere and now she said she had found the perfect place, a four-bedroom house with gardens and swimming pool, fifteen minutes from the centre of town. Emma couldn't wait to see it.

There was a shudder as the plane's wheels made contact with the runway and then they slowly taxied up to the terminal. Ten minutes later, they were disembarking into the warm Malaga sun. This time, Mark had learnt his lesson and had packed only hand luggage so they sailed through the arrivals hall and past the baggage reclaim to the taxi rank. Soon they were speeding along the motorway towards Fuengirola.

Emma reclined her head against the seat.

"I'm really looking forward to seeing them all again," she said. "And viewing the new house."

"But first I want a hot shower and a change of clothes," Mark said. "Already I'm feeling like a damp rag. And we've only been here fifteen minutes."

They had booked into the Alhambra once more and Emma had emailed Claire to tell her of their arrival time. She was waiting for them in the foyer, full of excitement.

They all embraced.

"Hey, you both look so well!" Claire said as she held Emma at arm's length.

"Not as well as you," Mark said wryly. "Unfortunately our suntans have faded in the grey Dublin rain."

"Plenty of time to top them up again," Claire replied with a grin. "How long are you staying?"

"Two weeks."

"I have a car waiting. As soon as you're ready I'll take you up to view the house."

"That's perfect," Emma said. "I'm dying to see it."

"I think you're going to like it. It was an old farmhouse but it has been completely renovated. Everything is brand new, appliances, everything. And it has spectacular views over the whole area."

"Can you give us ten minutes to get changed?" Mark asked.

"Sure. I'll wait in the bar."

They were back again within the appointed time. Emma had changed into a white skirt and brown T-shirt and Mark was now wearing a loose sports shirt and jeans. They got into Claire's car and started the journey up the hill towards Mijas.

"I want to catch up on all the news," Emma said. "Tell me what's been happening."

"Well, Maggie is still conducting a *ménage à trois* with Snuffy and Ricky. She can't decide which one she really loves. And she's been appointed Director of Entertainments for us. Did I tell you that?"

"I don't think so."

"Well, she has. She's now in charge of hiring the cabaret acts."

"What?"

"Oh, yes," Claire said excitedly. "We now stay open till midnight and every evening we have entertainment. Snuffy runs the bar but he also plays guitar at night with the Black Pimpernels. They're the resident band."

"My God," Mark said, "you've really changed the place!"

"You know that we've trebled the takings. Pedro's Bar is now firmly on the tourist map. People come from all over just to have a beer."

"And what about Maria?"

"She's in charge of the food. But we have a new cook who does all the heavy stuff. Maria's role is to oversee the operation. It means she has more time to spend at home with her sister. She's in her element bossing the new man around."

"How is her sister?"

"Improved enormously. That visit to the hospital was the best thing that ever happened to her. They really keep an eye on her now. She goes several times a week."

"So everything is turning out okay?" Mark said.

"Except for Antonio and Miguel. You heard about them?"

"Yes," Emma said gravely. "Three years each for fraud."

"They're lucky it wasn't more. The judge took into account their guilty pleas and Miguel Martinez's confession."

"And what about Kevin?" Emma asked with a grin. "The man who made it all possible?"

Claire smiled. "As you know, Kevin is in overall charge. But he spends most of his time on the restaurant. It's turning into a major success story. We're booked out most evenings. Recruiting Carlos as the chef was a big coup for us."

"And you and your property agency?"

"It's something I've always wanted. I'm happy to say that business is brisk. I get a lot of inquiries from Ireland and my mother is going around Dublin proudly telling everyone who will listen that her daughter is now a Managing Director."

"That's brilliant."

Claire glanced at her coyly. "I've something else to tell you. Kevin and I have moved in together. Saves rent. And when things settle down, we're planning to get married."

Emma gave a whoop of joy. She pulled Claire close and kissed her. "I'm so happy for you. Congratulations!"

At last, the car pulled up beside a dirt track and they got out.

"Here we are," Claire said, taking a bunch of keys out of her bag. "Take your time to look around."

The house was magnificent. It stood behind a high wall with beautiful gardens of orange and lemon and olive trees. Outside the back door there was a splendid swimming pool and a deck for sunbathing. A little tiled patio held a wrought-iron table and chairs. It would be perfect for eating breakfast on a bright, sunny morning.

Inside, the house had been completely restored. Emma and Mark wandered around the rooms uttering cries of satisfaction. There was a fully equipped kitchen, a dining-room and comfortable sitting-room. The master bedroom had an en-suite bathroom and a balcony with fantastic views over the mountains and the sea.

"I'm absolutely gobsmacked," Emma said in admiration. "You must be a mind-reader."

"Yes," Mark agreed. "It's exactly what we've been looking for."

"Take some time to think about it. There's no rush."

"We don't need to think about it," Emma said. "This is exactly what we want."

"Are you sure?"

"Absolutely."

"Well, in that case, we can have a contract for you in a couple of days' time. Is that okay?"

"Perfect," Emma said. "I'll ring Luis this afternoon and tell him."

On the way back to the hotel, Claire asked casually: "Have you guys got anything scheduled for this evening?"

"Nothing particular," Mark replied.

"That's good," Claire grinned mischievously. "The staff

385

of Pedro's Bar have something planned for you. A special Welcome Back party. It's arranged for eight o'clock. Can I tell them you'll be there?"

"Do we have any choice?" Mark laughed.

When they returned to the hotel, they had a snack at the bar. Emma was anxious to spend some time sunbathing and Mark agreed to join her. They stretched out on the sunbeds and Emma gave a sigh of contentment.

"I'm so happy to be back, Mark. Everything is turning out so well."

"You're right. That house is fabulous. I can't wait to move into it." He leaned across and kissed her. "There's only one thing left to make it all complete."

She took off her glasses and blinked in the sun. "What's that?"

"I'll tell you." He leaned forward and whispered in her ear.

Emma let out a squeal of delight. She immediately sat up and flung her arms around him. From the surrounding sunbeds, a few faces looked up in amazement.

They were ready to leave at half past seven, all dressed up formally for the occasion – Emma going for broke in a full-length turquoise dress and heels. Claire had offered to pick them up again but they told her it would be simpler to get a cab. Tomorrow, Mark planned to hire a car.

On the short journey to Pedro's Bar, they discussed the evening that lay ahead. But when they arrived, they were totally unprepared for the sight that awaited them.

Pedro's Bar was at least twice the size it once was, with a whole new counter and deck area where the old structure once stood. And beside the bar was a spanking new building with a large sign proclaiming: *Pedro's Restaurant.*

As they stepped out of the cab, they found the staff lined up to greet them. At once, they were swamped by people kissing and hugging them and shaking hands. Kevin, magnificent in a dinner jacket, stepped forward to welcome them. Snuffy shook hands and Carlos, in his chef's apron, came forward and made a little bow. A figure pushed out from the crowd. It was Maria, looking happier than they had ever seen her. She walked up to Emma and presented her with a bouquet of flowers.

"Oh, Maria," Emma said. "They're lovely."

The old woman beamed with pleasure. "I pick them myself. When you first come, I was so afraid you were going to close us down. But now I am so happy. All because you are such a generous lady."

Emma kissed the old woman gently on the cheek. "Thank you, Maria. Those are very beautiful words."

"They are true words. And they come from the heart."

Emma felt a lump rise in her throat. She held the old lady's hands and stared into her grey eyes. "I know they are, Maria. And I will always remember them."

At last, they managed to make their way inside the restaurant, where they found a long table set up in the middle of the room.

Once they had all sat down, Kevin filled their glasses with wine.

"I want to propose a toast. To Emma and Mark! Welcome back to Fuengirola!"

There were shouts and cheers as everyone drank from their glasses.

Emma got to her feet. "Thank you, everybody. I am truly overwhelmed by the warmth of your reception. And by the transformation that I see around me. I would like to return the toast."

She raised her glass.

"To Pedro's Bar! May it thrive and prosper!"

Everybody clapped and poured more wine. As the applause slowly died away, there was a creaking sound. People turned to see Mark push his chair aside and stand up.

"I have something to say too and I want you to be the first to hear it. This afternoon, I entered into certain negotiations with Emma."

A silence had now fallen on the room.

"As a result of these discussions, I am delighted to announce that she has consented to marry me."

There was a surprised hush and then the room erupted. People whistled and cheered and stomped their feet. Hands reached out to congratulate them. A champagne cork popped. Up on the stage, Maggie had appeared dressed in her Tina Turner outfit, swinging her microphone and belting out "Simply the Best".

Mark turned to Emma.

"I don't think there's any more to say, is there?"

She shook her head.

He took her in his arms and held her in a long embrace.

THE END

If you enjoyed *The Beach Bar*, don't miss out on
Hotel Las Flores, also published by Poolbeg.

Here is a sneak preview of Chapter one . . .

HOTEL
Las Flores

Chapter 1

Any girl who has ever been dumped by a man would have
sympathised at once with Trish Blake. Just this morning,
her lover of ten months, Henry Doran, had rung to tell her
he was ending the relationship. The phrase he used was
"announce closure" which was typical of Henry Doran who
rarely spoke English when he could use jargon he had
picked up on a training course somewhere. It was all part of
his carefully cultivated image: the flash suits, the casually
slicked-back hair, the Armani aftershave, the briefcase, the
Diners cards, the arrogant self-confidence and the spouting
of sales talk on every available occasion.

Being dumped by Henry Doran wasn't entirely unexpected
and it wasn't the worst thing that had ever happened to
Trish. Which doesn't mean it wasn't painful and didn't dent
her morale. He had called her at exactly two minutes to
twelve, knowing she had her weekly sales conference at
noon. He began by telling her how much he appreciated the
relationship, that the sex was wonderful, that he would never
forget her as long as he lived but sadly his wife was getting

suspicious and, well, he had the kids to think about and anyway hadn't they both agreed at the outset that it was only a fling?

Trish listened with sinking heart as he galloped to the inevitable conclusion. She realised with dismay that she was hurt by the brutality and coldness of the conversation. What a way to end a relationship! He hadn't even the decency to buy her a nice dinner and tell her to her face. Why hadn't he been really brave and broken it off by text message? A rubber duck would have shown more backbone.

But she hadn't interrupted or argued. She had read somewhere that the best course in these situations is to let the other person sweat. And she had experienced a certain sadistic pleasure in imagining Henry Doran perspire as he wriggled and twisted and finally slithered away like the miserable worm that he was.

'Good riddance to bad rubbish,' she muttered under her breath as she grabbed her files and rushed off to her meeting, feeling downcast and flustered and a good ten minutes late.

Why hadn't she told him about the other news she had received this morning? That she was pregnant? She hadn't told him because she knew in her heart that it wouldn't have mattered. If anything, it would have made him panic and run even faster. She was going to have to deal with the baby problem on her own. She would have to devise some explanation. And this was going to present a major problem. For Trish hadn't slept with her husband for almost a year.

She recalled the thrill she felt at the first hint that she might be pregnant. She was thirty seven years old and had recently become aware that time was running out. She had been married for fifteen years and, despite irregular hurried sessions of mechanical sex with her husband Adrian, nothing had happened. Not even a late period. Indeed, she had been on the verge of asking Adrian to go for a sperm test when she bumped into Henry Doran.

Henry was a rep for a computer company that did business with the auctioneering firm where she worked. They met at a lunch after a sales deal, in a smart restaurant in Temple Bar where the portions would have left a gerbil feeling hungry but everybody raved about the decor. He was seated next to her, dominating the company with talk of his sales conquests while the wine waiter kept pouring the chilled Chardonnay.

He was tall, with broad shoulders and smouldering brown eyes and a cute dimple in the centre of his chin. Mid-thirties, Trish calculated. For some reason, her eyes were drawn to the gold wedding band on the third finger of his left hand. She knew it instinctively. It was like the Law of Gravity. Good-looking men like Henry Doran were *always* married.

By half past three everybody had drifted back to work and only Trish and Henry remained. He poured the last of the wine and they tipped glasses together in a toast.

"Nice lunch," Henry said, stretching his long legs and loosening his tie. "Been here before?"

"Once or twice," Trish confessed. She didn't want to tell him that she hated the place with its snooty waiters and overpriced menu and dainty portions that made you want to grab a hamburger on the way home.

"Well, my boss will be happy. That's the second contract this week."

"I take it you work on commission," Trish said.

"Oh, it's not just about commission," Henry said dismissively. "It's reputation. When word gets around that I'm shifting product, the competition will set the hunters on me."

"Hunters?" Trish asked, thinking maybe he meant bloodhounds.

"Yes. The head-hunters. They'll be lining up to offer me jobs. That's what business is all about, nowadays. Reputation."

"I see," Trish said.

Henry grinned like a happy schoolboy and drained his glass. "Aren't you going back to work?"

Trish looked at her watch. She was feeling happy after all the wine. "Not much point now. I'll catch up in the morning."

Henry's eyes twinkled. "So how about cutting this place and getting a proper drink somewhere?" He leaned closer and smiled seductively. "Just you and me."

Why not? Trish thought. He's better company than waits for me at home. A lonely night watching TV soaps while Adrian remains locked in his study revising his bloody novel that has already been rejected by twenty publishers.

"Okay," she said. "Where will we go?"

They went to the Octagon Bar in the Clarence Hotel where Henry Doran ordered vodka and tonics.

"You're a very attractive woman," he said after the waiter had delivered their drinks.

"Thank you. You're not bad-looking yourself."

"Well, I try to keep trim," Henry said, taking the compliment in his stride. "I pump iron. Hit the bricks a couple of times a week. I used to play rugby, you know."

"Really?" Trish said, pretending to be interested.

"Old Belvedere. Friends say I could have made the national squad. But I was just too busy with other things."

"That's life for you," Trish said, realising how inane she sounded.

She swallowed a mouthful of vodka and felt it warm her stomach. Now that she knew what was going to happen, she felt amazingly relaxed. She just wished he would make his move quickly so that she could get home in time to make supper for Adrian.

"What does your husband do?" Henry inquired.

"He's a teacher. But he really wants to be a writer. He's working on a novel."

"That sounds very interesting."

"He hasn't got a publisher yet. What about you? What does your wife do?"

Henry suddenly lowered his eyes and looked grave. "She's dying. The Big C."

Trish almost spilt her drink. She felt her heart jolt. Surely he wasn't serious? "That's terrible. Poor woman. Is there nothing can be done?"

"Afraid not. She's seen all the top specialists. They say her case is hopeless. It's only a matter of time."

"And do you have children?"

"A boy and a girl."

"That's awful. I didn't realise."

"It is hard," Henry conceded. "We have absolutely no sex life." He turned his smouldering eyes on her. "Which is why you'd be doing me a major favour if you came to bed with me. You could look on it as an act of mercy."

They took a room in the hotel. Henry paid by credit card and ordered a bottle of Veuve Clicquot to be sent up with Room Service.

Trish had a shower and, when she emerged from the bathroom, Henry had stripped down to his Hugo Boss underpants. Her first impressions had been correct. He had a beautiful body: strong muscles, hard stomach, tight ass. And hair! My God, it was everywhere. It covered his arms and legs and curled like barbed wire along his chest. Trish felt her knees go weak at the sight.

He handed her a glass of champagne, then bent his handsome face and whispered, "You don't know what this means to me."

Trish felt a delicious shiver run along her spine as he wrapped his manly arms around her and led her to the bed.

The sex was marvellous. Henry was a practised lover. There was none of the mad urgency she had expected. Instead, he was careful and patient. He took his time. And the stamina! When he got going, Henry performed like a racehorse. At last, when they had finished and lay side by side in the twisted sheets, Trish felt a lovely warm glow envelop her whole body.

Henry ran a wet finger along her breast and gently squeezed a brown nipple. "Thank you," he said. "You were marvellous. You just absolutely light up my dials."

What the hell is he talking about? Trish thought and closed her eyes.

He called her at work a week later and asked her to go for a drink. Trish had been expecting this and every morning she had packed fresh underwear in her bag for just such an eventuality. They met in a little pub off Grafton Street.

Henry presented her with a single red rose and kissed her softly on the cheek.

"I've missed you terribly," he said. "I've been thinking about you all the time."

"I've thought about you too," Trish said. She wondered if she should ask about his dying wife but decided against it. It would only break the mood.

Henry ordered the drinks and casually took her hand and placed it on his crotch. Frantically, she pulled away.

"For God's sake," she hissed, "not here in full public view!"

But it had excited her. She could feel the blood pounding in her brain.

"I want you so much, I could eat you," Henry said.

"Can't you at least let me finish my drink?" She gulped at her glass.

This time, he took her to an apartment at Charlotte Quay which belonged to a friend. There were stunning views across Dublin Bay and in the distance they could see the green nose of Howth Head shining in the evening sun. Henry suggested they have a bath together.

Trish thought it a wonderful idea. He ran the taps and they got in, sipping vodkas while the room filled up with steam. Afterwards, he got her to put on some black stockings and a little white basque he had bought. Trish found it terribly exciting. She thought of the dull sex she had with Adrian and wondered if she had married the wrong man.

The relationship developed into an affair. Each morning when she logged on at work, an e-mail awaited her. Sometimes they were witty, other times passionate. Frequently, they were downright obscene and she hurriedly deleted them. He phoned every day. They had lunch together in quiet out-of-the-way bistros. They went shopping. They went to the cinema, driving over to the north-side where no one would recognise them.

And, once a week, they went to the apartment at Charlotte Quay and made wild, sensuous love. Trish couldn't believe what was happening to her. She felt rejuvenated. She giggled like a giddy schoolgirl. She blushed whenever his name came up in conversation. She woke every morning as if she was seeing the world with fresh eyes for the very first time.

Even Adrian, engrossed in his novel, noticed the change in her. One morning as they had breakfast together in the kitchen of their terraced house in Sandymount, he stared across the table and said: "My God, Trish. You look resplendent. What's come over you?"

She smiled intriguingly and said: "I've just realised how lucky I am."

And then they heard the thud in the hallway as the

postman delivered the mail. Adrian came back carrying a battered jiffy-bag and a face like a gravedigger's shovel.

"Bad news, darling?"

Adrian sat down mournfully and poured a cup of tea. "They've rejected it again. They say the dialogue's all wrong."

And the moment of intimacy – or potential intimacy – passed.

Love was the one word that was never mentioned between Trish and her new lover. Early on, Henry had said to her: "You know I can never leave Louise? Not with the condition she's in."

"Of course," Trish laughed, light-heartedly.

"It wouldn't be fair. Not with all she's going through."

"No. It wouldn't."

"There's no reason why two people can't simply enjoy each other's company and give each other mutual pleasure from time to time. We're sophisticated people. And this is the 21st century, for God's sake."

"That's right."

Her acquiescence seemed to cheer him up. He cuddled close. "I'm so sorry we didn't meet sooner. You're ideal for me. Did I tell you I sold another package today? That's six this month so far."

His remark got her thinking. What would have happened if she had met Henry Doran instead of Adrian? Would they have married? Would they have had children? She longed for a child. And, as she approached the Big Four O, as Henry called it, she felt a little ball of fear tighten in her chest.

Because she had no children, people assumed she was too busy with her career. But it wasn't true. She desperately wanted a baby. Once she had even written under an assumed name to an agony aunt in one of the Sunday papers asking for advice. The agony aunt replied that thirty-seven wasn't too old to have a child. Lots of women were doing it. She gave the address of a pregnancy clinic. Trish went and had a series of tests. The doctor told her she was perfectly fertile and there was no reason why she shouldn't get pregnant. Which meant the problem had to lie with Adrian. She thought sadly of her husband. What was happening to him? Why had the dashing man she had married turned into a bad-tempered middle-aged recluse whose only interest in life was his bloody novel?

They had met twenty years before in college where Adrian had been auditor of the Debating Society. He had looked so handsome in his flared trousers and Zapata moustache that he swept her completely off her feet and when they graduated she couldn't wait to get married. Adrian got a job teaching English in St Ignatius's Comprehensive College. He explained to friends that it was only a temporary measure till he decided what he *really* wanted to do. She found a position as a trainee agent with a major auctioneering company.

In the beginning, everything was bliss. There was the excitement of the new house with its distant views of the sea from the bathroom window and the gay round of dinner parties with other young married couples from college. They had enough money for a foreign holiday every year and a car which Adrian quickly commandeered, leaving Trish to get the bus into her job at the auctioneering firm.

But she soon discovered that the glamour of the debating hall had cloaked Adrian's innate dullness. He had no style or dress sense. He took to dressing in baggy corduroy trousers and check shirts. He wore hush puppies and polka-dot cravats. She had to tell him when to get his hair cut. Worse, he was awful in bed. He had absolutely no imagination and the sex was often over before she was even aware it had begun. She endured him but got no pleasure. Adrian seemed to regard sex as just another bedtime chore like putting the cat out and locking the doors securely.

And school quickly got him down. He would sit at the kitchen table marking essays and groaning loudly as he scored and scratched with his red biro.

"Can't spell. Wouldn't know an iambic pentameter if it stood up and bit them. Why am I wasting my time like this?"

Trish would attempt to soothe him. "We all have difficult moments at work, darling."

"Moments? Who said anything about moments? This is all the bloody time! From when I arrive in the morning till the last bell goes at four o'clock. It can't be done. How can I instil an appreciation of English Literature into a bunch of gurriers who think Lord Byron is the guy who runs the rock concerts at Slane Castle?"

The idea of writing had come about by accident although Adrian later claimed it had always been a lifetime ambition. A famous American novelist called Sheldon O'Neill had arrived in Dublin to research a book and track down his ancestral roots. Trish was given the task of finding suitable accommodation for the great man while he stayed in Ireland. She eventually discovered a renovated farmhouse in County Wicklow with views over Glendalough. Sheldon O'Neill was delighted. As a reward, he invited Trish and Adrian to dinner at Patrick Guilbaud's restaurant in Merrion Street to celebrate.

Here, while they dined on lobster and wild salmon, Sheldon O'Neill regaled them with stories of the wonderful life of an internationally renowned writer – the interviews, the travel, the publishers' lunches. And of course, the money. Adrian's eyes stood out on stalks.

He joined a writers' group. They met once a week in a pub in Ranelagh. Each participant had to prepare a piece of work and then the others would read it and give their comments. It was like a refuge for battered wives. Everybody was eager to support everybody else. Adrian would come home afterwards beaming with pleasure.

"I read them my short story tonight. Must say it went down a treat. Reggie Arbuthnot said it reminded him of early Hemingway. Same sort of rugged, descriptive prose."

Trish encouraged him. It gave him something to look forward to and took his mind off school. He spent more and more time in the spare bedroom which he had fitted up as a study. He bought a word processor and installed a desk and easy chair and a jam-pot filled with sharpened pencils. Most evenings, he sat in there happily typing his short stories.

Then he decided he was going to write a novel.

He announced it solemnly one Saturday evening after dinner when he had poured himself a large glass of brandy.

"Of course, it's a massive undertaking. I envisage something on the scale of Dickens. Or Pasternak. A groundbreaking work that will shatter the cosy consensus of modern Irish writing. We're looking at a big book here, Trish. Two hundred thousand words. I've even got the title. I'm calling it *The Green Gannet*."

It didn't sound like a very good title to Trish. "What will it be about?"

"The Famine."

She felt her heart sink. There had been so many books about the Famine.

"Are you sure? It's such a painful period in Irish history. It would require a really sensitive approach."

He raised an eyebrow. "Are you suggesting that I can't write sensitive prose?"

"Not at all," Trish rushed to mollify him. "It's just such a big task you're taking on."

"I'm ready for that. That's where the challenge lies."

"And it *has* been done before."

Adrian had a gleam in his eye as he swirled the brandy in his glass. "Not the way I plan to do it. I'm going to deconstruct the myths. It will be narrated through the eyes of a 160-year-old man who has lived through the events and is discovered alive in a bog in Connemara. He will report on the Famine at first hand. This novel is going to cause a sensation. Irish writing will never be the same after it hits the bookshops."

He was so clearly carried away with the idea that Trish hadn't got the heart to argue.

"And don't you see? This is my ticket out of that goddamned school. When *The Green Gannet* is published to world acclaim, I will never again have to stand in front of that mob of ungrateful gobshites and explain that *The Ancient Mariner* is *not* a pub in Ringsend."

He set about it with gusto. He drew up a draft outline of the novel and sent it off to Sheldon O'Neill for his comments. Mr O'Neill duly replied. He said the idea struck him as sound and he thought it had potential. But he gave Adrian an important piece of advice. "*Take it slowly. This is an ambitious novel in its scope and theme. There is no necessity to rush.*"

It was exactly the encouragement Adrian required. He went out and bought several large boxes of paper and each night and every weekend he barricaded himself into his study and Trish could hear the sound of the keyboard tap-tap-tapping away inside.

Adrian read the early chapters to the writers' group and their response was overwhelming. One member compared it to Dostoevsky. Another said it had echoes of Proust.

"They're going to give me a big head, if I'm not careful," Adrian laughed modestly over breakfast the next day. "These are only early drafts. They require revision. But they all like it and that suggests that I'm certainly on the right track."

He worked like a maniac through the winter and into the summer. After fourteen months, the novel was completed. The word counter on Adrian's computer showed it came to 333,872 words. He wore out three ink cartridges printing it and spent a fortune having copies made and bound at a stationer's shop in Nassau Street. Then he started looking for a literary agent to represent him.

"That's the way it works nowadays," he said knowledgebly. "No serious publisher will even look at your work unless it's been submitted by an agent."

He bought a copy of *The Writers & Artists Yearbook* which contained a list of all the agents in the UK and Ireland.

"Should I go for a big agency or a smaller, more personal one?" he asked Trish.

"I know absolutely nothing about it," she confessed.

"A big agency carries more clout but then a smaller firm would be able to give me more personal attention."

He fretted about it for a week and in the end selected the first agency in the book. It had an address in London. He carefully packaged the manuscript and enclosed a covering letter.

It cost €20 for postage. Adrian waited confidently for the response he knew would launch his literary career.

Nothing happened. After six weeks, he could contain himself no longer. He got on the phone to inquire if the package had arrived safely. A secretary informed him that they had indeed received Adrian's work but they had a policy of not accepting unsolicited manuscripts and if he wanted it returned would he please send them a cheque to cover postage. Adrian was outraged.

He tried another agency. This time, he sent an advance letter explaining who he was and giving a brief synopsis of *The Green Gannet*. He got a reply saying they were very sorry but they were oversubscribed and were not taking on any new clients. Adrian opened a bottle of Beaune that they had been saving for a dinner party and proceeded to get drunk.

A few days later, he picked himself up and started again. This time, he chose a small agency. He calculated that they would have fewer clients and would therefore be eager to sign him up. From the description in *The Writers & Artists Yearbook,* it seemed to Trish that it was a one-man band working out of a backroom. But they replied, asking to see the work. Adrian was overjoyed. He packaged it neatly and enclosed what he considered to be a witty covering letter. Then he settled down to wait.

A month went by and there was no response. Adrian grew impatient. He consoled himself with the thought that the novel was probably being considered by the board of the agency who were devising a strategy for placing it with a major publisher. But when the time stretched into two months, he decided to ring. A man with a superior accent left him hanging on while he went away to make inquiries.

He came back after five minutes and said that the manuscript seemed to have gone astray and would Adrian mind awfully submitting it again.

Adrian groaned and sank into a deep depression.

His behaviour grew increasingly bizarre. Some nights he would sit up till the early hours working on his manuscript. There were mornings when he was late for school or went into work unshaven and unwashed.

He decided to dispense with the service of an agent altogether and deal directly with the publishers.

"Why give these buggers 15 per cent of my money?" he said haughtily. "I'm the one doing all the work."

The manuscripts went off in large jiffy bags and came back regularly unopened. Various publishers read the novel and rejected it. Sometimes they offered advice. More often they didn't even bother to do that. Adrian grew obsessive. Each rejection letter sent him into a fury.

"Just wait till *The Green Gannet* is published to rave reviews. Wait till I win the Booker! There'll be blood all over the carpets when the directors discover that these bastards have rejected my novel without even reading it. Oh, they'll be a sorry bunch then!"

His confidence, once adamantine, began to crack. He took to revising and rewriting, hacking out whole chapters and then changing his mind and inserting them again. He stopped going out to visit their friends. He ate his meals at odd hours and left Trish to dine alone in the kitchen. Finally, he moved a camp bed into his study and forsook the marital bedroom altogether.

Trish watched helplessly. She didn't know what to do or who to turn to for advice. She still maintained a strong affection for the man she had married when she was twenty-two. But he had changed beyond all recognition. She busied herself with her work. And she sought solace in occasional affairs.

It was in this mood that she had fallen in with Henry Doran and now he had thrown her over. No point fretting about it, she decided. It was bound to come to an end sooner or later. At least she had achieved something she had longed for. She was pregnant! There was no doubt about it. She had bought herself a pregnancy-testing kit and the positive result had sent her rushing off to her doctor who confirmed it. She was six weeks pregnant.

Trish wanted this baby. She wanted it more than anything else in the world. But how was she going to explain it to Adrian? He was crazy already. If she told him the truth, it would probably send him over the edge completely.

She had a hurried lunch in a sandwich bar while she pondered her options. Could she seduce Adrian into bed and then pass the child off as his? It would be difficult but not impossible. But it couldn't be done while he remained at home, obsessed with his damned novel. And then the solution came to her like a flash of blinding light. She gave a little squeal of delight and then quickly suppressed it when the couple at the next table turned round and stared.

She quickly finished her meal, collected her bag and headed out to the street. Five minutes later she was in a travel agency.

"I'd like to book a holiday," she said to the eager young woman behind the desk. "For two people."

"When would you prefer to travel, madam?"

"Next week," Trish said.

Adrian's school was breaking up for the Easter holidays on Friday. The timing was ideal.

But the woman didn't appear too encouraging. "You've left it rather late."

"You must have something," Trish said, desperately. "I don't mind where it is."

The woman scrolled through the computer for a few minutes and then seemed to brighten up.

"I've just the place. Tenerife. The weather will be ideal at this time of year."

"I'll take it," Trish said quickly, in case the woman changed her mind.

"It's a one-bedroom self-catering apartment."

"Single or double beds?"

The woman checked the computer again. "Double. Is that all right?"

"Perfect," Trish said. "What's it called?"

"Hotel Las Flores," the young woman replied. "The Flowers Hotel."